CRIME INVESTIGATION

The ultimate guide to forensic science

Parragon

Bath • New York • Singapore • Hong Kong • Cologne • Delhi
Melbourne • Amsterdam • Johannesburg • Auckland • Shenzhen

This is a Parragon book
This edition published in 2011
Parragon
Queen Street House
4 Queen Street
Bath BA1 1HE, UK

ISBN 978-1-4454-3507-7

Editorial and design by
Amber Books Ltd
Bradley's Close
74–77 White Lion Street
London N1 9PF
www.amberbooks.co.uk

Project Editor: James Bennett
Design: Joe Conneally
Picture Research: Kate Green

A copy of the CIP data for this book is available from the British Library.

Printed in China

Contents

Introduction

'We all think of death as the ending. For forensics, it's just the beginning.'

Nancy Haley, Supervisor,
Forensic Toxicology Laboratory,
Department of Health, Rhode Island, USA

CRIME AND JUSTICE SEEMED SIMPLER IN THE EARLY NINETEENTH CENTURY BEFORE MODERN COMMUNICATIONS AND EFFICIENT TRANSPORTATION. Criminals were normally easier to apprehend because they lived in small communities with their victims and any eyewitnesses – the hit-and-run crime would have to wait for a modern infrastructure. And when suspects were arrested and tried, convictions were normally based on public opinion and even resulted from pressures put on the defendant, including torture. This easy justice, however, was often injustice in the years before standard police procedures and scientific evaluations of evidence.

Today's criminals use modern technology including emails, mobile phone messages, and even television appearances. Ian Huntley, who murdered two ten-year-old girls in Soham, Cambridgeshire, was soon on a BBC news programme coolly speaking about the community's shock. However, the investigative tools of forensic science have also advanced at a remarkable pace. Infrared spectrometers identify fibres left by suspects, CT scanners pinpoint weapons in suitcases, and DNA solves 'cold cases' that are decades old. Introduced in the 1980s, DNA testing has been recently refined to obtain results from only a few cells, ten times fewer than conventional DNA testing.

EVERY CONTACT LEAVES A TRACE

To the trained eye, a crime scene is filled with clues that can be obvious or mysterious. They involve physical evidence like fingerprints, hair, blood, fibres, drugs, paint or soil. Arthur Conan Doyle's fictional detective Sherlock Holmes, who first appeared in 1887, emphasized the importance of miniscule evidence. He searched for fingerprints, analyzed blood, and examined documents. The idea that 'every contact leaves a trace' was stated in 1920 by Dr. Edmond Locard, a French police officer and forensic scientist who ten years earlier had established the world's first crime laboratory in Lyon, France. His concept, now known as Locard's Exchange Principle, is the

Left: A forensic scientist collects fibre samples for microscopic examination as part of a criminal investigation. Fibres from clothing and carpets are among the most common items of trace evidence that are recovered.

Left: *Photographs of this gun, an item of evidence, are needed for use in court. A ruler shows the scale. The gun will also be test-fired to provide bullets and cartridges for comparison with those taken from the crime scene.*

Above: Forensic scientist checks for fingerprints on a bottle at a crime scene. His protective suit prevents contamination of the evidence.

key to modern forensic science. In practice this means physical evidence will be exchanged during any physical contact between a suspect and his victim or the crime scene. A criminal might leave his fingerprints or a hair at the scene, and take away carpet fabric on his shoes.

Such evidence is carefully collected and turned over to forensic scientists who handle such diverse crimes as identity theft, kidnapping, burglary, arson, rape and murder. If someone has died, forensic pathologists calculate the time and cause of death, and a nameless victim can be identified by a variety of methods, which include fingerprints, a dental match and facial reconstruction in clay or by computer.

The forensic laboratory is often the key to a successful police investigation. The lab results should indicate if a crime was committed and, if so, tests can verify evidence that helps convict the person or persons responsible. Placing a suspect at the crime scene is a basic goal of forensic work. That connection is often a clear sign of guilt, as when fresh tyre marks are found at the scene of an arson attack.

EVIDENCE IN COURT

The name 'forensic science' means science related to crime and courts of law. The word 'forensic' goes back to the Latin *forum* where legal matters were settled. Forensic experts, indeed, are called to testify in court cases by both the prosecution and the defence. The trail from a crime scene to a courtroom has a sequence that is well established, which can involve specialists in several forensic fields working closely with law enforcement officers. The scientific tools and techniques they use are impressive, but lab results have to be evaluated by highly trained professionals possessing knowledge, experience and intuition.

The following chapters will look at how evidence is collected at crime scenes, the ways of determining the time and cause of death, of identifying unknown victims and suspects, what tools and tests are used in the modern forensic laboratory, the way DNA profiling has revolutionized the fight against crime, how forensic scientists solve white-collar crimes, and what drives a criminal mind. The final chapters present a history of forensic detection and an overview of specialisms in the profession.

Left: A blood sample is shown on a microscope slide. A forensic serologist will use it for DNA profiling to try to establish a link between a suspect's blood and that found at the crime scene.

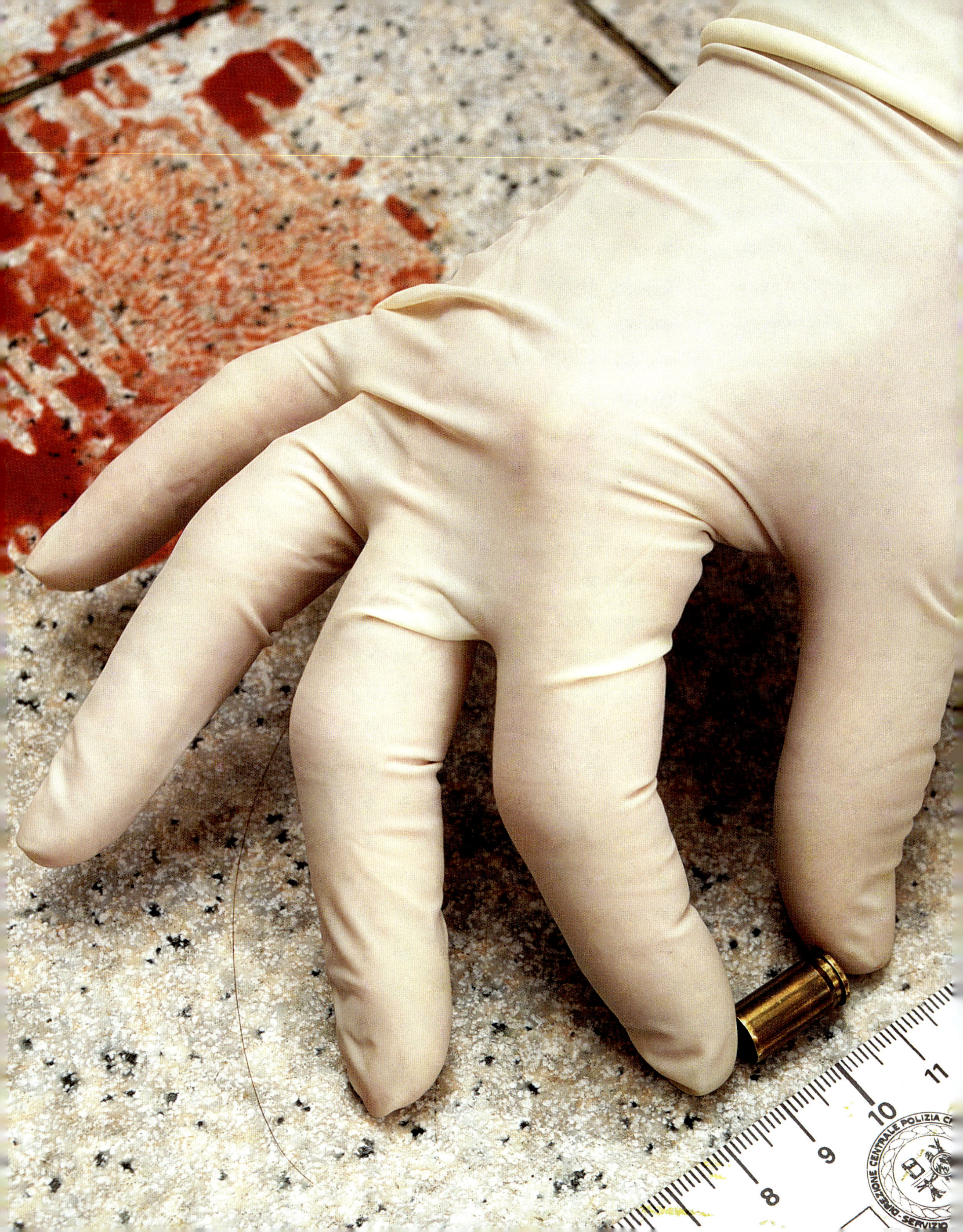
8
9
10
11
DIREZIONE CENTRALE POLIZIA
SERVIZIO

Chapter One

Forensic Science: The Facts

THE INVESTIGATION AND PROSECUTION OF A CRIME DEPENDS LARGELY UPON FORENSIC SCIENCE TO ASSEMBLE THE FACTS THAT PROVE A CRIME OCCURRED AND THAT A CERTAIN SUSPECT OR SUSPECTS COMMITTED IT.

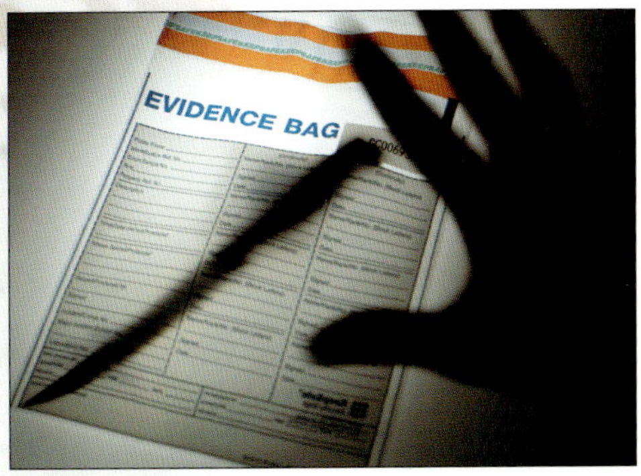

Evidence bags are required at crime scenes to protect items from contamination as they are collected and shipped to a forensic laboratory.

Important evidence collected at the crime scene may include fingerprints, footprints, spent bullets and trace evidence such as hairs, fabrics, skin, blood and other stains. However, some of the biological evidence such as DNA might not be visible to the naked eye.

This evidence will be carefully conveyed to a forensic laboratory to be examined by specialists working in such fields as pathology, toxicology, serology, odontology and DNA analysis. Their forensic tools will range from the familiar microscope to the complex DNA scanner and mass spectrometry instrument.

Among the key evidence that can be retrieved from a scene are cartridge shells (far left) and fingerprints (left).

Forensic Evidence

A crime cannot be solved without evidence. Confessions and circumstantial evidence sometimes prove untrue, but physical evidence can provide an airtight case against a suspect.

Guilty verdicts have been achieved by an expert's testimony that involves a single hair or a piece of fibre. For this reason, a forensic scientist's primary focus at a crime scene is to discover these small pieces, known as 'trace evidence', with other examples of evidence, including skin, gunshot residue and dust.

Fingerprints are sometimes described as trace evidence, as well as the prints of palms and soles at the crime scene. Fingerprints can be removed to be compared to those already on file in a database or to prints taken from suspects. They are also valuable in identifying an unknown victim. Prints made by shoes, gloves and tyres are also extremely useful. In addition, investigators search for marks left by tools such as those used for breaking into a house.

FIREARMS

If a firearm has been deployed in a crime and recovered, forensic scientists will use chemicals and microscopes to examine the gun and its projectiles. When bullets or shell casings are matched to the firearm of a suspect it is strong evidence.

DOCUMENTS

In a variety of criminal cases, a document examiner provides another type of forensic identification. This involves written evidence such as a kidnapper's note, an altered will, account book or lottery ticket, as well as a forged signature on a cheque or a forged passport. Besides analysing the handwriting, a document expert may be called upon to determine the age and source of the paper and ink.

Of course, evidence can be found away from the primary crime scene. This is why careful searches are made of a suspect's home and vehicle, as well as sites associated with the victim.

Numbered crime scene markers are used to indicate the position of every item of relevance such as this discarded gun. Each position is logged before the evidence is removed for analysis in a forensic laboratory.

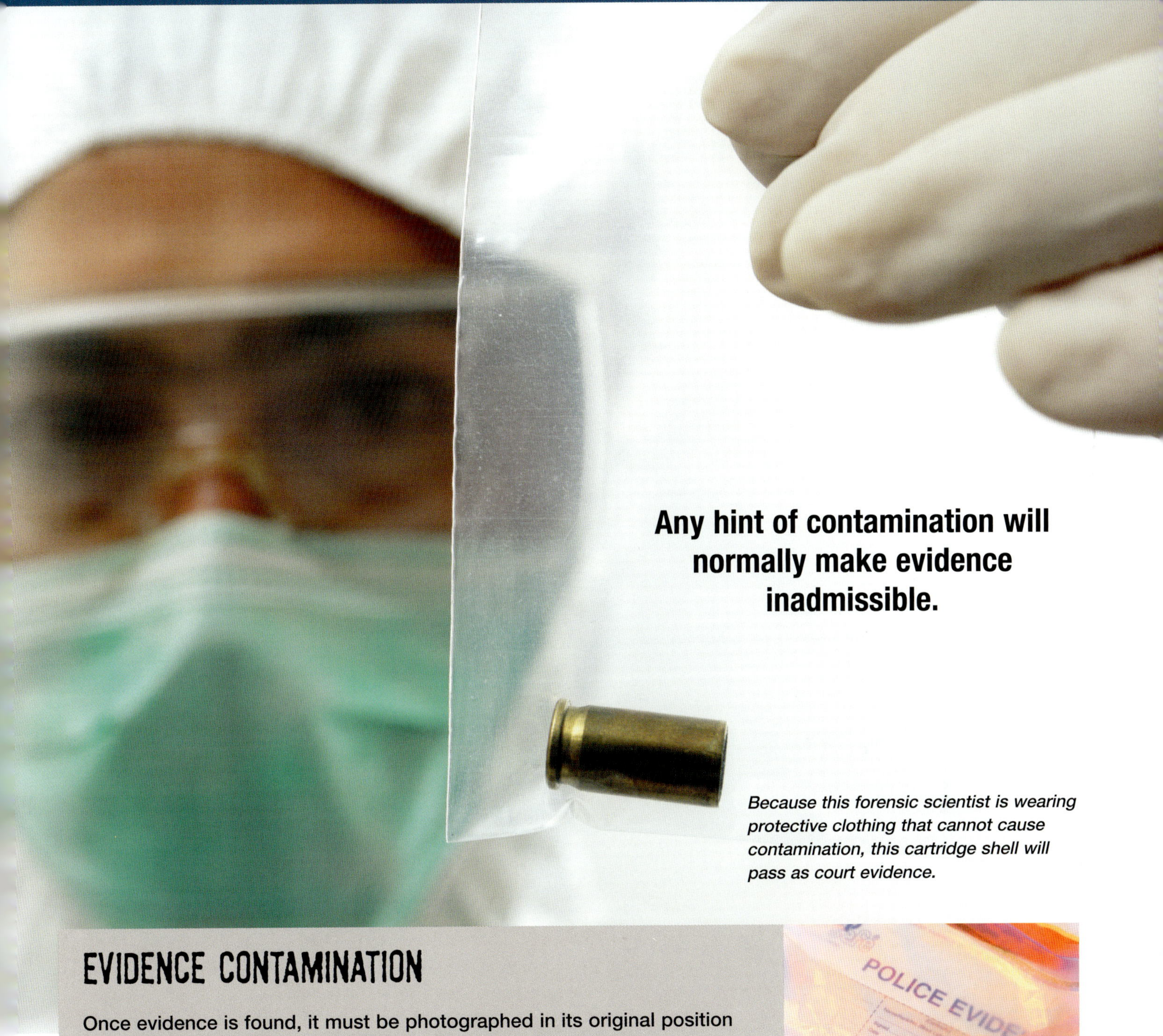

Any hint of contamination will normally make evidence inadmissible.

Because this forensic scientist is wearing protective clothing that cannot cause contamination, this cartridge shell will pass as court evidence.

EVIDENCE CONTAMINATION

Once evidence is found, it must be photographed in its original position and placed in separate clearly labelled bags or containers. These are transported to a forensic laboratory for examination and later may be presented as exhibits in court. All this must be done without the items becoming contaminated in any way whatsoever. This can happen, for instance, if a fibre from an investigator's clothes is transferred onto the victim's clothes, or if the evidential object is dropped on the lab floor. Any hint of contamination will normally make evidence inadmissible in court. The best way to avoid this complications is to set up a 'chain of custody' for those who handle the evidence – the fewer the better – by keeping a documented 'continuity of evidence' record of its movement.

National Forensic Services

The developed nations of the world have established modern and efficient forensic science services that have had remarkable success in working together on international cases.

The United Kingdom has a Forensic Science Service (FSS) within the Home Office where it was created in 1991 from regional forensic laboratories. It now oversees those six labs in London, Chepstow, Birmingham, Chorley, Huntingdon and Wetherby. The National Firearms Unit (NFU) is based in Manchester. There is also a Forensic Science Agency of Northern Ireland and four labs in Scotland for the areas of Grampian, Strathclyde, Tayside and Lothian and Borders. Private companies also offer forensic laboratory examinations and are often employed in court cases by defence and prosecution teams. The UK's largest, LGC, is headquartered in Teddington, Middlesex and has more than 500 employees. Over 150

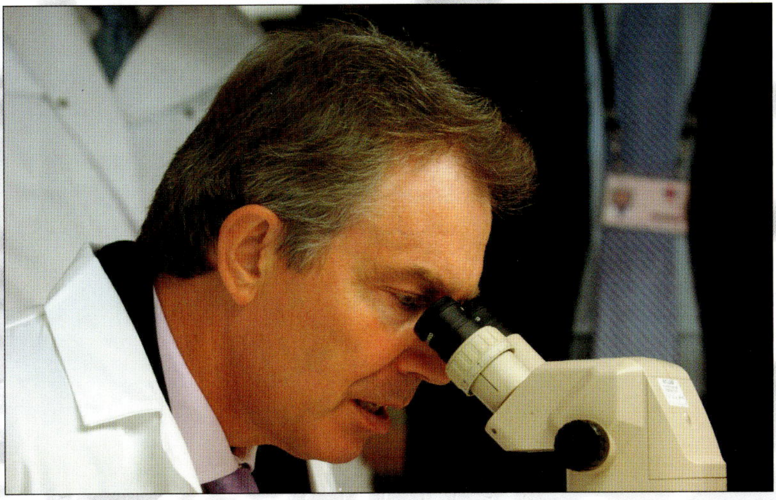

Left: Prime Minister Tony Blair looks into a microscope during his visit in 2006 to the Forensic Science Service headquarters in London.

Below: A scene of crime officer (SOCO) adds labels to collection tubes. These hold swabs containing saliva samples that are used to recover DNA.

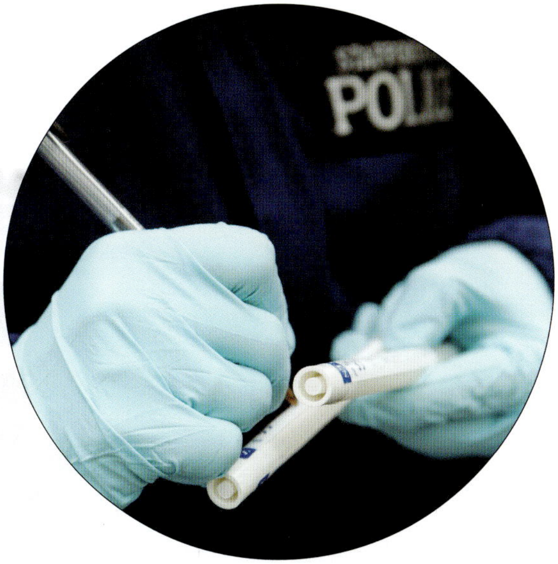

years old, it was the Laboratory of the Government Chemist before being privatized in 1996. In 2005 it acquired Forensic Alliance Limited (FAL), then the UK's largest private sector provider of forensic science services. The newly combined group has eight laboratories all around the country as well as a specialist firearms facility.

In the United States, the Federal Bureau of Investigation (FBI) Laboratory in Washington, DC, was established in 1932 but back then was known as the Technical Laboratory. It now has a Combined DNA Index System (CODIS), which is a national computerized database available to the 50 individual states, all of whom have their own DNA databases of convicted offenders. The laboratory also runs a Forensic Science Research and Training Center in Quantico, Virginia.

The Royal Canadian Mounted Police (RCMP) has the Forensic Laboratory Services as part of its National Police Services in Ottawa where the National DNA Data Bank is located. The RCMP's forensic laboratories are in Vancouver, Edmonton, Regina, Winnipeg, Ottawa and Halifax, while Ontario and Quebec have their own laboratories.

EUROPEAN FORENSICS

Criminal justice and law enforcement in the twenty-first century has to deal with perpetrators who can communicate worldwide in an instant and, especially in Europe, move effortlessly across borders. To combat this, national agencies of law enforcement and forensic science work closely together, sharing the latest science and technology. The European Network of Forensic Science Institutes (ENFSI) promotes co-operation between the forensic labs from 32 European countries.

A leading provider is the UK's Forensic Science Service (FSS), which has assisted over 60 countries. The first organization in the world that developed a national criminal DNA database, its expertise is available to forensic facilities, police forces and government organization around the world. The service also sends experts to different countries to train forensic scientists in their own laboratories.

The FSS maintains the world's most extensive database containing abstracts of forensic science literature, with more than 70,000 records. This covers problems encountered in analytical laboratories and such various topics as DNA, computer crime, documents examination and arson investigation.

Types of Forensic Specialities

Forensic science is a broad practice that embraces science used for legal purposes, and its practitioners range from physicians to laboratory assistants.

Their speciality may deal with human remains such as cadavers, bones, hair and teeth or with inanimate evidence such as fingerprints, firearms, detonators, wills and cheques. Some of the major specialities, which may include subspecialities, are:

FORENSIC PATHOLOGY:

This involves autopsies by licenced physicians of bodies that have not yet decomposed. This postmortem examination of the external and internal parts of the deceased is done to establish the cause and time of death. If murder seems evident, the pathologist often visits the crime scene to view the position of the victim. Living victims are also examined in such cases as assault and rape to determine injuries and their causes.

FORENSIC ANTHROPOLOGY:

This is concerned with postmortem examinations of the remains of human bones, usually to identify the deceased and hopefully establish the cause and time of death. This study can determine the age, sex, height and race of a victim, as well as injuries and illnesses.

FORENSIC ODONTOLOGY:

This specializes in the examination of teeth, which are the hardest and most durable substance in the body. When a corpse is badly decomposed, therefore, the best means of identification is often by matching the victim's teeth with dental records. Odontologists also compare a suspect's teeth with bite marks on a victim or on food left at the crime scene.

FORENSIC TOXICOLOGY:

This is the scientific study of poisons and drugs used in murders and other criminal cases such as date-rape drugs. Tests are also run on the living to determine if such substances caused them to act violently or drive dangerously.

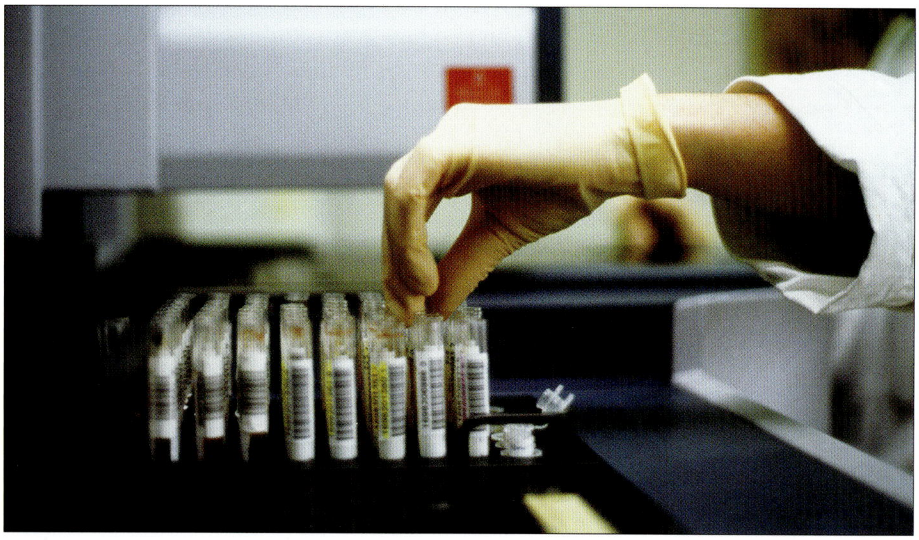

A laboratory technician in France selects a blood sample for testing. The samples are carefully kept in bar-coded tubes to assure the correct identifications.

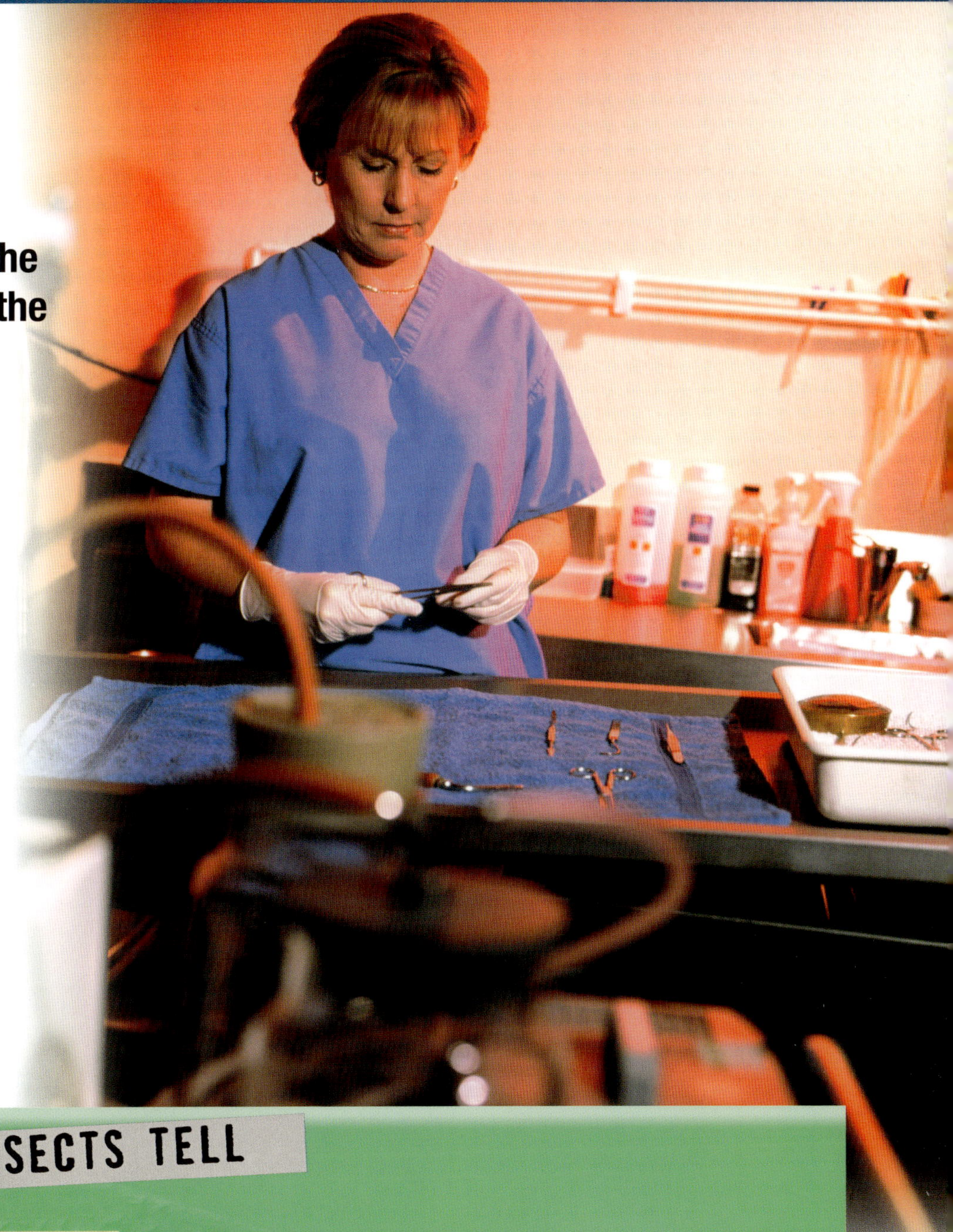

If murder seems evident, the pathologist will often visit the crime scene.

FORENSIC SEROLOGY:

This is the field that examines blood and other bodily fluids such as saliva and semen. Among the serologist's tests are blood typing and DNA profiling.

FORENSIC ENTOMOLOGY:

This concerns the study of flies and other insects on a corpse, since their known life cycles can be used to estimate a victim's time of death.

WHAT FLIES AND INSECTS TELL

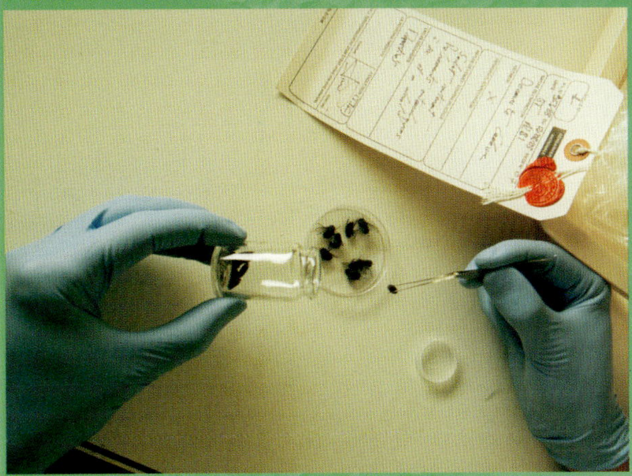

A forensic entomologist uses a technique that dates back to about thirteenth-century China. It was known then that looking at the stages of development and sizes of insect larvae on a body could establish the time of death. Tests on their larvae can also reveal a poison, because they take poison up from human tissue. This is important for toxicological tests because body fluids and soft tissues are soon gone from a corpse.
The type of insects can also indicate a body was moved from the insects' natural habitat, as some flies prefer laying eggs indoors or outdoors, and others always choose shade or sunlight. The concentration of insects on a part of the body may show where wounds are located.

Three Forensic Murder Cases

Forensic investigations have convicted criminals in a variety of ways. Three famous cases involved tooth marks, documents and DNA tests.

TED BUNDY

Theodore 'Ted' Bundy was a charming young American known to have killed 15 women, although he claimed it was from 40 to 50. On 15 January, 1978, he murdered two female students at Florida State University. Six days later, he was arrested for driving a stolen car, and his identity was revealed as a murder suspect who had escaped from a Colorado jail in 1977.

Ted Bundy (centre) finally faces justice after being charged with the killings of two female students at Florida State University.

A former law student, Bundy defended himself, but was faced by the prosecution's photograph of a bite mark discovered on the left buttock of one of the sorority girls. Dr Richard Souviron, a forensic odontologist, testified that Bundy's teeth matched the bite mark exactly. This was the key evidence that led to his conviction and his execution in 1989.

HAROLD SHIPMAN

British Dr Harold Shipman is estimated to have killed 236 of his patients over 24 years from 1974 to 1998, possibly making him the most prolific serial killer ever. He was only caught after forging a new will for Kathleen Grundy before killing her in 1998. This left £386,000 to Shipman, cutting out Mrs Grundy's daughter. Detective Superintendent Bernard Postles made an intense examination of the will, determining that the victim's name was forged and the phraseology and quality were not hers. The document was typed, and the police matched the imprint of the letters to Shipman's typewriter. Sentenced to 15 consecutive life sentences, he hanged himself in jail in 2004.

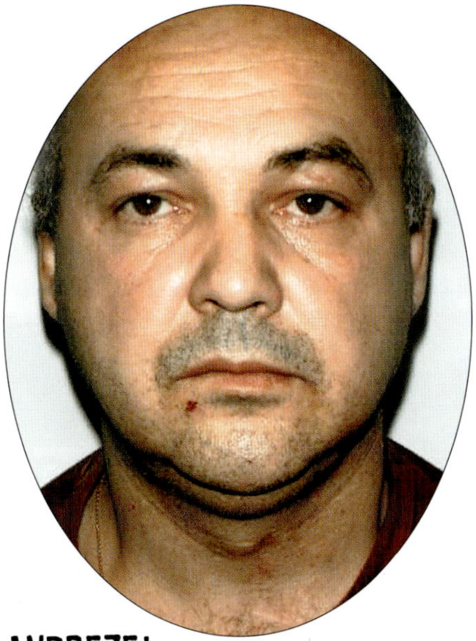

The paedophile Andrezej Kunowski, seen in this Metropolitan Police arrest photograph, was sentenced on 31 March, 2004, to life in prison for strangling Katerina Koneva.

ANDREZEJ KUNOWSKI

Polish-born Andrezej Kunowski, an illegal immigrant in Britain, had sexually attacked some 30 children and young women in both countries. He strangled 12-year-old Katerina Koneva in 1997 at her home in London, and the only evidence was a hair on the girl's cardigan.

Kunowski had previously served ten years in Poland for 27 sex attacks and was again jailed there in 1995 for raping a 12 year old. A judge allowed him to go free the following year for a hip operation and he fled to London. In 2002 he was jailed for raping a Korean student. His DNA was taken and matched the sample from Katerina as well as DNA from his final Polish rape. Kunowski was sentenced in 2004 to life without parole.

FORENSIC JARGON

Forensic scientists use their own jargon created from medical, scientific, police and legal terms.

Here is a brief sample:

Blood source: a victim who has bled.

Bull's-eye injury: an injury on a body that has the shape of the weapon used.

Cast-off blood: blood marks from a victim who has moved or been moved.

Cold hit: a matching of physical evidence with a sample kept on a database.

Crime-scene staging: changes made in a crime scene by the criminal to cover up evidence.

PERK (physical evidence recovery kit): the scientific kit used to collect evidence at a crime scene.

Trace evidence: small pieces of evidence left at a crime scene, such as dust, skin, hairs or fabric.

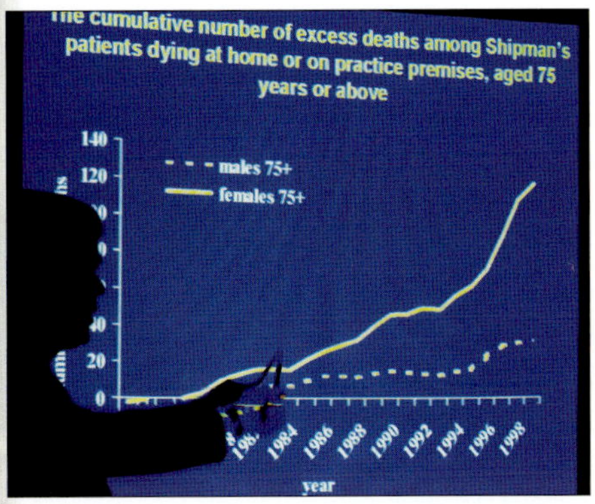

Richard Baker, professor of Quality in Health Care at the University of Leicester, delivers his report on the deaths attributed to Harold Shipman, who was jailed for life for killing about 236 of his elderly patients.

Chapter Two

The Scene of the Crime

A CRIME SCENE CONTAINS THE BASICS OF A CASE: THE VICTIM(S) AND SOME EVIDENCE. This is where the forensic scientist immediately begins to work with others who will be involved in the investigation such as the police, fire inspectors and witnesses. The forensic officer on the scene is a fieldworker who is variously titled a crime scene investigator, crime scene examiner, crime scene analyst, scenes-of-crime officer, criminologist or some similar name.

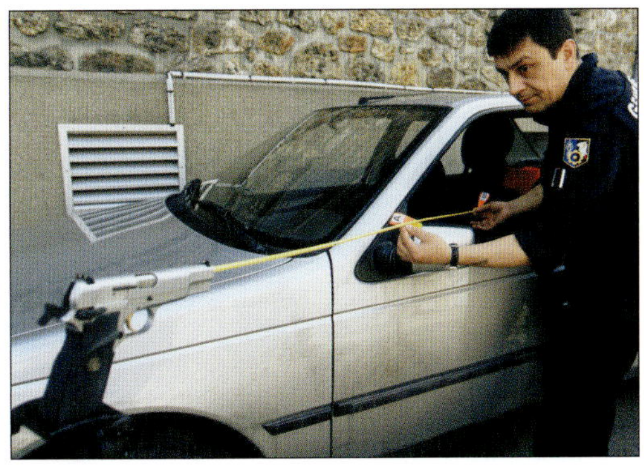

Careful measurements must be made of a bullet's path in a car shooting.

A primary crime scene is where a crime takes place, such as a murder, while a secondary crime scene is a site related to the crime such as a burial site or a vehicle used to transport the body. Normally more evidence is found at the primary scene, but sometimes that site is not known. This was the case when five prostitutes were murdered in December 2006 in Ipswich. Their bodies were in nearby rural areas, but police did not know where they were murdered. With no crime scene evidence, police arrested Steve Wright after talking to prostitutes' customers. In February 2008, he was convicted and given life without parole.

The solution to a crime will depend on observing proper procedures. A scene needs to be secured and recorded, evidence found, witnesses and suspects identified and interviewed and the crime reconstructed.

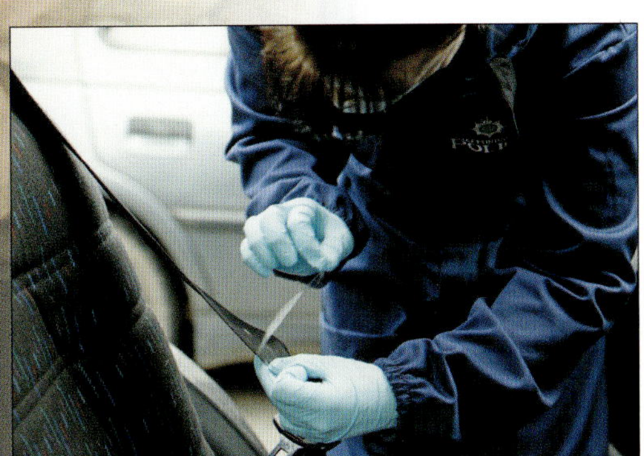

Time is well spent by forensic investigators at a murder scene (far left). Lifting fingerprints from the interior of a car requires delicate work.

Securing the Scene

When a building is on fire, vehicles collide or miners are trapped underground, onlookers are drawn to watch the tragedies unfold. The news media will also rapidly converge on such a site.

Public curiosity can create difficulties, and it becomes a significant problem when a murder or other major crime has been committed. Officials needed to sort out the situation will already occupy the scene. This may include police, forensic scientists, firemen, physicians, ambulance personnel and possibly more specialists such as bomb disposal experts.

The size of a crime scene can be limited to one room or spread over an extensive area, as happened when more than 1000 police and soldiers had to search 2189 sq km/845 sq miles of Scottish countryside in 1988 after a Pan American flight was bombed over the village of Lockerbie, causing the death of 270 people.

FIRST OFFICER ATTENDING

The immediate job for the first policeman on the scene, known as the first officer attending (FOA), is to help any victims who are alive.

NICOLE SIMPSON AND RONALD GOLDMAN

The murder trial of footballer and actor O. J. Simpson involved the stabbings of his former wife, Nicole Simpson, and her friend, Ronald Goldman. It was a small crime scene: just the walkway leading to her apartment. The first two officers on the scene determined that the victims were dead and, with three more officers, they secured the scene, created a sign-in sheet and, by the time two detectives arrived, there were already 18 officers present. A police photographer joined them but could only take area shots until the civilian forensic scientist arrived.

Detectives then went to O.J. Simpson's house, declaring it too a crime scene. From there the police criminalist collected blood spots and a bloody glove. Despite this and other evidence, Simpson was acquitted in 1995 after a televised trial that lasted more than eight months.

If they are injured, they must be medically assisted immediately, even if this destroys evidence. A victim should not be cleaned up, however, until a forensic officer has checked for bloodstains, hair and other trace evidence.

The first authorities on the scene will also detain any possible suspects and eyewitnesses, taking down their statements. They should be kept separate to avoid having trace evidence transferred from one person to another. If someone had reported the crime, they should be interviewed, detained and denied access to the crime scene. Perpetrators have been known to report their crime to appear innocent and gain entry in order to confuse the scene. A crime area should also be sealed off from onlookers to prevent evidence from being contaminated or lost. The police will cordon off the site, normally marking the perimeter with tape, and will restrict the areas of access, logging in all visitors and recording what they remove. Tents may be erected to protect the scene from the elements and onlookers.

Below: Wreckage of the bombed Pan American airline lies on Scottish soil after 270 lives were lost.

Above: Scene of crime officers (SOCOs) investigate a shooting. Police tape marks out the boundaries of the crime scene. The SOCOs are wearing paper suits, overshoes and masks to prevent contamination of evidence.

Suspects and witnesses must all be kept separate to avoid trace evidence being transferred from one person to another.

Preventing Contamination

It is important to ban the general public who might leave footprints and fingerprints, which would have to be ruled out of any investigation. Even the movement of family and friends needs to be controlled.

Controlling the scene is especially difficult when a crime is committed in a public urban setting. This was the case when the controversial Dutch filmmaker, Theo Van Gogh, was murdered in 2004 by an Islamic extremist on an Amsterdam street, and occurred on a greater scale with the terrorist bombings of transport systems in Madrid in 2004 and London the following year. In such cases busy public areas must be sealed off and made secure, often for several days.

PROTECTIVE UNIFORM

Investigators allowed onto a crime scene have to be sensitive to the danger of cross-contamination. They wear a white protective uniform that includes a mask,

HOW INSPECTORS CONTAMINATE SCENES

A recurrent problem with contaminated evidence at crime scenes involves inspectors leaving their own trace evidence, including DNA, at the scene and even on the victim. Many unidentified profiles in DNA databases that were thought to belong to perpetrators have proven to be from officers on the scene.

In a 2003 murder case in New South Wales, Australia, an unknown DNA profile was found on the victim's jumper that did not match the suspect. Then in 2005, the same DNA profile was found after a violent armed robbery. When police who handled both cases were examined, the DNA was matched to a forensic services investigator.

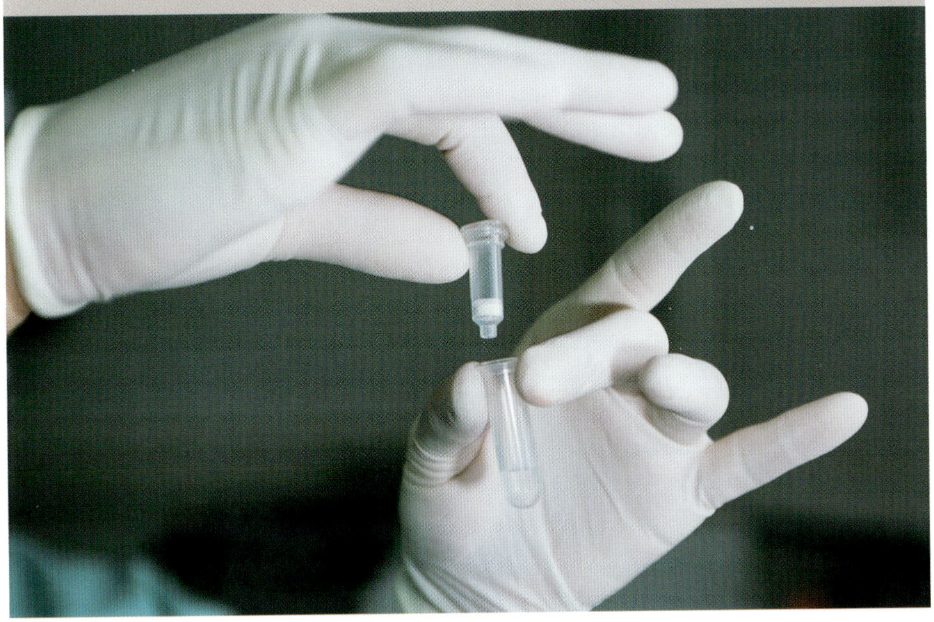

surgical gloves and plastic overshoes. If officials need to pass through part of the scene to reach the focal point such as a victim, a common approach path will be designated to protect any evidence. A homicide victim and normal objects should not be touched or moved before the forensic scientist arrives at the crime scene. The position of a door or window, for example, could be crucial to solving a case. Officials will also stop anyone else altering the scene, for example, as in the case when a crime survivor or family members wants to try to put a room back in order.

If more than one crime scene exists for a case such as a victim being murdered at one location and buried at another, a forensic scientist must try to avoid covering both scenes and risking cross-contamination. If only one person is available to examine both areas, he or she should undergo decontamination before switching to the other site.

JONBENET RAMSEY

Sympathetic officers are sometimes lenient when confronted with distressed family members. This happened after the murder of six-year-old JonBenet Ramsey in 1996 in Boulder, Colorado. Her father discovered the body in the basement, and police allowed him to carry it upstairs. They also permitted friends to move freely in the house. The evidence was therefore badly compromised, and the case remains unsolved.

The laboratory work on the JonBenet Ramsey murder case included an intense examination of a ransom note, but its author was never identified.

Recording the Evidence

Sketches, oral tapes, videotapes and notes are taken at a crime scene. A police or forensic photographer, however, who records the overall view, including the surrounding area and small evidential details, does the best documentation.

An item of evidence is filmed next to a ruler to indicate the size and again alone, in case the ruler had been covering up further evidence. Other references can be used in the photo to indicate size such as a pen or coin.

The photographer is usually one of the first allowed through the site, because the undisturbed scene must be recorded before victims are taken to the morgue or hospital and objects are removed to forensic laboratories. Photos also record fragile evidence such as latent fingerprints that may be ruined during their recovery and evidence such as a cigarette stub that may alter over time. Close-up images will be taken of wounds on a corpse or injured person. After a body has been removed, photos should be taken of the area where it lay.

Recording the scene by video has the advantage of adding comments, but still photographs present the sharpest images and are the easiest to handle in a courtroom. Each shot is labelled with a number, the location, the date and time taken and information about the processing. All this must stand up in court when a clever attorney questions whether someone may have tampered with the prints during the process.

DIGITAL CAMERAS

The advent of digital cameras has introduced the ability to enhance images. This type of camera can remove the background confusion if fingerprints are blurred when overlapping a patterned background, as found on a stamp, bank note or ticket. Such a change, however, carries the suggestion of manipulation, and some juries may discount the value of that evidence.

WHY TAKE NOTES?

Notes are valuable because they can record the sequence of actions taken by officials, whose names and titles are listed along with the times they were at the scene. A written description has the advantage of recording changes at the scene during the investigation. Lists can record several facts about each item of evidence: the object and its description; when and where it was discovered; and by whom. One list can serve as a log of photographs taken, describing them, their location, when and where they were taken and the name of the camera operator.

SKETCHY EVIDENCE?

Sketching is still used to indicate spatial relationship at a crime scene between objects or with an object and a corpse. Sketches are particularly clear, because unimportant items will not be shown and wounds on a body can be emphasized. Sometimes sketches are the only record available of the undisturbed crime scene, if a body has to be removed before the photographer arrives.

Finding Evidence

A crime scene needs to be searched quickly and thoroughly. If evidence remains after police remove their security restrictions, it will be compromised and unusable.

Most sites remain sealed off for a day or more, but this can vary according to the crime. In Canada police barred entrance to the international wing of Jean-Lesage Airport in 2007 in Quebec City for three hours after a false X-ray alarm, while the street in a Vienna suburb where Natascha Kampusch escaped after eight years of captivity in 2006 was closed for several days.

Investigators use their experience and common sense when probing through a site for clues. The crime-scene manager and scene of crime officers (SOCOs) will be trained in forensics. The police collecting evidence wear protective kits. They may advance in a line across an outdoor area or crawl along an indoor scene shoulder-to-shoulder conducting a fingertip search. A geometric search pattern may follow a spiral route towards or from a corpse,

DR DAVID KELLY

An example of high standards in a crime-scene search involved the death of Dr David Kelly, an employee of the UK Ministry of Defence, who committed suicide in 2003 after being named as the source criticizing the British government's statement on weapons of mass destruction in Iraq.

When his body was discovered in a wood, a Home Office pathologist and forensic biologists looked at the scene. Police teams conducted a thorough four-hour fingertip search 10 m/33 ft on either side of the scene's approach path they had established and also searched a radius of 10 m/33 ft around Dr Kelly's body. It was then removed and a 30-minute search was made of the ground where it had been. Nothing of significance was found.

while large areas can be divided into quadrants to be searched in a straight line or a criss-cross grid pattern.

If evidence might be both outside and inside a building, the former is searched first due to the possibility of rain and wind ruining the items. The search will also concentrate on the criminal's probable entry and exit paths.

FINDING EVIDENCE IN ISRAEL

In Israel the criminal identification technician (CDT) is responsible for finding the physical evidence at a crime scene, as a complement to an investigator's work. In this initial examination, field kits are used to seek evidence such as fingerprints, footprints and bloodstains. The CDT also documents the scene of the crime with photographs and drawings. The technician then transfers the evidence to laboratories located at the national facility in Jerusalem for tests. On some occasions, the CDT is asked to testify in court about the evidence found at the scene and to provide expert opinions submitted to the court as evidence.

Right: Israeli forensic experts examine the scene of a suicide bombing that killed eight people in Tel Aviv in April 2006.

Collecting Evidence

First, evidence that is fragile or in danger of contamination such as fibres and hair, must be attended to. This trace evidence can be collected from areas such as carpets and floors, furniture and car seats, using a special vacuum, tweezers, clear adhesive tape or by hand.

Clothes and other textile products can be simply shaken or brushed to recover hairs. In all cases wearing surgical gloves will avoid any transference of an investigator's DNA to the evidence.

Fingerprints are among the best evidence that can be recovered. They are a personal signature, and have been accepted in court cases for more than a century.

Argentina saw the first person convicted of murder by the use of fingerprints, Francisca Rohas, who killed her two sons in 1892 and cut her own throat trying to blame the crime on an attacker who had broken in.

Visible prints are classified as either patent prints, such as those stained with blood, grease and paint; or as plastic prints, which are impressions in some soft material such as putty, soap and dust.

Others indicators of a suspect's presence at a crime scene are footprints and tyre tracks. If both are left in soft ground, they can be photographed, cast in plaster, lifted and then compared with known shoes and tyres belonging to a suspect. If shoe prints are found on a floor or other hard surface, they can be detected the same way as fingerprints are, by applying a powder. Such shoe marks can be lifted by a fabric covered with a sticky gel or by using an electro-static device.

Fingerprints on a scarf are revealed here using a laser technique. The fingerprints are dusted with a chemical that fluoresces when exposed to laser light. This technique is useful because it works on porous surfaces.

LATENT FINGERPRINTS

Latent prints, which are invisible, are still detectable because light can reveal any sweat or oil on a surface left behind by fingers. When an angled beam of ultraviolet light, or a laser, is shone over the prints they will fluoresce, or glow. Latent prints can also be made visible by applying a powder, often carbon black, white or grey aluminium to the prints, using a soft brush. If marks have been absorbed on porous surfaces such as paper, magnetic powder can be applied by an applicator that does not touch the surface. All prints are then carefully lifted by a transparent tape and mounted.

Scales are placed over a can of fizzy drink to be photographed at a crime scene. The can has been dusted for fingerprints.

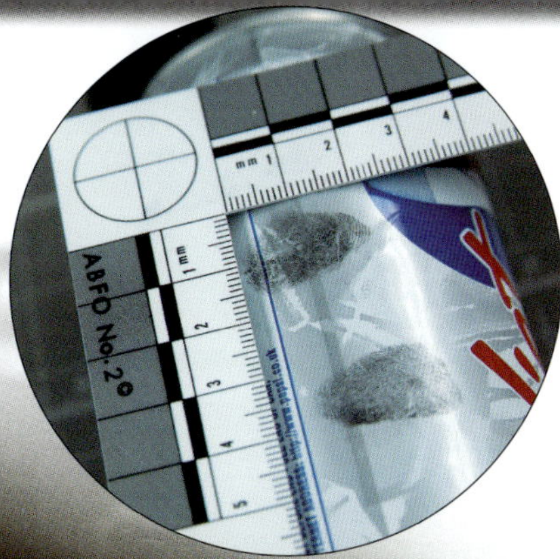

CRIME-SCENE TOOLS

GENERAL-PURPOSE SCIENTIFIC TOOLS

- **Exposing evidence:** magnifying glass, torch, and laser, infrared and ultraviolet lights
- **Recovering prints:** aluminium and black powders, black and grey magnetic powders, soft brush, magnetic applicator, gel fingerprint and footprint lifters, clear lifting tape, white latent print cards
- **Collecting trace evidence such as hairs, fibres and fluids:** tweezers, utility knife, scissors and cotton swabs
- **Making casts of tyres, footprints and tool marks:** casting plaster, mixing bowl and spatula
- **Packaging evidence:** permanent pen, evidence labels, plastic and paper bags and glass tubes

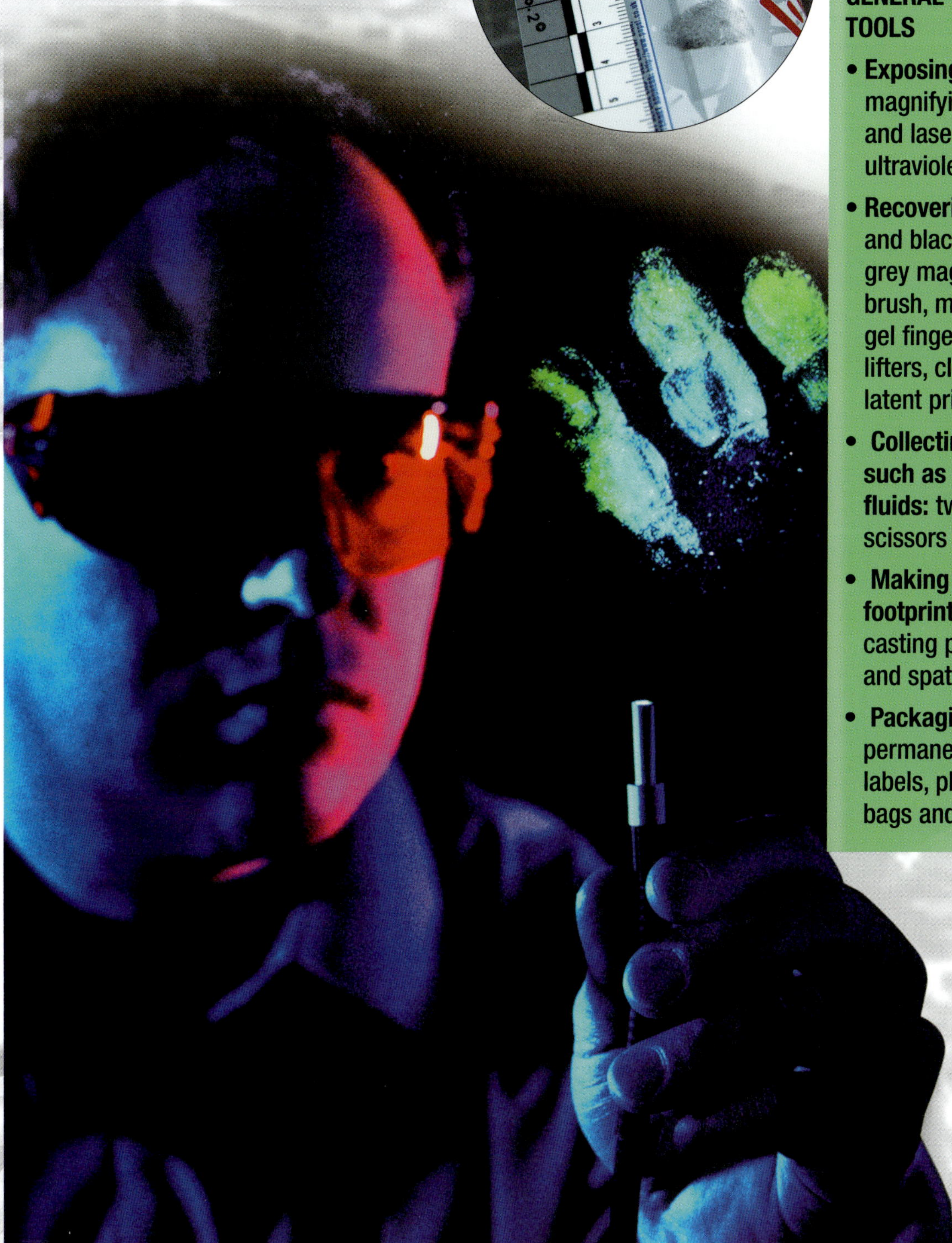

Forensic researchers wear special glasses to see the faint glow of fingerprints (shown in green) that are triggered by a flashing fluorescent lamp.

Protecting Evidence

Careful packaging must be used to protect any evidence. Plastic and paper bags, plastic bottles and envelopes are used for dry trace evidence, while airtight containers are normally used for liquids.

To avoid damage and deterioration by mould and mildew, moist biological evidence should be dried before packaging, or put into containers that are not airtight. All biological stains deteriorate with time, so items of clothing are dried before being packaged in separate bags, and are handled carefully to avoid disturbing trace materials. Blood samples at the scene can be put into a glass tube, sealed and placed in a bag. Hair samples are put into an envelope, which is then sealed.

All containers are labelled with a case or exhibit number, the item's identity, the date, time and location

KEEPING DNA

Police forces are reconsidering policies on storing evidence now that DNA can reach into the past to find perpetrators or free the wrongly convicted.

In 2004 a Canadian review committee wanted to test DNA on hair used to convict two men of killing a 16-year-old girl in 1990. However, the police had destroyed the single strand of hair because the law did not require them to keep evidence beyond 30 days after appeals had been exhausted.

In the USA in 2006, a bipartisan Constitutional Project committee recommended that DNA evidence be retained and tested for as long as it could 'establish innocence or avoid unjust execution'.

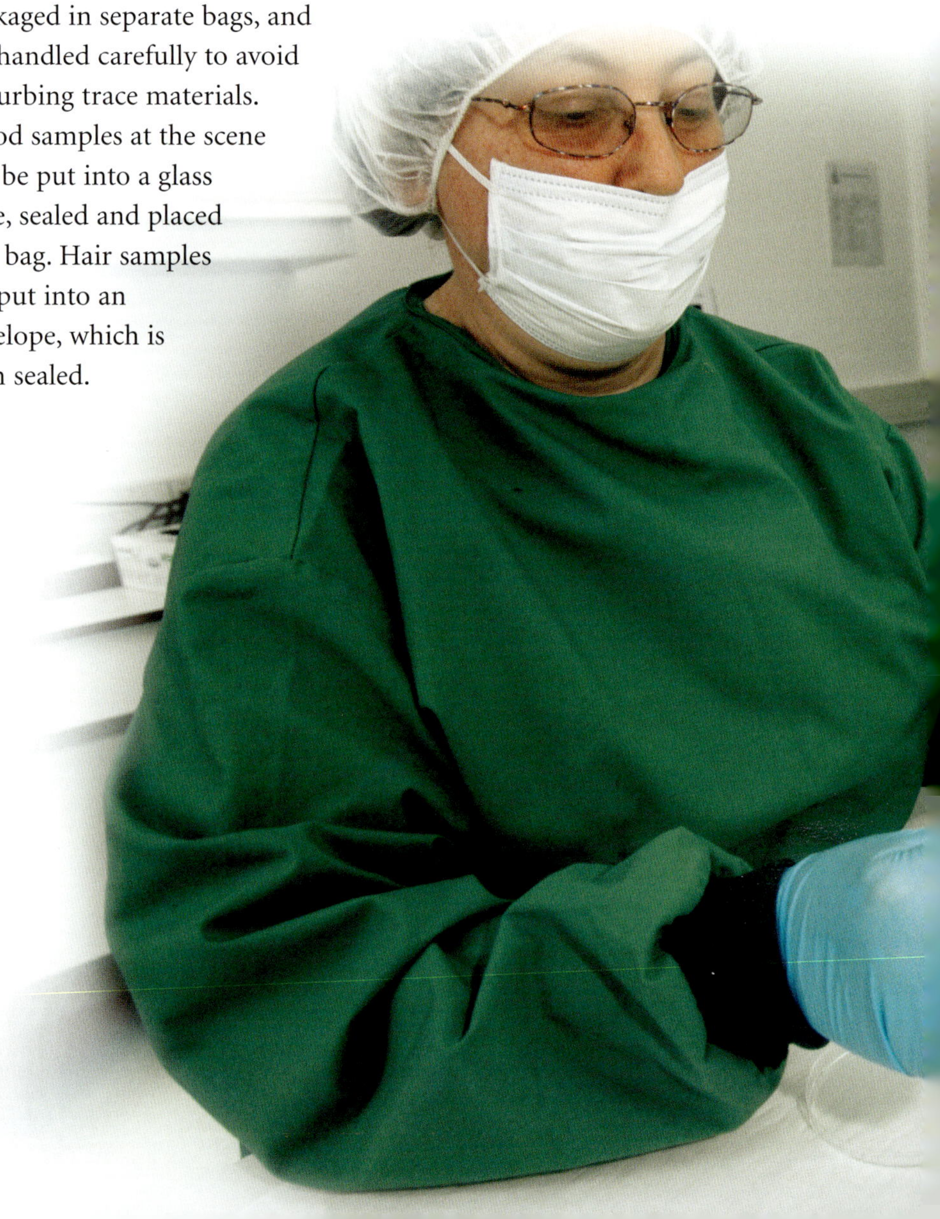

it was found, and the initials of the inspector who found it.

Even after all the precautions of safe packaging have been taken, evidence may be ruled inadmissible in court if a record is not available showing that the items were kept secure during their journey from the crime scene to the forensic lab and then the courtroom. This list, called the 'chain of custody', is the record of every person who handled the evidence and had put their initials and the date on the container. This assures that the evidence has not been removed, added to, replaced or altered.

OVERLOOKING THE BROKEN CHAIN

It is important to maintain the chain of custody, but judges sometimes overlook a broken chain. This happened in 2004 in Michigan when a court of appeals heard a defendant's claim that the chain of custody had been broken when cocaine supposedly seized from him was left, unsealed and unmarked, overnight in the police officer's car.

The court ruled the break had happened, but said there was no evidence of mistaken exchange, contamination or tampering, because the officer testified the package had remained inside his locked car in the locked glove compartment until the following morning when he sealed it and placed it in an evidence locker.

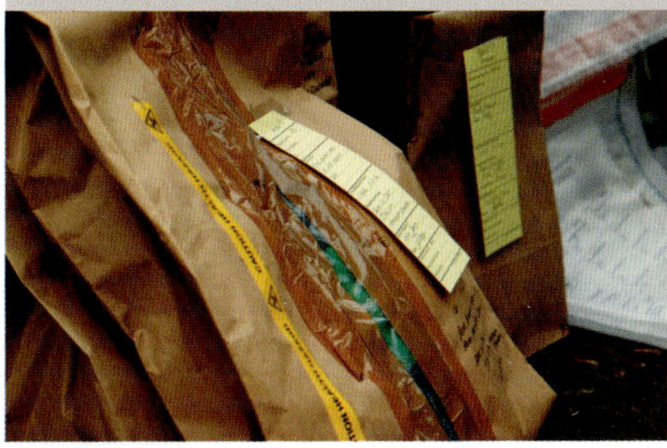

These labelled paper bags contain forensic evidence. Paper packaging is used to prevent condensation and contamination from bacterial growth.

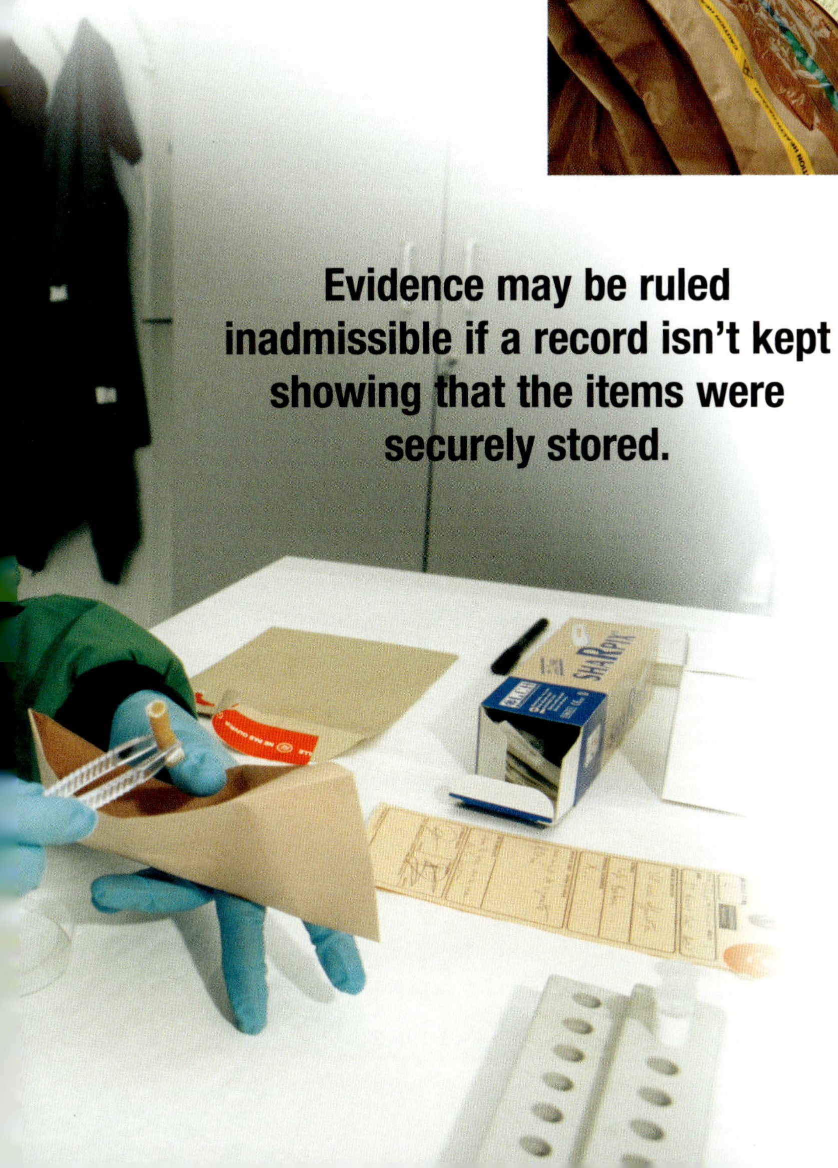

Evidence may be ruled inadmissible if a record isn't kept showing that the items were securely stored.

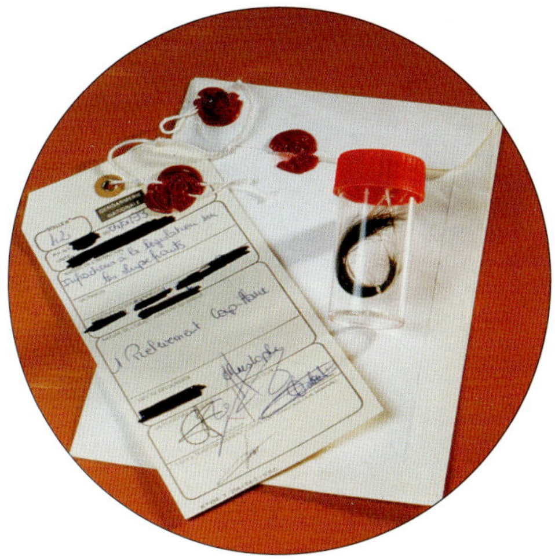

A forensic scientist (left) removes a cigarette stub from a sealed bag of evidence collected at a crime scene. A vial of hair sample (above) rests on a record sheet that has been sealed with wax to prevent tampering.

Reconstructing the Crime

A primary goal of police and forensic investigators at a crime scene is to reconstruct the crime. They define what the crime was, the sequence of events, who was present and their positions and actions.

This involves getting a feel for the scene and the evidence, interviewing any witnesses, suspects and surviving victims, and then using scientific methods and logical reasoning. Criminal profiling will be added to understand why the crime happened and what this reveals about who may have done it.

RECONSTRUCTIVE EVIDENCE

Clues as to what happened are known as reconstructive evidence. The direction of shoe prints, fingerprints or tool marks on a window or door, the position of blood splatters and bullet trajectories and the victim's wounds, which can indicate the positions of the attacker and victim, can all be used to piece together the crime.

A deceased individual slumped in a dining-room chair with a wound to his temple and a gun resting on the floor below his outstretched arm may seem to be a clear case of suicide. However, an examination uncovers wounds to the back of his head, scuff marks indicating a struggle and traces of skin under the victim's fingernails. Therefore, the original assumption of suicide quickly changes into a murder investigation. No fingerprints are uncovered on the gun but latent prints are on the door of a cabinet containing silver pieces. Investigators propose their theory: the victim surprised a burglar intent on stealing the silver. They struggled until the assailant struck the victim down, shot him and arranged the suicide scene, being forced to leave the silver behind.

This is an example of a staged crime scene, where the perpetrator leaves false clues to mislead investigators. Such cases could also

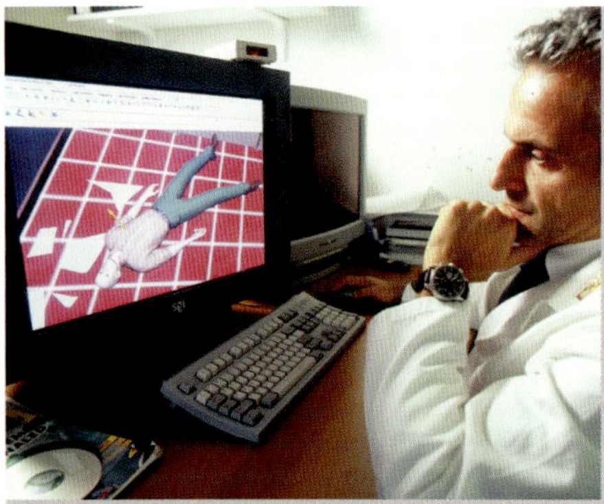

Forensic investigators can calculate bullet trajectories by creating a three-dimensional computer reconstruction of a crime scene.

RECONSTRUCTION CLUES

When retired Group Captain T. P. Singh, his wife, Shibani, and sister, Ajit Kaur, were murdered together in 2006 in Chandigarh, India, forensic experts helped police reconstruct the crime. Tracks showed that the perpetrator killed the man, followed by his wife and sister, which indicated one or a few assailants. The wife had thrown a flower vase at the assailant(s) and her hair had been pulled, indicating she had fought back. Two gunshots were found in the man's body, showing he had tried to escape. The lack of a forced entry led police to Singh's son, Pawandeep, who confessed and named two associates in the murder.

include a husband killing his wife with several blows and then positioning her body at the bottom of the stairs to indicate an accident, an arsonist who sets a fire to consume the body of a murder victim or a person involved in insurance fraud, hiding their own valuables and staging a burglary by scattering contents from drawers and breaking a window.

The BBC 'Crimewatch' programme re-enacts (above) the stabbing of Abigail Witchalls in Surrey in 2005, and a gendarme (left) checks a dummy used to recreate the 1999 murder of Isabel Peake in France.

The Modus Operandi

As well as evaluating the physical evidence, criminologists also reconstruct a crime by looking at the perpetrator's *modus operandi* (MO), which is his or her normal way of committing the same type of crime.

JUERGEN BARTSCH

Serial criminals normally repeat the same sequence of actions. Juergen Bartsch, a young homosexual, killed four boys in Essen, Germany, from 1962 to 1966, each time luring a slim, dark-haired victim into a cave or similar type of shelter. He also mutilated their bodies in the same manner, including decapitation, castration, gouging out their eyes and cutting open their bodies to empty the abdominal area. He was estimated to have attempted more than 100 further homicidal attacks. Bartsch was caught in 1966 and remained in a psychiatric hospital until his death in 1976.

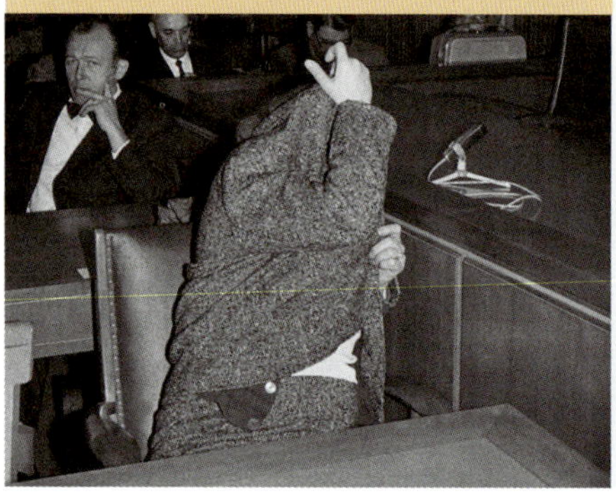

This involves decisions that include the weapon preferred, the method of entry, whether the perpetrator disconnects the telephone and whether items are taken after a victim is attacked or killed. Each criminal also has a signature comprised of actions done in addition to those needed to commit the crime. For example, an offender may always talk quietly to the victim, inflict torture or write messages on a mirror.

Investigators will also look closely at the victim and the timing of events leading up to the crime. Family and friends will be interviewed concerning the victim's background and personal relationships, while searches are made of medical, education and employment records, including police files if relevant. If there is a question of possible suicide, profilers will determine if there were alcohol, drug or other problems.

Each criminal has a signature comprised of actions made in addition to those needed to commit the crime.

CAROLINE DICKINSON

The case of the 13-year-old British schoolgirl, Caroline Dickinson, raped and murdered in France in 1996 while on an activity holiday with her school, demonstrates how a perpetrator's method of operation will lead him to the same type of scene to commit a crime. Caroline was killed in a youth hostel dormitory, and five years later Francisco Arces Montes of Spain was arrested in Miami, Florida, for a lewd act in another youth hostel dormitory. DNA tests in the USA matched the sample collected at the French scene. Montes was extradited to France, convicted in 2001 and later confessed.

Files at Interpol were searched after the murder of schoolgirl Caroline Dickinson in a French youth hostel room (left).

RE-ENACTMENTS

Police, victims, criminals and even actors sometimes act out a crime during an investigation or confession. When four young men were killed in northern Rio de Janeiro, Brazil, in 2003, police said they were drug dealers, but a re-enaction of the event proved them to have been innocent bystanders.

In Waihou, New Zealand, in 2005, a woman charged with murdering her husband in 1988 showed police how she dragged him to a shallow grave and even how his body landed on top of her after she fell into the hole she had dug.

Handling Witnesses and Suspects

Because the human memory is a fragile entity, it is best for witnesses to a crime to be identified and interviewed at the scene of the crime. Yet, even at the scene, memories have proved to be fairly unreliable.

Witnessing a crime can place an individual in an excitable state. And being probed by the police will add a great deal of stress, especially if the witness is worried about being a suspect.

Before forensic science, witnesses were often the only way of linking a suspect to the crime. If today's courtroom testimony by a crime-scene witness contradicts that of an 'expert witness' who has conducted forensic tests, the jury will inevitably believe the latter. A lawyer will have a much easier time disputing an ordinary person's eyesight than the results of a DNA profile.

DETAINING WITNESSES

Police powers to detain witnesses at a crime scene vary considerably. In Uzbekistan investigators can detain anyone they deem to be a 'witness' and that person does not have the right to a lawyer during detention, which can be extended by the prosecutor without consulting a judge. Any answers obtained from such a witness can be used as evidence in a court case. In the USA, however, powers to detain witnesses are in doubt and often unresolved in the various states. Witnesses cannot be arrested under the Fourth Amendment's prohibition against unreasonable search and seizure, but they can be detained if 'special needs' or 'suspicion-less detention' is crucial to a case.

THE NEW YORK SOLUTION

True suspects at the scene can be arrested and taken to a police station for interrogation. The difficulty is in separating suspects from innocent witnesses. In 2005 the New York Police Department (NYPD) launched a Real Time Crime Center constantly staffed by officers. They immediately access information about a crime scene and potential suspects and send the results by email, fax or telephone to first responders on the scene.
In the spring of 2008, New York's $500 million Citywide Mobile Wireless Network became operational after a seven-month pilot, so officers can instantly download identifying data like fingerprints and mugshots, which will allow them to detain suspects at the scene.

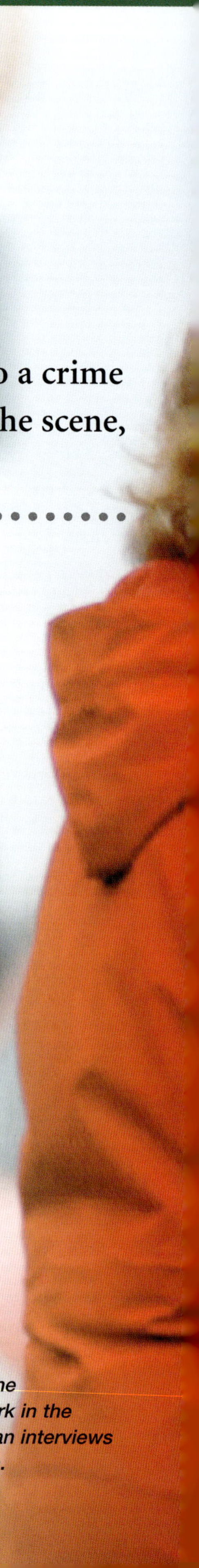

Right: As members of the emergency services work in the background, a policeman interviews a witness to a car crash.

Above: New York officers interview customers leaving a Harlem restaurant after a shooting in 2005 injured two bystanders.

WITNESSES VS DNA

Linda Razzell, a 41-year-old mother of four, went missing in Swindon in 2002, and bloodstains were later found in the car of her estranged husband, Glyn. Her body was never found, but six witnesses called police to say they had seen her after the disappearance. One, a friend who knew her well, said they made eye contact, and she was sure it was Linda.

Although this information was presented during the court case in 2003, the jury was more impressed with DNA tests that identified the blood in the car as hers. Glyn Razzell was convicted and sentenced to life imprisonment.

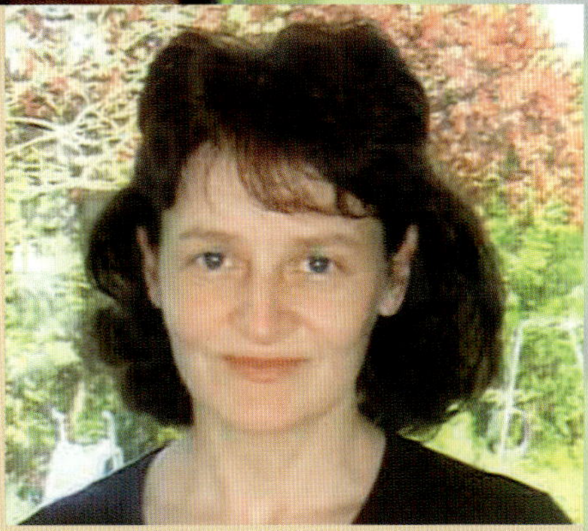

Linda Razzell had already taken her husband to court twice for assault and feared that he would kill her.

Witnesses Who Made a Difference

All types of crimes are regularly solved through witnesses. Having viewed a crime, many people give confused accounts. But law enforcement depends heavily on eyewitnesses, so one of the police's first acts after a crime is to make an appeal for the public's assistance.

Several people, who identified the perpetrators but unfortunately missed the opportunity to intervene, witnessed one of England's most shocking crimes. James Bulger, a two-year-old from Merseyside, was abducted in 1993 from a shopping centre when his mother's attention was diverted. Within two hours he was dead, his body found on a railway track after he had been violently attacked with stones, bricks and a metal object.

James was seen on a camera with two boys, and several witnesses saw the three on their two-mile trip to the crime scene, all assuming they were brothers or friends. Some noted injuries to James' head, some described him as crying and extremely distressed, but others said he was laughing. A woman who queried them was told they had found the toddler and were taking him to the local police station. Even more witnesses saw the three at a railway bridge. The 10-year-old abductors, Jon Venables and Robert Thompson, were convicted by this conclusive evidence in 1993, and imprisoned in an institute for young offenders until 2001. In 2010 Venables was returned to prison for downloading child pornography and violating several terms of his release.

SHARP EYES

Another abduction case in the USA in 2007 had a happier ending when information from a sharp-eyed observer led to the rescue of two young boys, one of them held captive for more than four years. Michael Devlin, 41, grabbed Ben Ownby, 13, as he left his school bus in a suburb of St Louis, Missouri, but one of Ben's friends leaving the bus saw a dilapidated white truck speeding away and gave a detailed description to the police. Four days later, officers had traced the vehicle to Devlin and were surprised to find both Ben and Shawn Wilcox, who had been kidnapped by Devlin in 2002 when he was 11 years old.

Police are especially trained to interview witnesses, many of whom may be traumatized by a crime or worried that they may be suspects.

'PEELING AN ONION'

Although they generally arrive at the crime scene after the police have secured it and are in the process of conducting interviews, forensic investigators can also question victims, witnesses and suspects.

A crime scene analyst with the Las Vegas Metro Police Department noted, 'My job is to ask what the story is. It's like peeling an onion – I take it one layer at a time. I listen to everybody and then look at the evidence to see what it says, and if it denies or corroborates somebody's story. I'm not on anybody's side – not even the side of the detectives against the arrestees. My job is to find the truth through the evidence and to document that truth.'

Police (far left) investigate the railway track where James Bulger's body was found. A surveillance camera caught images of Bulger holding hands with Jon Venables as he was abducted from a shopping centre near Liverpool.

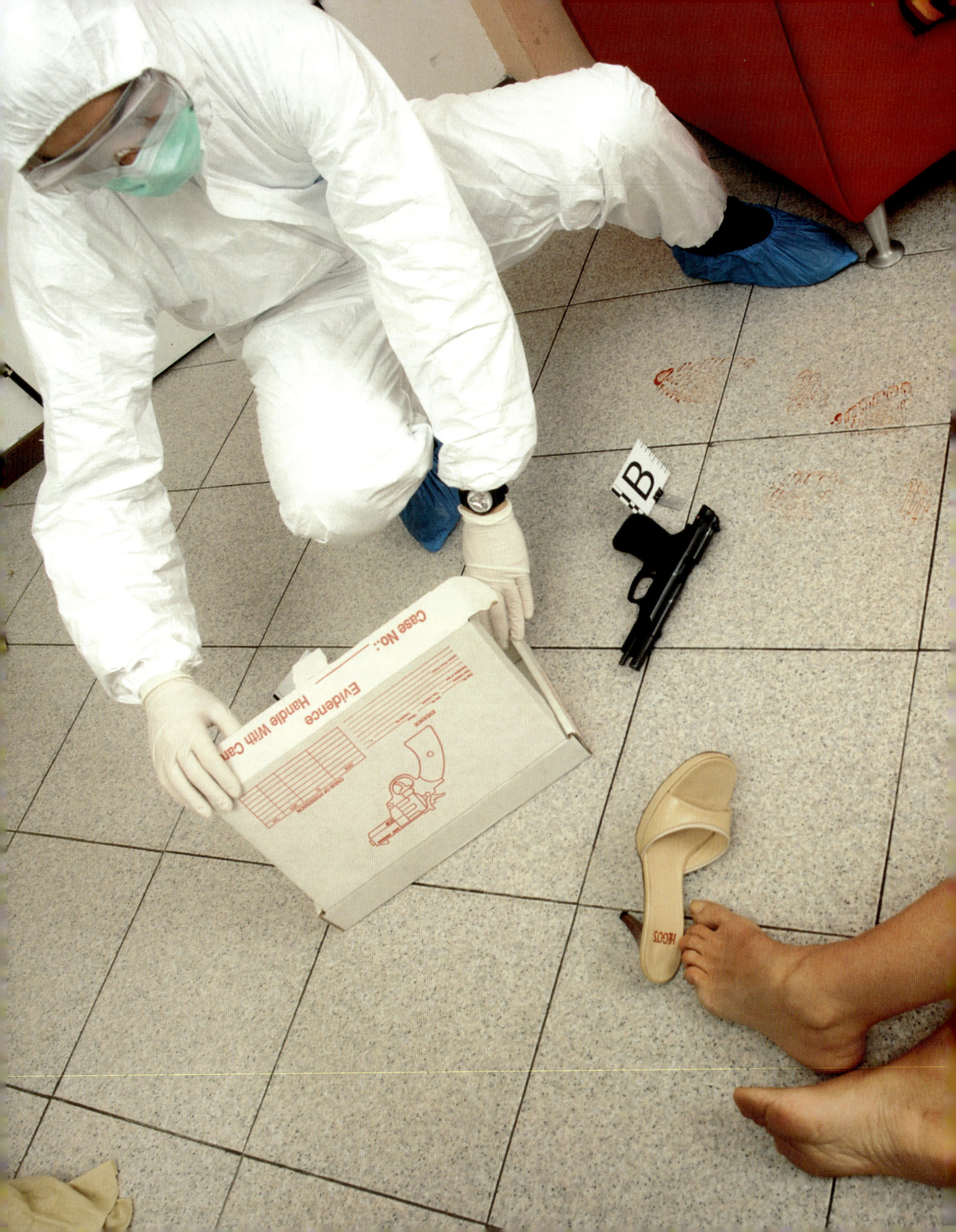
B
Case No.:
Evidence

Chapter Three

Details of Death

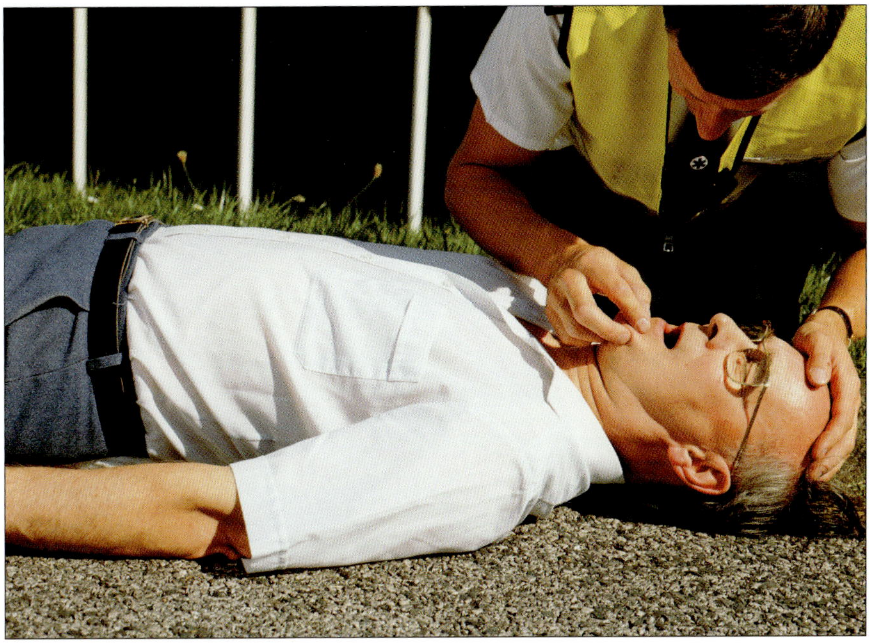

A man is found unconscious under suspicious circumstances. The first priority is resuscitation, but if this fails, the location will become a possible crime scene.

MOST DEATHS OCCUR BY NATURAL CAUSES, BUT THEY CAN ALSO BE THE RESULT OF AN ACCIDENT, SUICIDE OR HOMICIDE. Only the last will turn the place of death into a crime scene, and forensic scientists must determine as quickly as possible if murder has been committed. A pathologist's examination is superficial at this point, but checks will be made for rigor mortis and for fluids or marks on the body. Finding other clues will involve examining the position of the body and patterns of bloodstains. The immediate surroundings will be examined for marks, blood specks and items that may have been used in the crime.

The skull of a murder victim in a forensic laboratory is numbered along with other bones for identification.

Checking for Life

When a body is discovered, the priority is to check for vital signs such as a pulse, heartbeat and breathing. A medical examiner will use a stethoscope to attempt to find a faint heartbeat.

A CORONER AT THE SCENE

Disagreement exists as to whether a coroner is actually needed at a crime scene, because some believe a coroner hinders the work. During the inquiry into Dr Harold Shipman's murders, the forensic pathologist Dr Peter Acland said a coroner at the scene of death could contaminate evidence and make decisions that complicate the investigation. Dr Acland added that he had never known the involvement of a coroner to benefit a crime-scene investigation. Michael Burgess, representing the Coroners' Society, added that he saw potential problems with a coroner being physically present at the death scene. However, he said that a coroner or someone separate from the police should be there with the power to authorize an autopsy of the body.

Michael Stone, arriving at the High Court in London on 18 January 2005, was found guilty of murder.

Any slight indication of life calls for resuscitation or other critical medical treatment, and this takes priority over the arrest of a suspect and the possible contamination of evidence. This has been obvious during terrorist attacks such as the Madrid bombings of 11 March 2004. Badly injured victims can seem lifeless, so great care must be taken in examining a body for life. When a man brutally attacked Dr Lin Russell and her two daughters, Megan and Josie, with a hammer in 1996 on an isolated lane near Canterbury, Kent, one of the two police officers first on the scene, Constable Richard Leivers, checked for signs of life and found none. Dr Shaun Russell, the husband and father, was told of the discovery and informed that all of his family had died. However, as the police surgeon, Dr Michael Parks, arrived at the murder scene, Constable Leivers noticed that the body of nine-year-old Josie moved.

'I had ascertained that the female adult was cold and had no signs of life,' Dr Parks reported. 'I immediately diverted my attentions to the child. She moved when I touched her and felt warm. I reassured her and after a brief period of reflection I asked PC Leivers to pick her up. She was semi-conscious and had clear head injuries.'

The girl had lain barely alive next to the dead bodies of her mother and sister for an hour. Although Josie Russell suffered severe head injuries, she made an amazing recovery. Her interview by police was videotaped and presented as evidence at the trial of Michael Stone, who was convicted of the murders in 1998 and given three life sentences.

Josie Russell recovered at home after the hammer attack that killed her mother and sister. Police on the scene first thought she had died.

Resuscitation or other critical medical treatment takes priority over the possible contamination of evidence.

Resuscitation

Police and emergency services are well equipped to treat crime victims, and it is the duty of the first officer attending to give aid immediately to anyone still alive.

An ambulance should be called if the victim is unconscious or slipping in and out of unconsciousness or has difficulty in breathing, is experiencing a heavy blood loss, a deep wound such as a stab wound, severe burns or another serious trauma.

When victims might have neck injuries, they are placed on their backs, and an officer then checks if the chest is rising and falling. If no breathing is detected, the officer can give mouth-to-mouth resuscitation. If the victim is breathing, he or she is placed on their side with the lower arm stretched out in front of them and the hand of the upper arm under their cheek.

It is important to make sure oxygen is circulating to the victim's brain, so the officer checks for blood circulation by pressing two fingers lightly to one side of the victim's windpipe to feel for a pulse in the neck. If a pulse of at least one beat per second exists, mouth-to-mouth resuscitation continues. If there is no pulse or a slow one, an officer starts cardio-pulmonary resuscitation (CPR), which is a continuation of the rescue breaths combined with chest compressions.

Often two officers will be on the scene to attempt to revive a victim and summon medical help. If a member of the public arrives first, comfort and some first aid should be given to the victim and emergency calls made.

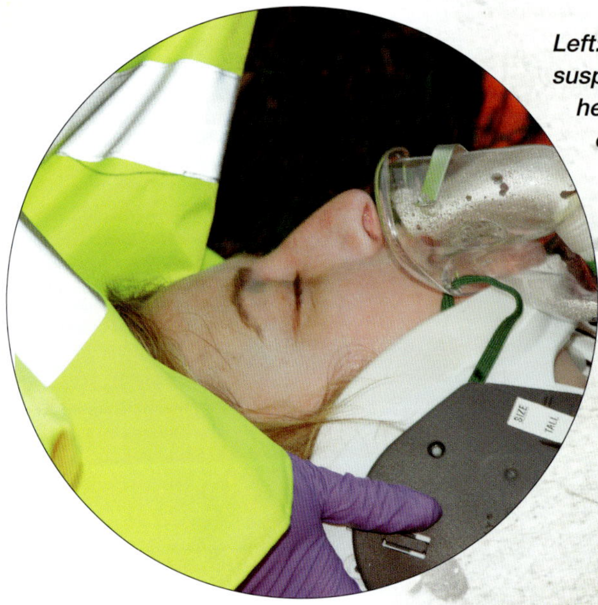

Left: Paramedics treat a woman with a suspected neck injury by holding her head and using a rigid cervical collar and oxygen mask.

Right: First aid for a stopped heart involves chest compressions and mouth-to-mouth resuscitation.

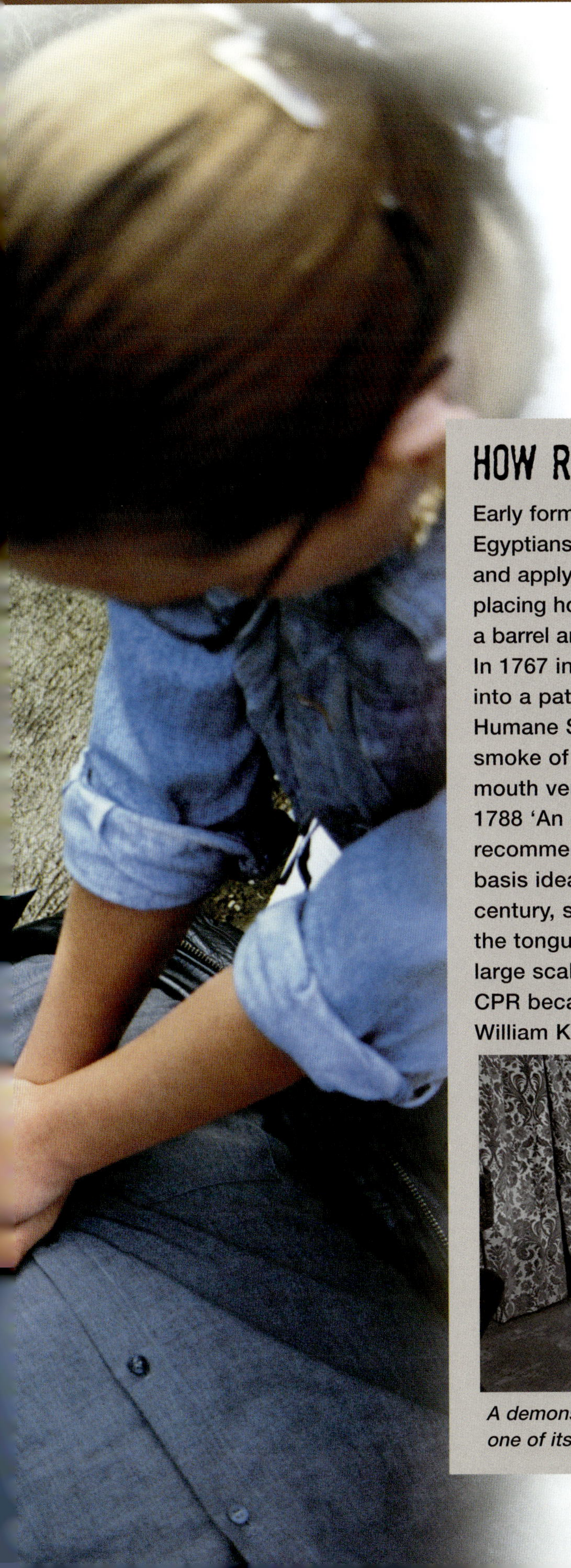

If there is no pulse, or a slow one, an officer starts cardio-pulmonary resuscitation.

HOW RESUSCITATION EVOLVED

Early forms of attempted resuscitation were not pleasant. The ancient Egyptians have recorded their efforts of hanging patients by the feet and applying pressure to the chest. Other early methods included placing hot ashes on the chest, whipping the victim, rolling him over a barrel and stretching him over a trotting horse.

In 1767 in England and Europe, a bellows was used to blow smoke into a patient's mouth and even rectum. That year, the Dutch Humane Society issued guidelines that included 'insufflation of smoke of burning tobacco into the rectum' but also 'mouth-to-mouth ventilation'. An English physician, Charles Kite, published in 1788 'An Essay on the Recovery of the Apparently Dead' that first recommended electrodes to shock the body. Nevertheless, more basis ideas continued to flourish in Europe in the late nineteenth century, such as stretching the rectum and, in France, stretching the tongue. Mouth-to-mouth resuscitation was first promoted on a large scale in the US military during World War II, and the use of CPR became standard in the 1960s, introduced by the US doctor William Kouwenhoven.

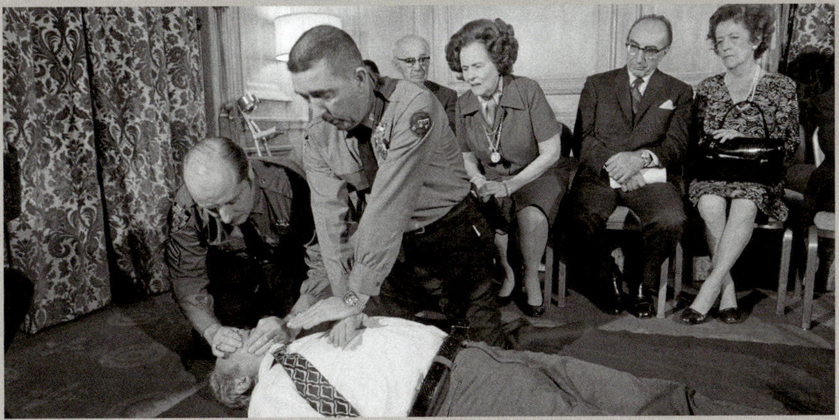

A demonstration of CPR by the New York Police Department is watched by one of its pioneers, Dr William Kouwenhoven, in 1973.

Examining a Body at the Scene

A forensic pathologist examines a body found at a possible crime scene before it is removed to the morgue. The first examination may be done with the corpse *in situ*, or it may have to be moved for a proper examination.

This is why the original undisturbed position of the body is photographed, videotaped or sketched first.

The pathologist carries only a notepad and pen to the scene, but the crime scene manager or medical examiner provides any other necessary items such as a thermometer, swabs for the removal of a sample of any fluids or marks on the body or clothes, and containers for storing evidence.

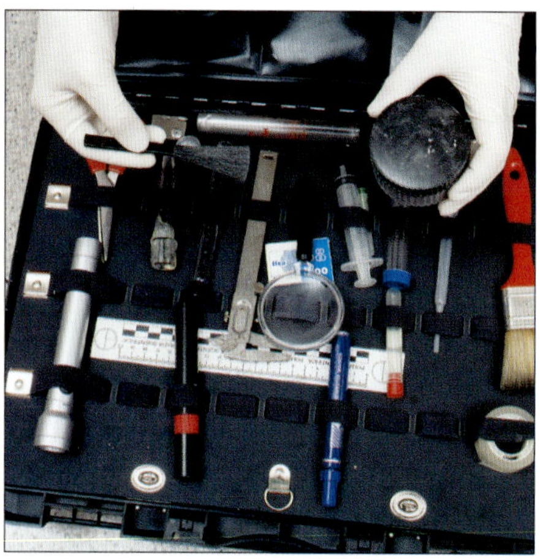

A forensic investigator, gloved to avoid contamination, removes a container of fine powder from a crime scene kit for fingerprint work.

The examination will concentrate on determining the time of death – this may be a vital clue in linking the murder to a suspect. The time of death, never an exact figure, will be more difficult to judge after the body is removed, an action that will also eliminate signs of rigor mortis.

It may be necessary to remove the deceased's clothing to check for discoloration of the skin. A dead person's skin in the lower regions begins to take on a pink-red colour, or lividity, due to blood settling. This begins some 30 minutes to 2 hours after death and is complete by 8 to 12 hours. This is caused by gravity, so a corpse lying on its left side has lividity on its left shoulder, arm, hip and leg. The overall skin also takes on a greenish tint after 48 hours because of bacteria. This becomes a marbled look after four to seven days. Dark skin, however, will not show these colours.

The temperature of the cadaver is measured with a rectal thermometer. After death, the temperature of the body's trunk will generally fall about 0.8°C/1.5°F for each hour.

CADAVERIC SPASM

Sometimes a corpse will have a kind of instant rigor mortis called 'cadaveric spasm'. This happens when the muscles were being used with great exertion while dying, as during a struggle or while running hard. This is why the victim might have a death grip on a weapon. A cadaveric spasm, of course, can add confusion to the time of death.

RIGOR MORTIS

A pathologist at the crime scene will check for this stiffening of the body by carefully trying to move the arms and legs, neck, jaw and eyelids. Rigor mortis normally occurs from 30 minutes to 3 hours after death, taking hold first in the eyelids, jaw and neck, then progressing downwards. The whole body is affected within 8 to 12 hours, the stiffness continues for up to 18 hours, and is gone after a further 6 to 12 hours. Sometimes at low temperatures, rigor mortis will not even be present.

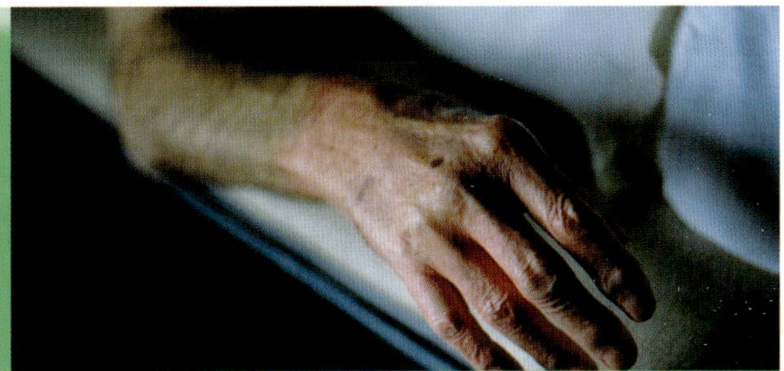

It is extremely important for a pathologist to investigate the body of a crime victim as soon as possible after discovery. By the time a body reaches the morgue, vital information will have been lost.

The Decaying Body

A corpse is sometimes found several weeks after the victim has died, and this poses problems for a pathologist estimating the time of death. Help will no longer come from rigor mortis, body temperature and lividity, so the rate of decay will have to be used.

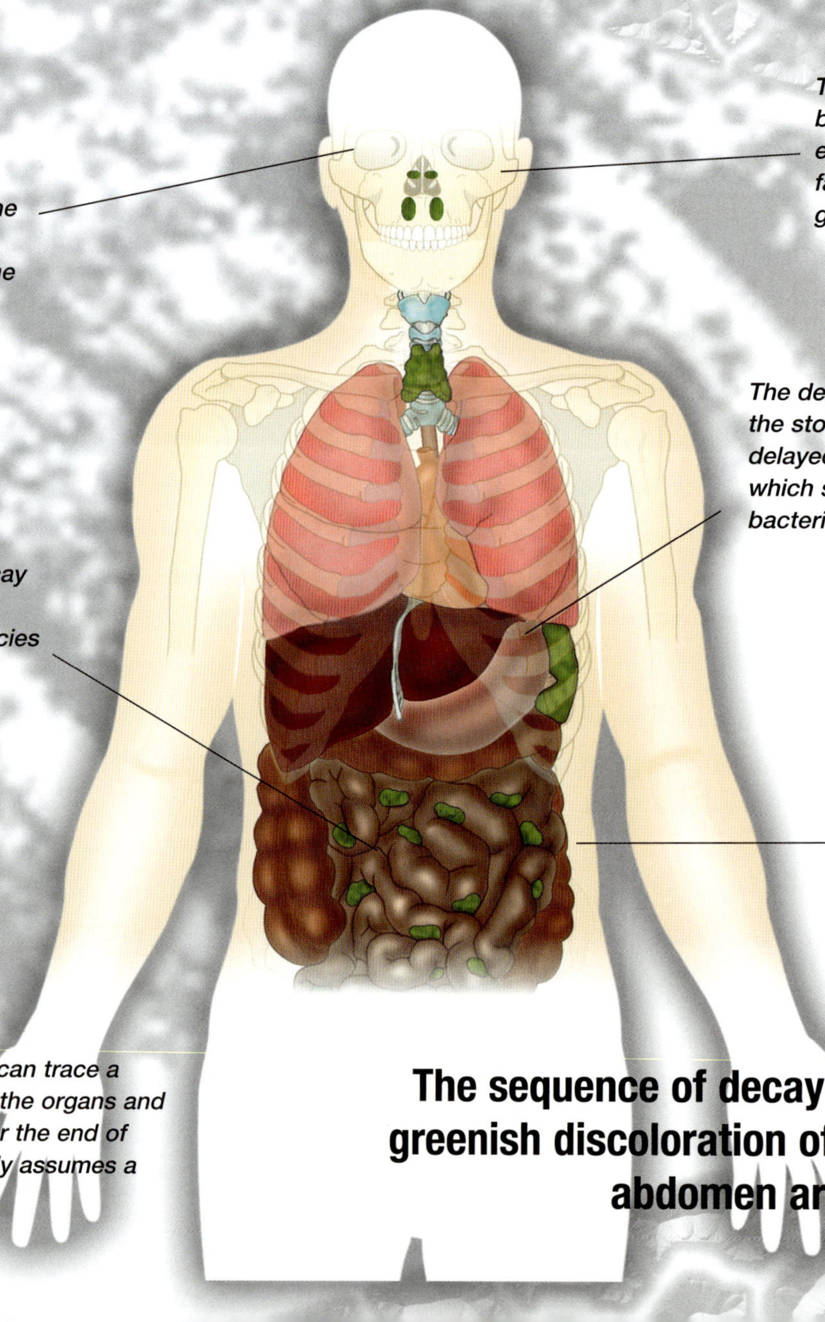

Forensic pathologists can trace a body's decay through the organs and other soft tissues. Near the end of decomposing, the body assumes a greenish-black colour.

The sequence of decay begins with a greenish discoloration of the skin in the abdomen area.

Even the rate of decay can change according to the surrounding temperature and humidity, because, for example, a body in the open also decays faster than if it was buried or was immersed in water. More complications arise if the murderer waited a period of time before burying the victim, or if he moved it later.

Bacteria and the chemical breakdown of the body's cells and tissues, known as autolysis, cause postmortem decomposition, or putrefaction. These processes begin immediately after death, but they may not be visible until two or three days have passed. The sequence of decay is unpleasant, even for a veteran forensic scientist. It begins with a greenish discoloration of the skin in the abdomen area, and this spreads to the upper body and head. After three days gases from the decomposition cause bloating, with the swelling appearing first in the face. The skin then begins to marble, showing a pattern of blood vessels, which resemble a web, near the surface. The skin also develops blisters filled with liquid or gas; when they burst, the skin loosens. Fluids of decomposition drain from the mouth and nose, and the body soon splits open.

Many factors can influence a corpse's rate of decay, including the victim's weight. For example, overweight people decay faster, so the process is not as reliable as tests conducted on someone who is recently deceased.

SKELETALIZATION

When a body's soft tissues have completely decomposed, the forensic anthropologist is left with only bones to work with. This length of this skeletalization process depends on the climate. For example, it might take up to two years in France, but only take a few weeks in the heat of Kenya.
A complete skeleton will normally reveal the gender and race, as well as the general age and height of the deceased. Forensic odontologists can also help estimate the age at time of death by the development of teeth and their amount of wear.
The cause of death may be indicated by trauma such as a hole in the head or by natural causes such as disease. Forensic experts are seldom interested when a victim's bones are older than a century, because the murderer will likely be dead.

A skeleton is arranged in a forensic lab, with the bones numbered for accurate reference. These are the remains of a person abducted and murdered during the military rule in Argentina between 1976 and 1983. The hole in the skull is testament to a violent death.

THE DECAY OF INTERNAL ORGANS

Forensic pathologists can sometimes give a better estimate of the time of death by checking the internal organs, which decay in a known sequence. Bacteria attack the intestines first, and then decay moves to the liver, lungs, brain, kidneys, stomach (food and acid there can retard the growth of bacteria) and lastly the prostate or uterus.

Examining the Surroundings

The area surrounding a crime scene must be carefully searched for evidence or, in some cases, a corpse. Obviously, the access strip to be used by investigators should be examined first.

In all of the area, inspectors will take soil and plant samples that might also be found on a suspect's clothing. An outdoor area will usually be gone over by a police line moving slowly forwards. This environment is open to the elements and can change quickly, so it should be examined without delay.

If investigators suspect a body or weapon has been put under water, searches are required in lakes, ponds and rivers. Bodies and weapons may be buried, requiring searches using metal detectors, radar or sniffer dogs.

An immense area can surround crimes. In 2001, a British backpacker, Peter Falconio, was murdered in the Australian Outback. Police had to cover inhospitable terrain of half a million square miles in the Northern Territory, six times

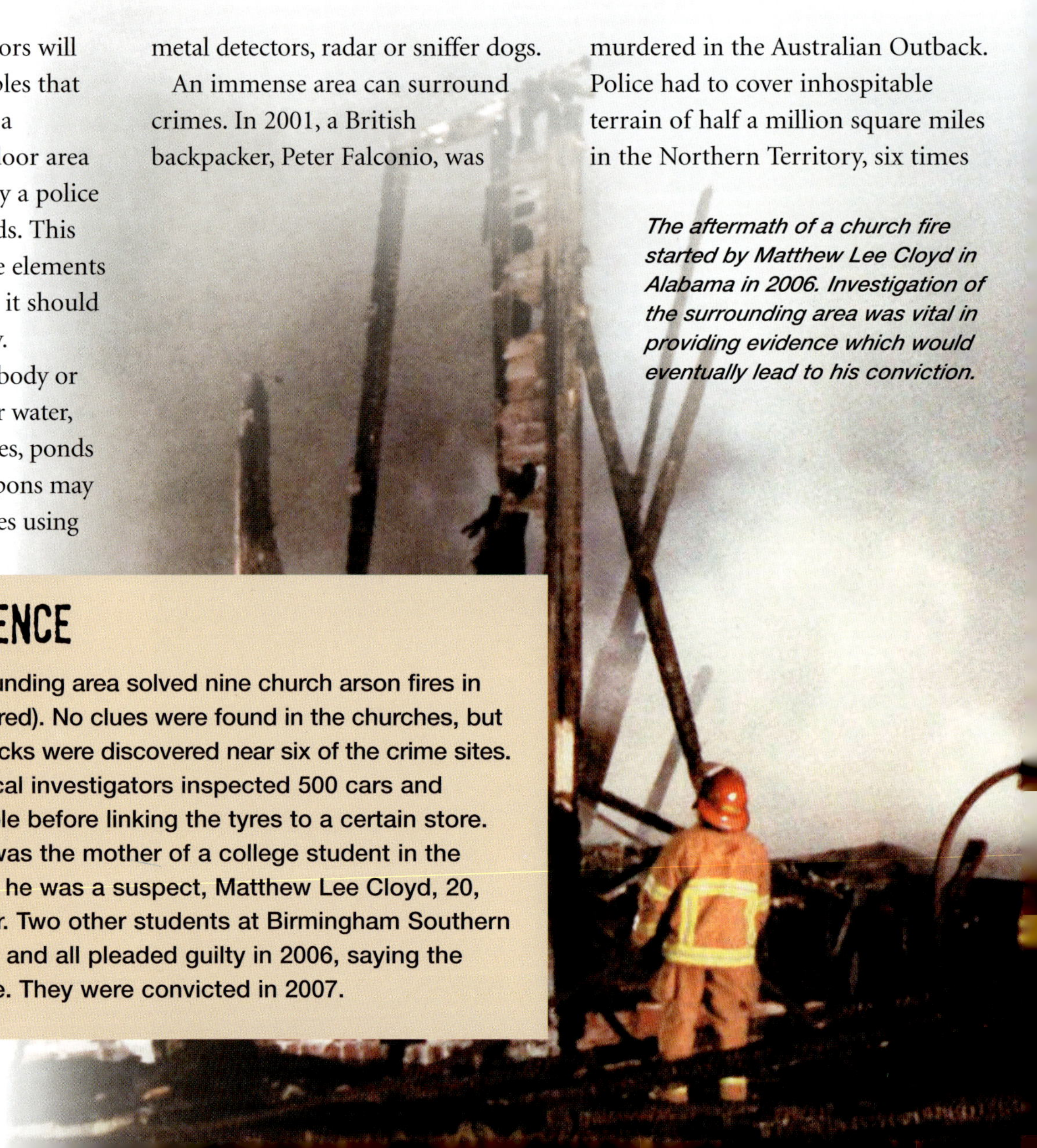

The aftermath of a church fire started by Matthew Lee Cloyd in Alabama in 2006. Investigation of the surrounding area was vital in providing evidence which would eventually lead to his conviction.

TRACKING EVIDENCE

Investigating the surrounding area solved nine church arson fires in Alabama in 2006 (pictured). No clues were found in the churches, but the same set of tyre tracks were discovered near six of the crime sites. Federal, state, and local investigators inspected 500 cars and interviewed 1500 people before linking the tyres to a certain store. One of its customers was the mother of a college student in the Birmingham area. Told he was a suspect, Matthew Lee Cloyd, 20, confessed to his father. Two other students at Birmingham Southern College were arrested, and all pleaded guilty in 2006, saying the fires were set as a joke. They were convicted in 2007.

the size of Britain. Aboriginal trackers, who know the land better than anyone, joined the search.

Peter Falconio and Joanne Lees were attacked by Bradley Murdoch at this deserted site in the Australian Outback. Lees escaped by hiding among the shrubs.

Bradley Murdoch attacked Falconio, along with his girlfriend, Joanne Lees. He shot Falconio dead and tied up Lees, who managed to escape into the dark night. More than two years later, Murdoch was arrested as a rape suspect. Dr Jonathan Whitaker, senior forensic scientist with the UK's Forensic Science Service, matched his DNA to that on cable ties used to bind Lees. Falconio's body has never been found, but Murdoch was convicted and sentenced to life in prison.

NATALEE HOLLOWAY

Crime scenes are difficult to search, but a worse problem is not knowing exactly where the crime occurred. Authorities on the Dutch Caribbean island of Aruba were faced with this when 18-year-old US student Natalee Holloway disappeared on 30 May 2005. Virtually the entire island was searched for two years. Aruban police drained a pond and scoured beaches, sand dunes, and a landfill site. Police cadets combed one square mile where she was last seen. Police from the Netherlands, US FBI agents, officers from Miami and divers joined in. In 2007, investigators dug around the home of a suspect. Holloway is still officially listed as missing.

Benvinda de Sous, the lawyer representing the family of Natalee Holloway, advertises the reward offered for information on her whereabouts.

Signs of Violence

Although conclusive proof of a violent crime can be obtained in a forensic laboratory, a forensic pathologist will make a careful examination of a corpse at the scene of death.

Below: This three-dimensional CT scan shows the fractured skull of a man involved in an assault. Direct brain damage and even death can result from such injuries.

Obvious signs include wounds made by gunshot and by blunt and sharp instruments. Cutting, stabbing and puncture marks are examples of defensive wounds that are normally found on the back of the victim's hands, inside the palms and the inner side of the forearms. Scrapes and bruises can also suggest a struggle.

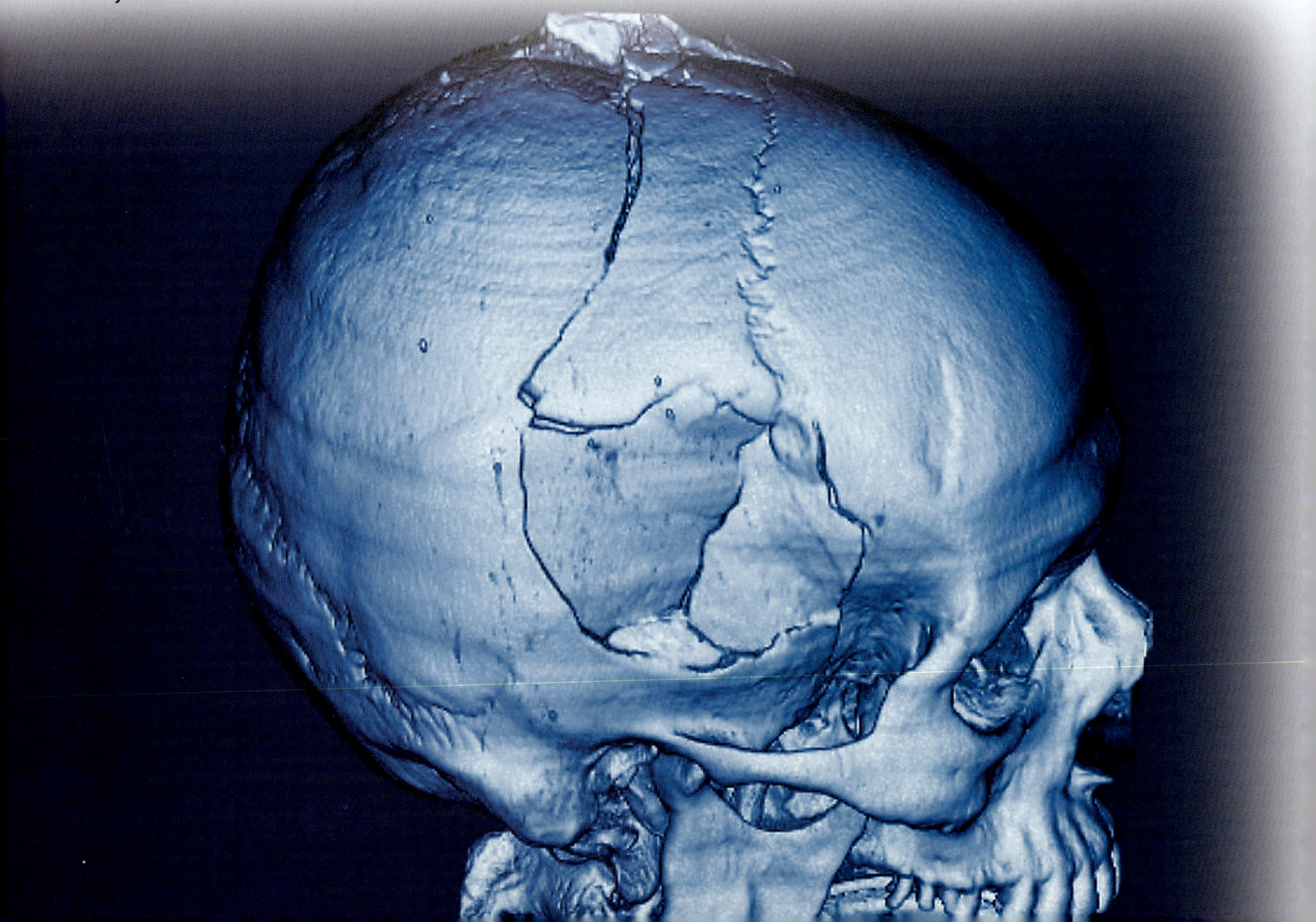

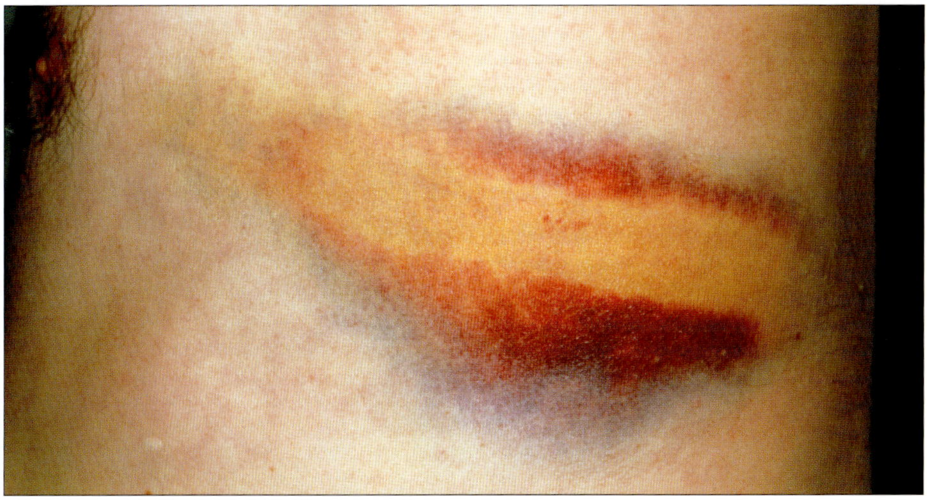

Bruising such as this could be the result of a beating with a club or baseball bat, and will be investigated carefully by a pathologist.

Violent marks on the body can also disprove an apparent suicide or accident victim. When the wife of a traffic policeman was found dead in front of her house in Cholurpalya, India, in 2004, it was ruled she committed suicide jumping from the balcony. However, a postmortem report found she had been strangled, and police arrested her husband and his father.

Other marks indicating violence include those made by ropes, tapes, bandages or other devices used to bind a victim, marks of a blindfold or gag and those associated with torture such as cigarette burns.

In some cases, despite having obvious marks and trauma, victims may deny they were assaulted, either to protect the perpetrator such as a spouse or out of fear of further violence. Police violence can be especially intimidating. The Asian Human Rights Commission has highlighted this such as the case of R. Don Nawaratne Bandara of Panadura, Sri Lanka. They say he was severely tortured by police in 2001 but withdrew his case against them because he feared for his life. The UN International Criminal Tribunal for the Former Yugoslavia also encountered many victims who refused to testify, citing their own safety. Its first case was dropped after a woman withdrew a rape charge because she could not be anonymous.

A LACK OF MARKS

Just the indication of overturned objects is sometimes enough to indicate foul play. When police in Hawaii discovered the body of a 40-year-old woman in 2000, there were no apparent physical marks of violence on her body but the nearby scene indicated a struggle, so they tentatively classified her death as a homicide. This initiated an immediate investigation, which led to an arrest.

TYPES OF WOUNDS

Forensic examiners encounter many different types of wounds, or lesions, and traumas caused by physical assault.

Some of the most common types are:

Abrasion: an injury in which the skin is scraped off

Concussion: a serious brain injury caused by a hard blow to the head

Contusion: a bruise in which the skin is not broken

Fracture: a break, crack or shattering of a bone

Laceration: a cut that is deep enough to need stitches

Trauma: a wound or a physical or emotional shock to the body

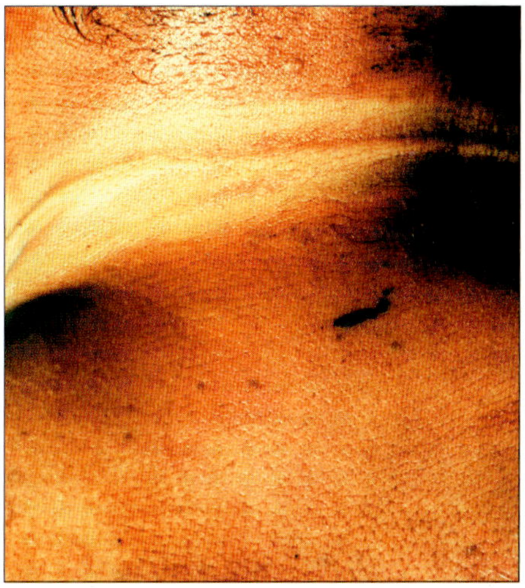

A murder victim has strangulation marks on the back of his neck caused by a thick cord. The appearance of the skin helps determine the time of death.

Signs of Abuse

Officials investigating a child's death have on occasion made discoveries of abuse. Maltreatment and a lack of proper care of children turns many death sites into crime scenes.

Each week in England, one to two children are killed by their parent or a caregiver and 16 per cent suffer serious maltreatment by parents; in the USA, an estimated 1500 children died in 2003 of maltreatment, three-quarters of these under the age of four. Child abuse has become less secret and reported cases are soaring. For example, in Japan in 2006 police investigated 297 cases, an increase of 33.8 per cent over the previous year.

GRIM DISCOVERY

In central Germany in 2000, the body of a child was discovered during an attempted eviction for rent arrears. The mother, a heroin user and prostitute living with her uncle, could not remember when she had last seen the child. She informed her uncle the child was with the grandmother, but also asked him how long someone could survive without food. Police at the crime scene found doors and windows tightly closed. The child's corpse was taken to the Institute for Legal Medicine at the University of Leipzig within one hour of its discovery. There were signs of malnourishment, and a forensic entomologist examined maggots on the body and estimated that the child had died about 14 days earlier. The estimate would have been more exact had the forensic expert been at the scene of the crime.

A wound caused by a cigarette burn in a child's skin is classified as a non-accidental injury.

VICTORIA CLIMBIE

When eight-year-old Victoria Climbie died in North Middlesex Hospital in London, the Home Office pathologist Dr Nathaniel Carey found 128 separate injuries and scars, many from cigarette burns, and declared this 'the worst case of child abuse I've encountered'. Victoria's parents had sent her from the Ivory Coast to live with her aunt, Marie-Therese Kouao, who ended up staying with Carl Manning in Tottenham, in north London. The girl was twice taken to the hospital's casualty department with injuries but the aunt's excuses were accepted. On the third visit Victoria died of malnutrition and hypothermia, and Kouao and Manning were found guilty of murder and both sentenced to life. An official inquiry found that agencies could have intervened on 12 occasions and possibly saved the girl's life.

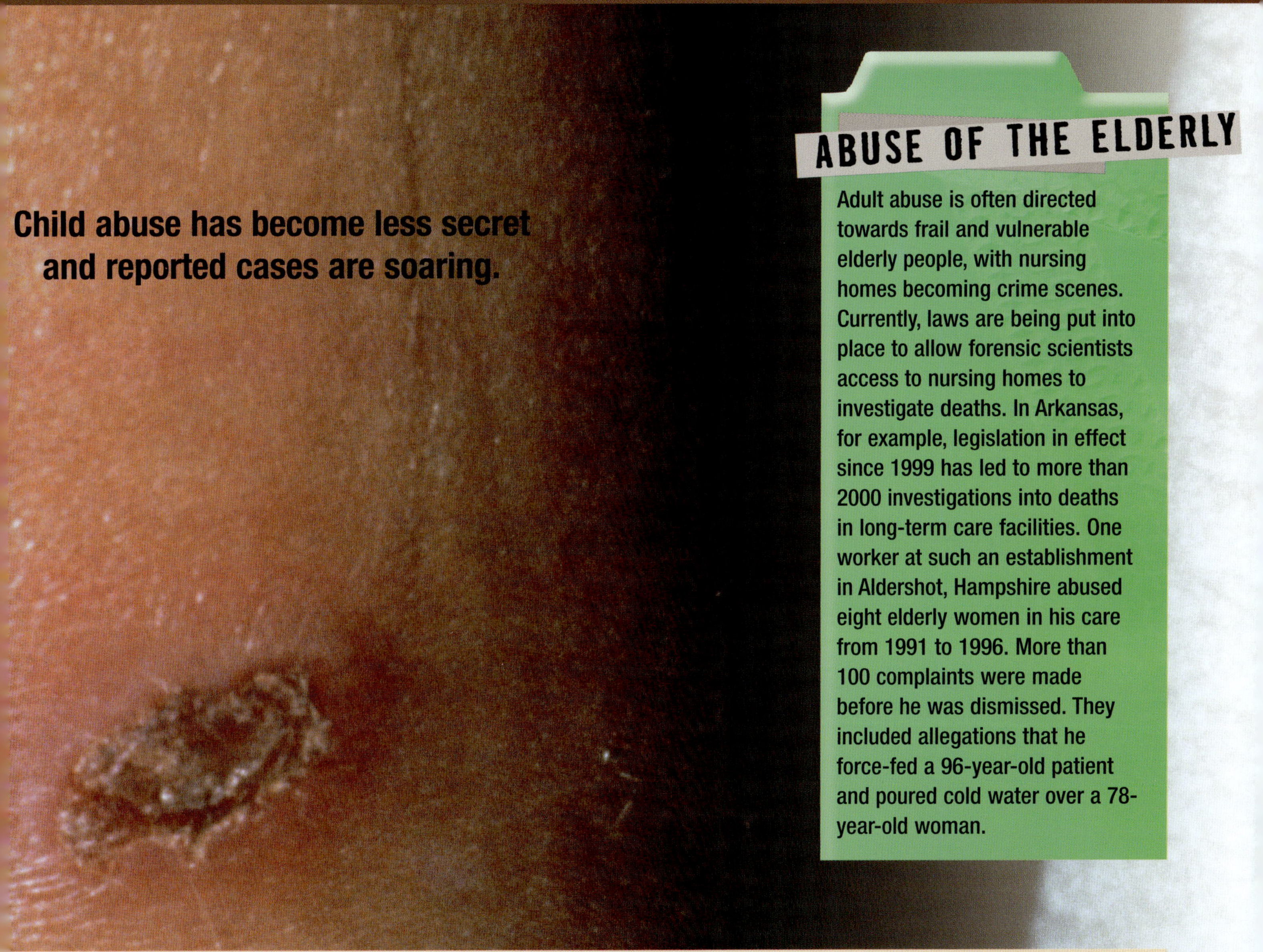

Child abuse has become less secret and reported cases are soaring.

ABUSE OF THE ELDERLY

Adult abuse is often directed towards frail and vulnerable elderly people, with nursing homes becoming crime scenes. Currently, laws are being put into place to allow forensic scientists access to nursing homes to investigate deaths. In Arkansas, for example, legislation in effect since 1999 has led to more than 2000 investigations into deaths in long-term care facilities. One worker at such an establishment in Aldershot, Hampshire abused eight elderly women in his care from 1991 to 1996. More than 100 complaints were made before he was dismissed. They included allegations that he force-fed a 96-year-old patient and poured cold water over a 78-year-old woman.

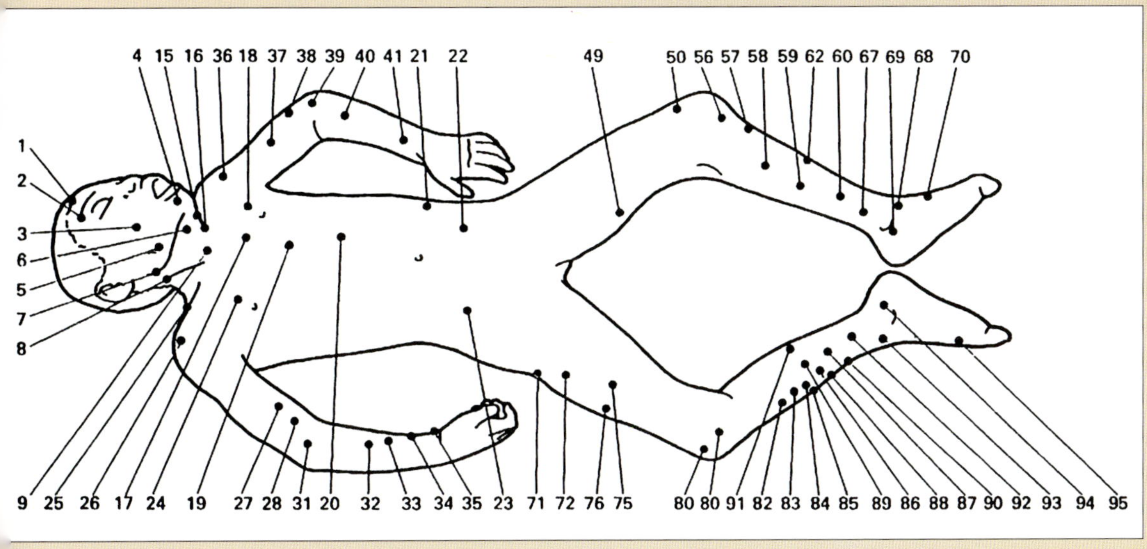

A diagram of the multiple injuries received by eight-year-old Victoria Climbie shows the brutality she suffered before dying. Such striking evidence has been successfully used in court cases to show the extent of a child's abuse.

A forensic pathologist checks medical instruments in the laboratory before coming up with an analysis.

Dr Carmela Coppolino in Florida. Her husband, Dr Carl Coppolino, an anesthesiologist, had injected her with the paralytic drug succinylcholine chloride.

A physician friend of Coppolino's wrongly ascribed the death to a heart attack on the death certificate because the murderer said his wife had suffered chest pains. Three weeks before her death, he had increased her life insurance from $10,000 to $55,000. Although the drug was thought to be undetectable in the human body, Dr Umberger had taken months to isolate it in the brain tissues of the victim. Coppolino was convicted of second-degree murder and served 12 years in prison.

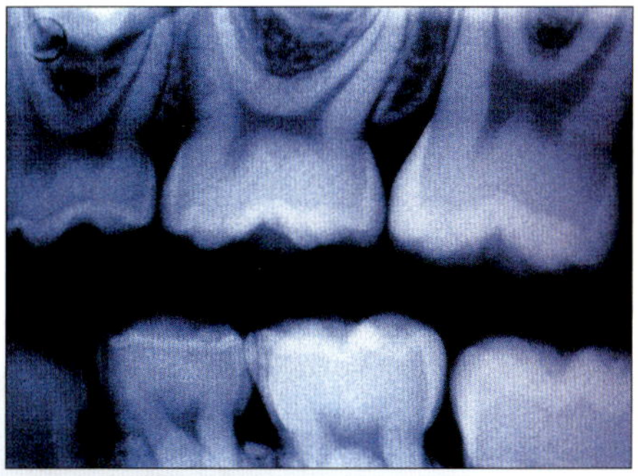

Dental X-rays have been used to solve cases that involved bites such as the death of Linda Peacock.

Only 1 of the 29 suspects had a rare dental disorder, which created pits in his teeth, leaving incriminating marks the victim.

Dr Carl Coppolino was convicted of killing his wife, Carmela, in 1965.

TOO MUCH EVIDENCE

Forensic labs throughout Canada were overwhelmed with evidence in the case of Robert Pickton, a pig farmer charged in 2002 with killing six women and facing a total of 26 murder counts. More than 200,000 DNA samples had been tested by February 2007. This followed a 20-month search of his 7-ha/17-acre farm, an area so large a mobile lab was set up on the farm for preliminary tests before evidence was sent to the six Royal Canadian Mounted Police labs, where additional staff were hired to process the items. Forensic work continued during his trial that lasted from January to December 2007 ending with a conviction and sentence of six life terms.

Fingerprints

Fingerprints will always be an uncontested form of identification because no two are alike and a person's prints do not change throughout life.

THE NIGHT STALKER

Richard Ramirez, 25, became known in Los Angeles as 'The Night Stalker' when he terrorized the city from June 1984 to August 1985. He sexually attacked and murdered more than a dozen victims, with almost as many surviving other attacks. After the last attack, a teenager wrote down his car's registration. The vehicle was located and fingerprints taken. The LAPD had a new AFIS system and matched Ramirez's prints within minutes. Ramirez was convicted and given a life sentence.

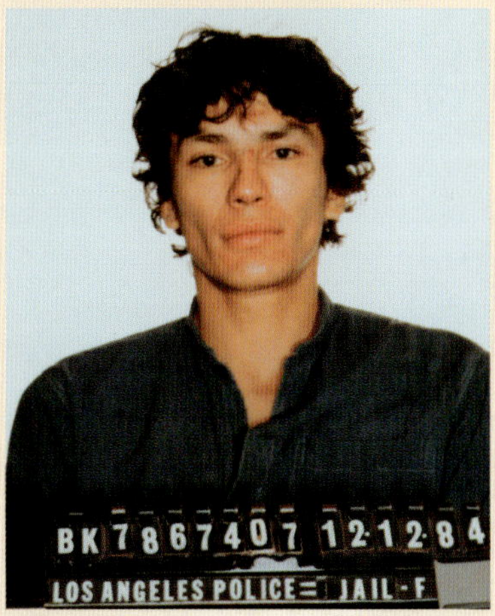

The first courts to convict a suspect by fingerprints were in Argentina in 1892 and in England in 1902. Then in 1903, the New York State Prison system began using them for criminal identification. Today fingerprinting remains a major source of identifying criminals, boosted by online databases containing millions of prints of known criminals.

Fingerprints are now being scanned electronically into databases, gradually replacing the traditional ink-and-card process. The computerized system, called the Automated Fingerprint Identification System (AFIS), is extremely fast, with computers now able to search through 500,000 prints in less than a

FINGERPRINT PATTERNS

The UK, US, and most other English-speaking countries use the Henry System for classifying 10-print collections, developed in 1899 by Sir Edward R. Henry with the British police in India. Three basic types of ridge patterns classify fingerprints:

Arches: these ridges, making up about five per cent of all patterns, rise above one another in the centre like an arch. There are plain arches and tented ones that rise more sharply.

Loops: these patterns, about 60 per cent of all patterns, are ridges that double back on themselves.

Whorls: these resemble small whirlpools revolving around a point, and make up some 35 per cent of patterns. There are four types of whorls.

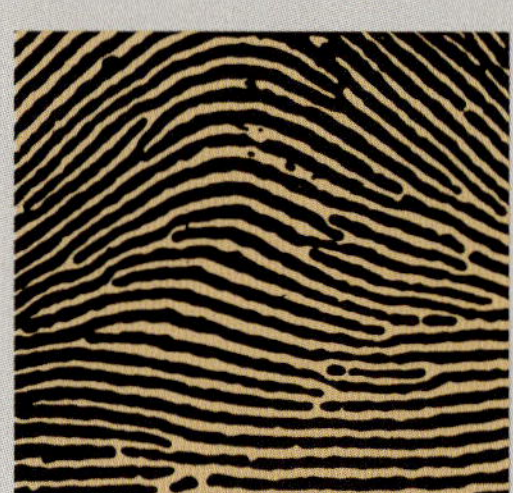
Arches

Loops

Whorls

second. The system scans prints and plots the positions of ridge characteristics, then compares this with prints in the database. It suggests possible suspects, but the fingerprint expert still makes the final decision. The AFIS is especially valuable in scanning partial prints, using digital enhancement for better contrast and sharpness. It is also able to suggest a match between the broken pattern taken at a crime scene and a complete one on the database.

Australia was the first nation to establish an automatic system. Its National Automated Fingerprint Identification System (NAFIS) was set up in 1986 and now holds 4.4 million 10-fingerprints and 11 million palm prints. The FBI developed their system in 1991 and today has 91 million sets of prints, while Britain's system linked all of its police forces in 2001 and it's National Fingerprint Database (IDENTI) now has some 19 million sets of prints.

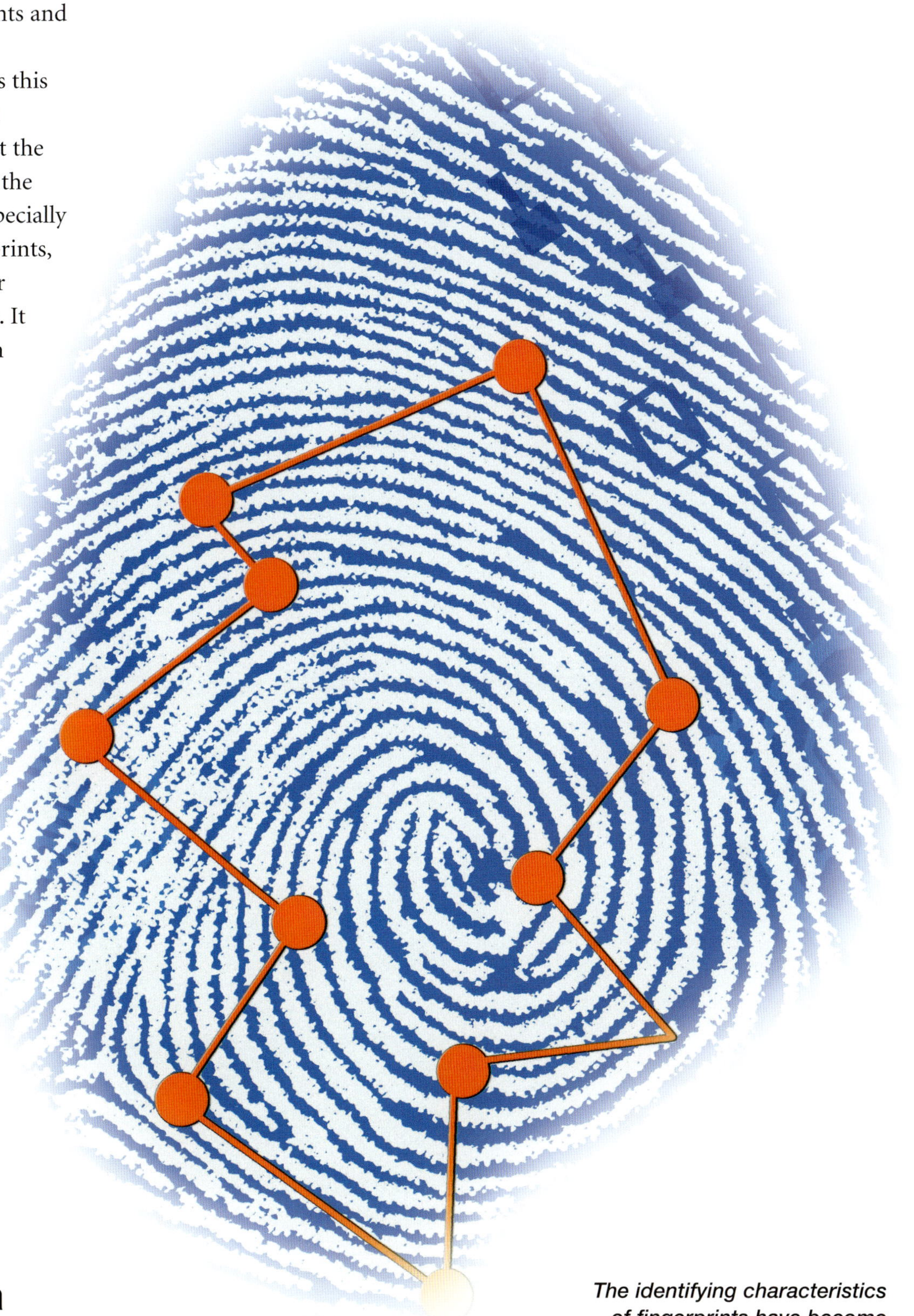

The identifying characteristics of fingerprints have become standardized.

In 1986 Australia was the first country to establish an automatic fingerprint ID system.

The History of Fingerprints

The first use of fingerprints for solving crimes is lost in the early mists of history. Certainly, in 100 CE the Roman attorney Quintilian proved a blind man, who had been framed by someone else's bloody palm prints, innocent of murder.

A more exact classification of prints was needed for complicated cases. Finger ridges were described in 1684 by the English botanist and physician Nehemiah Grew. Four British men also developed modern fingerprinting. In 1880 two published their interest in using them for identification: the Scottish physician Henry Faulds, then working in a Tokyo hospital, used printer's ink to record prints and thought about using them to identify criminals; William Herschel, a civil servant in Bengal, India, reported he had used them for identification since 1860.

The English scientist Sir Francis Galton *(pictured right)* suggested the system of grouping fingerprint patterns into arches, loops and whorls. Then in 1899, Sir Edward R. Henry developed today's modern classification system with subdivisions of Galton's pattern types. He was put in charge of Scotland Yard's new fingerprint branch in 1901. Juan Vucetich of Argentina also devised a classification system in 1904 that became used in Latin American and Spanish-speaking countries. In 1924 the FBI began what would become the world's largest fingerprint database, using the Henry system but adding numerous sub-classifications for more accuracy.

JAN PURKINJE

One of the first scientists to classify fingerprint patterns was Jan Purkinje (1787–1869), who was born in Libochovice, Bohemia (now part of the Czech Republic). In 1823, the same year he became professor of physiology and pathology at the University of Breslau, Purkinje classified fingerprint patterns into nine varieties: transverse curve, oblique loop, ellipse, central longitudinal stria, almond whorl, circle, oblique stripe, spiral whorl and double whorl. Purkinje received a modern compound microscope in 1832 to examine tissues. He discovered the sweat glands in 1833. At the university he established in 1839 the world's first department of physiology and in 1842 the first official physiological laboratory.

Today's classification system of fingerprint arches, loops and whorls was developed in 1899.

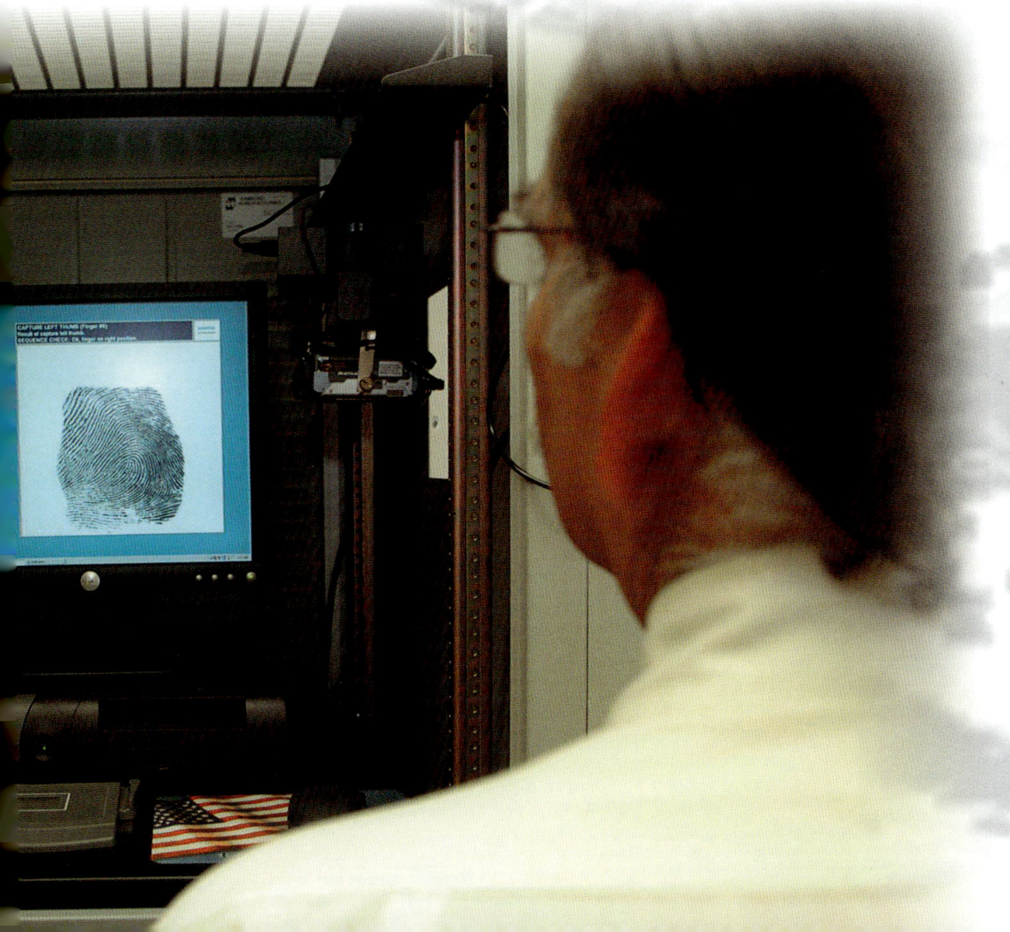

TRAINING

Fingerprint experts in the UK undergo a rigorous training programme lasting several years. They are trained and qualified by Centrex National Training Centre, a Home Office department that is independent from any police force. Its head is Mike Thompson, a fingerprint expert with over 32 years of experience. He said the centre emphasizes court testimony. 'Our training', he noted, 'makes clear to the fingerprint officers that their first duty is to the court and to explain in easily understood language how they reached their findings.'

The new digital fingerprinting system at the police station in Auburn, New York, is the latest refinement in capturing prints without using ink.

Trace Evidence

The trace evidence unit of a forensic science lab is the most diverse discipline. Any unknown material that cannot be placed in a specialist unit must go to the trace evidence unit for an attempt to identify it.

THE VALUE OF HAIR

Many cases are solved because hairs have been transferred between a victim and perpetrator. One individual hair can lead to a conviction. Hairs can survive years after a body has decayed, and they hold many secrets within one thin shaft and follicle. They can be a source of DNA, including valuable mitochondrial DNA (mtDNA) passed through maternal generations. Hair also records poisons such as arsenic, and past drug use, including alcohol and nicotine. As well, general racial types can often be determined from samples.

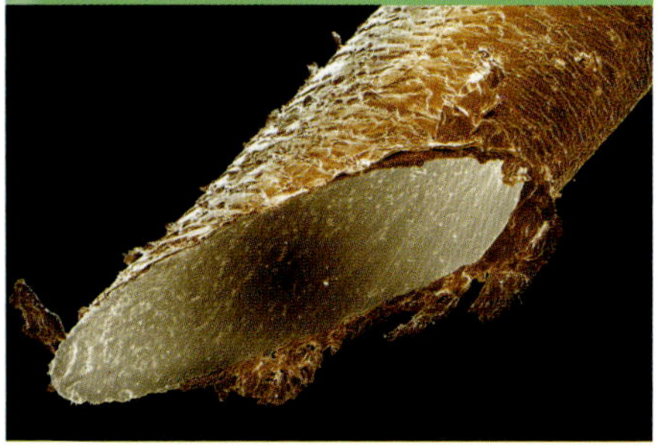

An examiner will have to investigate a range of items that will include hair, fibre, glass, paint, explosives, footwear and tyre impressions and arson debris. Personal items may include cosmetics, like lipstick, mascara and nail polish.

The FBI's Trace Evidence Unit maintains reference collections of human and animal hairs, natural and man-made textile fibres, fabrics, feathers, woods and seeds. Besides testing and matching nonhuman evidence, the Unit also helps identify

EDMOND LOCARD

The French forensic scientist Edmond Locard (right), the first to declare that 'every contact leaves a trace', gave a dramatic description of how trace evidence entraps a criminal:

'Wherever he steps, whatever he touches, whatever he leaves, even unconsciously, will serve as a silent witness against him. Not only his fingerprints or his footprints but his hair, the fibres from his clothes, the glass he breaks, the tool mark he leaves, the paint he scratches, the blood or semen he deposits or collects. All of these, and more, bear mute witness against him. This is evidence that does not forget. It is not confused by the excitement of the moment. It is not absent because human witnesses are. It is factual evidence. Physical evidence cannot be wrong, it cannot perjure itself, it cannot be wholly absent. Only human failure to find it, study, and understand it can diminish its value.'

arm, hair and face. Samples can be taken from the suspect, and a scanning electron microscope used to locate these tiny particles on hair or fibre. Residue on clothing can also reveal the distance between the shooter and victim, since the spread will be wider from a farther distance. Test firings on similar fabrics will give an accurate estimate of the distance.

MARKINGS ON SHELL CASINGS

After a bullet has been fired, a shell casing is left as evidence. A firearms examiner can compare a variety of marks left on the metal:

Striations: The barrel of each weapon leaves its unique pattern of marks that are used in comparisons. Striations run parallel to the length of the bullet.

Firing pin: Dents will be made by a firing pin in the soft metal base of a casing. Seeing where the firing pin struck helps identify the type of gun used.

Rifling: These are spiralling grooves inside the barrel, which are used to spin the bullet. Their angle and direction, clockwise or anti-clockwise, help identify the type of weapon and match the shell to a gun.

Two spent hollow bullets show their distinctive striations and markings. These can be used to identify a gun.

Some criminals file off the serial numbers of guns, but the metal will retain the original indentions below the surface.

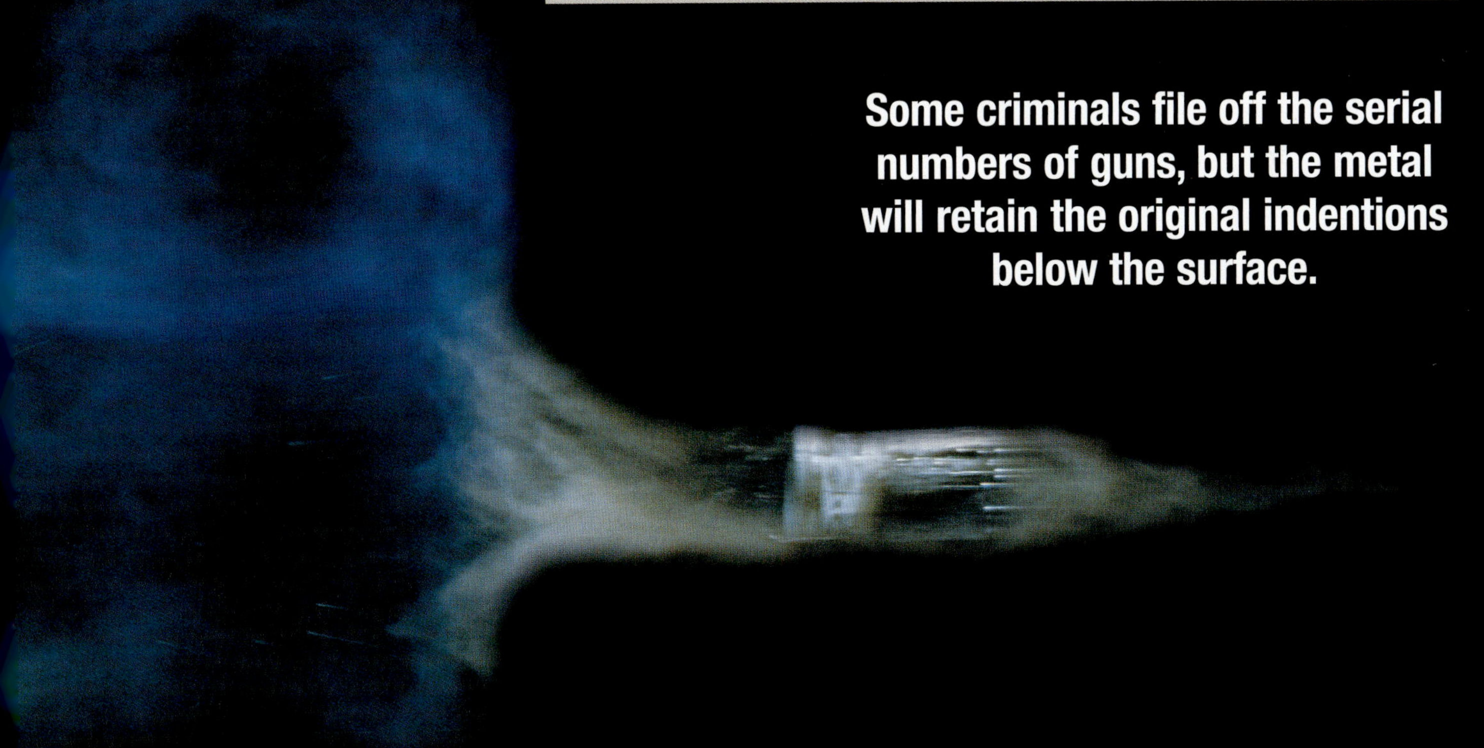

A high-speed photo shows a cartridge after discharge from the muzzle of a 12-bore shotgun.

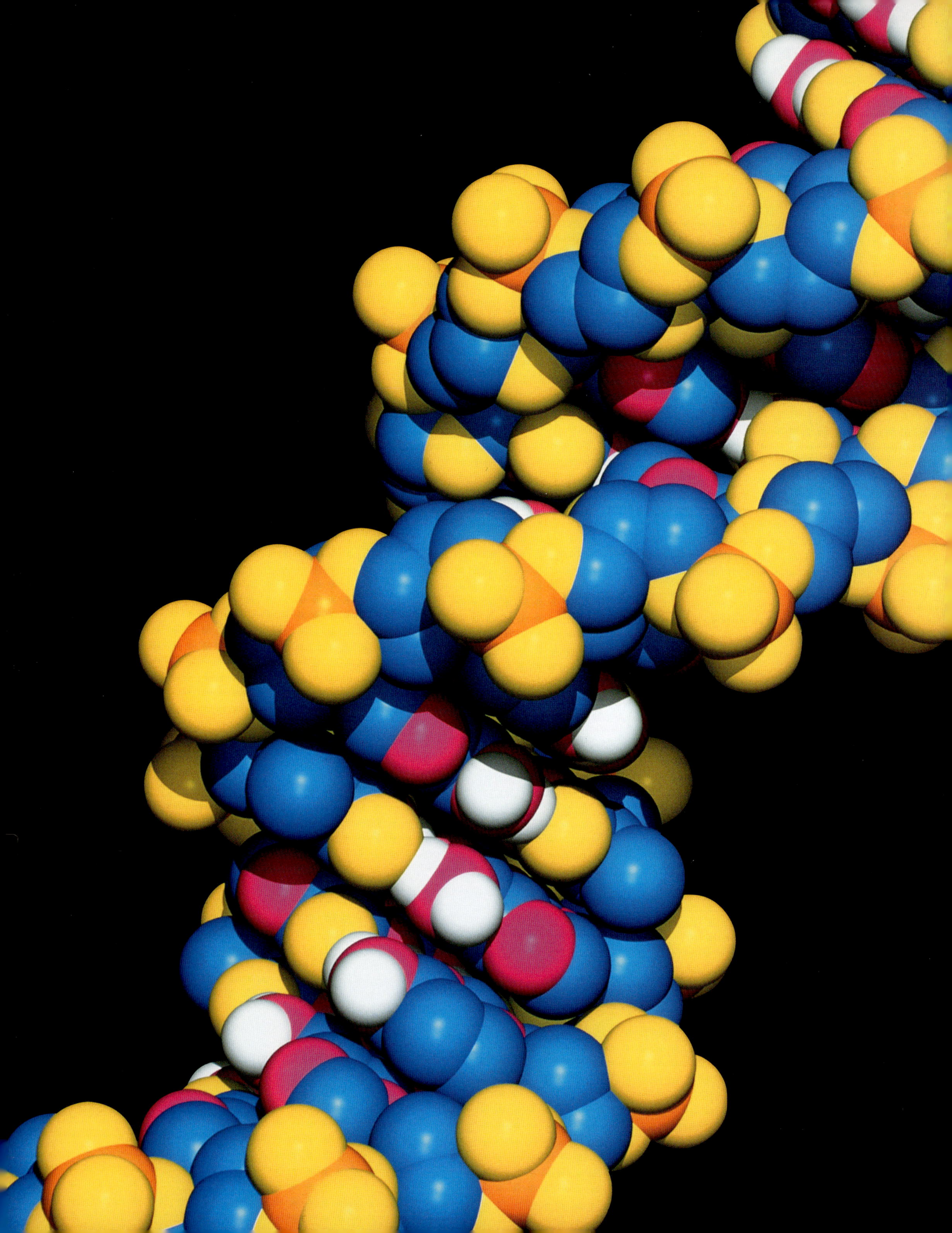

Chapter Five

DNA and the Criminal

DNA TESTS ARE THE MOST TRUSTED EVIDENCE IN legal history. A better chance exists of finding and matching DNA to a suspect than using fingerprints, because criminals can avoid leaving prints by wearing gloves or wiping away the incriminating marks. DNA, on the other hand, can be extracted from microscopically small trace evidence that a perpetrator cannot even see. Today in Britain, for example, 70 per cent of all forensic tests are DNA ones.

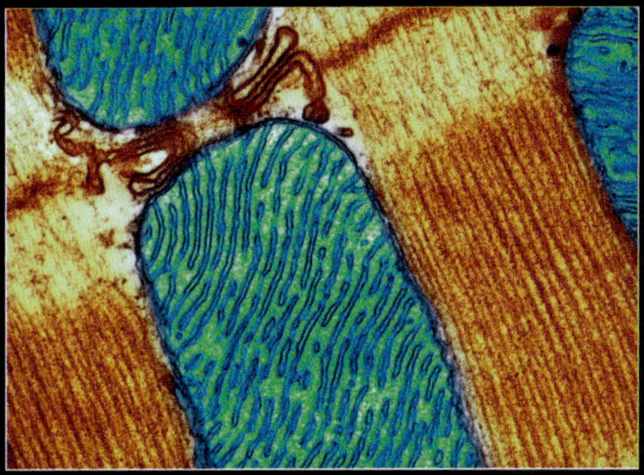

Mitochondria in a heart muscle are coloured blue in this transmission electron micrograph (TEM). Mitochondria DNA (mtDNA) is a more abundant DNA type.

Two scientists, Britain's Francis Crick and the American James Watson, identified the double helix structure of DNA in 1953. In 1984 the British geneticist Alex Jeffreys discovered genetic fingerprinting, and this led two years later to the first court case in which a DNA sample convicted a suspect, the murderer Colin Pitchfork. In 1987 DNA evidence was allowed in a US court case.

Advances continue to be made in DNA recovery and testing. The 1990s saw the emergence of mitochondrial DNA (mtMDA) testing in forensic casework, which is valuable when the biological evidence is degraded or small in quantity. As well, mtMDA lasts so long that accurate tests can be made on ancient skeletons. Another new technology, developed by the UK's Forensic Science Service, is DNA Low Copy Number (DNA LCN) testing, which can be used to obtain profiles from samples containing only a few cells.

Computer artwork on a strand of DNA shows colour-coded atoms: carbon (blue), oxygen (yellow), hydrogen (white), nitrogen (magenta) and phosphorous (orange).

What is DNA?

Deoxyribonucleic acid, or DNA, is a 2-m/6-ft long spiral within every nucleus of our body's cells, which number about 60 trillion. It is located in the nucleus, so it is referred to as nuclear DNA.

DNA has a double helix structure that looks like a twisted ladder formed into long strands called chromosomes. Inside the spiral are three billion connecting rods that add the 'rungs' to the ladder. Known as bases, these are of four different types, which are known as guanine (G), cytosine (C), thymine (T) and adenine (A). The order in which they are positioned along the strand is unique in each person, with the exception of identical twins.

The double helix is formed from pairs of bases, with C only pairing with G and A with T. This never varies, so when DNA replicates itself, all new strands are exact copies. One person's DNA has six billion bases that create three billion base pairs.

A small section of the DNA spiral contains our individual genetic code, the genes that give us our looks and characteristics such as curly hair or blue eyes. However, forensic scientists are only interested in the large remainder portion of the spiral. Although it seems to do little and is called 'junk' DNA, the short sequences of the base pairs repeat themselves, and this varies greatly among people, allowing individuals to be identified.

Besides nuclear DNA, another type in most cells is mitochondrial DNA (mtDNA), so named for being located in another part of the cell, the mitochondrion. It is arranged in a circle much smaller than the linear nuclear DNA. While nuclear DNA is inherited from each parent equally, mtDNA comes only from the mother, which is vital for tracing direct ancestry.

SIR ALEC JEFFREYS

DNA fingerprinting was discovered and named by the British geneticist Alex Jeffreys on 10 September 1984 in his lab in Leicester University. He was alone in the darkroom when an X-ray image in the developing tank suddenly gave him the idea that each person has a unique DNA pattern and that this could be used for criminal cases. Born in Oxford in 1950 and graduating from the university there, Jeffreys was knighted in 1994. He remains amazed at his own discovery. 'It is the most powerful criminal investigation tool there is', he said. 'If you had told me all that 20 years ago, I would not have believed it.'

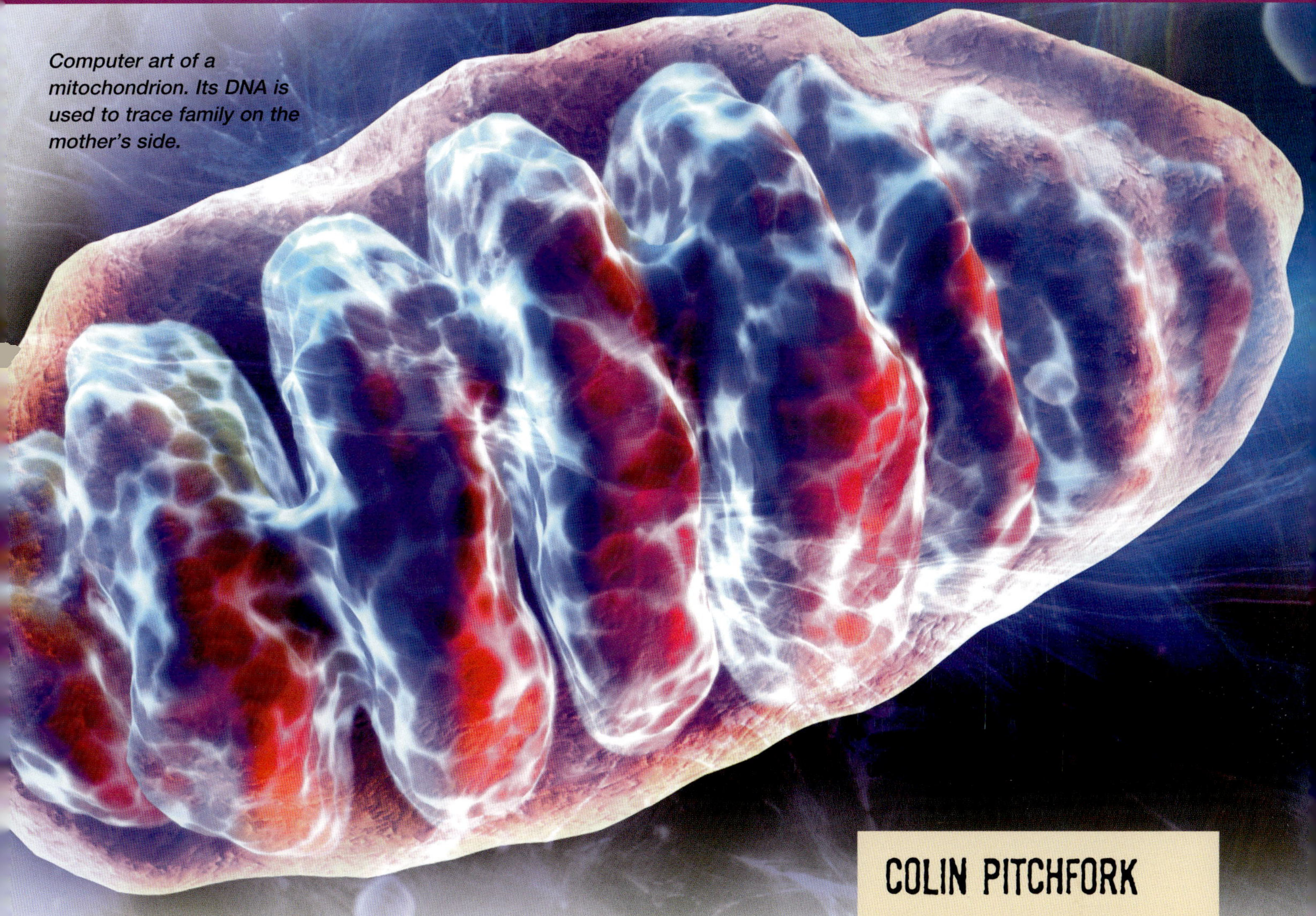

Computer art of a mitochondrion. Its DNA is used to trace family on the mother's side.

'DNA fingerprinting is the most powerful criminal investigation tool there is.'

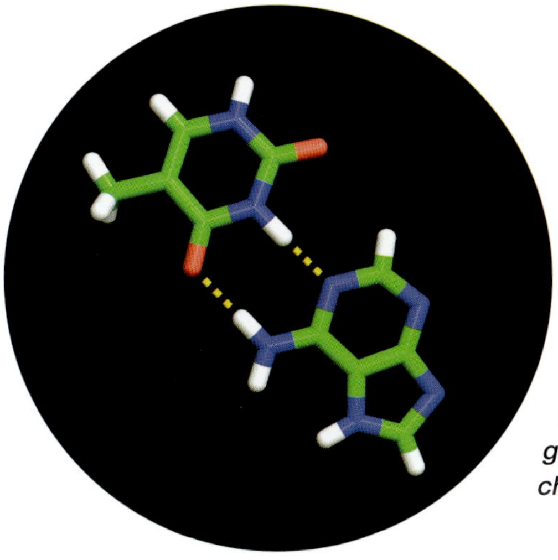

Computer artwork of an A-T (adenine-thymine) base pair. A-T is one of the two base pairs found in DNA (along with C-G (cytosine-guanine)). The positioning of these base pairs along the DNA chain gives organisms their individual characteristics.

COLIN PITCHFORK

The rape and murder of two 15-year-old girls in Narborough, Leicestershire, in in 1983 and 1986 led to the first forensic application of DNA profiling. Blood samples were taken from the male population of the area, but no match turned up. However, when a woman overheard Ian Kelly boasting he had given a sample for Colin Pitchfork, a local baker, investigators took Pitchfork's sample and it matched. He then confessed and in 1988 was sentenced to life imprisonment.

The History of DNA Research

DNA was discovered in 1869 by the German medical researcher, Johann Friedrich Miescher, at the University of Tübingen, working under Felix Hoppe-Seyler. Undertaking research with white blood cells, he isolated a white, slightly acidic substance he called nuclein.

Miescher worked on his discovery for the remainder of his life, believing that the proteins in chromosomes were responsible for heredity.

His discovery took place at about the time that the British scientist Charles Darwin, and the Austrian botanist and monk, Gregor Mendel, were also publishing papers on genetic theories.

THE GENOME

The complete set of DNA within a cell is called its genome. The name combines 'gene' and 'chromosome' and was coined in 1920 by the botanist Hans Winkler at the University of Hamburg. Human chromosomes have from about 50 million to 300 million base pairs. Each chromosome contains up to thousands of genes for making proteins. Each gene in the human genome makes an average of three proteins.

All humans and primates share a large amount of the genome, so our DNA is identical to that of chimpanzees.

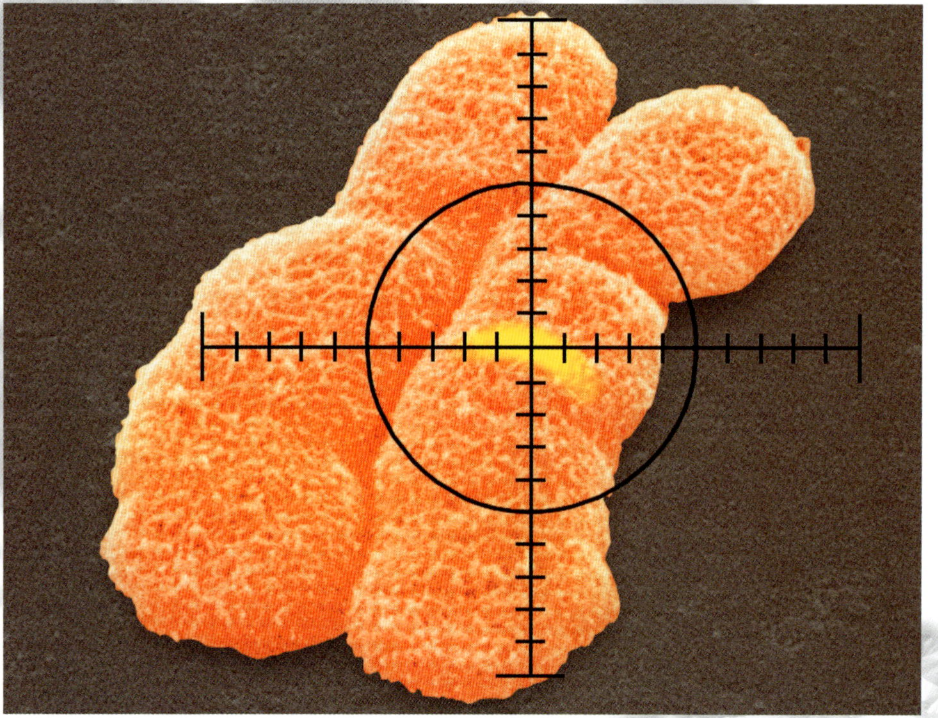

A coloured scanning electron micrograph (SEM) shows a targeted gene (yellow) on a human chromosome that contains DNA.

FRANCIS CRICK AND JAMES WATSON

The discoverers of DNA's structure came from totally different backgrounds. Francis Crick (right in photo) was born in 1916 near Northampton, and studied physics at University College, London. In 1949 he joined the Medical Research Council Unit at the famous Cavendish Laboratory in Cambridge and worked on the structure of proteins.

James Watson (left in photo) was born in 1928 in Chicago and studied zoology at the University of Chicago. He gained a PhD in zoology in 1950 from Indiana University. He became interested in the structure of DNA after attending a symposium in 1951 in Naples, Italy.

Crick and Watson became friends, and the American joined Crick in Cambridge in 1951. That year their first effort to understand the DNA structure failed but two years later they discovered the double-helical configuration. Both were awarded the Nobel prize in 1962 for their discovery.

In 1928 the British medical officer Franklin Griffith found that genetic information could be transferred from bacteria cells killed by heat to live ones. He called this 'transformation'. Subsequently, in 1944 American bacteriologist, Oswald Avery, identified the transforming agent as DNA when he destroyed DNA and found that transformation would not occur. As previously mentioned, James Watson and Francis Crick discovered the molecular structure of DNA in 1953 and Alex Jeffreys discovered genetic fingerprinting in 1984.

In 2003 the Human Genome Project to identify all of the 20,000 to 25,000 genes in human DNA was finally completed after 13 years. This project, co-ordinated by the US Department of Energy and the National Institutes of Health, was able to determine the sequences of the three billion chemical base pairs that make up human DNA.

In 2003, after 13 years, the Human Genome Project identifying all of the 20,000 to 25,000 genes in human DNA was finally completed.

A technician removes frozen cell lines from cryostorage for the Human Genome Project.

Taking DNA Samples

The normal method of collecting DNA samples is by swabbing the mouth. The swab is put into the mouth and moved across the inside of the cheek to collect cellular material.

This will usually take about 15 minutes. In many countries trained police officers are supplied with DNA kits that contain everything needed to take a sample, including two swabs and disposable gloves to prevent contamination.

DRAGNET

Mouth swabs are also used in a 'sweep' or 'dragnet' of people living

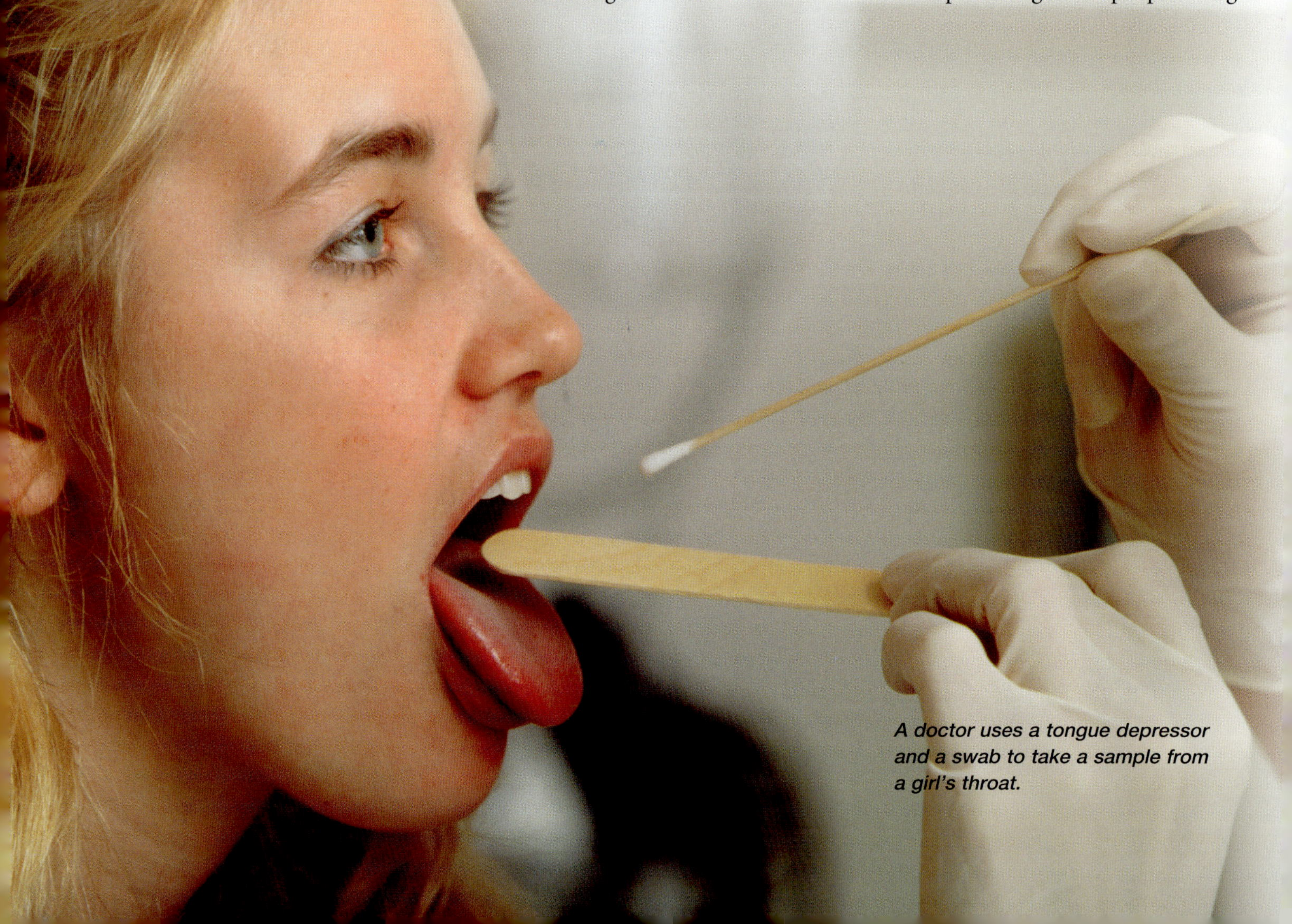

A doctor uses a tongue depressor and a swab to take a sample from a girl's throat.

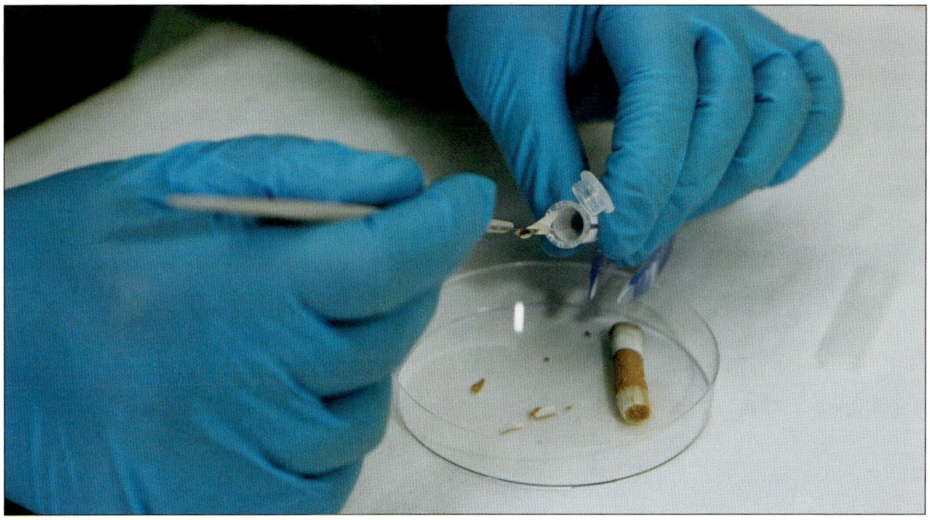

A forensic scientist takes a sample from a cigarette stub to see if traces of DNA from saliva can be found to identify the smoker.

in the area of a crime. In the USA, samples from 2300 men were taken in 1994 in Miami, Florida, when six prostitutes were murdered, and in Baton Rouge, Louisiana, 1200 men were tested in 2003 during the hunt for a serial killer. The sweeps failed to find the criminals who were arrested by other means, and a 2004 survey at the University of Nebraska at Omaha found that only 1 in 18 sweeps identified the perpetrator.

Mouth swabs for other offences will sometimes lead to an unexpected connection with a previous crime. This happened in 2006 when Sukhdarshan Singh was arrested for drink driving and police took a mouth swab. His DNA matched the sample taken 18 years before when a woman was raped in Bridgend, Wales. Singh was jailed for four and a half years.

At a crime scene without suspects, common sources of DNA are trace samples of blood, semen, saliva, sweat, hair follicles, bone and skin. In fact any biological sample with cells is a potential DNA source. Samples are carefully preserved for comparisons with the mouth swabs of suspects and with DNA databases.

BIN LADEN'S DNA

In 2002 the American CBS network reported that the FBI had obtained samples of Osama bin Laden's DNA and were checking it against tissue and body parts on the battlefields of Afghanistan. The sample supposedly was obtained from strands of his hair. One Canadian-led mission that year into the Tora Bora region excavated some 23 graves of al-Qaeda fighters following speculative reports that bin Laden had been killed. DNA samples were taken from the corpses for identification, but the terrorist leader was not among them.

TERESA CORMACK

Patient police in New Zealand tested DNA in a murder case three times in 14 years, certain that advances in the science would eventually lead to the killer. Six-year-old Teresa Cormack was murdered in 1987. DNA swabs were sent to Britain for testing, but they contained insufficient material. More tests in the 1990s were unsuccessful. Then, in 2001, a tiny amount of saved semen was tested with advanced DNA technology. Blood samples were taken from the local male population, and Jules Mikus proved a match. Hairs stored for 14 years were sent to the USA for mitochondrial DNA testing and confimed the match. Mikus was found guilty in 2002.

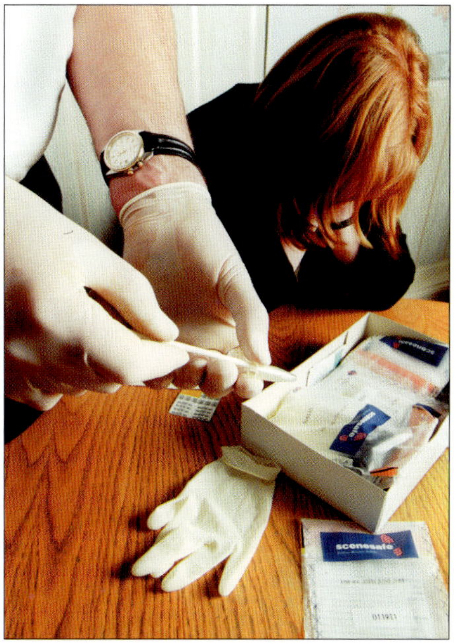

A swab is used to take cells from the inside of the cheek for a DNA sample.

Amplifying DNA

When identifying genetic fingerprints, a forensic scientist may want to make copies of small amounts of DNA, because some methods of analysis need more DNA than may be in a sample.

Polymerase chain reaction (PCR) is a technique that amplifies (multiplies) DNA, allowing scientists to create millions of copies in about two hours. The American scientist Kary Mullis conceived of it in 1983 (see box), and most DNA profiling today is based on his process.

PCR, which has informally been called 'molecular photocopying', amplifies specific regions of a DNA strand such as a single gene, part of a gene or a non-coding sequence. The PCR process is extremely sensitive, so specific analyzes can be made of tiny amounts of crime-scene DNA.

The process uses the polymerase enzyme for copying instead of a living organism such as yeast. The DNA sample is mixed in a test tube with salty water, polymerase, the four bases and primers (two DNA fragments that attach the sides of a target sequence). This mixture is heated to separate the sides of the

KARY MULLIS

The inventor of PCR, Kary Mullis, was born in 1944 in Lenoir, North Carolina. He gained a degree in science at the Georgia Institute of Technology and a PhD in biochemistry from the University of California at Berkeley.

Mullis joined the Cetus Corporation of Emeryville, California, as a DNA chemist in 1979. While there, he conceived of the PCR idea in 1983 while cruising along a motorway. In 1993 he received the Nobel prize for discovering PCR. Today he is a researcher at the Children's Hospital and Research Institute in Oakland, California. Writing in *Scientific American*, Mullis summed up the simplicity of PCR: 'Beginning with a single molecule of the genetic material DNA, the PCR can generate 100 billion similar molecules in an afternoon. The reaction is easy to execute. It requires no more than a test tube, a few simple reagents and a source of heat.'

A forensic expert at ICI Cellmark Diagnostics in Oxfordshire separates fragments of DNA into bands.

double-stranded DNA and then cooled to let the primers bind to their complementary sequences on the separated strands, and to let the polymerase extend the primers into new complementary strands. The mixture is repeatedly heated and cooled to multiply the DNA exponentially.

Polymerase chain reaction amplifies DNA, allowing scientists to create millions of copies in about two hours.

The banding pattern of lengths of DNA sequencing is revealed under ultraviolet light.

THE GREEN RIVER KILLER

Gary Ridgway was an infamous serial killer who, from 1982 to 1998, murdered 48 women, mostly prostitutes, and dumped many in the Green River near Seattle, Washington. When police caught up with him, he gave a DNA sample, but the semen samples from his victims were too small to test. His saliva sample was stored, and the advent of PCR allowed forensic testing of the amplified DNA in 2001 that matched Ridgway's. He pleaded guilty, and confessed to more murders than anyone else in US history. He was sentenced to life without parole.

How DNA is Matched

To compare DNA samples an investigator first uses agents such as a chloroform and phenol mixture to separate the DNA from other material in the cell nucleus.

The PCR process will normally amplify this sample. A fluorescent dye is used to tag each DNA fragment.

The double-stranded fragments are converted by chemicals into single strands and separated by length using electrophoresis, in which an electrical current is passed through a sample to move it through a gel or narrow tube, separating the fragments into a series of bands.

VNTRS AND STRS

Forensic investigators check these bands for base sequences that are repeated. The two types are Variable Number Tandem Repeats (VNTRs), which can be hundreds of base pairs long, and Short Tandem Repeats (STRs), which are normally three to seven base pairs long.

PEAK PROFILE

A scanner system reads the sequence: a laser beam causes the dyed fragments to fluoresce, and these flashes are registered on a colour-sensitive detector. The results are displayed as coloured peaks on a graph. A crime scene DNA will be displayed next to a suspect's sample, and investigators check the results visually or by computer. A match is indicated if the profile of peaks is the same.

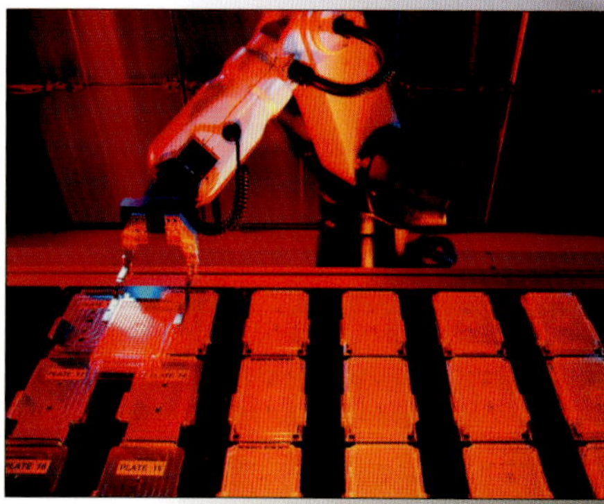

A robot arm picks up a tray of bacterial colonies that clone human DNA fragments for use in the Human Genome Project.

A SPEEDIER DNA ANALYSIS

About three hours is required for the replication of DNA by polymerase chain reaction (PCR) to produce a sample large enough to analyze. A new system developed at the University of Michigan, however, will cut the time needed back to only 40 minutes. The DNA mixture must be heated to 95°C/203°F, allowed to cool to 50–60°C/122–140°F, and then heated to 72°C/162°F for the PCR process to work. This must be done as many as 30 to 40 times to get a sufficient sample. The new device uses convection, which keeps the DNA mixture moving in a steady, circular flow within a few minutes. This is done by placing it into a Plexiglas well between two plates held at constant temperatures: 95°C/203°F at the bottom and 50–60°C/122–140°F at the top.

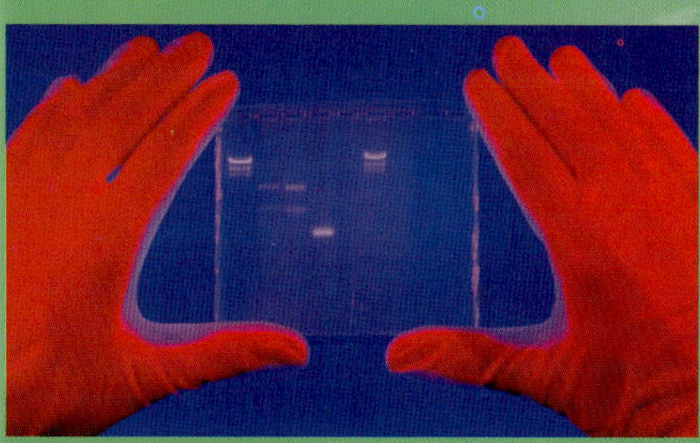

MISINTERPRETING DNA

Forensic experts can draw widely varying conclusions about DNA matches. When Dr Bradley Schwartz was accused of hiring a hit man to kill his former medical partner, the trial in 2006 turned on disagreements about DNA statistics.

The Department of Public Safety testified that the hit man's DNA matched samples from the crime scene, and only 1 in 20 million people could have such a connection. A DNA expert for the defence reduced those to 1 in 1658, saying the DNA at the scene had been misinterpreted. But when DNA expert Bruce Budowle of the FBI was called in, he put the number at 1 in 13,000. Dr Schwartz was convicted and is serving a life sentence.

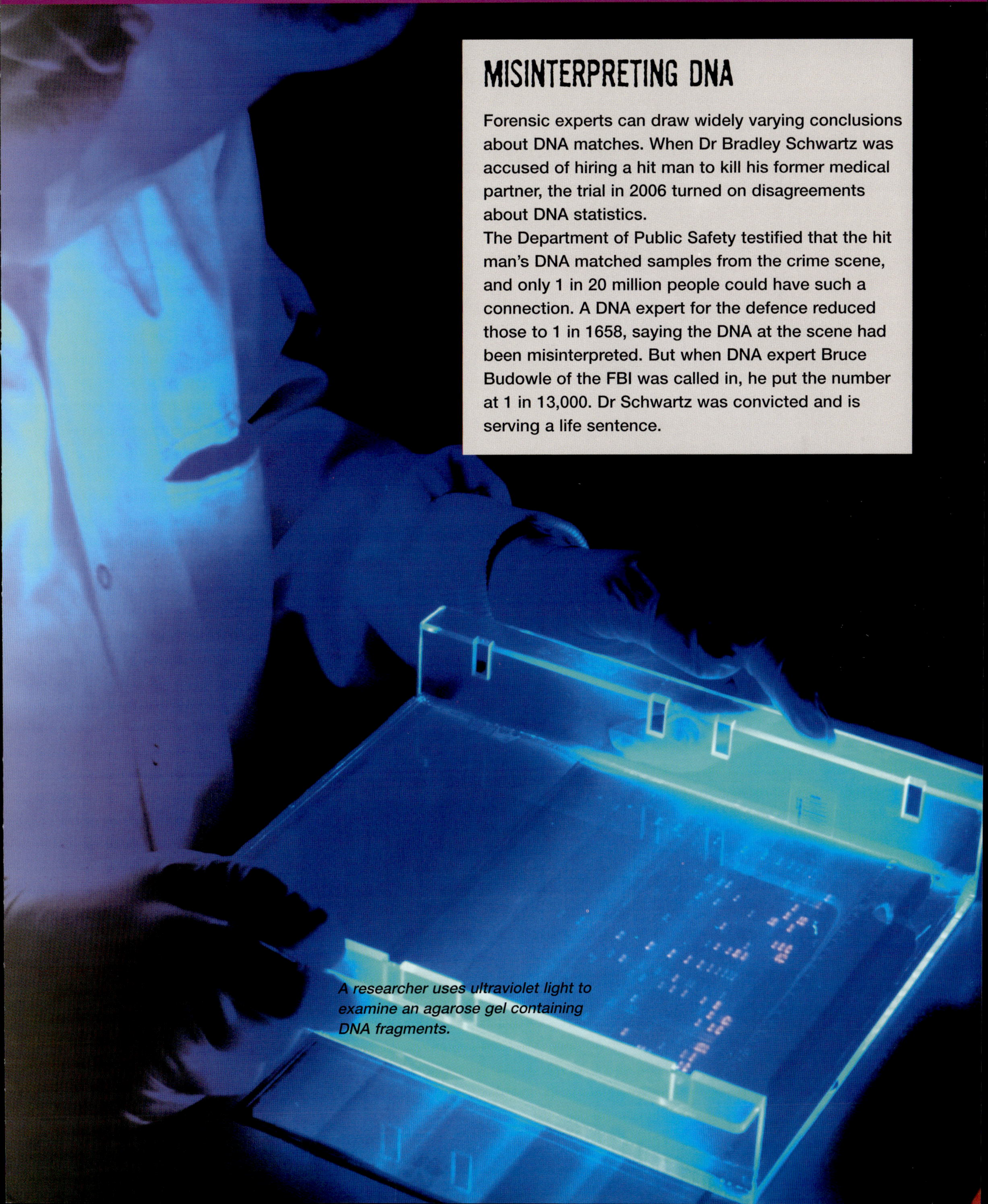

A researcher uses ultraviolet light to examine an agarose gel containing DNA fragments.

Two Cases of Familial DNA

Michael Little, 53, was killed in March 2003 when someone threw a brick down onto the bonnet of his lorry as he drove on the M3 in Surrey.

In 2003 Craig Harman became the first person in the world to be convicted through familial searching.

A forensic scientist prepares an agarose electrophoresis gel used in DNA separation techniques.

AFTER INNOCENCE

The true story of prisoners exonerated by DNA evidence was the subject of the movie *After Innocence* that won the 2005 Special Jury Prize at the Sundance Film Festival. The documentary followed seven men and their emotional journeys back into society. It also featured Barry Scheck (pictured) and Peter Neufeld, founders of the Innocent Project, which has helped exonerate prisoners through DNA testing. The movie was described by *Variety* as "remarkable stories that highlight injustice, courage, and endurance."

In a court case in 2007 in the United States, Steven Avery became the first prisoner convicted of murder by DNA who had been previously freed by DNA from another conviction. He had been behind bars for 17 years of a 35-year sentence for sexually assaulting and beating a woman in Manitowoc, Wisconsin. After DNA testing arrived, hairs at the crime scene were matched to another man in prison. Avery was exonerated in 2003 and two years later the Wisconsin legislature passed the Avery Bill to prevent wrongful convictions. On the same day, 31 October, Teresa Halbach went missing. Her remains were uncovered, and DNA bloodstains in her vehicle matched Avery's blood.

The Angola penitentiary is one of the world's largest with more than 5000 inmates and two death row units.

THE PRICE OF FREEDOM

In 2007 an American exonerated by a DNA test was awarded $3.9 million in Louisville, Kentucky. William Gregory, 59, had already collected $700,000 from the state to settle his claims against the state forensic examiner who had testified against him.

Gregory was convicted in 1993 of raping one woman and attempting to rape another. He spent seven years behind bars before being freed in 2000 after DNA tests on hair found at the crime scene showed he was innocent.

Lab-on-a-Chip

One of the latest advances in DNA testing is a miniaturized device known as a lab-on-a-chip. These portable micro laboratories can be used to speed up DNA tests by automatically analyzing samples.

The simple, low-cost portable instruments will make DNA analysis more widely available.

One version developed at the University of Michigan is a glass and silicon chip, which is far less expensive than conventional methods of analyzing DNA in a specialized lab, but just as sensitive. In contrast to lab equipment it is virtually a hands-free instrument. All components are contained on a single chip that includes systems for measuring and mixing microscopic liquid samples of DNA with reagents, moving the mixtures to a temperature-controlled reaction chamber, separating the DNA molecules by size through gel electrophoresis, and determining the results with an on-board fluorescent detector.

Another lab-on-a-chip version was funded by the space agency NASA and developed at the California Institute of Technology. The device can be altered to perform rapid DNA tests, though it was primarily created to perform blood tests in space for astronauts, which had not been possible previously because of the large size of blood-analysis instruments.

Lab-on-a-chip technology is being taught in American and British universities. It will be an undergraduate subject at the new state-of-the-art forensics research centre at the University of Teesside, Middlesborough, and was a main topic of discussion when forensic experts from the UK and Europe attended a crime conference there on 8 June 2005 to mark the opening of the centre.

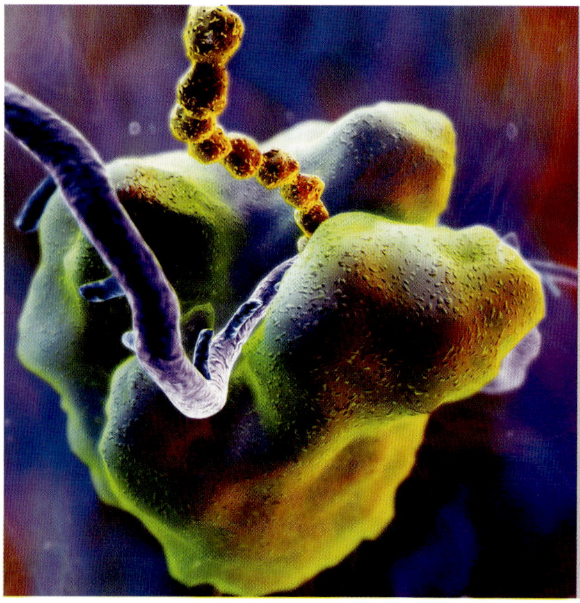

DNA BOOST

A new forensic technique piloted in 2006 by the UK's Forensic Science Service (FSS) could solve tens of thousands of 'cold cases', which have lain dormant in police files. The computer-based software-analysis system is expected to boost the FSS crime detection rates by more than 15 per cent and will continue to be used for new cases. Known as DNAboost, it enables investigators to work with a poor-quality sample of DNA, or one that lacks the necessary quantity. It also allows investigators to work with DNA with a mixed profile, which is a sample that has more than one person's DNA on it. Previously, forensic experts had been unable to split the profiles of mixed-profile DNA.

In contrast to most laboratory work, lab-on-a-chip DNA tests can be done on a single silicon chip.

A scanning electron micrograph shows part of a microfluidic microchip used for DNA analyses.

DNA AND THE CRIME NOVELIST

Some 3000 specialists from around the world who deal with DNA attend training programmes each year at a private institute, which was the brainchild of best-selling crime novelist Patricia Cornwell. Having first worked in Virginia's crime lab for years, she donated $1.5 million, matched by state funds, to start the Virginia Institute of Forensic Science and Medicine in 1999 near Richmond. It is a private non-profit institute, where about 800 people have completed continuing-education seminars since its doors opened. Annual fellowships of $23,000 are offered to some students to enable them to study for up to 50 hours a week.

Novelist Patricia Cornwell worked for four years in the medical examiner's office in Virginia.

Chapter Six

Identifying a Body

Forensic experts identified bodies on Thailand's island of Phuket after the devastating 2004 tsunami.

A CORPSE IS OFTEN ANONYMOUS, FOUND WITHOUT ANY CREDIT CARDS, DRIVING LICENCE OR OTHER MEANS OF IMMEDIATE IDENTIFICATION. In major tragedies such as natural disasters, air crashes or terrorist bombings, the victims will be separated from their personal and travel documents. If nobody comes forth to enquire about the missing or to identify the remains, the case becomes a forensic puzzle.

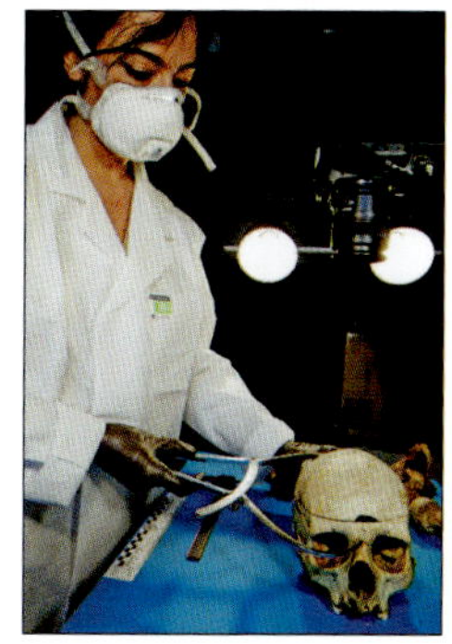

A forensic scientist uses calipers to measure a skull. This can be used for a facial reconstruction to help identification.

DNA has become the standard test for identification, but investigators still struggle when confronted with near total destruction. The terrorist attacks on the World Trade Center on 11 September 2001 led to the recovery of almost 20,000 body parts. The identification task came to an end in February 2005, with 1585 of the total 2749 victims being identified. The families of the remaining 1164 victims were told that DNA technology was not yet sufficient for more results. The DNA samples had been degraded, subjected to intense heat, water and bacteria.

Identities were also lost in the South-east Asian tsunami of 2004, which killed more than 200,000 people. Although DNA samples were taken soon after the deaths, the same DNA degradation meant only five per cent were identified this way. Instead, dental records and fingerprint examinations were relied upon. By contrast, when hurricane Katrina hit the US in 2005, the majority of the approximately 1500 victims were identified by DNA and other forensic methods, as well as by personal effects.

New York Port Authority Officer Tony Basic examines evidence on 29 April 2002 from the World Trade Center terrorist attack of 11 September 2001.

Identifying Crime Victims

Most homicide victims are easily identified, being killed at home or nearby by someone close to them. Other victims are known before they die such as a child who has been abducted.

Yet it is not uncommon for authorities to be baffled by the unknown remains of a victim. The process of identification can take anywhere from days to years, and, ultimately, some bodies are never given a name.

Forensic identity searches rely on several sources, often in combination. They include DNA, dental records, fingerprints, personal effects such as jewellery and clothing, tattoos, birthmarks and scars, as well as the person's age and race. The description is soon given to the news media, normally along with an artist's sketch of the deceased. In skeletal remains a forensic sculptor may do a facial reconstruction in clay.

REMOVING SIGNS

Visual clues are not always possible to recreate. If the remains are old, have been disturbed by animals or decomposed by the weather, it can cloud the identification process. Criminals often attempt to remove signs of identification by using fire, quicklime or acid. In extreme cases, they may mutilate or dismember the body, cutting off the victim's fingers, hands or even the head.

In rare cases a living victim may be unidentified. Examples involve infants and very young children, victims in a coma or suffering memory loss, and even crime victims who want to remain anonymous.

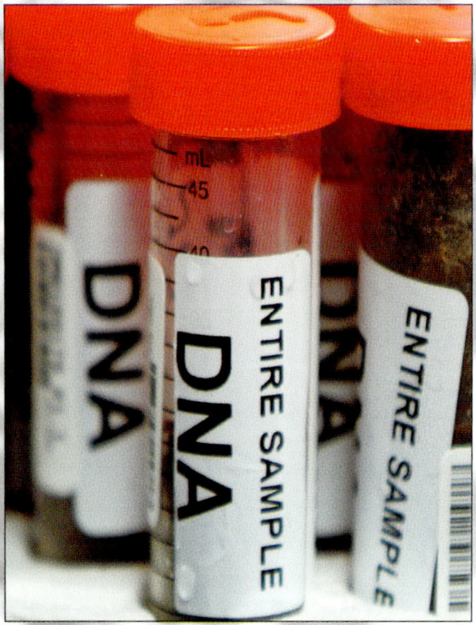

Vials with DNA samples provided by relatives of the 9/11 victims are stored in the New York City morgue.

WHEN VIEWING FAILS

Matters seem certain when relatives or friends view a body for identification purposes, but this is sometimes unreliable. The body may be burnt or disfigured. Or the person identifying can be emotionally upset, too squeamish to take a proper view or may not have seen the victim for years. In some cases the viewer may give a false identification to cover a crime or gain an inheritance.

Murders have even been committed in order to falsely identify the body. In a US case Joseph Kalady, facing trial for producing fraudulent documents, killed William White in 2001. Kalady's brother, Michael, falsely identified the body as Kalady's. Investigators, however, identified White through fingerprints, and Kalady was charged with murder, dying in prison in 2003 before the trial.

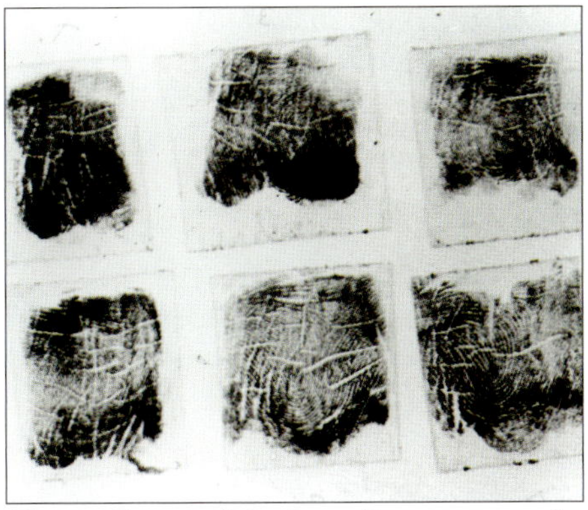

These fingerprints from the corpse of the 'Black Dahlia' identified her as Elizabeth Short.

LIVESCAN FOR THE DEAD

In 2006 the University of Leicester, working with the Leicester Constabulary and the Institute of Legal Medicine at the University of Hamburg, demonstrated the first use of an electronic hand-held device to recover fingerprints from the dead. It was developed from the larger Livescan computer device that takes prints from fingers pressed against a coated glass platform.

The Home Office introduced Livescan itself to all police forces in 2007. The state of California has not accepted inked fingerprint cards since 2005, only Livescan images.

A US official checks fingerprints of a tourist crossing from Canada to Niagara Falls, New York.

Identifying Tsunami Victims

The world's largest disaster victim identification programme occurred after the 2004 tsunami struck South-east Asia. Interpol and 20 national police forces came together on the island of Phuket, Thailand, to examine forensic data.

From 2005 to 2006, nearly 2000 personnel from 31 nations were involved with help from labs in the UK, Sweden, China and Bosnia. By 2006 nearly 3000 of 3750 unidentified victims had been named using fingerprints, dental records and DNA samples. DNA was able to identify only 800 of the victims because the extreme heat had decomposed their corpses.

The forensic experts developed a way of recovering fingerprints from corpses. Fingers were removed and placed in boiling water to make the rigid skin pliable. Corporal Wayne Oakes of the Royal Canadian Mounted Police explained: 'It re-hydrates the digits and enables the technician to then, in most cases, get a print that can possibly result in identification.'

For comparisons fingerprint records from the various countries came from criminal databases, national ID cards or homes of any victim who was unidentified. 'The sort of thing we are looking for', said Interpol fingerprint specialist Mark Branchflower, 'is a glass of water that somebody had the night before they went on holiday, which they left beside their bed.'

FBI DISASTER SQUAD

The FBI Disaster Squad was formed in 1940 to recover and identify victims of disasters. Its 49 members are highly trained forensic examiners from the FBI Laboratory, and each trains for nearly two years in fingerprint science.

By 2006 they had assisted in 230 disasters involving 10,687 victims and had identified 6809 victims by fingerprints, palm prints or footprints. (These totals do not include their work on the 9/11 attacks in 2001 and the tsunami of 2004.)

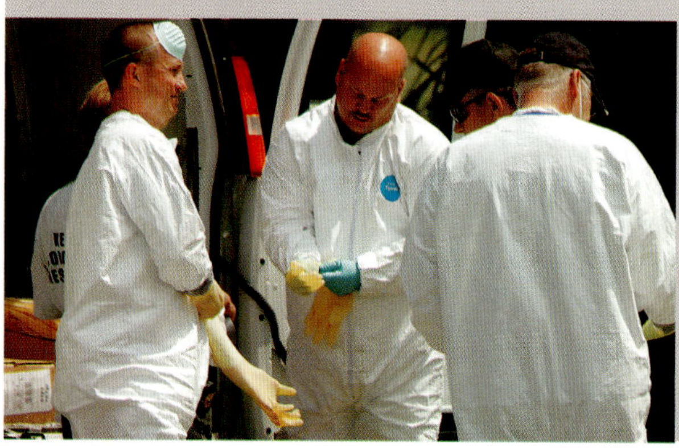

One of their largest challenges was Hurricane Katrina in 2005. In the two months following, the Disaster Squad had identified 155 bodies through fingerprints, aided by the Fly Away Identification Team of the US Criminal Justice Information Services and by the Louisiana State Police.

The Disaster Squad also analyzes latent fingerprints submitted by law enforcement agencies across the USA, and trains federal, state and local partners how to collect latent prints.

Fingers were placed in boiling water to make the rigid skin pliable, so that prints could be taken.

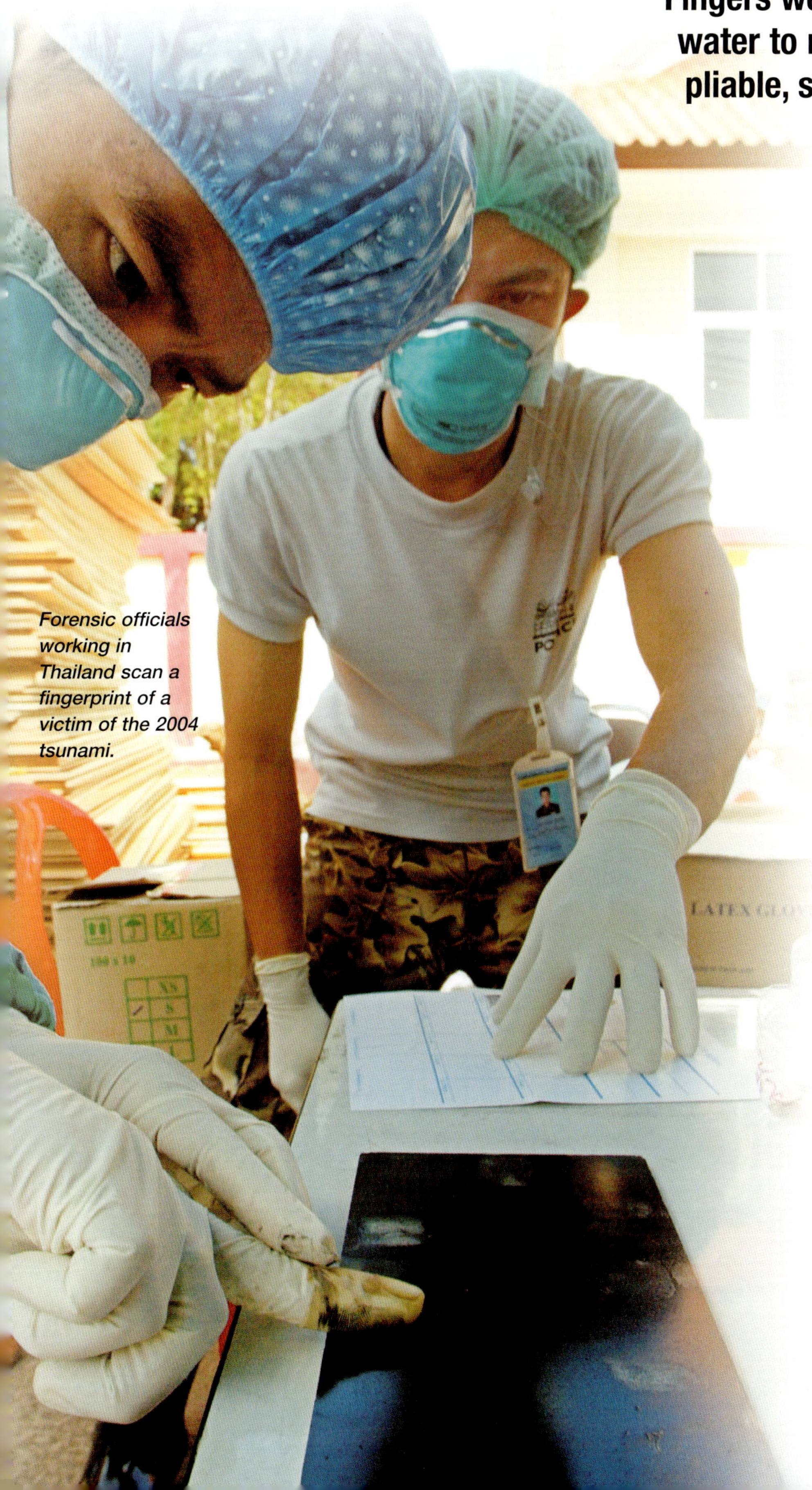

Forensic officials working in Thailand scan a fingerprint of a victim of the 2004 tsunami.

INTERPOL'S FINGERPRINT GUIDE

Interpol's Disaster Victim Identification guide notes that no international standards or agreements currently exist for the identification of disaster victims, and this can create doubts between countries concerning methods used. It advises that it may be more expedient in disasters to file and compare fingerprints by sex, race and age. The fingerprint expert, it adds, should keep a consecutive list of fingerprints by date, time and reference number, also including his or her comments.

A coroner's team remove a body for identification in New Orleans, Louisiana, in the aftermath of Hurricane Katrina in 2005.

Dental Identification

Dental records are extremely valuable in establishing an unknown identity. Teeth are especially hard and almost indestructible, remaining after burial in earth and water for years and even surviving fire.

The impressions of each individual's teeth are different, due to chips, fillings, misalignments and missing teeth. Dentists routinely make notes about the surfaces of each patient's 32 adult teeth. A comparison with dental records, which most people

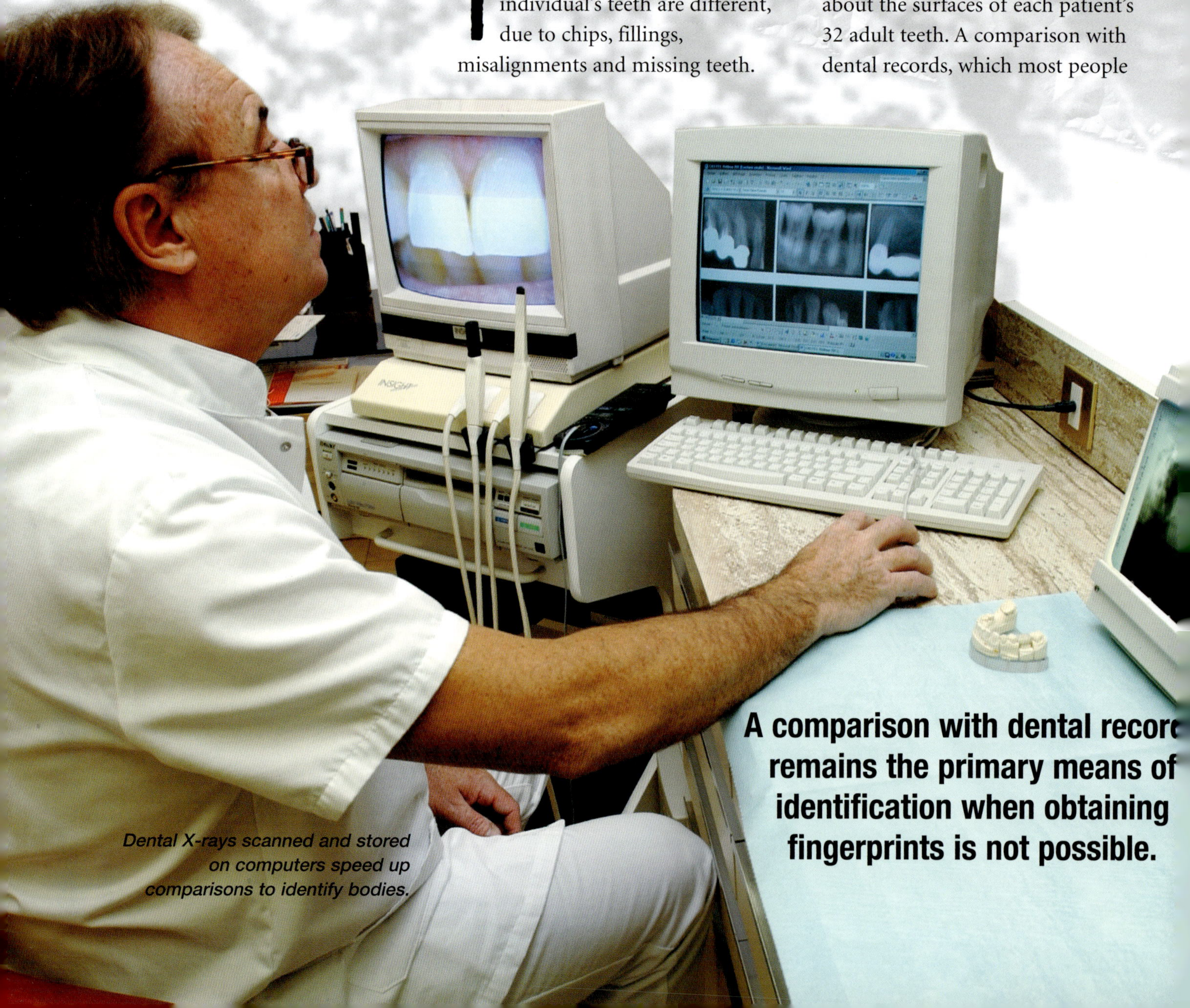

Dental X-rays scanned and stored on computers speed up comparisons to identify bodies.

A comparison with dental recor remains the primary means of identification when obtaining fingerprints is not possible.

have, still remains the primary means of identification when obtaining fingerprints is not possible. DNA technology, in contrast, is expensive and often obtaining results takes weeks or months. Dental records are also much cheaper to enter onto a computerized database.

In identifying crime victims, a total and accurate dental examination should be made, including X-rays of the teeth and jaws, which can now be done at the crime scene using a portable instrument. Forensic odontologists can compare several areas with dental records, including the number of teeth, cavities and fillings, bridges, restoration, spacing and special details such as an overbite or overlap of teeth. As well, the materials and methods used in dental work can indicate the country where the treatment was administered.

DENTAL IDENTIFICATIONS IN HISTORY

The unique marks of teeth have been used throughout history: The Roman emperor Nero identified his mother Agrippina, whom he had murdered in 59 CE, by her teeth. William the Conqueror used to bite the wax seals on his letters with his crooked teeth to verify they were from him. The first formally reported case of dental identification was for John Talbot, the Earl of Shrewsbury, who fell at the battle of Castillon in France in 1453.

Sir John Talbot died on 17 July 1453 at the Battle of Castillon during the Hundred Years' War.

The American patriot Paul Revere was able to identify his friend Dr Joseph Warren 10 months after he was buried, a victim of the 1775 Battle of Bunker Hill in Massachusetts. This was an easy identification, because Revere had fashioned dentures for Warren. In 1865 a dental identification was made of John Wilkes Booth, the assassin of President Abraham Lincoln.

The first disaster victims to be identified by their teeth were killed in a fire in 1849 at the Vienna Opera House. Dental records were also used to establish identity after 126 rich Parisians were killed in 1897 in a charity bazaar fire.

PROBLEMS OF DENTAL IDENTIFICATIONS

Despite the hardiness of teeth and the prevalence of dental records, problems may be encountered with this type of identification. In some cases investigators encounter partial or no dental records, or may fail to recover all teeth and their restorations. Even the improvement of dental health, thanks to the increasing use of fluoridation, works against identification because it means people generally have fewer cavities and restorations. In addition, laws also exist in some countries, such as the USA, to protect medical records and therefore may slow an investigation slightly.

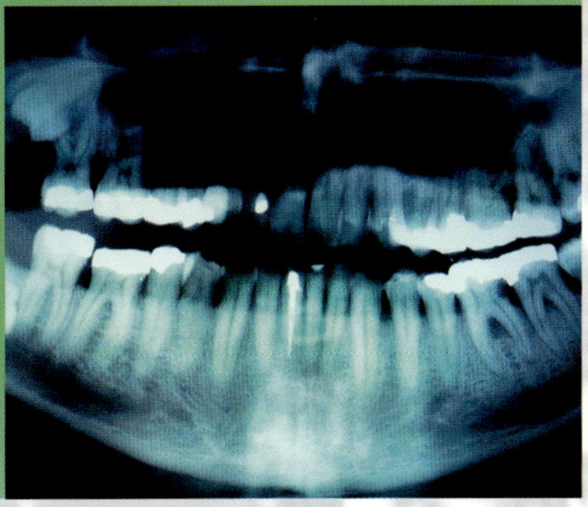

Dental fillings help identifications. The white areas in the teeth of this 45-year-old man show teeth with fillings.

Dental Identification Cases

Forensic dentists provide the key to identifying bodies that have virtually been destroyed by time or violence. An example of the former was the discovery in May 2002 of the skeletal remains of Chandra Levy in a park in Washington, DC.

A policeman closes off the area where the skeletal remains of Chandra Levy were found.

Chandra Levy had been dead for just over a year, so the remains had to be identified through dental records provided by her family. She was a former US government intern whose affair with California Representative Gary Condit ruined his career. The murder case remains unsolved.

Terrorist bombs invariably require dental or DNA identification. The explosions on London's underground and a bus on 7 July, 2005, created special identification problems because many of the bodies were jumbled together and badly damaged. Forensic experts took weeks to identify those killed.

Extra efforts also are made when foreigners die and dental records must be obtained from their country. This happened in Naples, Italy, on 26 May 2006, when the body of a man with a kitchen knife in his abdomen was found in a storm drain below a manhole. His body was greatly decomposed, but three days later dental records had identified him as Lewis Brooks Miskell, a Canadian diplomat based in Vienna, Austria, who had disappeared in early March at the start of an Italian holiday. The killing remains a mystery.

HELENA RANTA

Finland's Helena Ranta is, at the age of 64, one of the world's most renowned forensic dentists. Working in the Department of Forensic Medicine at the University of Helsinki, she was involved in identifying Russia's murdered Tssar Nicholas II and his family, looking for victims of Saddam Hussein, identifying victims of the tsunami in Southeast Asia and testifying at the trial of the former Serbian president, Slobodan Milosevic.

During her work identifying bodies in Bosnia-Herzegovina, she had to dodge snipers' bullets, and once ordered US forces to use their tanks to protect her working group. Nothing has deterred her important occupation, including death threats to cancel a trip to the Balkans. 'I sleep well at night', she said. 'If there are threats, there are arrangements for dealing with them.'

TOOTH PRINTS FOR CHILDREN

Tooth printing for children has been adopted in several US states as a means of identification in case a child is abducted. It is part of a Child Identification Program (CHIP) that includes DNA and fingerprints.

Because many children have no cavities or dental work, Dr David Tesini of Natick, Massachusetts, developed a system using thermal plastic wafers. It is warmed until pliable, a child bites on to the wafer to leave his or her tooth prints. Once the wafer hardens, the record is preserved. The state of Massachusetts, alone, has had more than 1500 dentists volunteer their time for the programme, and 37 school systems in the state participate.

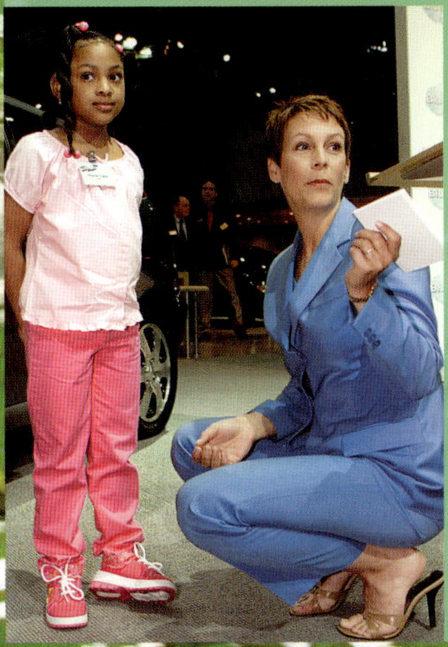

Actress Jamie Lee Curtis announced a child ID programme in 2001.

Skin Marks

Some of the most distinctive marks of identification are found on the skin. Birthmarks, scars and tattoos are easy to recognize, such as the red birthmark on the forehead of the former Russian president Mikhail Gorbachev.

Such marks have been important indicators throughout history. King Harold's body was identified after the battle of Hastings by a tattoo over his heart, reading 'Edith and England'.

TATTOOS

Tattoos, in fact, have now become acceptable body decorations, including those worn by celebrities such as David Beckham. Their permanence and their prevalence among criminals has proved to be a blessing to police. Especially helpful are the chosen names or slogans, as used by gang members. When identifying corpses, investigators try to match the tattoos to the known work of tattoo artists. Sometimes pigments from the skin are even extracted and analyzed to trace the source. Another recent trend, piercing the ears, nose, eyebrows and other body parts, is also a strong indicator for identification.

'SCARFACE'

Forensic investigators also look for scars acquired from operations, plastic surgery or fights. The gangster Al Capone was nicknamed 'Scarface' after his cheek was cut with a knife during a dispute in his early days. Birthmarks have fine identifying characteristics because they have irregular shapes, and skin blemishes such as moles have been used to identify bodies.

NATASCHA KAMPUSCH

A pale and distressed 18-year-old girl ran to an elderly man on 23 August 2006 in Vienna, Austria, saying she had escaped after being kidnapped and held captive. Her name, she said, was Natascha Kampusch. This was verified by her family who identified her by a scar on her upper arm that went back to an operation she had as a child. The identity resolved one of Austria's most famous criminal mysteries. Hours after her escape, the man who had snatched her from a Vienna street and held her for eight years, committed suicide by throwing himself in front of a train.

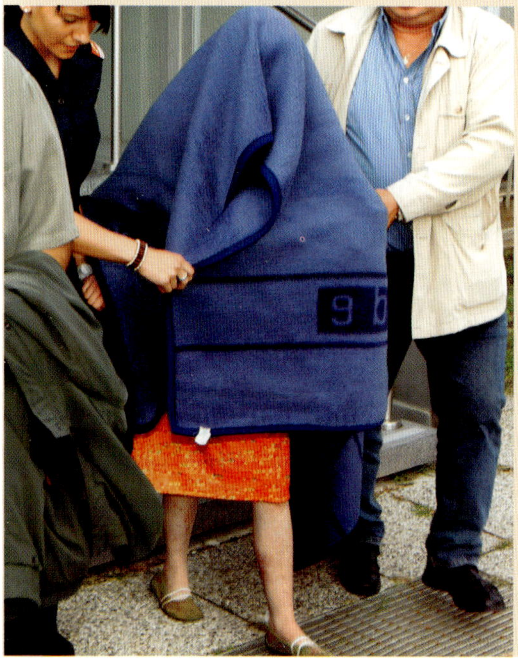

Covered by a blanket, Natascha Kampusch is escorted by police on the day she escaped.

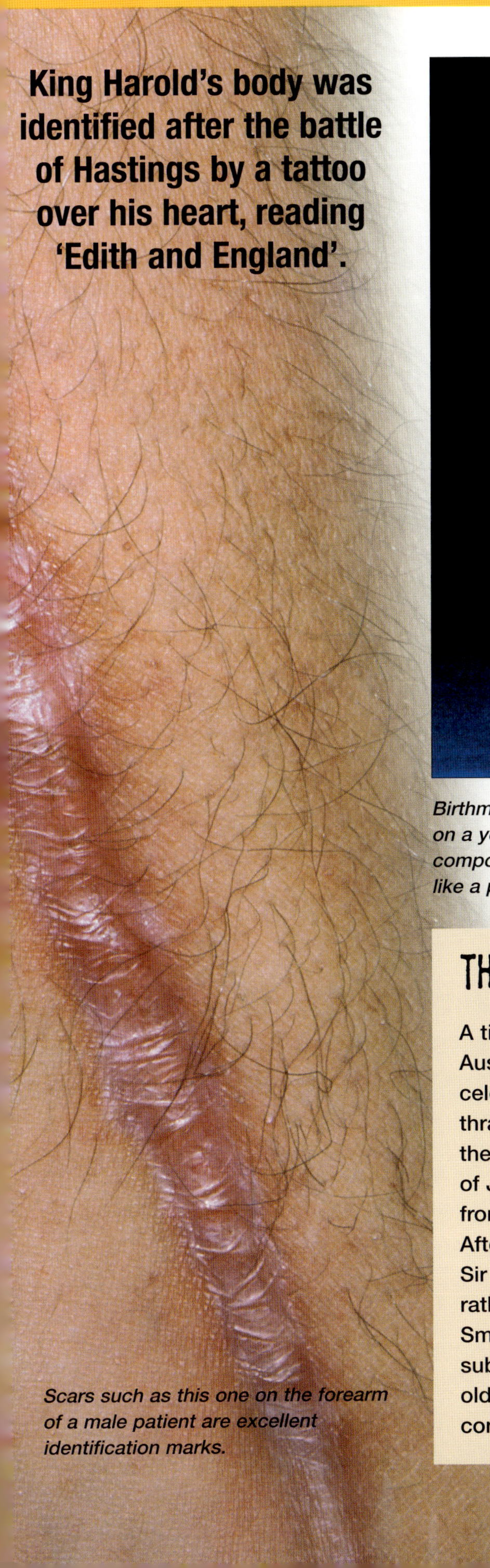

King Harold's body was identified after the battle of Hastings by a tattoo over his heart, reading 'Edith and England'.

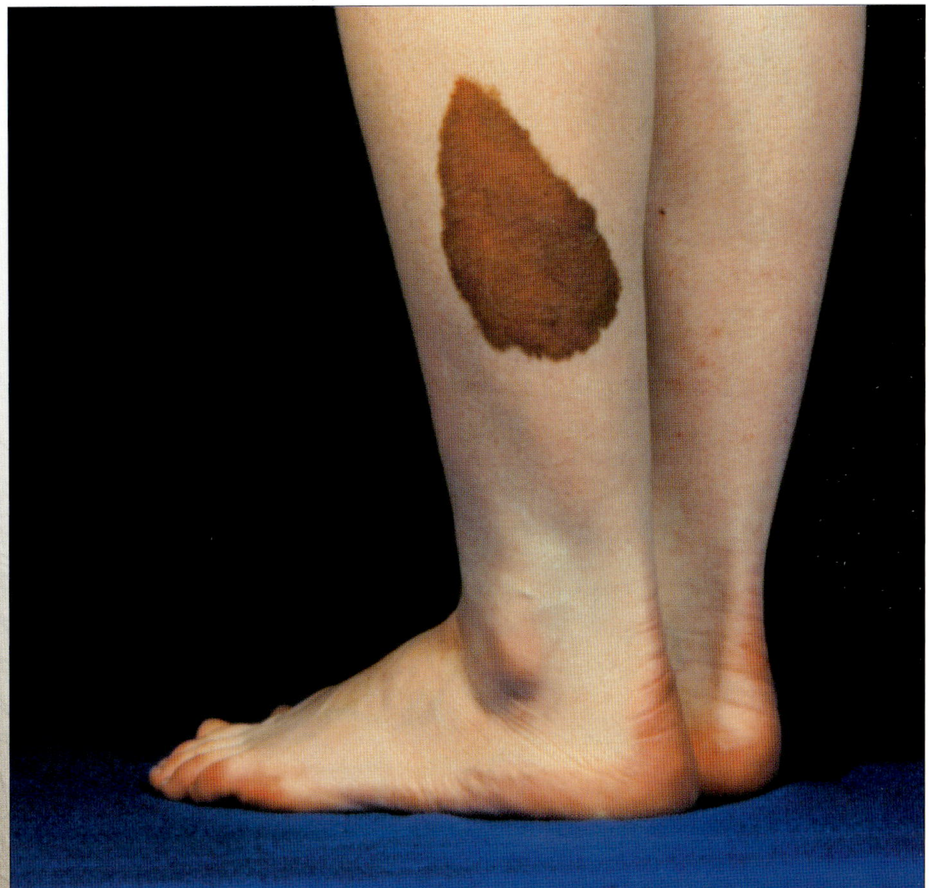

Birthmarks have led to numerous identifications such as this large pigmented one on a young woman's calf. These will occur in different forms, with some composed of small blood vessels, including the strawberry mark, and some being like a port-wine stain.

THE SHARK ARM CASE

A tiger shark caught by fishermen was an attraction in Coogee, Australia, on 25 April 1935 at the nation's annual Anzac Day celebration. Fun became fear, however, when the animal suddenly thrashed about and coughed up a tattooed human arm. Searches for the rest of the body all failed. The fingerprints were found to be those of James Smith, a construction worker, and his wife identified his arm from the tattoo showing two sparring boxers.

After this identification, the renowned English forensic pathologist Sir Sydney Smith examined the arm and said it had been cut off rather than bitten off by the shark. This indicated murder, because Smith had been involved in the drugs trade. A key witness was subsequently murdered, and an inquest was abandoned due to an old law that said a body was necessary and 'a limb does not constitute a body'.

Scars such as this one on the forearm of a male patient are excellent identification marks.

Indications Within the Body

Clues to identification are sometimes hidden inside a corpse. The victim may have had a disease, accident or operation, and these signs are normally discovered in an X-ray or during an autopsy.

The evidence of diseases such as tuberculosis, AIDS and cancer has identified bodies. Bones damaged by disease are good indicators, with identifications made from osteoporosis, the progressive myeloma and childhood deformities such as scoliosis and rickets.

Among the easiest clues to identity are artificial implants such as pacemakers, heart valves, defibrillators and artificial hips. These all bear engraved serial numbers, which can be traced back to a hospital where the operation took place. In 2004 in Florida, the body of a 35-year-old female investment banker was found encased in cement in a suitcase under the house of an unlicenced cosmetic surgeon. She was identified by the serial numbers on her breast implants. In another Florida case in 2007, a prosthesis metal rod in one leg identified a 73-year-old man.

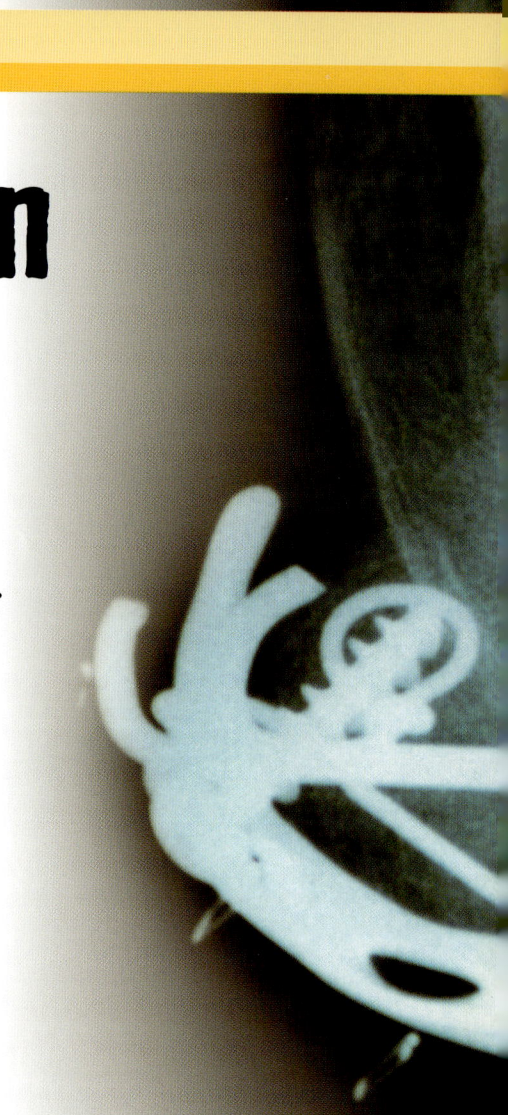

This X-ray, revealing metal pins supporting a fracture of an arm, could lead to an identification.

Artificial implants such as pacemakers and defibrillators bear engraved serial numbers, which can be traced.

NEFERTITI

A mummy unearthed in 2003 in Luxor's Valley of the Kings, in Egypt, may be the Egyptian queen, Nefertiti. The team, led by Dr Joann Fletcher, a specialist from the University of York, took X-rays that showed a female pelvis and the disease of lumbar scoliosis. The joints were fused, showing it was an adult. Dr Fletcher said the complete X-rays should establish any diseases, injuries and even the cause of death.

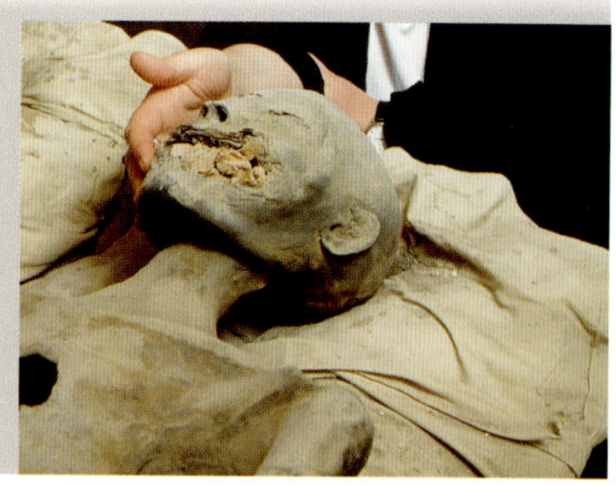

WHAT BONES TELL

An examination of skeletal remains can go far in identifying the victim by class characteristics. The gender can be determined with good accuracy because of male-female differences in the pelvis, skull and femur. Age can be estimated for children up to the age of five by the amount of bone that has formed to replace cartilage, and the process of bone fusion between the ages of 5 and 25 is another indicator. When a skeleton is complete, a victim's height can also be estimated.

IDENTIFICATIONS IN HISTORY

Injuries have led to identifications throughout history.
When the Scottish missionary and explorer David Livingstone died in 1873, his body was embalmed in what is now Zambia, and taken on a 1600-km/1000-mile journey to the African coast. Back in England, a broken bone in his shoulder, caused by an encounter with a lion, positively identified him.
Modern instruments can also peer into the past. When the French queen Marie Antoinette was executed, her son, Louis Charles, was kept in prison until he died of tuberculosis in 1795. Several people later claimed to be Louis. The heart of the imprisoned man had been preserved, and mtDNA tests were conducted in 2000. The result was matched to a lock of Marie Antoinette's hair, proving he was her son.

Facial Reconstruction

When only a skull is recovered from a nameless crime victim, forensic sculptors may be called in to reconstruct the face in modelling clay, a highly skilled procedure.

The likeness of a living person is difficult to recreate, but the skull gives an indication of the form and contours needed. The 'American model', devised in the USA, uses knowledge of the tissue depth that covers the various bony landmarks of a skull. There are from 20 to 35 tissue depths to contend with around the face, and the forensic artist has known measurements for gender, different ages and ethnic groups.

The process begins with small wooden depth pegs, often cocktail sticks, fixed to the skull or a cast at the different tissue depths. Strips of clay 'muscles' are applied, with their thickness measured to the height of the pegs. The sculptor then fills the gaps between the strips, smoothes out the clay, removes the pegs and begins modelling the nose (the most difficult because of the lack of bone), eyes, mouth, ears, chin and jowls. Prosthetic eyeballs are placed into the eye sockets to increase the realism of the look.

The artist must make several guesses, including the plumpness of the face, hairstyle, structure of the eyelids and facial expressions. As well, there may be only just a portion of recovered skull, the shape of which must be filled in.

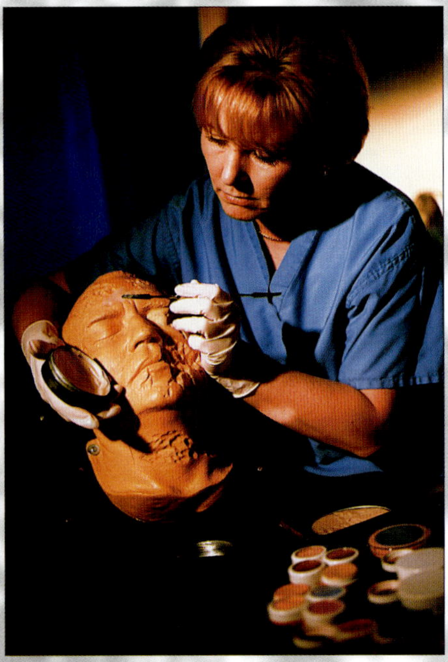

A forensic sculptor carefully works on a model of a dead person's head. Such models can be used to construct a likeness of a person from their remains, aiding in the identification process.

COMPUTER FACIAL RECONSTRUCTION

Digital reconstruction is the latest tool in identifying crime victims. A scan is taken of the skull as it rotates on a turntable, and the computer programme creates a digital skull that can be manipulated on the screen. The technician then selects a computer tomography (CT) three-dimensional scan of a real person estimated to be the same race and about the same age. As this scan is digitally merged with the one of the skull, it adjusts to correspond and moves its facial tissue into a shape that resembles the victim. The hair and eyes are estimated and added to provide a life-like image. Computer reconstruction has the value of giving a view from any angle, but retains the limitations of clay reconstruction.

The Unit of Forensic Art, opened in 2005 at the University of Dundee, has a groundbreaking program that allows the user to 'feel' the surface of the reconstructed face on the screen.

The skull gives an indication of the form and contours needed to recreate the likeness of the living person.

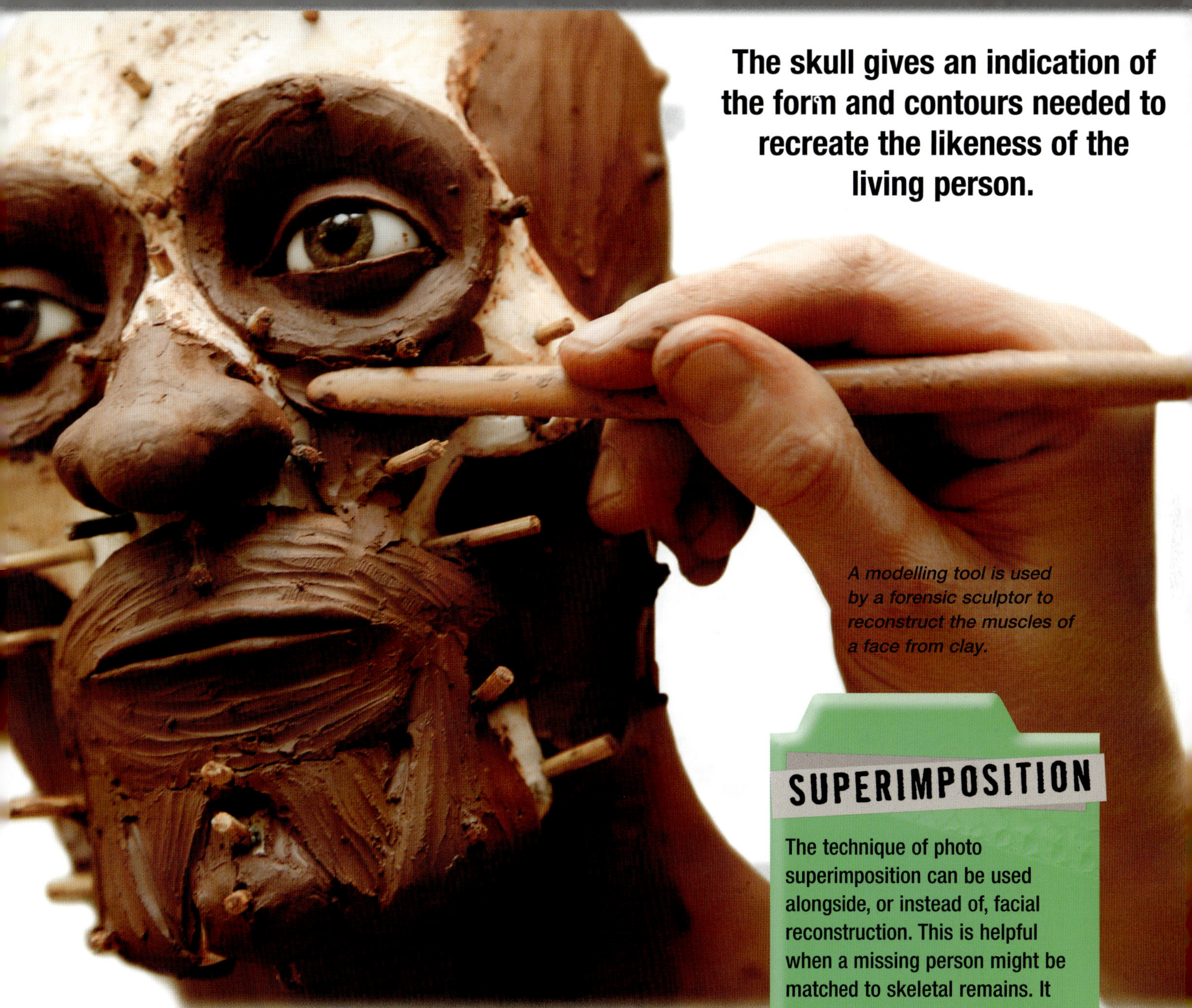

A modelling tool is used by a forensic sculptor to reconstruct the muscles of a face from clay.

A human skull reassembled with wax. Forensic experts rebuild skulls to enable facial reconstructions when there are no other means of identifying the remains.

SUPERIMPOSITION

The technique of photo superimposition can be used alongside, or instead of, facial reconstruction. This is helpful when a missing person might be matched to skeletal remains. It involves photographing the skull onto transparent film, and then superimposing this image over a photo of the individual. Matches can be seen in the teeth and key bony features such as the supraorbital ridges above the eyes. Today's computer techniques have made the process much easier to manipulate.

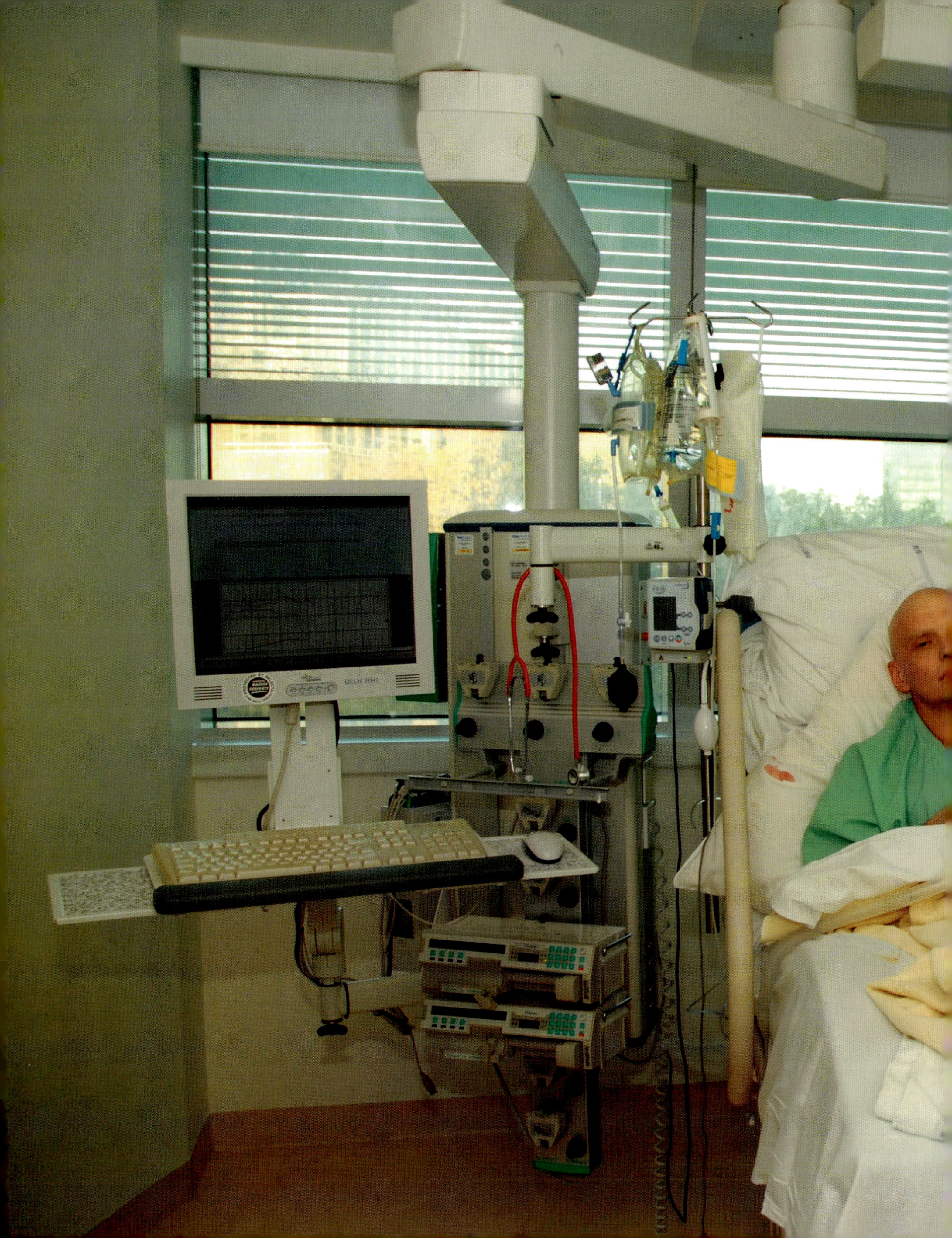
UCLH NHS

Chapter Seven

Cause of Death

HOMICIDE, SUICIDE, ACCIDENT, NATURAL CAUSES. ONLY THE FIRST CREATES A CRIME SCENE AND, IF POSSIBLE, FORENSIC INVESTIGATORS MUST QUICKLY DECIDE THE CAUSE OF DEATH.

A violent assault will be obvious, but many cases will not be that simple. It is the coroner in England and Wales, however, who must officially decide the manner of death, including if a crime has been committed. This is based on the evidence of the pathologist, who will normally give an opinion on whether the scene indicates a homicide.

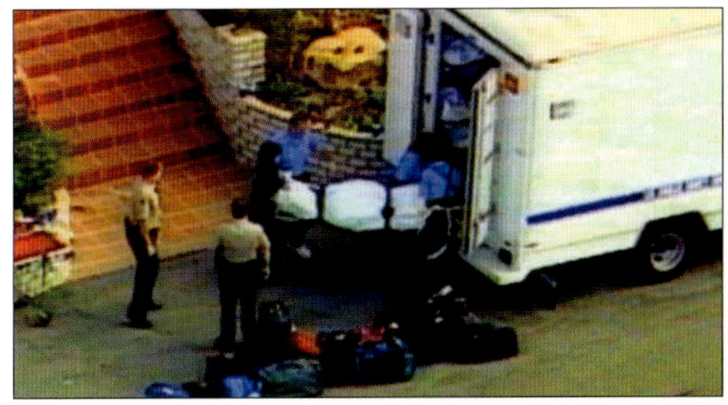

Officers remove 39 bodies after the mass suicide in 1997 of members of the Heaven's Gate cult near San Diego, California. They left a video describing their plan.

A forensic exam may find that a skull fracture was the cause of death, but the coroner must declare the manner of death such as an assault with a hammer, which would give the police a homicide case. These decisions are made easier by related forensic evidence such as a weapon, blood splatters or a forced entrance.

Has an apparent suicide been staged by a murderer? Was a fatal drug overdose an accident or administered by another? Was a fire death caused by arson? Pathologists help answer questions such as these after investigating the body and scene, or they may require laboratory work such as DNA or toxicology tests. Often it may take an autopsy, a postmortem examination, to reveal the truth. The latter is ordered by a coroner in England and Wales and by the procurator fiscal in Scotland.

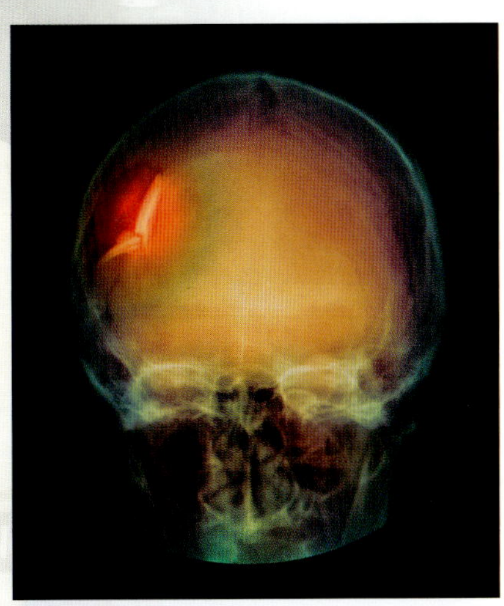

A coloured X-ray shows a skull fracture as red in the upper left-hand side. A forensic scientist would say the cause is due to a high-energy impact from a blunt object.

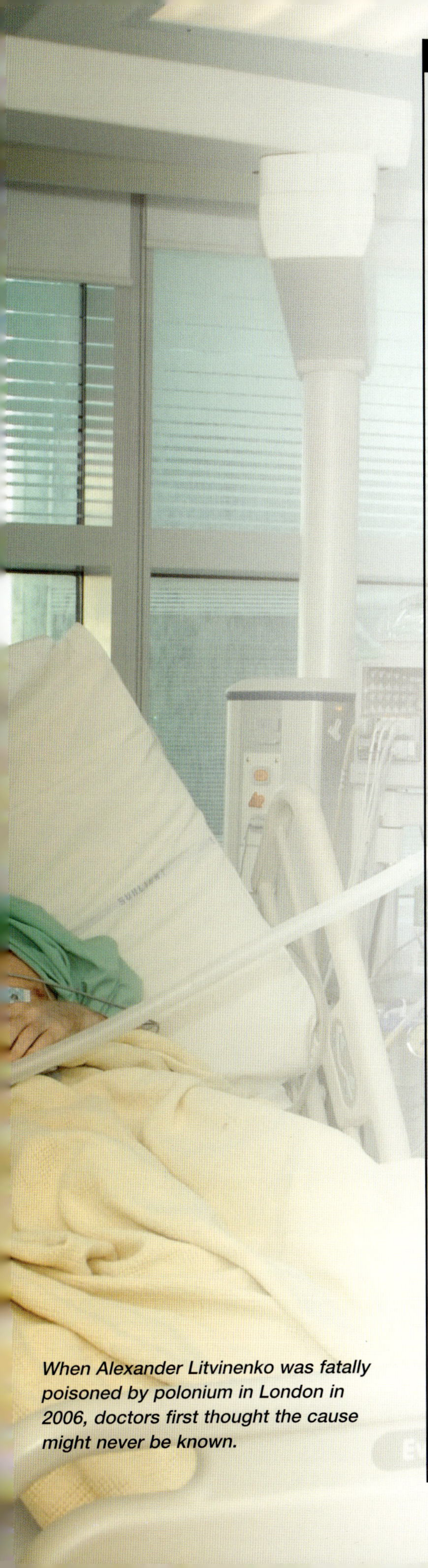

When Alexander Litvinenko was fatally poisoned by polonium in London in 2006, doctors first thought the cause might never be known.

The Forensic Pathologist

The forensic pathologist can be the most important scientist in an investigation because he or she knows several medical disciplines and will most likely be involved throughout a case.

This can begin at the crime scene, where the pathologist may be able to give an opinion on both the cause and manner of death after viewing the evidence *in situ*.

MYSTERY POISONING

Such was the case when two British children were found dead in 2006 in a Corfu hotel bungalow alongside their comatose father and his partner. Dr Stephanos Gasteratos, the Corfu hospital pathologist, said this was most likely a case of a strong poison, but not food poisoning. There were no signs of forced entry, struggle or other clues. Toxicology tests revealed they had died of carbon monoxide poisoning, traced to an overheated boiler.

As the investigation moves to the lab, a forensic pathologist will consult with other specialists, such as a forensic toxicologist if poison is suspected or a forensic odontologist for dental identification. Forensic pathologists also perform autopsies to gather evidence about sudden and apparently unexplained deaths. They write up the results and submit a report, along with photographs and documents, to the coroner. Their findings are based on the police investigation so the report will be able to serve as proper evidence in court.

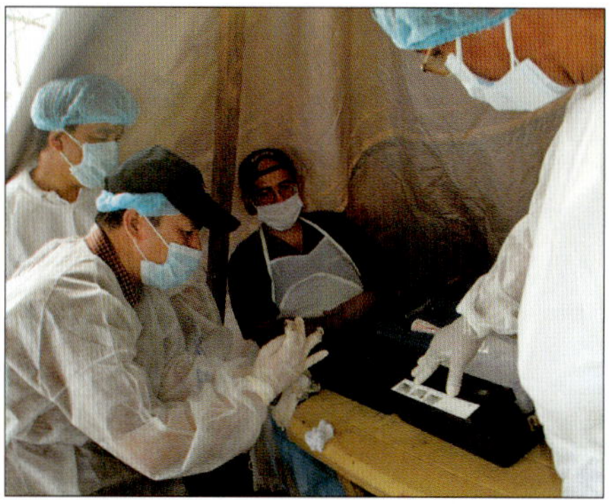

Forensic pathologists work to identify mudslide victims in the Philippines in 2006. Fingertips were removed for fingerprints.

TOOLS OF THE PATHOLOGIST

A pathologist works in three main areas and requires different tools and equipment for each:

Crime scene The initial investigation on site requires a kit containing items like a fingerprint brush, aluminium dusting powder, lifting tape, magnifying glass, cotton swabs and small containers for samples. The pathologist will also need protective clothing and work with police equipment, such as body bags.

Laboratory A pathologist usually heads a crime laboratory and has access to all available equipment, from electron microscopes to test tubes and complex analysis instruments. Much of this work involves collaboration with colleagues in their areas of specialization.

Autopsy room Here the pathologist is on the familiar ground of a surgeon aided by assistants. Because the morgue is an operating room for the dead, the tools consist of items such as a scalpel, bone cutters, cranium chisel, handsaw and brain knife.

Forensic pathologists perform autopsies to gather evidence about sudden and apparently unexplained deaths.

THE REAL SHERLOCK HOLMES

When Arthur Conan Doyle was a medical student at the University of Edinburgh in 1877, he was impressed by one of his professors, Dr Joseph Bell (above), who was a pioneering forensic pathologist. Doyle became his assistant and was able to absorb his tutor's keen eye for details. Bell would often observe the walk and accent of strangers and identify where they came from and their professions.

Later, when Doyle created his fictional sleuth, Sherlock Holmes, he loosely based him on Dr Bell, who supposedly would say, 'It was elementary', when diagnosing a patient.

A forensic pathologist seeks a conclusive result by analyzing a sample under a microscope.

Two Pathology Cases

On 1 May, 1999, the Nigerian asylum-seeker Marcus Omofuma died after three Austrian policemen bound and gagged him during a flight from Austria to Sofia, Bulgaria, where he was to fly to Nigeria.

At the policemen's trial, three forensic pathologists gave their opinion on the cause of death. The Bulgarian forensic pathologist, Stojcho Radanov, said the taping of Omofuma's mouth and binding of his thorax caused his death. The Viennese forensic pathologist Christian Reiter decided a heart weakness caused it. The German forensic pathologist Bernd Brinkmann said it was asphyxiation. The policeman were first suspended but argued that gagging was a normal practice, and Omofuma had been aggressive in resisting his deportation. They were each sentenced to eight months' probation for involuntary manslaughter.

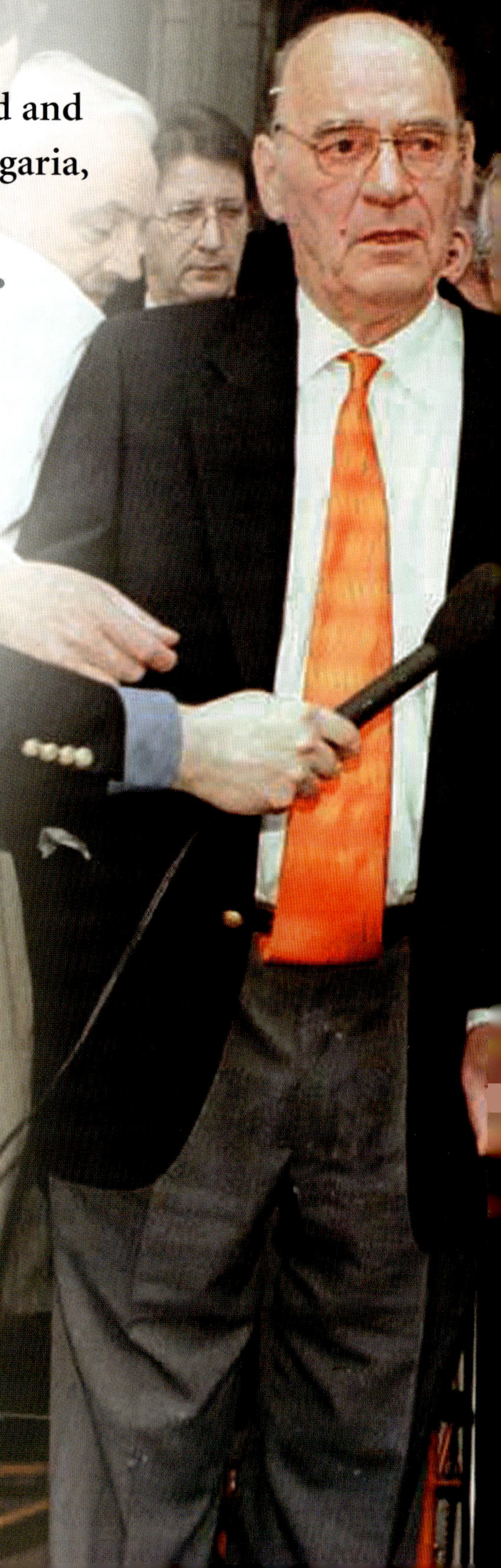

THE PATHOLOGIST IN COURT

The forensic pathologist, like all scientific experts, is normally giving evidence for the prosecution on a cause of death. In the public's eye this tends to look like science being used to secure a conviction, and the pathologist has been unfairly called 'a policeman in a white coat'.
In fact the scientist is considered by the court system to be impartial, and this is normally accomplished. The cause of death is given, and the judge or jury must decide if the facts are true. The forensic expert uses simple descriptions for complicated matters, and he or she informs the court on its scientific limitations, so its members will not jump to conclusions.

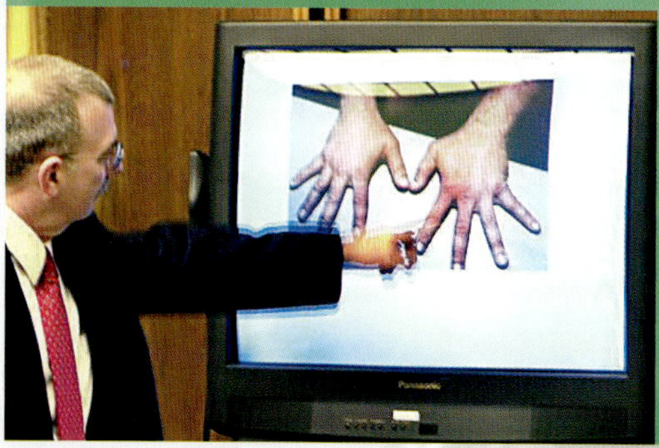

US pathologist Dr Ira Kanfer points out injuries in a 2002 Connecticut trial.

WRONGLY CONVICTED

Pathologists have also freed prisoners who were incorrectly convicted. Patrick Nicholls was sentenced to life in 1975 for murdering 74-year-old Mrs Gladys Heath, a family friend, that same year at her home in Worthing. Nicholls claimed he had found the body at the bottom of the stairs, but two pathologists concluded that she had died of a heart attack after being suffocated, and then severely beaten about the face.

After Nicholls had served 23 years in jail, Professor John Crane, a pathologist in the Irish Republic, reviewed his case. Crane said the victim's facial injuries were trivial and probably came from a fall caused by her heart attack. Nicholls' conviction was therefore quashed in 1998. 'They have stolen a third of my life, haven't they?' Nicholls said.

Patrick Nicholls stands outside the High Court building after winning his appeal in 1998.

THE DEATH CERTIFICATE

The cause and manner of death are recorded by a medical practitioner on the death certificate, based on standards set by the World Health Organization. The certificate can be issued immediately if the death is natural, or it may have to wait for a postmortem examination if the cause is unknown or suspicious. If a body is to be cremated, a second medical exam is needed before a death certificate can be issued.

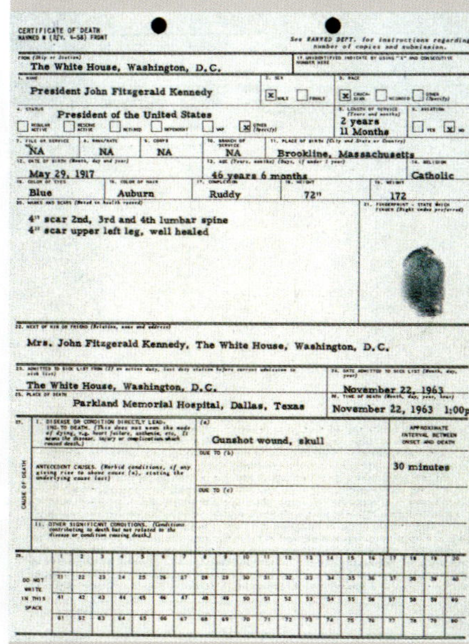

CERTIFICATE OF DEATH

The White House, Washington, D.C.

President John Fitzgerald Kennedy

President of the United States

2 years 11 Months

NA NA NA NA

Brookline, Massachusetts

May 29, 1917

46 years 6 months

Catholic

Blue

Auburn

Ruddy

72"

172

4" scar 2nd, 3rd and 4th lumbar spine
4" scar upper left leg, well healed

Mrs. John Fitzgerald Kennedy, The White House, Washington, D.C.

The White House, Washington, D.C.

November 22, 1963

Parkland Memorial Hospital, Dallas, Texas

November 22, 1963 1:00p.m

Gunshot wound, skull

30 minutes

President John F. Kennedy's death certificate was signed by his personal physician Dr George Burkley on 22 November 1963.

Pathologists have also freed prisoners who were incorrectly convicted.

The Postmortem

A postmortem examination is used to establish the cause of death. It will involve more than the opening of the body. A photographer will also be present to photograph the body laid out in the morgue.

A photographer will be present to photograph the body laid out in the morgue. The first photos will record the corpse in the clothing worn when found, and each time the pathologist removes a piece, another photo will be taken.

Before the dissection, the pathologist will measure and weigh the body and record the age, sex, race and hair and eye colours then the pathologist will check the clothes for trace evidence, check for marks on the skin, collect a sample of hair and clip or scrape the fingernails. Swabs will be taken from the mouth, rectum and sexual organs. X-rays may also be taken, because these will reveal the size and shape of knife wounds and how, for example, bullets moved through the body.

Dissecting the body normally follows a set routine. An incision is made, organs such as the heart and lungs removed and weighed, the abdomen examined and samples taken from the stomach. The skull is then opened to view the brain. Finally the organs are returned to the body, which is closed with sutures and released to the family for burial.

CHRIS PENN

When the actor Chris Penn died unexpectedly in Santa Monica, California, on 24 January 2006, an immediate postmortem examination was unable to determine how he died. There were no obvious signs of foul play or suicide. However, the 40-year-old younger brother of actor Sean Penn had a history of drug abuse.

A Los Angeles coroner ordered a blood toxicology test. When this was added to the earlier autopsy, it was found that Penn had died of an enlarged heart and the effects of mixing several medications.

Chris Penn died the day before his film, The Darwin Awards, *premiered at the Sundance Film Festival.*

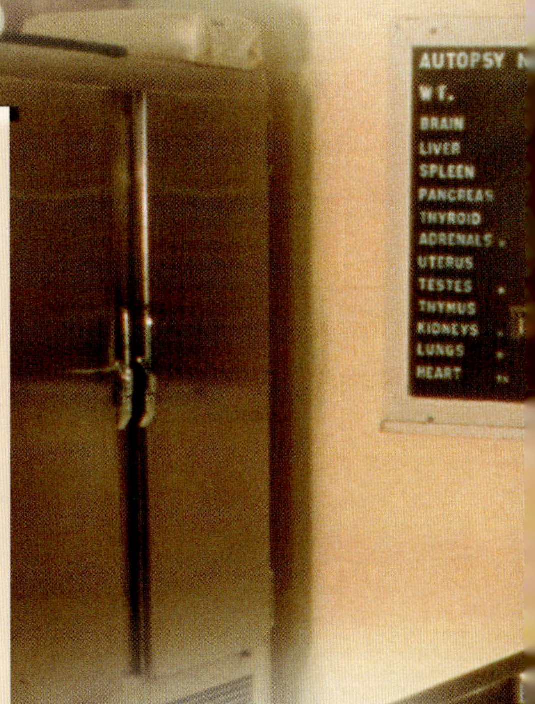

This autopsy room in a hospital morgue has scales used to weigh the major organs.

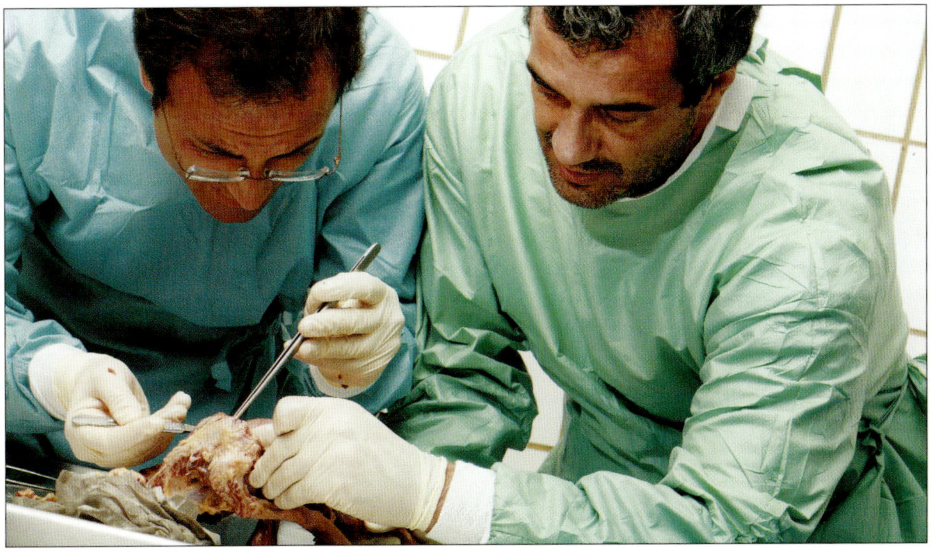

These forensic pathologists wear latex gloves to dissect the shoulder of a cadaver during an autopsy. Others present at the examination may include a police witness and an exhibits officer who examines materials on the body.

Before the dissection, the pathologist will measure and weigh the body.

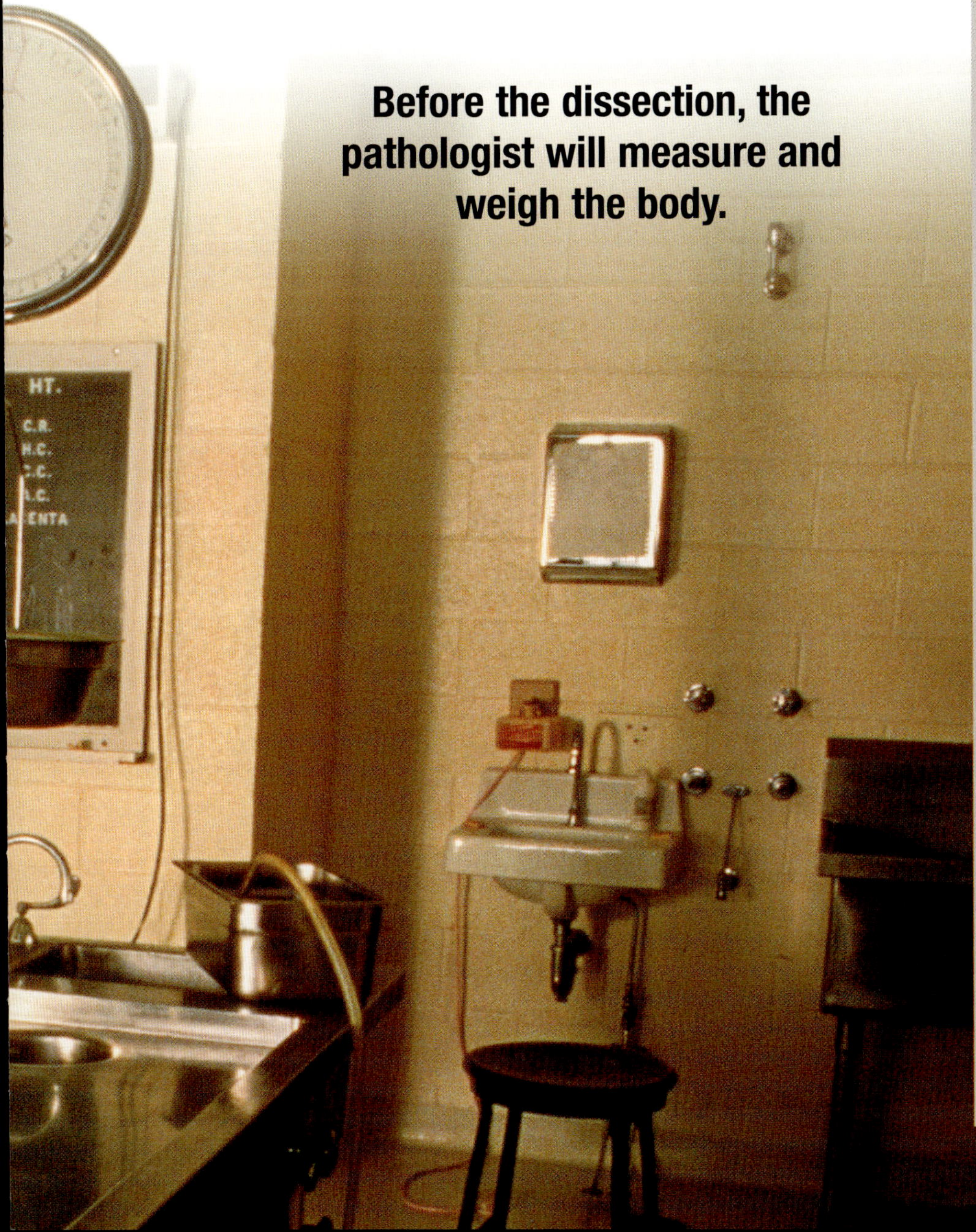

A MUSLIM AUTOPSY

Although Islam requires that a dead body be buried quickly without cutting or disturbing it, the Maldives' government approved that Muslim country's first autopsy in April 2007 after a request by the relatives of the deceased. This followed the death of Hussain Salah, a Maldivian opposition activist. His Maldivian Democratic Party accused prison authorities of beating him to death. A government spokesman said Salah had been released from prison from a narcotics charge, and his body was found floating in the sea. The government flew Salah's body to Sri Lanka for the autopsy. Dr LBL De Alwis, the chief judicial medical officer of Sri Lanka, conducted the postmortem examination and found that Salah drowned. He said minor injuries to the nose, face and left leg could have been sustained in the water. 'There were no major injuries to bones, soft tissue, or internal organs,' he said, 'and therefore death by physical violence is excluded.'

Dissecting the Body

A dissection begins with an incision down the front of a cadaver, but the manner of the cutting will depend upon whether the death seems natural or suspicious.

If natural, one simple incision is made from the larynx to the pubic region, and the organs will be removed for examination. If the deceased is a possible victim of crime, a cut in the shape of a T or Y is done to provide better access to the body cavity.

The ribs and clavicles are cut and the breastplate removed. Samples are taken of fluids such as blood, bile and urine for analysis. All of these could reveal any drugs taken hours before the death.

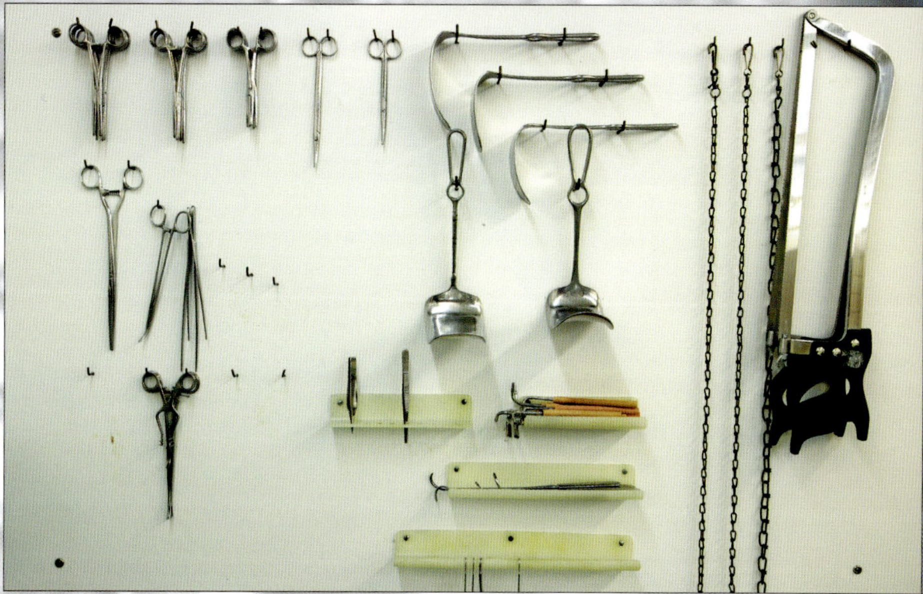

Autopsy instruments include the bone cutter and cranium chisel.

A pathologist may remove the major organs together such as the heart, lungs, trachea and oesophagus, but they are sometimes removed separately. The organs are weighed, and samples taken for microscopic examination. The contents of the stomach and intestine are inspected and samples also taken for toxicological tests.

Cutting the scalp and then sawing open the skull reveals the brain. The pathologist views the brain in place and then removes it for a closer examination. Thin slices of the brain tissue are removed to be examined microscopically.

Although the torso is normally dissected first, if there is evidence of the victim having been strangled, the pathologist will begin the autopsy with the head and neck.

TWO TYPES OF AUTOPSIES

If a death is presumed to be unknown or suspicious, a legal authority asks for a medico-legal autopsy, sometimes called a forensic autopsy. The unknown death will often have no foul play suspected. Only pathologists who are on the Home Office list can carry out this type of autopsy in England and Wales.

A clinical autopsy, also known as an academic or hospital autopsy, is performed to verify a cause of death that is usually known such as cancer or a stroke. They are also used to judge the effectiveness of treatment, study the processes of a disease and educate medical students and personnel. These autopsies cannot be performed without the consent of the next of kin of the deceased.

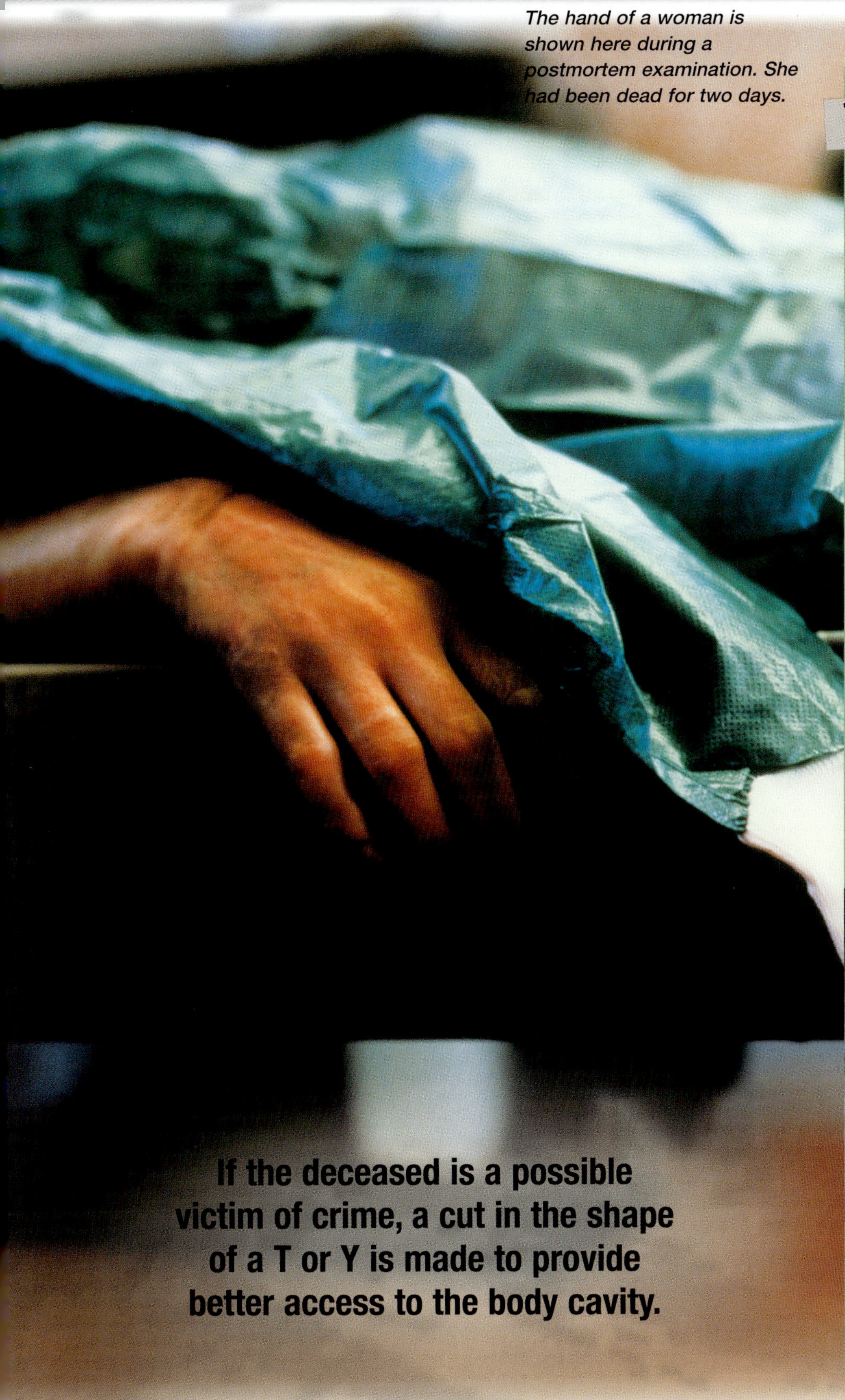

The hand of a woman is shown here during a postmortem examination. She had been dead for two days.

THE FIRST AUTOPSIES

Around 300 BCE, the Greek anatomist Herophilus was conducting dissections to teach human anatomy, and a century later the Greek physician Erasistratus of Ceos began using them in order to understand diseases. In the late 1400s the Italian physician Antonio Benivieni published the first book concerning anatomical pathology, *Remarkable Hidden Causes of Disease*. In the eighteenth century, the French physician Marie François Xavier Bichat conducted more than 600 autopsies.

Sir William Osler, a Canadian physician, was a great promoter of the autopsy in the late nineteenth century. He wrote that investigating the causes of death in this manner to prevent and treat disease 'is one of the highest objects of the physician'.

The French pathologist Marie-Francois Xavier Bichet (1771–1802) worked in a Paris hospital for the poor and founded modern histology, the study of tissues.

If the deceased is a possible victim of crime, a cut in the shape of a T or Y is made to provide better access to the body cavity.

Trace Evidence

Although trace evidence is more associated with identifying a suspect, it is also of value in finding the cause of death. Both mysteries can be solved at the same time.

For example a trace of arsenic in soup will confirm the cause of a victim's death and point to the spouse as the prime suspect. Other cases have identified the cause but not the criminal. When the former Russian spy Alexander Litvinenko died in London in 2006, pathologists found traces of polonium 210, a lethal radioactive substance, but police could only theorize over a Russian connection.

Traces of drugs near bodies are strong indicators of an overdose. Autopsies also turn up traces within a body that will overturn the original conjecture of death. This occurred in a Florida case in 2005. In Wellington, a husband and father, aged in his late forties, died in his sleep apparently of a heart attack. An autopsy, however, found he had overdosed on a combination of cocaine and oxycodone.

Homicides can also be revealed by drug traces in the body. In 2006 Daniela Toledo do Prado brought her convulsive daughter, Vittoria, to a hospital in Sâo Paulo, Brazil, saying she had drunk milk that had gone off. After the child died of heart failure the next day, doctors found a suspicious white powder on the girl's tongue. The mother said it was milk, but tests identified it as cocaine. Traces were later found in the baby's bottle, and the mother was charged with murder.

MARILYN MONROE'S AUTOPSY

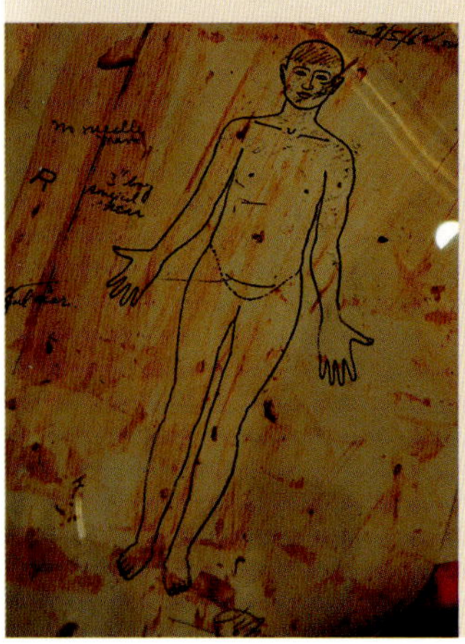

Marilyn Monroe died on 4 August 1962, and her autopsy was conducted by Dr Thomas Noguchi. Afterwards Coroner Theodore Curphey said she died from an overdose of barbiturates. Traces of the drug pentobarbital (sleeping pills) were discovered in her liver and chloral hydrate in her blood. He ruled her death a 'probable suicide.' Despite this many still believe it was accidental and conspiracy theorists say it was murder.

The autopsy consisted of a Y-shaped incision. A sample of blood was taken, and the liver, kidney, stomach and contents, urine and intestine were saved for further toxicological study. Her brain was weighed at 1440g/50.79oz and her heart was 300g/10.58oz.

This sketch was part of the Coroner's Autopsy Report on Marilyn Monroe's death. The report was featured in an exhibit about the star in the Hollywood Museum.

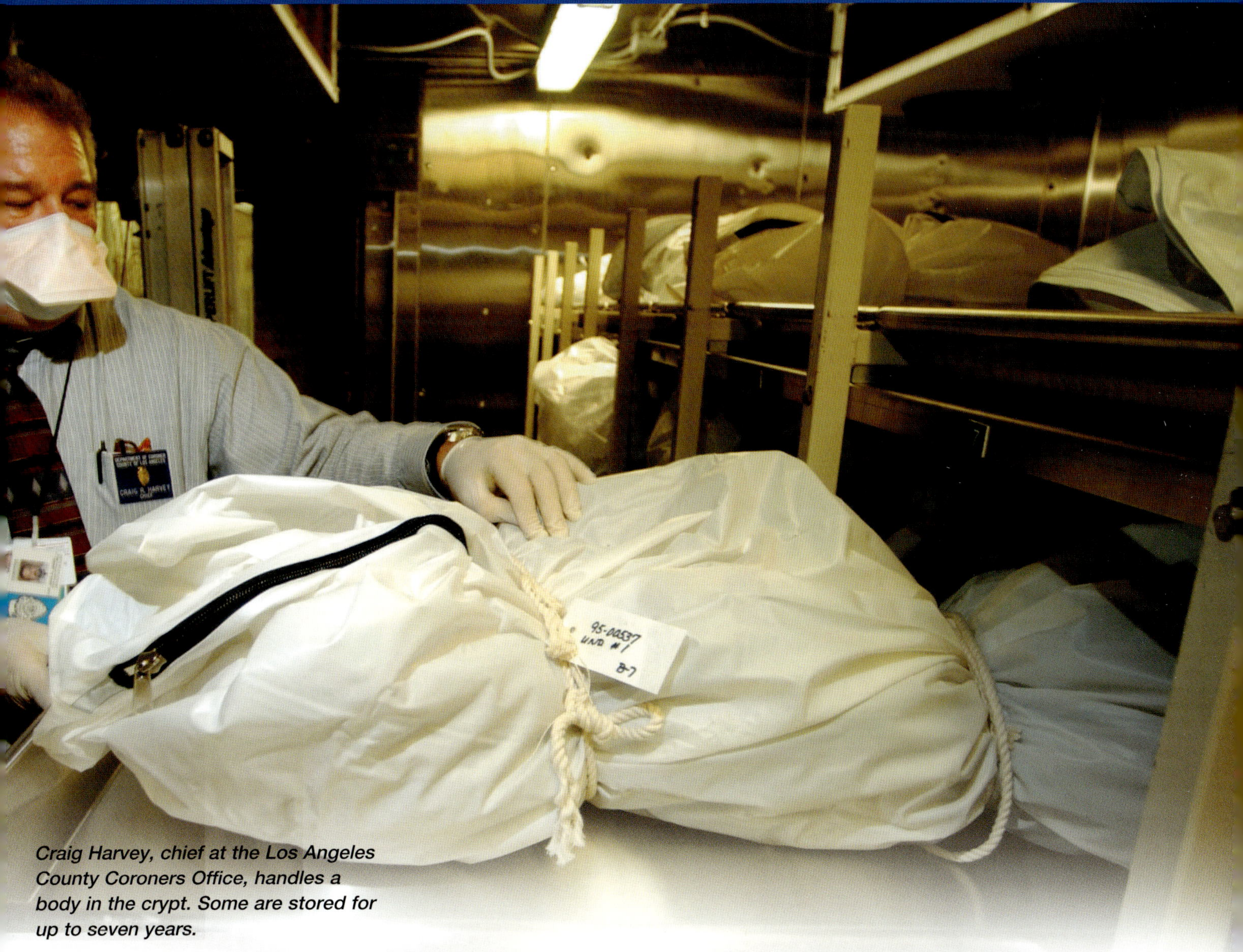

Craig Harvey, chief at the Los Angeles County Coroners Office, handles a body in the crypt. Some are stored for up to seven years.

HOW HAIR TRAVELS

Forensic research carried out in Australia reveals that hair found at a crime scene may not indicate a suspect, since it could have been transferred several times. Josephine Dachs investigated how hair clings to different fabrics while she worked in forensic services at the Australian Federal Police. The results were published in the journal *Forensic Science International.*

Dachs found that hair is easily passed on in a car, by contacting someone else or even through washing clothes. For her research she attached stray hairs to people who then went about their normal activities. A lot was lost in the first hour or so through movement, but several stayed put for some time.

Los Angeles County Coroner Dr Lakshmanan Sathyavagiswaran presents evidence during the 1995 O. J. Simpson murder trial.

Two Historic Cases

Was the Egyptian pharaoh Tutankhamun, who died about 1350 BCE, murdered? Ever since his tomb was excavated in 1922 by the British archeologist Howard Carter, scientists have tried to solve this question.

In 1968 a team from the University of Liverpool took skull radiographs of the mummy and discovered a piece of bone in the skull cavity. Professor R. G. Harrison, who led the investigation, said: 'This could mean that Tutankhamun died from a brain haemorrhage caused by a blow to his skull from a blunt instrument.'

By 2005, however, a team headed by Egyptian archaeologist Zahi Hawass took a 15-minute CT scan of the mummy that produced 1700 images. It revealed no evidence of a blow to the back of the head, only a hole apparently drilled by embalmers. A fracture on the left leg was scanned and the most likely cause of death was the result of gangrene.

NAPOLEON

Recent DNA tests have indicated that the French emperor, Napoleon Bonaparte, was murdered. He died on 5 May 1821 after being banished to the remote Atlantic island of St Helena. The original diagnosis had been death from stomach cancer.

The new scientific evidence was presented to the French senate in 2000 by a dozen French toxicologists, coroners, police

Napoleon Bonaparte (1769–1821) was defeated by Britain's Duke of Wellington at the battle of Waterloo in 1815 and exiled to St Helena.

Egyptian archaeologist Zahi Hawass examines a mummy, one of many that require identification.

forensic scientists and cancer specialists. His valet had kept a lock of the emperor's hair, and forensic tests by the FBI and other laboratories found arsenic levels hundreds of times higher than normal. They also revealed that the arsenic had been ingested over a period of four months.

ARSENIC POISONING?

The theory of death by cancer had been questioned previously, because Napoleon was fat when he died, and when his body was returned to Paris in 1840 for burial it was perfectly preserved, a symptom of arsenic poisoning. Suspects include his British captors, led by the island's governor Hudson Lowe, and Charles Tristan, Marquis de Montholon, exiled with Napoleon, and aware the emperor had had an affair with his wife.

WHO ARE CORONERS?

Coroners in England and Wales are normally lawyers but doctors are chosen for some cases. A coroner is an independent judicial officer whose duty is to find out the medical cause of a death if it is unknown and to enquire into the cause when the death is sudden, unexpected or unnatural.

Los Angeles Deputy District Attorney Gregory A. Dohi (left) asks Jeffrey Gutstadt, medical examiner with the Los Angeles County Coroner's Office, to identify bullets at the 2003 murder trial of actor Robert Blake, who was found innocent.

UNKNOWN CAUSES

It is not always possible for a coroner or medical examiner to determine the cause of death. Most US states follow a reporting system similar to Michigan after an investigation fails to discover the cause. The examiner must write 'Based upon autopsy, toxicology and a thorough investigation of the circumstances, a cause of death cannot be explained.' Unknown deaths are labelled as 'sudden death' when witnessed but unexplained, and 'found body' for unwitnessed and unexplained deaths.

Non-Criminal Deaths

The correct identification of a homicide is vital. If a criminal death is wrongly registered as a suicide or attributed to natural causes, the murderer is not punished and may strike again.

Conversely, if a non-criminal death is judged to be a homicide, much police time will be wasted. The latter happened in the parachute death of Stephen Hilder, with the police arresting two people and searching ten months for a murderer who did not exist.

A verdict of death by natural causes covers many situations: old age, fatal diseases and accidents that range from drug overdoses to traffic fatalities. An inquest will be held only if the death is unexpected or its cause unknown. Among the most difficult non-criminal deaths to analyze are suicides, so suspicions should always be present in a suicide investigation.

CAUSES OF DEATH

The causes of homicide deaths such as a bullet in the head can be straightforward, but in deaths by natural causes it is generally more difficult to find the underlying manner of death. The cause may be a heart attack, but it could have been the result of any number of events, from jogging to robbery. Studies have found that physicians completing death certificates often put down coronary heart disease as a default cause when the specific cause cannot be determined. This is particularly true when elderly people die. Heart disease remains the most common official cause of death in the world's developed countries.

DEATH BY SELF-NEGLECT

When a lottery millionaire, Philip Alan Kitchen, aged 58, was found dead in 2002 at his home in Burnt Green, Worcestershire, an inquest turned in the unusual verdict of 'death from self-neglect', although he had died of bronchial pneumonia. The principal cause was spending long periods of time without moving.

Kitchen had won a £2 million jackpot three years earlier. The former master carpenter had a history of heavy drinking and had not eaten properly for six weeks before his death. Pathologist Paul Geddy said Kitchen had first-degree burns to his thighs and lower back that had turned to blisters due to spending several months immobile on his sofa.

Right: The British skydiver Stephen Hilder (upper left, in black) links with members of the Army Parachute Association during a dive in 2005. A week later he fell to his death. It was ruled an open verdict.

DISPUTING AN AUTOPSY

Family members almost never challenge the results of an autopsy, but this happened with the French postmortem examination of Henri Paul, who drove the car that crashed in 1997 in Paris killing Princess Diana, Dodi Al Fayed, and himself. Mohammed Al Fayed, Dodi's father, disputed the French findings that the driver was drunk. He believes the crash was a homicide and alleged that the autopsy failed because blood samples could have been switched or taken from the wrong corpse. In 2006, French authorities responded, saying they had now verified the results by DNA tests. A British inquest in 2008 blamed the negligence of the driver and paparazzi.

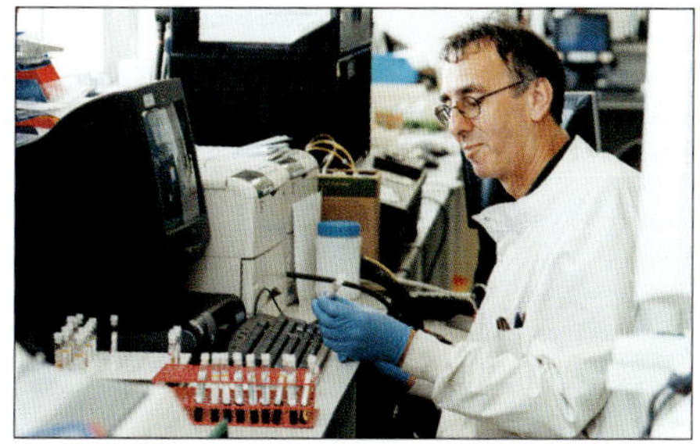

A forensic pathologist analyzes a blood sample to determine if a death was from natural causes.

Suicide

Authorities often misdiagnose suicides or, being unsure, declare an open verdict. It is indeed difficult to determine if an overdose or motor fatality is a case of self-destruction.

Attempts are made by some families to conceal a suicide death, perhaps from religious reasons or because insurance policies would be jeopardized. Murderers, as well, have frequently tried to mask their crimes by faking a suicide, and a pathologist would need to look carefully to detect homicide in a drowning case if the victim bore no signs of violence because he was drugged beforehand.

SELF-INFLICTED

Despite such problems more than 30,000 suicides are recorded each year in the USA. About one-quarter of the suicides leave notes. Forensic pathologists can also be fairly certain when confronting traditional suicide methods. A death by inhaling carbon monoxide from the exhaust pipe of a car is a simple case if the body shows no sign of physical distress or a struggle. These cases are normally suicides, as are hangings, although a bruised body will arouse suspicions. Homicides represent a small percentage of poisoning deaths because of modern detection methods, so the vast majority are accidents or suicides. Self-inflicted gunshot deaths, which are the most common form of suicide in the USA, can be detected by the position of the bullet hole and the bullet's angle of trajectory (see Sabow box).

The carbon monoxide in car exhaust fumes has been frequently used in suicides. Changing the shape of the exhaust pipe would make it more difficult to attach a hose.

JAMES SABOW

Family members and other physicians frequently dispute an official ruling of suicide. US Marine Colonel James Sabow was discovered dead in 1991 in his backyard at the El Toro, California, Marine Corps Air Station. A bullet fired from a shotgun had blown his head apart.

The coroner and three military investigations ruled he killed himself, but Sabow's brother, Dr David Sabow, believes he was murdered and in 2005 a San Diego gunshot-residue expert, Dr Bryan Burnett agreed. He said the blood-spatter patterns and a total absence of gunshot residue on the victim's hands showed he was murdered. As well, he noted, smears on Sabow's hand indicated it was moved twice after his death. The US press continues to debate the colonel's uncertain cause of death.

Despite many celebrity deaths being ruled non-criminal, conspiracy theories always abound.

Above: The wreckage of James Dean's Porsche belies the rumour that he was not travelling fast enough to be killed.

CELEBRITY DEATH CONSPIRACIES

Despite many celebrity deaths being ruled non-criminal, conspiracy theories always abound. Many believe that the suicide of Marilyn Monroe was a murder instigated to cover up her affairs with President John Kennedy and his brother Robert. The heroin overdose suicide of Kurt Cobain, lead singer with Nirvana, is claimed by some to have actually been a murder with a shotgun and heroin overdose.

Theorists also contest deaths that have been ruled accidental by coroners. They say the damage found on the Porsche that took actor James Dean's life supposedly reveals that the speed the car was travelling at was not fast enough to kill him.

Fans grieve outside the building where singer Kurt Cobain died.

Italian Prosecutor Pietro Grasso shows photofits of mafia boss Bernardo Provenzano in 2005. He was captured a year later after more than four decades on the run and is now serving a life sentence.

Chapter Eight

The Criminal Trail

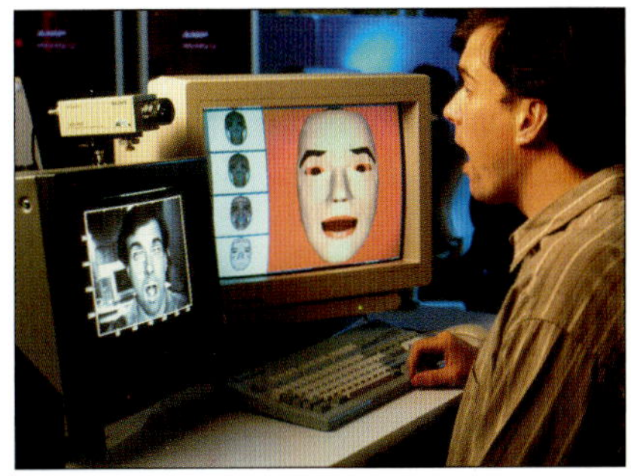

A scientist works with a computer that recognizes expressions to create a facial 'map'.

THE FOREMOST GOAL OF A FORENSIC INVESTIGATION IS TO IDENTIFY ONE OR MORE SUSPECTS WHO COMMITTED THE CRIME. THIS IS DONE USING PHYSICAL EVIDENCE THAT LINKS THE PERPETRATOR TO THE VICTIM AND/OR THE CRIME SCENE. This process may begin with a search for a face captured on a CCTV surveillance camera or an eyewitness description that is recreated by a forensic artist. A faceless crime, however, may rely entirely on trace evidence.

During a criminal investigation nobody is ruled out as a suspect, even the person who reported the crime. Even such evidence as bloodstains, a suicide note or a confession that appears to be reliable must be questioned. In order to have any impact in the courtroom the forensic expert's conclusions should be as certain as possible. A scientist can point out strong evidence leading to a suspect but cannot directly attribute guilt to anyone.

The laboratory expert has a great responsibility in drawing scientific conclusions that may incarcerate a person for life or, as in the USA, lead to his or her execution. In identifying a suspect for the police and an impressionable jury, a forensic scientist should only state the facts and let the opposing lawyers argue their merits. After all a homicide victim's hair on a suspect's coat may have been exchanged at their meeting months before the murder. Or the murder weapon owned by a suspect could have been stolen and used by another, the killer.

Closed-circuit television (CCTV) cameras, such as this one mounted on a wall, act as deterrents and have helped solve many cases.

The Forensic Artist

In the world of modern technology, the sketchpad is not dead. Photofit composites and E-FIT computer programmes are now available to create a criminal's facial features.

After the 1995 bombing of the US Federal Building in Oklahoma City, which killed 168 people, an FBI forensic artist, Raymond Rozycki, met for two to three hours with a witness.

To create an accurate sketch Rozycki showed the witness the FBI's facial catalogue. It contains photographs of faces broken down by the overall shape and separate characteristics such as eyes, eyebrows, cheeks, chin, ear and hair. Each of the 25 categories has 16 different photographs. After the parts were selected and combined, Rozycki used further details from the witness to fine-tune the drawing. The witness described the man who rented the van that carried the bomb. The resulting sketch Rozycki made identified the bomber as Timothy McVeigh, and he was soon apprehended.

CCTV EVIDENCE

Artists are also asked to make sketches from surveillance-camera evidence in order to clarify and simplify the images. This happened after a suicide car bombing on 2 March 2006, near the American consulate in Karachi, Pakistan, which killed one diplomat and four other people. A day later, the Pakistani police artist drew a sketch from camera images and eyewitness accounts.

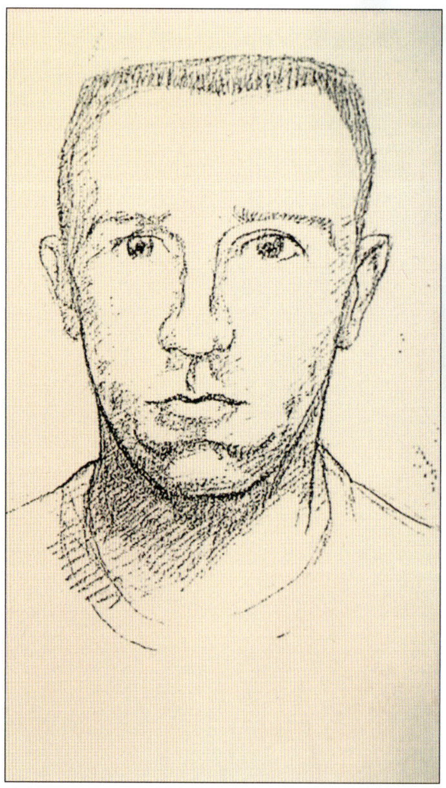

The sketch by FBI forensic artist Raymond Rozycki produced a striking resemblance to the bomber Timothy McVeigh.

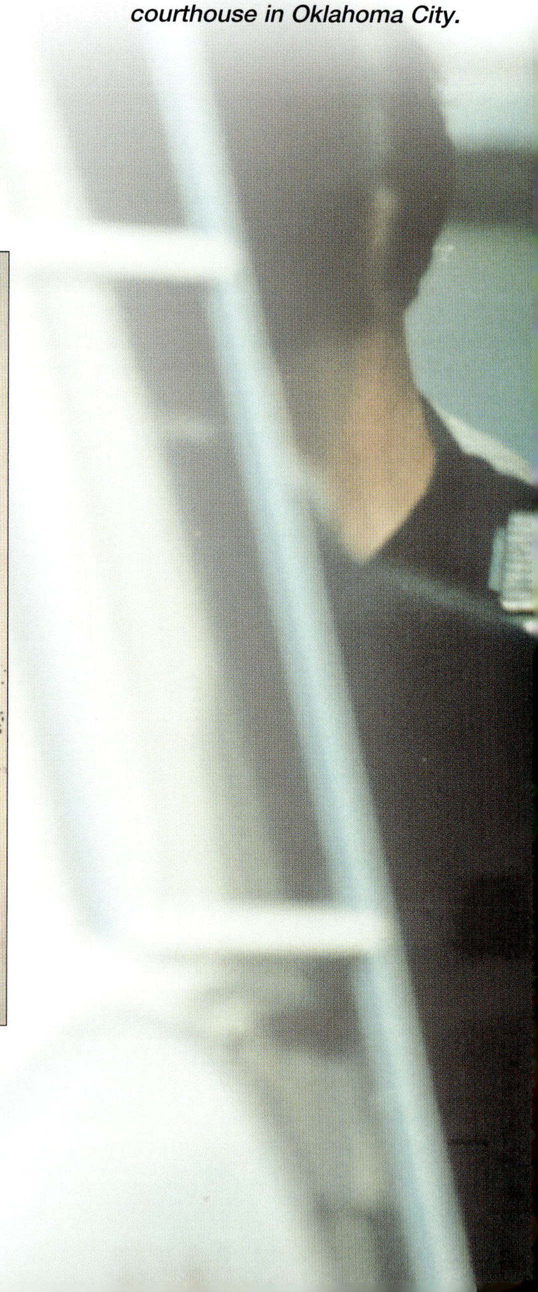

Timothy McVeigh is escorted in 1995 by authorities to the courthouse in Oklahoma City.

ARTISTIC AGEING

Forensic artists also help find people who have been missing for several years. This is done by 'age progression'. The artist uses photographs and knowledge of the growth of bone structure to create a sketch of how the person might have aged, as seen in this computer imaging of Elvis Presley. Such artists work, for instance, for the UK's National Missing Persons Helpline.
One manner of estimating advanced age involves siblings. If the missing person has a brother or sister, the artist can use a photograph of the sibling and merge it with an old photo of the missing person. A computer programme will show how the face might have matured.

With the help of the eyewitness, the artist was able to produce a sketch that identified the bomber as Timothy McVeigh.

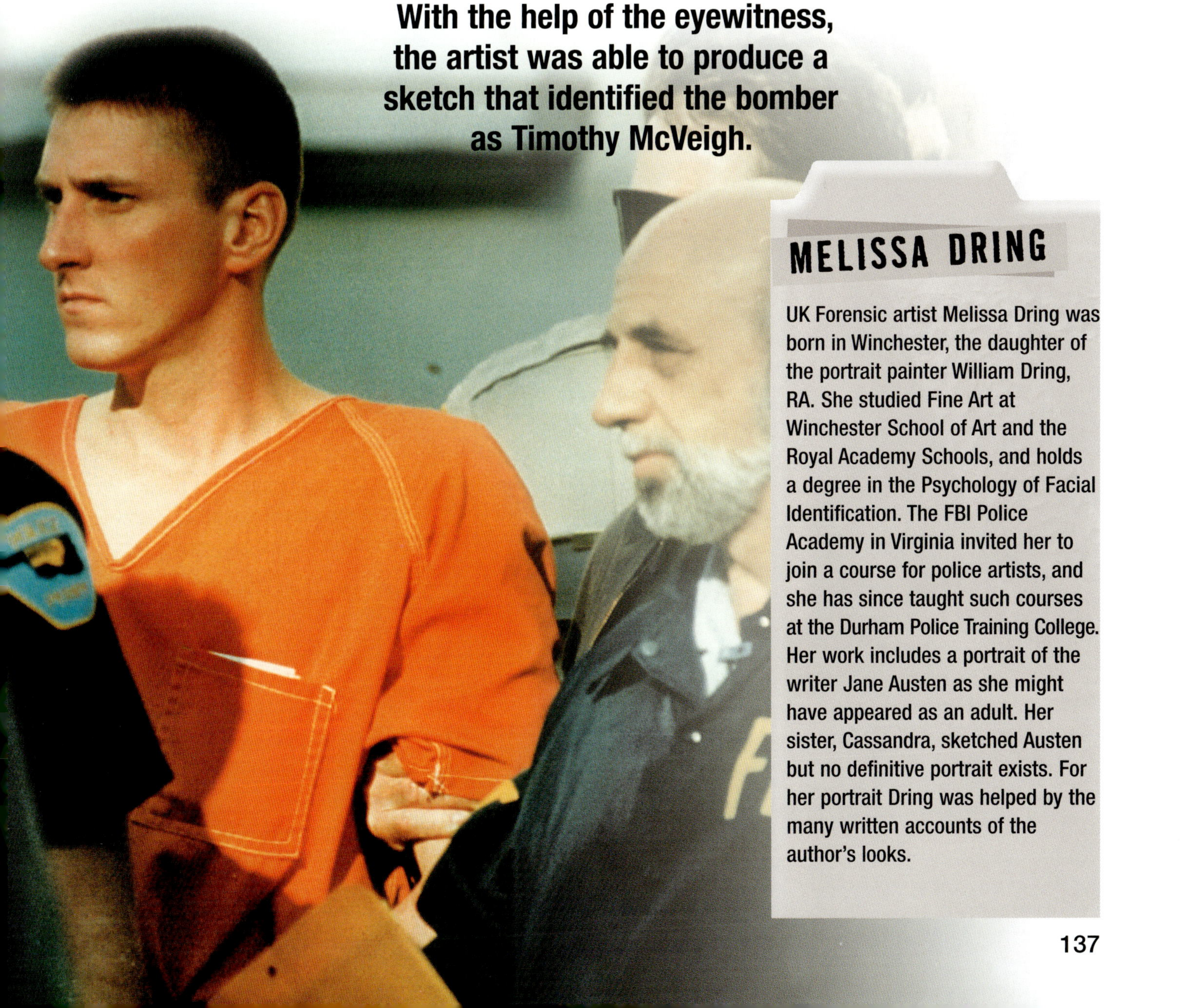

MELISSA DRING

UK Forensic artist Melissa Dring was born in Winchester, the daughter of the portrait painter William Dring, RA. She studied Fine Art at Winchester School of Art and the Royal Academy Schools, and holds a degree in the Psychology of Facial Identification. The FBI Police Academy in Virginia invited her to join a course for police artists, and she has since taught such courses at the Durham Police Training College. Her work includes a portrait of the writer Jane Austen as she might have appeared as an adult. Her sister, Cassandra, sketched Austen but no definitive portrait exists. For her portrait Dring was helped by the many written accounts of the author's looks.

E-FIT Programmes

The reconstruction of a suspect's face was done by identikit and from 1970 mostly by photofit. Both require a witness to select a series of different facial features and fit them together like a jigsaw puzzle.

Identikit uses sketches, and photofit uses photographs. With the advent of computers, the old system, which produced rather disjoined images, was replaced by the electronic facial identification technique, commonly known as E-FIT, a name coined by Janina Kaminska at the Home Office in 1984.

Detective Chief Inspector Stuart Mace talks with the press after releasing E-FIT images of the suspect who shot a 19-year-old woman in Walthamstow, London, on New Year's Day 2002 to steal her mobile telephone. The victim was left with a gash on her forehead and recovered.

An E-FIT software programme, which stores hundreds of facial features, is used by such law enforcement agencies as Scotland Yard, the FBI and the Royal Canadian Mounted Police. This computerized photofit system is also a feature of the BBC's Crimewatch television programme.

In 2005 advanced E-FITs were unveiled in London at a conference on crime-fighting technology. The software now uses a genetic algorithm to mutate a screen image as the witness gives the description. This cuts down the old selection of parts from hours to minutes.

One system, EigenFit, has been developed at the University of Kent, and another, EvoFit, at the University of Stirling. Both packages produce nine random faces based on the gender, race and hairstyle of the suspect. The witness chooses the closest likeness, and the face evolves according to additional details fed in to the system. A more realistic face is created by the programme's attention to variations in a face's shape, shading and the relationship between the features.

STUYVESANT TOWN RAPIST

Detective Stephen Mancusi, the senior forensic artist with the New York Police Department, has had many successes. However, the most unusual one involved the 'Stuyvesant Town Rapist', who had raped four women in that residential area of Manhattan.

The last victim recalled the rapist's features and worked with Mancusi on a composite sketch. It was quickly printed on posters and distributed around the city. A Bronx assistant district attorney spotted one and immediately recognized her half-brother, Anthony Mane. He was arrested, convicted and sentenced to up to 40 years.

Above: A crime victim (left) works with a police artist to create a computerized image of the criminal.

IRA BOMBERS

When Teresa Redmon began working as a forensic artist for the Kentucky State Police in 1994, she created her composite sketches of criminals and missing persons by drawing them by hand. More recently the police have invested in software technology, and Redmon chose E-FIT because it was the one that focused solely on law enforcement and, she notes, contained the world's largest database of hairstyles, facial features and other attributes. From the first 14 E-FIT composite faces she created, the police made ten arrests, and the overall successful rate now is 80 per cent. Today, as she travels in Kentucky working with state and local police, she carries along her laptop computer loaded with E-FIT and other face composite systems.

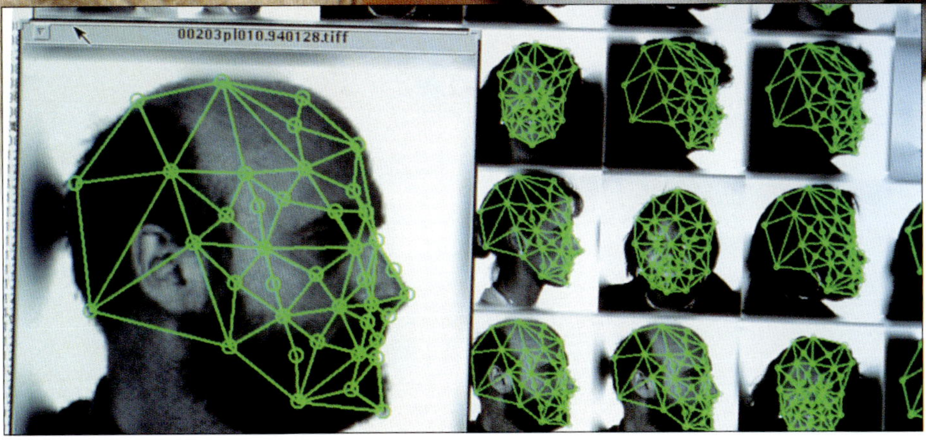

A man's head is overlaid with a contour map to produce a computerized facial image. The grid compares specific points.

Surveillance Cameras

They may give fuzzy, jerky images, but closed-circuit television (CCTV) cameras have proved invaluable in identifying criminals and tracing the last movements of victims.

Closed-circuit television (CCTV) cameras, such as the one pictured left, beam their images back to monitors in a security control room.

SWISS VANDAL

Surveillance cameras in Thailand caught a drunk Swiss man spraying black paint on several portraits of the Thai king Bhumibol Adulyadej and this led in March 2007 to a sentence of ten years in prison. Oliver Jufer, 57, at first blamed a German who had left for the Philippines, but decided to confess after the cameras recorded his vandalism. He could have received 75 years, but the judge reduced the sentence because he had confessed. Jufer has lived in Thailand for a decade, and the 79-year-old monarch had studied in Switzerland. The king had previously said he would pardon anyone jailed for insulting him.

Technical advances now allow the captured faces of suspects to be compared with mug shots by using imaginary points, or 'landmarks', on the faces.

Cameras have also been successful in locating vulnerable missing persons and for preventive surveillance, such as locating football hooligans in a crowd.

WATCHING THE POLICE

There are an estimated 25 million CCTV cameras in the world. In 2007, Britain led all countries in having up to 4.2 million, with a city person's image captured about 300 times a day. Some worry this is an invasion of privacy, but the Association of Chief Police Officers (ACPO) said many safeguards are in place to stop abuses by officers. 'The police use of surveillance', said ACPO's Graham Gerrard, 'is probably the most regulated of any group in society.'

In some areas of Britain, CCTV has reduced crime by 95 per cent. The Wakefield District of West Yorkshire has 166 cameras, having spent £1.3 million on new ones from 2007 to 2010, adding a mobile CCTV van in 2010.

SURVEILLANCE SLIPS

The value of CCTV is especially appreciated when cameras fail. This occurred during the London bombings of 7 July 2005, when the camera was not working on the bus that was attacked. Police have stressed that tapes must be changed daily and tested, and that the time and date displays need to be correct.

A CCTV camera observes passengers on a London bus. These cameras, used as deterrents and for evidence of crimes, were installed on all London buses in 2007.

SHOPLIFTING

Private surveillance cameras are making it much easier to catch shoplifters. One of the famous catches was American actress Winona Ryder who was filmed in 2001 in the Beverly Hills Saks Fifth Avenue store as she stole more than 20 items worth $5,560. A Saks security guard, who operated the cameras from a basement control room, played the videotape during Ryder's trial in 2002. It showed her entering a dressing room in the store's luxury boutique carrying a red bag, then leaving with the bag looking much larger. She also bought items during her hour-and-a-half visit. The cameras helped convict Ryder, who was given a three-year probation, 480 hours of community service, $2,700 in fines, and ordered to pay Saks for the stolen items.

CCTV Cases

Many arrests come from surveillance cameras in private businesses. This is what caught Paul Agutter, known as the 'Safeway Poisoner'. A biochemistry lecturer at Edinburgh's Napier University, he tried to poison his wife's gin and tonic drinks in 1995 with atropine in order to marry his lover.

To throw the blame elsewhere he placed bottles of tonic injected with the poison on supermarket shelves. CCTV footage revealed him putting the tonic on a shelf in Safeway's Edinburgh branch. He was convicted and received a 12-year sentence. Released in 2002 after seven years, he became employed as a part-time lecturer on philosophy and medical ethics at the University of Manchester.

Police can also manoeuvre surveillance cameras to target high-risk situations. A junior off-duty police officer, Noel Duke, saw a girl walking home alone at 3.15am. in Doncaster. He notified colleagues who trained CCTV cameras on the area and captured Dieter Graw grabbing the girl and trying to carry her off into the bushes. Graw released her when she screamed and struggled. Police were on the scene seconds later, and he was arrested and sent to prison for four years.

Footage from CCTV proves to be solid evidence in court. When a gunman went on a shooting spree in north London, injuring two people, cameras filmed him. John Laidlaw, 24, was caught on camera as he rampaged through London's Finsbury Park underground station brandishing a gun as onlookers cowered in fear. The footage was shown to jurors at his trial in 2007, and he was found guilty and sentenced to life with a minimum of 15 years in prison.

Above: A CCTV camera stands out among a city's lights. Britain has the most cameras per head of population, and the USA is quickly increasing its numbers.

Left: CCTV is frequently used in conjunction with mirrors to provide a 360-degree view for security officials.

CCTV+YOUTUBE=ARREST

A clip from a security camera in Hamilton, Ontario, Canada, was placed on video-sharing website YouTube in December 2006 and led to an arrest in a murder case. The camera had captured young men outside a hip-hop club where a 22-year-old man was killed. Hamilton was a Canadian pioneer in video surveillance, putting cameras in high-crime areas in 2002.

ECURITY IN STOCKHOLM

ockholm Transport has invested $29,000,000 in CCTV systems to ake the Swedish capital's public transport the safest in the world. e security overhaul came after rising instances of vandalism and saults on bus drivers.

the spring of 2006 Stockholms Localtrafik (SL) announced the stallation of 1500 cameras in its underground and rail stations. Four onths later 1200 more cameras were put in place, and in October it aced cameras in buses, taking the total number of cameras to more an 15,000. Cameras, alarms and warning systems are linked to a ntral security station.

Connecting Victim and Suspect

When a crime is not directly witnessed, linking a suspect to the victim must solve it. In some rare cases this is not even enough, because an innocent person may be found holding the murder weapon as he stands over the body.

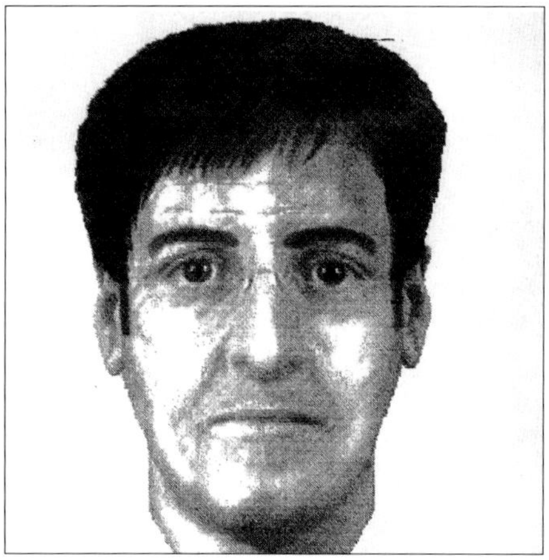

Police released this E-FIT image in 1999 of the suspected murderer of the BBC presenter Jill Dando.

Still, connecting the perpetrator to the crime in some way will normally lead to a conviction. The link is most often DNA, fingerprints or trace evidence. A guilty verdict is virtually assured by forensic proof showing that items such as hair, fibres or blood have been exchanged between a victim and suspect.

Most murderers are close to the victim such as spouses and lovers. Others have no previous relationship, as is the case in many kidnappings. And a lack of a relationship is what makes contract killings so difficult to solve. The instigator of the murder has an established alibi and is not the real murderer. They are often caught, however, when either the hired hit man or a go-between contacts the police with information.

Forensic awareness has helped some parents recover their children. A mother in Philadelphia, Pennsylvania, USA, regained custody of her daughter in 2004 after a six-year kidnapping. Seeing the child at a birthday party, she took a hair sample and sent it to a DNA lab that verified the identification and led to the kidnapper's arrest.

THE WEAPON CONNECTION

Possibly the most blatant evidence of guilt is the murder weapon handled by a suspect. Ballistic tests, as an example, linked the rifle used to kill ten people in the Washington, DC, area in 2002 to John Allen Muhammad and Lee Malvo, helping convict them. Muhammad was sentenced to death and Malvo received several life sentences. Perpetrators make great efforts to dispose of incriminating knives and guns, and some are never located. This was the case when Sam Sheppard, the US doctor who inspired the television series and movie, *The Fugitive*, was convicted of his wife's murder in 1954. Nevertheless, the connection seemed strong enough when the coroner described the missing weapon as a surgical instrument.

Most murderers are already close to the victim such as spouses and lovers.

A policeman stands guard outside Jill Dando's home where she was shot on the doorstep.

JILL DANDO

One of London's most infamous murders occurred on 26 April 1999, when BBC television presenter Jill Dando was callously shot in broad daylight on her doorstep in what first resembled a contract killing. Police seemed baffled as the search stretched on for two years. However on 25 May 2000 they arrested Barry George, a known sex offender who lived 0.8km/½ mile away from her home.

George did not know Dando, but forensic scientists matched a strand of fibre found at the crime scene with his trousers. A single speck of residue from the murder gun was also found in Dando's hair and matched residue discovered in George's coat pocket. He was convicted and sentenced to life.

Domestic Violence

Forensic experts have less evidence to work with in cases of domestic violence. The violence often happens behind closed doors, and the alleged victim is often the only witness.

Since spouses are normally in constant contact, trace evidence is hardly needed to place the perpetrator at the crime scene or to make a link with the victim.

It is of value, however, in establishing the violence of murder. When suitcases containing the body parts of a man washed up in 2004 in Chesapeake Bay, Virginia, police arrested his wife after specks of human tissue were found on her shoes.

As in other cases forensic evidence is virtually needed for a conviction. Its lack in the murder trial of Hollywood actor Robert Blake in 2005 even overcame testimony of a stuntman who said Blake had asked him to 'snuff' his wife, Bonny Lee Bakley. She was found shot through the window of their car as Blake went into a restaurant, he said, to collect his gun. Forensic examiners could find no weapon, no gunshot residue on the actor and no blood on his clothing, so Blake went free.

SELF-DEFENCE

The lack of self-defence evidence is also crucial. Self-defence is a frequent plea by women who claim their husbands have been abusing them. Jane Andrews, the former dresser for Sarah Ferguson, the ex-wife of Prince Andrew, used it in 2001. The evidence, however, failed to back up Andrews' claim that her

FAMILY CONTACT

Because family members often find the body and have contact with it, evidence is contaminated and a case can become complicated. Sion Jenkins was accused of murdering his foster daughter Billie-Jo in 1997 in Hastings after she was beaten to death on the patio with an iron tent peg. A case was built on 150 blood spots on his clothing, but the defence argued that these were caused by air being released from the girl's lungs as he moved her. His former wife also accused him of violence towards her.

Although he was convicted of murder in 1998, appeals finally brought about Jenkins' release in 2006 when the jury failed to reach a verdict in his third trial.

Self-defence is a frequent plea by women in murder trials who claim their husbands have been abusing them.

murdered boyfriend, Thomas Cressman, had stabbed himself on a kitchen knife she was holding for protection. It was found that she had first struck him with a cricket bat. She received a life sentence.

KITCHEN KNIFE

The self-defence plea also failed for Susan Polk after she stabbed her millionaire psychotherapist husband to death in Orinda, California, in 2002 and then declared she had suffered years of abuse. She said she grabbed a kitchen knife from her husband as he attacked her, but the autopsy revealed she had no defensive wounds, and she was sentenced to life, with the recommendation that she serve at least 16 years.

Jane Andrews arrives handcuffed at the High Court in London on 24 September 2003 .

Identification by Witnesses

Witnesses can be unsure and unreliable, but they are the key to countless arrests and convictions.

Witnesses provide the descriptions used by forensic artists. They recognize faces displayed on posters and television crime programmes, they attend line-ups to point out the perpetrator and they provide anonymous tips.

Problems do exist because anyone's memory may play tricks. Some witnesses, as well, may have reasons to make incorrect identifications. Therefore, a great effort is made to back up witness statements with physical forensic evidence. In 1994 in the USA, a 13-year-old girl identified Peter Rose of Lodi, California, as the person who had dragged her into an alley and raped her. In 2004 the girl admitted she had no idea who had attacked her and, after serving ten years in jail, Rose was proven innocent by DNA tests.

Testimony can endanger the life of a witness, and some have been murdered. Several UK police forces run dedicated witness support schemes, while the USA and Canada have legislated formal protection programs. Since it began in 1970, the US Federal Witness Security Program has given protection, relocation and new identities to more than 7500 witnesses and 9500 witness family members.

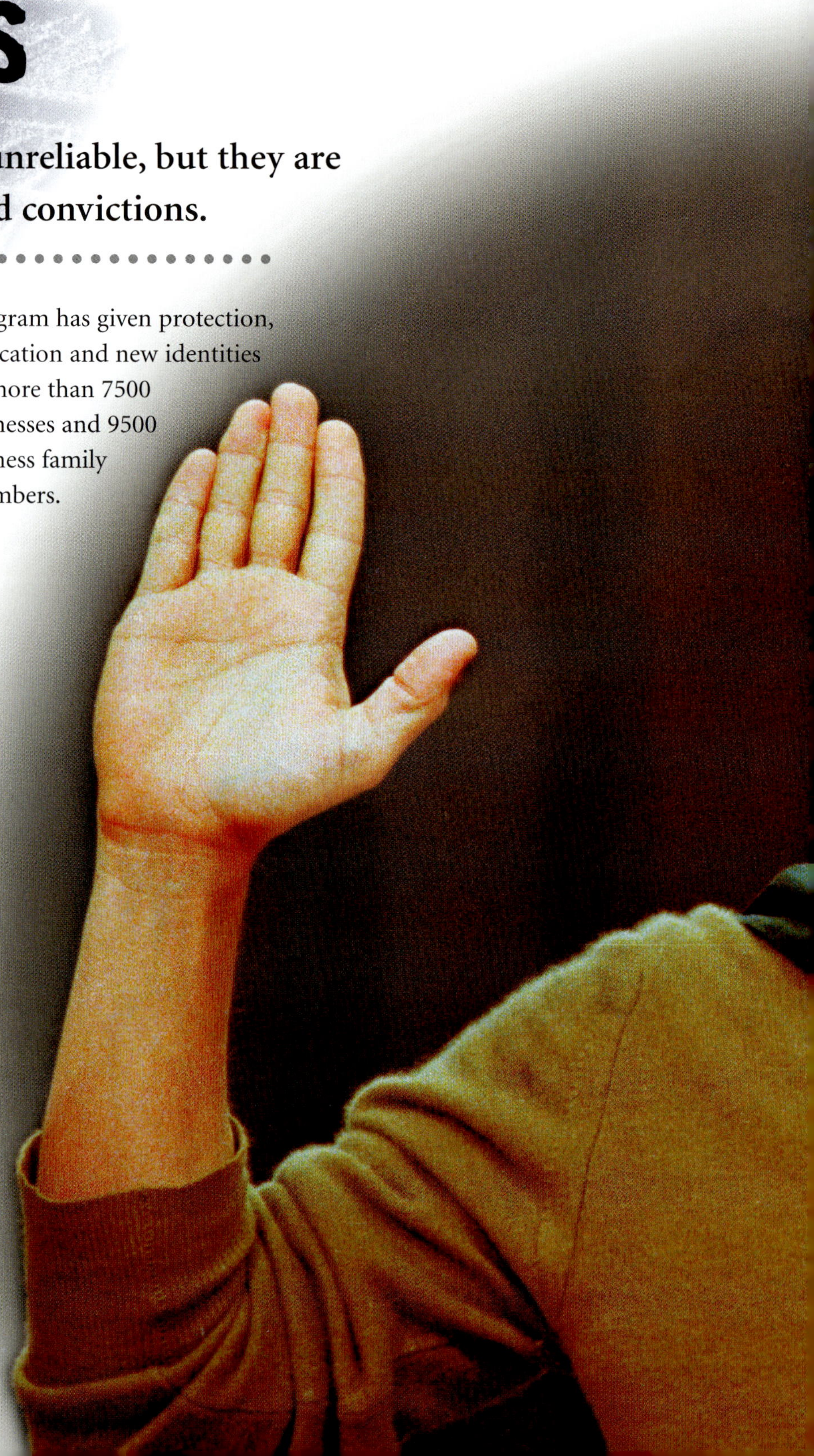

This pilot, being sworn in before giving evidence against Panamanian General Noriega in 1988, is wearing a hood to protect his identity.

'I WAS CERTAIN, BUT I WAS WRONG'

Writing in the *New York Times*, Jennifer Thompson described how convinced she was in making an identification after being raped in 1984. She had studied every detail on her attacker's face, and later confidently identified him from police photos, in a lineup and again during the trial in 1986. Because of this, Ronald Cotton was given a life sentence.

When another man, named Bobby Poole, bragged about the rape, police brought him to Jennifer who said she had never seen him before in her life. Eleven years after Cotton's conviction, in 1995, Jennifer gave blood so DNA tests could finally resolve the doubts. They proved she had identified the wrong man. Poole was the rapist, and he confessed. 'I live with constant anguish that my profound mistake cost him so dearly', she said after Cotton's release.

Some witnesses may have reasons to make incorrect identifications.

'IVAN THE TERRIBLE'

When John Demjanjuk was accused of being 'Ivan the Terrible', a notorious SS guard at the Treblinka concentration camp during World War II, the US extradited him to Israel in 1986. During his trial there, despite the passage of nearly 50 years, five witnesses identified him in court and six others also did so photographs. Even a former SS guard agreed.

In 1988, the court in Jerusalem sentenced him to death, but the Israeli Supreme Court decided, despite the witness testimony, Demjanjuk had only been proven to be a guard, not 'Ivan the Terrible'. Freed, he returned to the US which deported him to Germany in 2009 where his trial continued into 2011.

Expert Witnesses

When forensic scientists give evidence in court, they are known as expert witnesses. Because of their specialized knowledge, they can give both facts such as test results and also their opinions, which may be an estimation of the number of people eliminated by a certain DNA result.

Juries are often swayed by the clarity and confidence demonstrated by the expert witness.

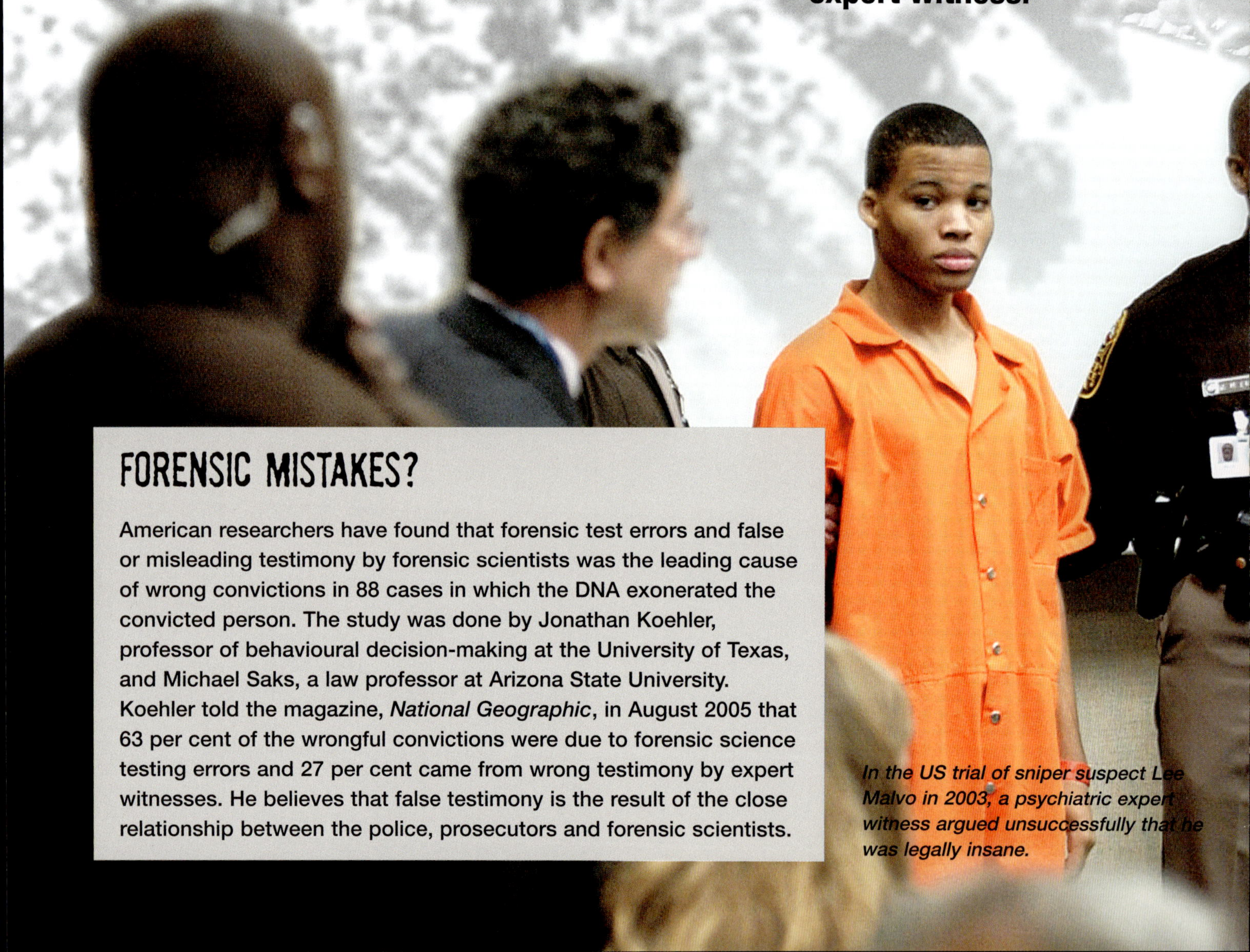

FORENSIC MISTAKES?

American researchers have found that forensic test errors and false or misleading testimony by forensic scientists was the leading cause of wrong convictions in 88 cases in which the DNA exonerated the convicted person. The study was done by Jonathan Koehler, professor of behavioural decision-making at the University of Texas, and Michael Saks, a law professor at Arizona State University. Koehler told the magazine, *National Geographic*, in August 2005 that 63 per cent of the wrongful convictions were due to forensic science testing errors and 27 per cent came from wrong testimony by expert witnesses. He believes that false testimony is the result of the close relationship between the police, prosecutors and forensic scientists.

In the US trial of sniper suspect Lee Malvo in 2003, a psychiatric expert witness argued unsuccessfully that he was legally insane.

An expert witness is different from a professional witness such as a police officer or security guard, who is also allowed by the court to present facts and opinions connected to their duties. The third type, a witness of fact, comes from the general public and has information about the events or people involved in a crime. A witness of fact cannot express opinions in court.

IMPARTIAL

Both the prosecution and defence may call upon forensic scientists to give testimony that will support their case, and many trials have forensic experts who present opposing facts and interpretations. Despite this, an expert witness is expected to be impartial and assist the court in dispensing justice.

CROSS-EXAMINATION

Forensic scientists on the stand will give their names, qualifications and experience before being examined by the side that called for their testimony. The expert will answer questions based on test reports he or she drew up. The opposing side's cross-examination will try to discredit any facts or interpretations detrimental to their case. Juries are often swayed by the clarity and confidence demonstrated by the expert during this cross-examination.

Some 80 witnesses arrive in the courtroom in Auxerre, France, in 2004 for the trial of Emile Louis, a suspected serial killer.

TALKING TO A JURY

Dr Henry C. Lee, an American who is one of the world's most famous forensic scientists, has investigated more than 6000 cases and testified at many trials. Interviewed by Courtroom Television's *Crime Library*, he gave this advice on presenting scientific evidence to a jury:

'You cannot use long words. The jury is intelligent. I approach them in a logical way to present scientific facts – only the facts. I don't get into speculation. Let the jury make its own decision. I use simple life examples. Instead of naming a chemical test, I just say "chemical test". I don't try to impress them. If a bullet wound is found in the upper body, I just say, "upper body" instead of "superior" or "anterior".'

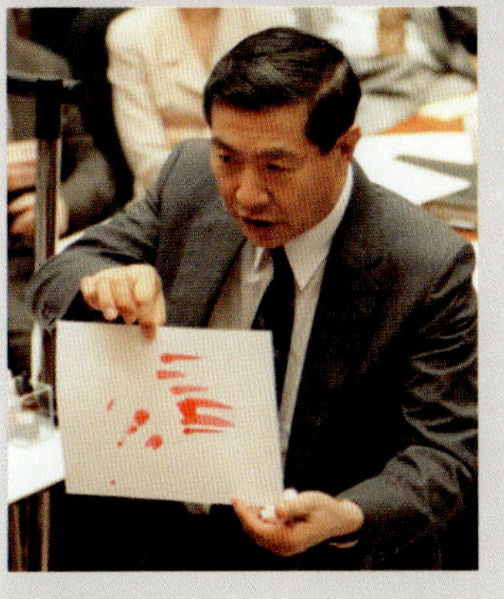

Dr Henry C. Lee shows ink smears to the jury in the 1995 O. J. Simpson trial to explain smear patterns of blood.

Organizers work at setting up a network at the sixth HOPE (Hackers on Planet Earth) Convention in 2006 in New York City.

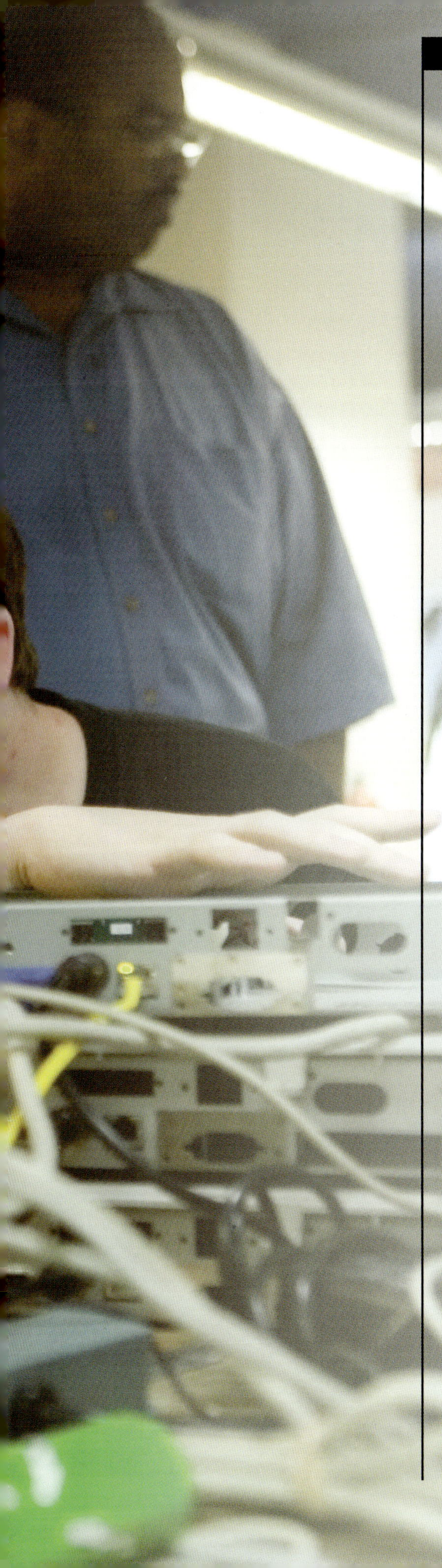

Chapter Nine

Crimes Without Violence

MURDER AND OTHER VIOLENCE AGAINST INDIVIDUALS STAND OUT AS THE MOST ABHORRENT CRIMES, BUT LIVES CAN BE RUINED BY AN ARRAY OF ILLEGAL ACTIVITIES. SUCH WHITE-COLLAR CRIMES AS OFFICE THEFT, EMBEZZLEMENT, BRIBERY, FRAUD, FORGERY AND COUNTERFEITING, ARE NORMALLY DEVISED TO STEAL MONEY OR PROPERTY.

A soldier cleans oil from rocks after the oil tanker Prestige *sank off the Spanish coast in 2002.*

Workplace fraud in the US has been estimated at more than $652 billion annually, with 30 per cent of business failures directly related to employee theft. Many cases are difficult to prosecute because the criminals use sophisticated systems to cover their tracks.

Around the world, police and forensic scientists are constantly refocusing their efforts to deal with evolving high-tech crimes such as identity theft. New forensic computer teams combat hacking, Internet fraud and the transfer of illegal money.

Crimes against the environment are also devastating. Pollution, wildfire arson, poaching and the trade in endangered species are a few of the activities pursued by authorities and processed through forensic labs.

British passports, like those from other nations, have been counterfeited and stolen. The Interpol database in 2010 listed 11 million stolen or lost passports. They are often sold to illegal immigrants.

Commercial Crimes

The US criminologist Edwin Sutherland coined the term 'white-collar crime' in 1939. He defined it as 'crime committed by a person of respectability and high social status in the course of his occupation'.

Commercial crimes do land high-profile executives in prison. In the UK, four executives with the Guinness drinks company were jailed in 1990 for attempts to manipulate the stock market. A year later media tycoon Robert Maxwell's death saved him from a similar fate for embezzling staff pensions. Homemaking guru Martha Stewart was imprisoned in 2004 for insider trading, and by 2005 executives from the bankrupt US energy corporation Enron were in jail for securities fraud. In 2007, two officials of Russia's bankrupt oil company, Yukos, were imprisoned for embezzling $13 billion.

Most business crimes are, of course, on a smaller scale, but the FBI estimates the annual loss at more than $300 billion. Embezzlement is among the most common and relatively easy to detect. Forensic investigators often trap embezzlers through forged signatures on checks and other recorded movements of money. In a Scottish case in 2006, Jackie Aitchenson was caught using Internet banking to embezzle £26,000 from a medical centre in Perthshire.

Opposite: Martha Stewart, America's homemaking advocate, departs Federal Court in New York City. She was convicted in 2004 of lying about a stock sale and received five months' imprisonment.

POSTAL FRAUD

Fraud is delivered straight into the home in the form of scams designed to obtain money, and these can frequently be traced back to the sender. They often appear in the form of a commercial misrepresentation, such as get-rich-quick promises and work-at-home opportunities. Other illegal mailings include fraudulent charities and religious organizations soliciting donations. In some fraud cases, merchandise that has been ordered and paid for is diverted on its way to the rightful owner. The latter, as well, has become a common type of Internet fraud.

Fake invoices are also a common scheme. In 2007, in Canada, the Toronto Police Service warned the public about letters being sent out claiming the recipient owed money in back taxes. The letters said payments by cheque could be made out to Stephen Smith at the Consumer Service Bureau. The police reminded the public that the government never asks for cheques payable to an individual.

Former Enron Chief Executive Jeff Skilling (center) arrives at a courtroom in Houston, Texas in 2006. He was found guilty of corporate fraud and received 24 years in prison.

Homemaking guru Martha Stewart was imprisoned in 2004 for insider trading.

CLUES TO FRAUD

Forensic scientists play a key role in investigating business fraud. They often detect it by examining questioned documents and identifying handwriting and signatures. According to Britain's Forensic Science Service, a document examiner can reveal altered documents, fake identities and false bank accounts by using chemical tests, specialized lighting and the enhancement of hidden entries. The sequence of documents can also disclose a history of events in an illegal business transaction.

Forensic tests, including DNA profiles, can link suspects to documents, computers and other office equipment. Valuable information can also be recovered from office security cameras, office computers, PDA palmtop computers and mobile phones, including mobile-phone site analyzes.

This file is at the computer forensics lab in Menlo Park, California, where fraud and other crimes are investigated.

Cases of Fraudulent Documents

Commercial fraud leaves a trail of paper that forensic investigators carefully trawl, looking for, among other clues, false documents and counterfeit signatures. As the following cases indicate, fraud is an international problem.

EVIDENCE OF FRAUD

According to the UK Association of Police Officers, if suspicions of commercial fraud are raised, there are three main ways of securing evidence:

- Papers and other documents should be kept as the fraudster left them. However they should be placed in clear bags or envelopes so they can be examined without obliterating forensic evidence.
- When a computer has been used in a fraud, it should not be used until a forensic scientist examines it. If that is not possible, the suspect files should be backed up.
- A record should be kept of any other facts and events such as conversations that aroused suspicions.

John Rigas, the former CEO of Adelphia Communications, talks to the media outside the courthouse in New York City in 2005. He and his son Timothy were convicted of stealing from the company, with Rigas receiving 15 years in federal prison and his son 20 years.

The UK's Serious Fraud Office worked with Cheshire police and the FBI to uncover a bogus high-yield investment scheme devised by Cheshire businessman Peter Barry Maude. Some 195 victims each sent a minimum investment of £12,500 to an account on the Isle of Man. But, instead, the money was used to pay for Maude's house and to make expensive purchases. He was sentenced in 2001 to six years in prison.

JOHN RIGAS

American examiners went through nearly 1000 documents that were presented to the jury during the 2004 trial of John Rigas and his son, Timothy, accused of a monumental fraud against Adelphia, the nation's fifth-largest television company. This included siphoning off $100 million for personal extravagances and hiding $2.3 billion in debt. False documents helped send the two to prison, with Timothy sentenced to 20 years and his father to 15 years.

Forgery and false documents were also uncovered by forensic experts in Israel, sending the former Knesset member, Ofer Hugi, to jail in 2006. In order to receive increased government funding he had fabricated lists of students and teachers for a technical college that did not even exist.

In Japan in 2007 Takafumi Horie, once head of the Internet firm Livedoor, was sentenced to two and a half years in prison after document investigators found he had falsified accounts to show a profit instead of the actual losses.

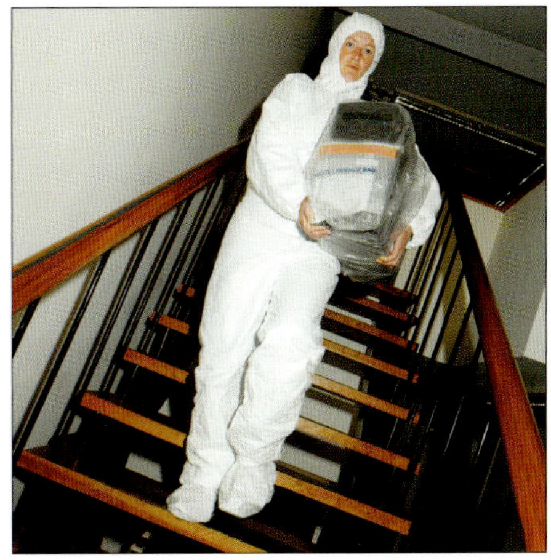

A crime officer removes a computer for investigation so forensic experts can access its hard drive for data stored there.

CANADIAN SCREENING

Although Canada has a long humanitarian tradition of helping refugees, it makes sure anyone entering the country undergoes document checks along with other security screening. Documents are looked at by Citizenship and Immigration Canada (CIC) working with the Canada Border Services Agency (CBSA), the Royal Canadian Mounted Police and the Canadian Security Intelligence Service. Responding to complaints that refugees have been admitted with false papers, the CIC said there are 'systems in place and expert personnel trained to detect fraudulent identification' and that refugees' documents are checked a second time before they become permanent residents.

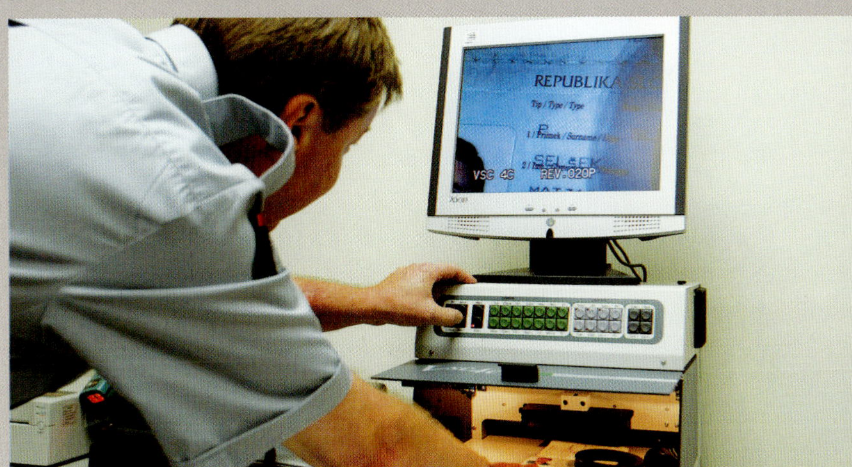

A Canadian immigration official checks the passport of a Slovak citizen entering the country.

Computer Crimes

The digital age has created the new field of computer crime, known as cyber crime. This immediately gave rise to computer forensic science, one of the fastest-growing disciplines within law enforcement.

The new forensic experts specialize in digital data used for an array of criminal activities, including hacking, identity theft, fraud, embezzlement, terrorism, software piracy, computer viruses and child pornography.

DELETED FILES?

The ease of accessing computer files contributes to crime – but also to investigating it. Investigators can read 'deleted' files recovered from a hard disk. They also can find deleted emails, hidden files and

TERRORISTS AND THE INTERNET

The Internet has become a major weapon for Islamic terrorist organizations such as al Qaeda. They use emails and coded messages to create a community of believers, send news of upcoming plans and spread fear through images of beheadings and bombings. For their part, government agencies maintain constant efforts to take down these websites, although terrorists are often one step ahead, moving to new ones. Still, police forensic experts have had impressive successes. In 2004 they picked up leads on a website that showed the execution of an American victim, Paul Johnson, and traced the clues to Abdel Azziz al-Muqrin, the former top operative of al Qaeda in Saudi Arabia, who was then killed.

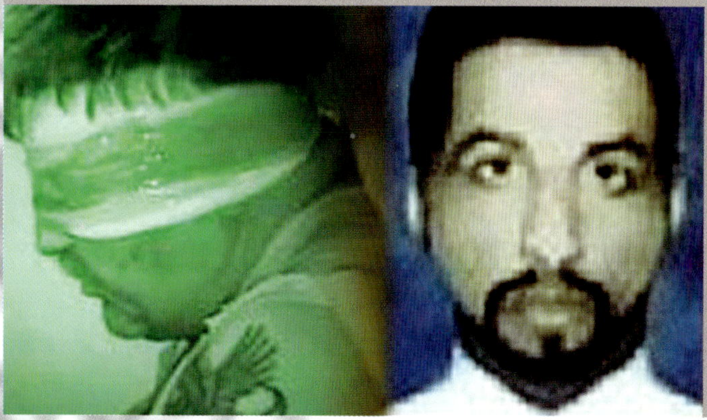

Paul Johnson (left) was a US helicopter engineer in Saudi Arabia. His beheading by a group led by Abdel Azziz al-Muqrin (right) was shown on an Islamic website.

folders, Internet activity and stolen data. Such services are available from the UK's Forensic Science Service, whose eForensic Solutions portfolio includes mobile-phone examinations. In the USA the FBI has a Computer Analysis and Response Team that co-ordinates its efforts with the Department of Defense Computer Forensic Laboratory. When forensic experts dismantle and examine computers that have been seized, they must photograph and note each part before investigating data on the hard disk. This documentation is needed to prove that the evidence was not contaminated.

UNTRACEABLE

One area in which investigators have been hindered by the switch from typewriters to computers is in tracing the source of a false document. Whereas each typewriter's letters had distinctive characteristics that could be read like its fingerprints, most computers use the same word-processing software, which is indistinguishable.

This computer equipment was taken as evidence on 7 January 2005 into the Silicon Valley Regional Computer Forensics Laboratory in Menlo Park, California.

SPYWARE EVIDENCE

Investigating the murder of wealthy American banker Robert Kissel in Hong Kong in 2003, a forensic computer specialist was aided by spyware Kissel had secretly installed on his wife's laptop. Nancy Kissel, also an American, was charged with serving her husband a milkshake laced with sedatives and then beating him to death.
Police officer Cheung Chun-kit found emails to the woman's lover and evidence she had searched the Internet for 'Sleeping Pills', 'Overdose Medication Causing Heart Attack', and 'Drug Overdose'. This evidence was combined with the discovery of her fingerprints on boxes of bloodstained clothes and bedding. She confessed, claiming in her defence that Kissel physically abused her, but in 2005 she was sentenced to life.

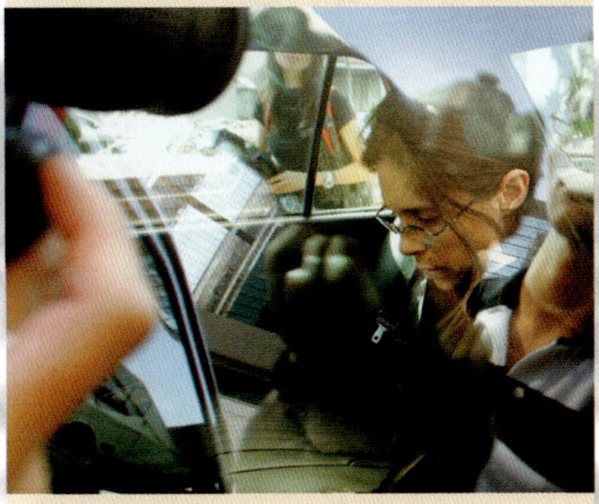

Nancy Kissel is surrounded by photographers as she leaves the High Court in Hong Kong on 3 August 2005.

Hacking

Hackers electronically break into computers to access information or sabotage the system. These attacks can compromise data, cost companies millions and endanger national security.

It is estimated that hacking costs more than £10 billion (about $19.6 billion) in the UK, and about $40 billion (£20 billion) a year in the US. In 2006, 87 per cent of large UK companies had security incidents, with the cost of the average incident being £12,000.

Hackers either exploit vulnerabilities in the software or hardware already on computers, or they install software that gives them access. Once they gain access to businesses, they download customer databases and credit card information. Many then notify the company in a veiled extortion threat by offering to patch the system against other attacks. The Ministry of Defence in the UK announced in February 2007 that its computer networks had been hacked into at least nine times since 2002, with five successful attacks taking place in 2006. Since some hackers are clever enough to leave no trace, computer security experts believe the real figure is probably higher. One estimate says China accounts for 30 per cent of programmes designed to infiltrate networks covertly. For its part, the US government in 1997 established the National Information Protection Center at FBI headquarters to detect hacking attempts as soon as they occur.

The UK Ministry of Defence announced that its computer network had been hacked into five times in 2006.

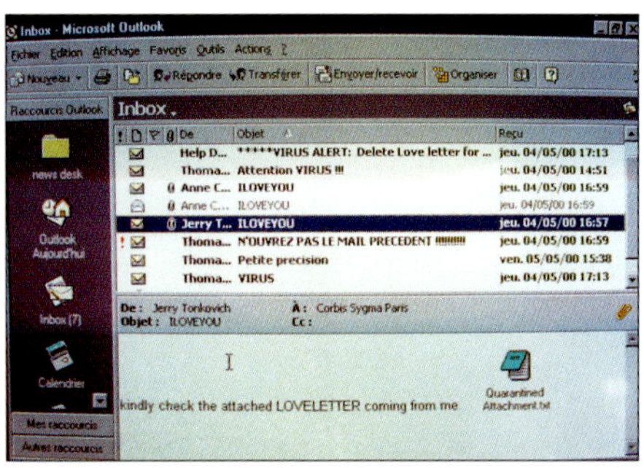

Left: 'I Love You' was an email whose attachment had a virus that spread computer havoc across Europe, North America and Asia in 2000.

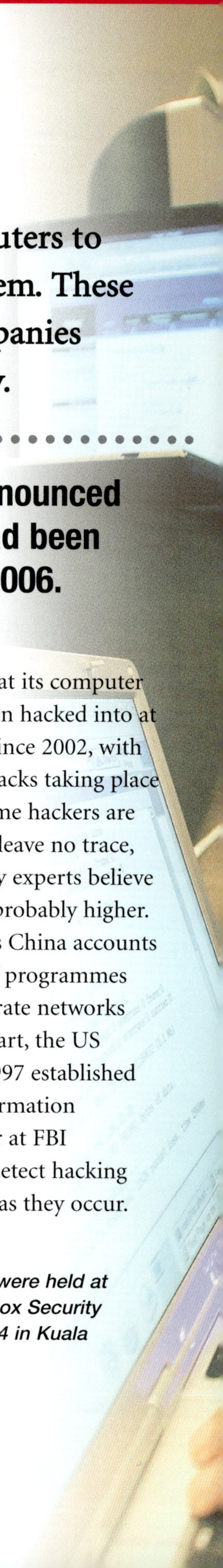

Hacking contests were held at the Hack-In-The-Box Security Conference in 2004 in Kuala Lumpur, Malaysia.

HACKING IN RUSSIA

The Russian government has dealt with large hacking cases by criminals and, it claims, spies. In 1994 Russian hackers broke into the computers of Citibank and stole more than $10 million from customers' accounts. The bank eventually recovered all but $400,000. In one of the worst 'spying' cases, Russian authorities in 2000 arrested a Lithuanian who allegedly spied for the CIA and Lithuanian state security by hacking into Russian security service computers.

GARY MCKINNON

It has been described as the 'biggest military computer hack of all time'. Gary McKinnon, a Scottish former hairdresser, was accused of hacking into 300 computers at a US naval station in New Jersey, and 97 more US military and NASA computers between 2001 and 2002. And he did it all from his bedroom in north London.

McKinnon was arrested under the Computer Misuse Act. The Home Office granted a US request to extradite him for trial, but in 2007 he continued his legal battle in the High Court against the order. He could face 50 years in prison if convicted in the US of sabotaging the defence systems.

McKinnon denied his intention was to disrupt security. The US charged, however, that he caused the naval bases network of more than 300 computers to become inoperable. McKinnon remained in the UK in 2010 for psychiatric evaluation.

The US Government says Gary McKinnon caused £350,000 damage to its computers by trying to access classified information.

Identity Fraud

Estimates in 2010 said identity fraud in the UK cost some £2.7 billion ($4.3 billion) to the economy, $4 billion in Australia and $191 billion in the USA, the main victim.

INSTANT CREDIT, INSTANT IDENTITY THEFT

Bob Sullivan is one of America's leading journalists covering identity theft, having written the book, *Your Evil Twin: Behind the Identity Theft Epidemic* (2004), and more than 100 articles since 1996.

A prime reason for US identity fraud, he says, is instant credit. 'US retailers waste no time throwing credit at anyone browsing high-ticket items in their stores', he notes. 'Imposters can get their hands on valuable plastic with as little as a Social Security number and a name.' And Sullivan knows the result: 'Just as consumers can drive off a car lot in an hour with a brand new $30,000 car, so can their imposters.'

Stealing personal information normally comes from the theft of a person's letters, credit cards or chequebooks. Even documents thrown out with the rubbish, such as bills, receipts and bank statements, can be used to steal someone's identity. A person who steals another's identity can use it to open bank accounts, withdraw funds from existing accounts and apply for credit cards, loans, state benefits and documents such as passports and driving licences. At worst, false

Chemists, biologists and toxicologists cooperate to find trace the sources of pollution.

customers into believing he was a legitimate waste operator. He charged up to £200 to illegally dump lorry loads of rubbish at a beauty spot in Devon. The Environment Agency and local authorities tracked him down and he was subsequently sentenced to 16 months in prison.

Corporations pay a dearer price. A US petroleum refinery located in Memphis, Tennessee, was fined $2.2 million in 2007 for violating the Clean Air Act. Investigators from the US Environmental Protection Agency found that the Williams Refining Company violated regulations about benzene emissions, a chemical that Congress has labelled a hazardous air pollutant.

A researcher in protective clothing analyzes the local environment with a magnifying glass, the result of an industrial chemical spill.

BROWNFIELD POLLUTION

Brownfield sites are urban areas that have a potential for new building developments. Major projects include the recent replacement of a former goal-gas plant in Amsterdam, the Netherlands, with a cultural centre and park, and the site for the 2012 Olympic Games in east London.
Many sites, however, are polluted by chemical contamination of the soil, and under a European Union Environmental Liability Directive, which came into force in 2007, the polluters have to be identified so they can pay for the cost of restoration. Environmental forensics will be employed, which should make the legal proceedings quicker and less expensive.

Environmental Crimes: Endangered Species

International agreements exist to outlaw the trade in endangered species and their body parts. Many Asians believe in cures requiring animal parts, which bring high prices for medicinal uses, such as rhino horn pills and tiger bone juice.

Endangered species also find their way onto restaurant menus, often under cleverly deceptive names.

Forensic tests such as DNA and serology can readily identify animal parts. Otherwise, authorities would have to catch suspects in the act of killing the animals or in possession of the carcass. Sometimes the killer turns out to be another animal. Bones, teeth, claws, tusks, hair, hides, furs, feathers, stomach contents, as well as poisons, arrows and bullets, are all items of evidence that may be examined forensically.

Because of the value of their tusks for ivory, elephants have always been a prime target for poachers. Despite an international ban on ivory in 1990, it is estimated that 216 tonnes were smuggled out of Africa in 2006, representing the death of about 24,000 elephants.

IVORY FINGERPRINTS

Forensic scientists are now obtaining DNA 'fingerprints' from stolen tusks that have been seized, and can trace them back to where they were poached. Samuel Wasser, at the Center for Conservation Biology at the University of Washington, supervises the extraction of DNA samples from ivory pulverized into a fine powder. The result is matched with DNA from wild elephants to ascertain the location they originated from.

When a large seizure of ivory was made in the port of Singapore in 2005, the crates came from Zambia, but officials there swore poaching was extremely rare. Wasser's DNA tests, however, traced it back to Zambia, a finding that forced the head of the Zambian wildlife department to resign.

Authorities recover piles of tusks of African elephants killed illegally. The ivory is sold for jewellery and supposed medicinal properties.

A WILDLIFE CRIME LABORATORY

The USA is the only country in the world with an official wildlife crime laboratory. The US National Fish and Wildlife Forensics Laboratory opened in 1989 in Ashland, Oregon, costing £2.3 million. Among its divisions is a genetics unit that conducts DNA and protein analyzes to identify unknown species, a pathology unit to verify illegal killings, a criminalistics unit using microscopic and chemical techniques to compare items of evidence and a morphology unit to trace wildlife parts back to the family, genus or species source.

A Chinese pharmacy display shows packets of tiger bone and dried seahorse alongside those of plant medicines. These 'remedies' can be produced in the form of powders, pills, tonics and oils.

DNA tests on whale meat in Japanese restaurants traced it to endangered stock.

ILLEGAL WHALE MEAT

Mitochondrial DNA tests run on 574 samples of whale meat in Japanese markets and restaurants found that nearly one-third of North Pacific minke whales being sold came from the endangered stock in the Sea of Japan. Marine biologists Scott Baker from the University of Auckland and Steve Palumbi from Harvard University reported in 2000 that this number is twice as large as expected from bycatch (whales killed accidentally). Some minkes, therefore, were possibly poached. The research results were disputed by the Japanese Fisheries Agency, but it said it would monitor the bycatch whales more carefully, and would use its own DNA testing.

Left: Japanese whalers cut blocks of meat from a 9.5-m/31-ft Baird's beaked whale at the Wada port in Chiba, Japan, in 2006.

Arson

Arson is considered to be a white-collar crime when the perpetrator sets a fire for financial gain, usually to collect insurance or to destroy company records. Financial arson is a serious crime that could accidentally kill.

The malicious setting of fires in the UK now averages 2,100 incidents each week.

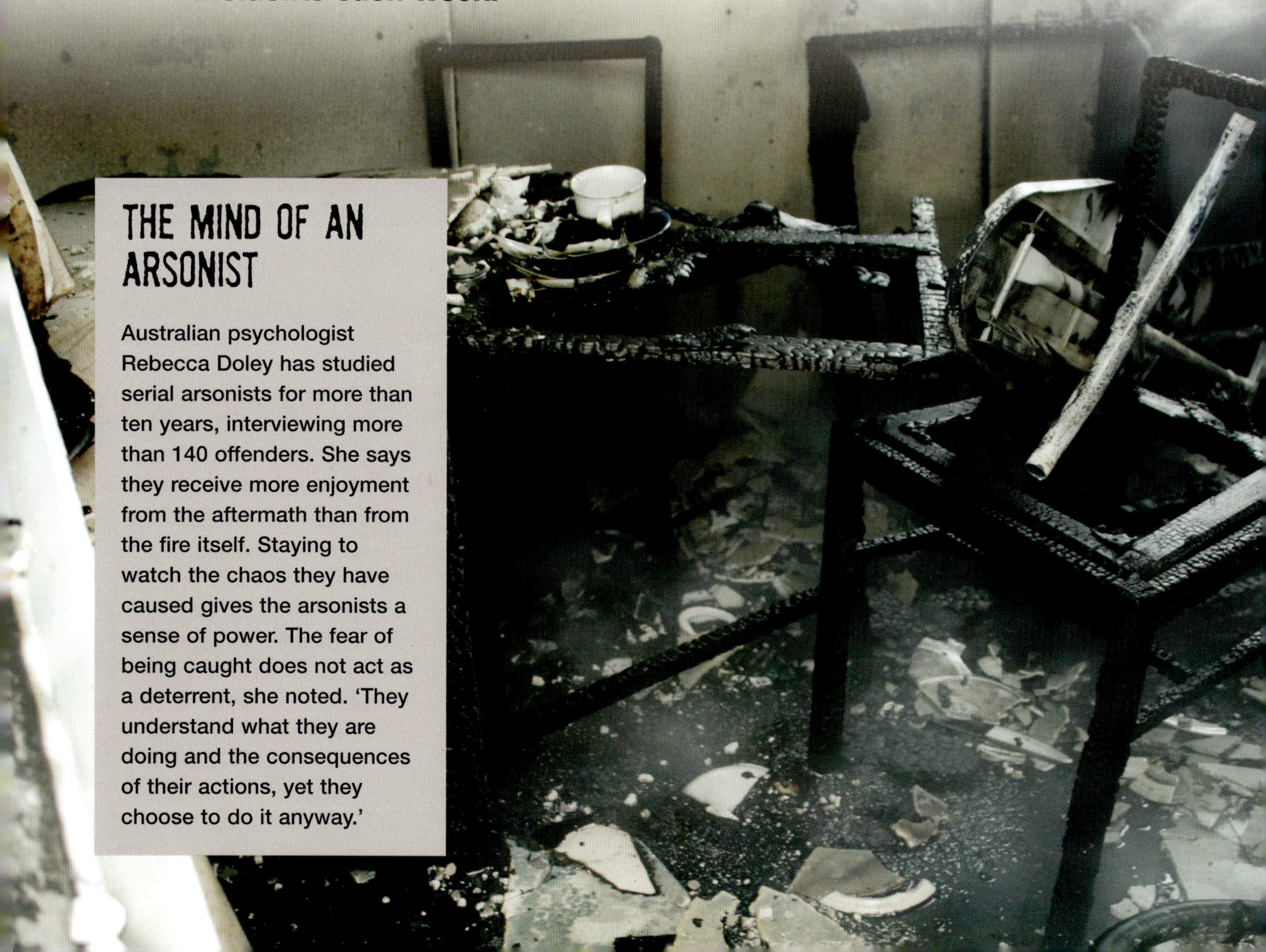

THE MIND OF AN ARSONIST

Australian psychologist Rebecca Doley has studied serial arsonists for more than ten years, interviewing more than 140 offenders. She says they receive more enjoyment from the aftermath than from the fire itself. Staying to watch the chaos they have caused gives the arsonists a sense of power. The fear of being caught does not act as a deterrent, she noted. 'They understand what they are doing and the consequences of their actions, yet they choose to do it anyway.'

The malicious setting of fires in the UK now averages 2100 incidents each week, including arson attacks on cars, and the last decade has seen 2.4 million recorded arson fires. The annual cost is estimated to be some £3 billion. In recent years the USA has annually recorded more than 63,000 arson offences with an average damage of £180,000 to industrial and manufacturing buildings. About 4000 people are killed and 20,000 injured by arson attacks each year in the USA.

Although most evidence would seem to be destroyed by fire, several clues can point investigators towards arson. Finding the 'seat' of a fire, or its point of origin, can reveal how it started and spread. Accidental fires spread upwards, creating a 'V' shape pointing down to its origin. Fire started deliberately may have several 'Vs' where an arsonist began separate fires. These may travel unnaturally across a floor, which indicates accelerants such as petrol or paint thinners were used. An accelerant that does not burn will leave an odour, and liquid accelerants create pool marks on the floor.

Arson investigators search burnt debris in a similar way to forensic examiners working through a crime scene. They identify and collect evidence, preserving it carefully for laboratory tests and court proceedings. They wear protective clothing, and their tools include digital and video cameras, notebooks and pens, knives, screwdrivers, hammers, crowbars, evidence tags and tape, and evidence containers.

Firefighters search carefully through the debris of a burnt house. Evidence that is collected from the scene can help distinguish arson from an accident.

A family often loses everything they own in a malicious arson attack.

ABORIGINAL FIRESETTING

It may seem like arson to some, but the practise of setting fires by Australian Aboriginals is not classified as such by the Australian government. These natives, who arrived in Australia some 50,000 years ago, were using fire for land management long before Europeans settlers arrived. The importance of these fires is evident by the different names the Aboriginals give to various types. Aboriginal peoples continue to light fires even when new agricultural practices mean that they are no longer needed or desirable. In some cases the fires can cause property damage or livestock losses. The Australian government considers this fire-setting not malicious in nature, since the bush is not set alight to destroy or damage property. It is therefore not classified as arson, excluding some Aboriginal people who might be guilty of traditional arson.

Wildfire Arson

Unlike fires intentionally set in buildings for various motives, wildfires tend to be random and the arsonist has no special investment or strong link to the targeted area.

For these reasons few perpetrators are convicted. While this is not an attack on another person, the unpredictability of wildfires can easily cause the deaths of firefighters and residents. The immense area covered by many of the fires hampers investigators, but they can still discover the point of origin by following the burn patterns. Forest fires, like house fires, spread outward in the shape of a 'V'. Investigators can retrace the direction of the fire by studying the sides of trees and even the way burnt grass is bent. Wind direction at the time of the fire is also taken into account.

ARSON BY FIREFIGHTERS

In rare cases a firefighter or forest worker may set a devastating fire. The worst wildfire in Colorado's history occurred in 2002 in Pike National Forest. A forest service employee, Terry Barton, burnt a letter from her estranged husband, and the blaze suddenly spread. It burned 55,485 ha/137,000 acres, destroying 133 homes, and caused nearly $40 million in damage. She claimed she had smelled a campfire, but fire inspectors testified she could not have done so from the distance she described.

Tamara Meredith, a forest service worker in Oregon, set 28 fires in the Umpqua National Forest in 1998 to earn overtime pay for fighting them. An electronic tracking device placed on her government-owned truck to trace her whereabouts caught her. Agents flying overhead monitored her progress, and saw Meredith stopping in an open area in the forest to light a wildfire. She served three years in prison and three years on parole.

Terry Barton is sketched at her bail hearing in June 2002 with federal judge Michael Wantanabe.

SEAT OF A FIRE

Once the seat of a fire is located, authorities are able to search for footprints, tyre tracks, matches and accelerants. Even then, it may be difficult to prove the fire was not an accident. Other innocent causes also have to be eliminated such as lightning or a downed power line.

Witnesses are sometimes available, but their view is normally from a distance. In California's San Bernardino Mountains in 2003, three witnesses saw occupants in a white van toss burning items onto the brush, starting a fire that consumed 36,969 ha/91,281 acres, destroyed 993 homes and killed six people. The arsonists were never found.

Forest fires, like house fires, spread outward in the shape of a 'V'.

Above: Smoke clouds rise from wild fires in the San Bernardino Mountains in California in late October 2003. Strong Santa Ana winds fanned the flames, helping to maintain and spread the dangerous fires.

Left: Trees burn during a forest fire at Weston, Colorado. Since trees are fuel for a fire, firefighters frequently down them ahead of an approaching fire.

PUBLIC REWARDS

In an effort to apprehend wildfire arsonists, the state of Florida offers rewards for tips from the public. The Florida Forestry Arson Alert Association, created by the state legislature, asks anyone with information about an arsonist to contact the Florida Division of Forestry. Rewards of $100 (£49) to $5,000 (£2480) are paid if the information given leads to an arrest.

These counterfeit Euro banknotes abounded after the switch from familiar national currencies.

Chapter Ten

Forgeries and Fakes

APPROXIMATELY ONE-TENTH OF ALL WORLD TRADE IS MADE UP OF FAKED PRODUCTS, AND MANY OF THESE ITEMS FUND ORGANIZED CRIME AND TERRORISM. EVEN THE MOST ACCOMPLISHED FORGERS, HOWEVER, LEAVE BEHIND CLUES THAT ASSIST FORENSIC SCIENTISTS IN THEIR INVESTIGATIONS.

THE SUNDAY TIMES

WORLD EXCLUSIVE: How the diaries of the Fuehrer were found in an East German hayloft

The secrets of Hitler's war

Formula spells peace for BL on Tuesday

The Hitler Diaries gained worldwide publicity before and after they were proven to be fakes.

Document experts examine the paper, ink and printing style to identify items such as counterfeit money and forged documents. The unaided eye and instruments such as a magnifying glass, stereomicroscope or infrared microscope can do this careful examination, which includes comparing handwriting and signatures. Multi-spectral video microscopes can also be used to reveal if documents have been altered.

Art forgeries may be brilliant enough to hoodwink gallery experts, but they will never pass a laboratory examination. Forensic tests can reveal the age of the paper or canvas, along with modern pigments, which are identified by X-ray diffraction. Infrared scanning detects overpainting and retouching.

Despite technology, forgeries continue to be successfully sold, based on the personal opinion of experts. This has happened with such various items as Faberge eggs, fossils and the diaries of Hitler.

Researchers use a computerized handwriting recognition system to compare the writing on two pieces of correspondence.

Counterfeit Money

Currency counterfeiting for financial gain and to destabilize economies is an ancient crime. The US dollar, the currency most used for global transactions, is copied the most.

Computers makes it possible for unskilled operators to produce excellent colour reproductions.

HOW TO DETECT COUNTERFEIT MONEY

Here are some general tips on how to examine money to identify counterfeit notes. On genuine currency:

- Serial numbers are evenly spaced and have a distinctive style.
- Fine lines on the borders are clear and unbroken.
- Some lines and other printing is embedded. Counterfeit notes have printing on top of the paper.

Used worldwide, the dollar is the main victim of counterfeiters.

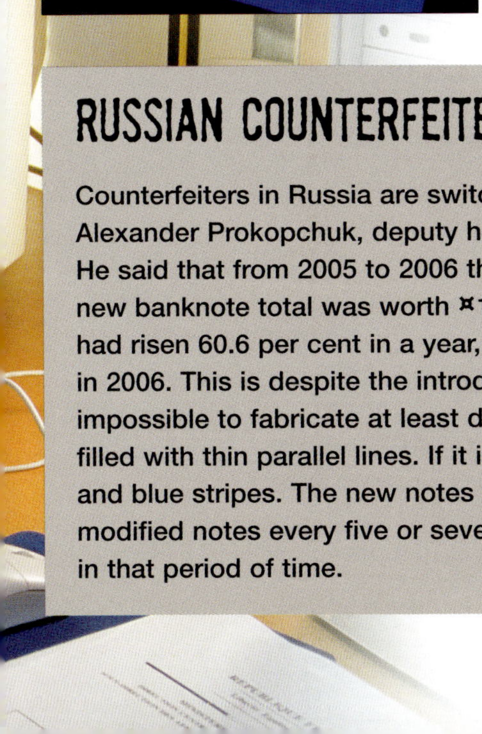

Left: An operator uses the RAPACE system to help detect counterfeit Euros. The system allows the operator and enquirer to communicate by telephone.

Below: Special fluorescent ink and strips glow bright blue and red under ultraviolet light to show this is a genuine Euro banknote.

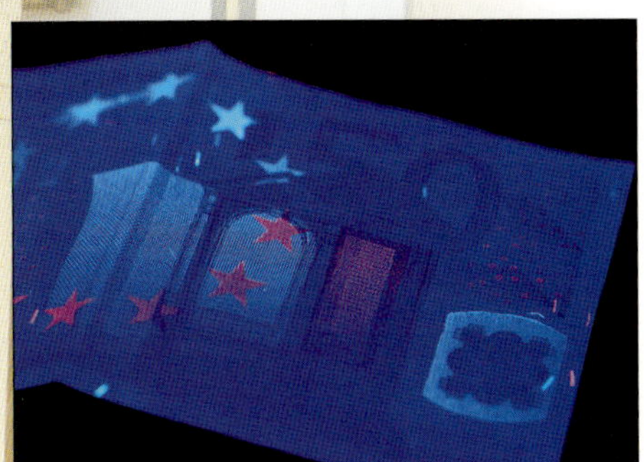

In 2006 some 50,000 euro notes were counterfeited each month. Forty-four per cent of the counterfeit copies were 20-euro notes and a further 36 per cent were 50-euro notes. The Forgery of Money unit of Europol, the European Police force, maintains a database on counterfeiters and another monitors the technical aspects of reproducing currency.

The problem has multiplied with the advent of easily available high-resolution printers and copiers. Computer-generated counterfeiting makes it possible for unskilled operators to produce excellent colour reproductions. Forensic examination, however, can detect the printed image resting on top of the paper's surface and, under a low-grade magnification of about 20x, small particles of toner can often be seen outside the image area.

National currencies, as well, have special protective marks such a micro printing and built-in ultraviolet features. A silver foil strip is embedded inside UK paper currency, US currency has tiny red and blue fibres embedded throughout, Canadian notes have a holographic strip and Australia now produces only polymer notes with a plastic substrate.

RUSSIAN COUNTERFEITERS LIKE THE EURO

Counterfeiters in Russia are switching from the dollar to the euro, it was announced in March 2007 by Alexander Prokopchuk, deputy head of Interpol's National Central Bureau at the Russian Interior Ministry. He said that from 2005 to 2006 the number of confiscated counterfeit banknotes rose from 979 to 1138. The new banknote total was worth ¤106,440. Prokopchuk also noted that the number of counterfeit ruble notes had risen 60.6 per cent in a year, with 118,000 notes worth more than 104 million rubles confiscated in 2006. This is despite the introduction in 2004 by the Russian Central Bank of notes 'which would be impossible to fabricate at least during the coming seven years.' The new rubles contain a watered silk stripe filled with thin parallel lines. If it is turned, the one-colour stripe will become multicoloured with yellow, pink and blue stripes. The new notes follow a recommendation by Interpol that all countries introduce new modified notes every five or seven years, since criminal gangs learn to make high-quality counterfeit notes in that period of time.

A Worldwide Counterfeit Case

The White House and US officials warned in 2006 that North Korea has sponsored the near-perfect counterfeiting of $100 bills that could erode the global standing of US currency.

The US Secret Service has seized some $50 million worldwide, and believes that much more is in circulation.

The notes, called Super Dollars, were first detected in the Philippines in 1989, and have spread to more than 130 countries. More than 170 arrests have been made, including several North Korean diplomats found carrying hundreds of thousands of the counterfeit dollars. In October 2006 US officials arrested and indicted Sean Garland, a leader of the Official Irish Republican Army, on conspiring with North Korea to circulate millions of fake dollars.

'A little bit of counterfeit currency of very high quality can go a very long way', said the US deputy assistant treasury secretary Daniel Glaser, who added it can cause people to 'lose their faith in the dollar, which is extremely important to the United State to maintain.'

As part of this case three men in the UK were jailed in 2002 for taking part in the largest counterfeiting of dollars ever uncovered by British detectives. The total distribution of the fake dollars worldwide was then estimated at $27 million.

COUNTERFEIT DETECTION MACHINES

Modern technology is allowing counterfeit detectors to keep pace with the technology that enables counterfeiters to produce more and more realistic fake notes. In Japan, banks, retailers, post offices and government departments use a small device that can scan a note in 0.7 seconds using a series of light-circuit, magnetic, laser and ultraviolet sensors. Manufactured by Matsumura Technology, the EXC-5700 and EXC-6700 check 76 points on a note. According to the company, it can yield an accuracy of 99.999 per cent, and can detect fake dollars, euros, yen and other currencies.

However, the detector requires constant updates to foil the counterfeiters. 'As soon as they figure out we've found a flaw in their counterfeits, they fix it and print more money,' said Yoshihide Matsumura, a counterfeit-currency expert and president of Matsumura. 'That's why we believe detection equipment should be updated frequently.'

An examiner uses a magnifying glass to detect if a US dollar is counterfeit. The US paper currency has coloured fibres enbedded in each banknote, so the counterfeited version will be revealed under a close examination. New security marks are constantly added.

selling them for years, and British police discovered 'boxes and boxes' of the documents in a house in London.

The ubiquitous American driving licence, used as a key source of identification in the USA, has also proven easy to acquire. In 2005, therefore, Congress passed an act requiring all states to deny a driving licence to those who cannot prove they are legally in the country. Several of the 9/11 suicide hijackers had obtained Virginia licences (needed to board an airplane) by establishing residency in that state. Other of those terrorists had a stolen Saudi Arabian passport, a fake Canadian passport, a stolen Social Security card and even possessed licences to transport hazardous materials.

Above: A French customs officer shows fake European Union ID documents, including passports and residence permits, at a press conference in 2006 in Ajaccio, southern Corsica. Many of these falsified documents had been seized in Corsica and southern France as they were about to be sold.

INTERPOL'S VIEW

'It's been proven in every single terrorist incident that a fraudulent passport has been used', according to Ron Noble, an American who heads Interpol.

'After September 11 if a citizen were to learn that a terrorist attack occurred by someone having entered their country with a stolen passport that was registered with Interpol but their country wasn't regularly checking it, I say governments would fall.'

Left: US immigration inspector Fred Ho shows a counterfeit passport enlarged by a microscopic camera at San Francisco International Airport in 2002. A system known as DataShare is being used at more than 300 US ports of entry to check photographs and information of visa holders.

Art Forgeries

The production of fake art has long been a lucrative business. Superficially, forged art 'masterpieces' are difficult to discern, even by some gallery, museum and auction experts.

Many cases can only be solved by forensic analyzes that look at the age of a painting and compare it with other genuine pieces by the same artist.

Cracking the surface paint with varnish or rolling the canvas often ages a fake painting. A stereo-microscope can detect this more recent effort, and X-rays will reveal if the cracking reaches each paint level. Ultraviolet radiation can determine the age of a varnish and also reveal any sketching, retouching, and painted-over areas.

X-RAYS

The type of pigments used can also help dating, because the years they were introduced are known. The modern chrome yellow pigment, for example, can be identified by a scanning electron microscope (SEM), because the modern version has been coated for the past 30 years to protect it from pollution.

Ceramic artworks are difficult to copy, and experts use thermo-luminescence to date them, since it measures the radiation the clay has absorbed since it was fired.

Copies of metal figures are easy to cast, but an SEM can differentiate metals used today from older ones. X-ray fluorescence will date metal pieces because they emit an X-ray spectrum of the alloy used to make it.

Right: A forgery of a painting by Lucas Cranach the Elder is exposed by ultraviolet light, which causes it to fluoresce. The dark areas have been retouched.

Above: A technician at the Doerner Institute in Munich, Germany operates the infrared scanner that found the forged painting supposedly by Lucas Cranach the Elder.

LASERS AND CERAMICS

A forensic scientist in Perth, Australia, is using lasers to trace pottery back to its kiln site to expose ceramic forgeries. Emma Bartle from the Center for Forensic Science at the University of Western Australia developed the scientific method to authenticate porcelain.

Bartle said forged Chinese Ming and Japanese Imari porcelain is a multimillion-dollar industry in South-east Asia. 'These modern fakes are so detailed and sophisticated', she noted, 'that gone are the days whereby trained experts can authenticate pieces using visual examination alone.'

The lasers analyze the porcelain's chemical composition to trace its origins back to production in China or Japan. 'Each site has a different combination of trace elements such as strontium and lanthanum, which is unique', she said.

Ultraviolet radiation can determine the age of a varnish and reveal retouching.

COMPUTER ANALYSIS

Professor Hany Farid and his colleagues at Dartmouth College in Hanover, New Hampshire, have developed a computer tool for analyzing digital images to detect art forgeries. Announced in 2004, the technique classifies paintings and drawings by a digital analysis of an artist's style. High-resolution digital scans break down an image into 'wavelets'. These are simple elements and can be analyzed by a complex mathematical model to check for consistencies between works of art or within a single one. When applied to 13 drawings, the technique automatically grouped the 8 real works of the sixteenth-century Flemish artist Pieter Bruegel the Elder, separating them from 5 modern copies.

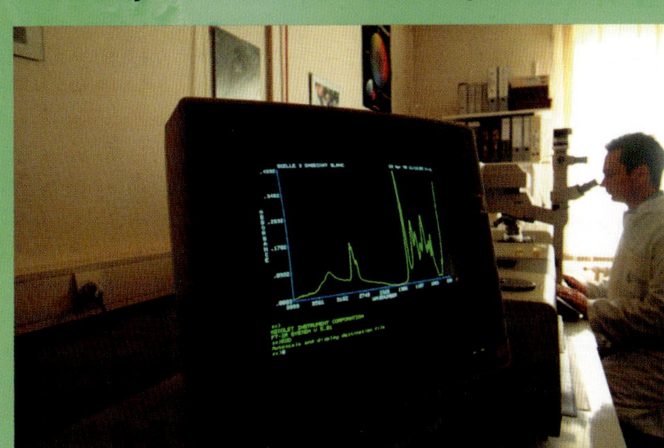

A popular method for detecting art forgeries is by using a spectrophotometer that can reveal the type of resin in the paint.

Successful Art Forgers

One of the most famous art forgers was an art restorer named Hans van Meegeren (1889–1947). Instead of copying existing masterpieces, however, he created entirely new paintings.

Van Meegeren created new paintings and attributed them to famous artists such as six fake paintings by Vermeer, which he said he had discovered. They supposedly earned up to $30 million, with one going to the Nazi leader Hermann Goering.

AGEING PROCESS

Van Meegeren turned to copying the masters because his works were not wanted and he disliked the art establishment. He invented a process to age paint film by dissolving phenol formaldehyde resin in benzene or turpentine and baking it. This produced the look of a work of art of the seventeenth century. After a decade of this he confessed to the forgeries. Forensic tests were made on his paintings, and traces of cobalt blue were found, a pigment not produced until the nineteenth century. He was charged with fraud, but died before serving his one-year sentence.

REVENGE

Tom Keating (1917–1984) was a London Cockney. Like van Meegeren, he was an art restorer who decided to create forgeries because his own paintings were unsuccessful and he wanted to upset wealthy art dealers. In the early

ELMYR DE HORY

One of the world's most talented art forgers was the Hungarian-born Elmyr de Hory (1906–1976). He studied art in Munich and Paris before being imprisoned by the Nazis in a concentration camp. He escaped from a prison hospital and bribed his way to Paris where he began to copy famous paintings, selling Picasso fakes to art galleries by claiming they came from his family's estate.

De Hory settled in Miami, Florida, in the 1950s, where his painting began to fetch extremely high prices at art galleries. After suffering depression and an attempted suicide, however, he returned to Paris in 1959 and then the Spanish island of Ibiza in 1962. Already a celebrity, he told his story to the American writer Clifford Irving who published his biography, *Fake! The Story of Elmyr de Hory the Greatest Art Forger of Our Time*. De Hory took an overdose of sleeping pills in 1976 after learning that the Spanish government intended to turn him over to French authorities.

Art forger Elmyr de Hory poses with one of his fakes, which he claimed he could 'knock off' in ten minutes.

1970s he estimated that 2000 of his forgeries were in circulation but refused to name them. They include copies of famous works by Rembrandt, Renoir, Degas and Gainsborough.

All this came to an end in 1970 when auctioneers discovered 13 suspicious watercolours by 'Samuel Palmer' for sale. Keating confessed and was eventually arrested in 1977. Two years later his trial was ended because of his poor health. He later presented a television series for Channel 4 on the techniques of the old masters. The year of his death, 1984, Christie's auctioned 204 of his works, and Keating's paintings now fetch up to £12,000 and more.

Above: To guard against charges of fraud Tom Keating placed clues in his paintings such as flaws in the artwork for investigators to find. He also used modern easily identifiable materials.

Right: The artist Hans van Meegeren works on a painting of Christ titled 'Teaching in the Temple.' Van Meegeren only confessed to the forgeries after he was arrested for collaborating with the Nazis. Tests by the laboratory of Belgian museums then confirmed the forgeries.

Fake Products

Throughout the world, the manufacture and sale of fake products has become an immense industry estimated to represent up to seven per cent of world trade.

Above: Nestle CEO Peter Brabeck-Latmathe at the 2007 meeting of the Business Action to Stop Counterfeiting and Piracy in Geneva, Switzerland.

Right: Michel Danet, secretary general of the World Customs Organization, displays fake goods in 2004 in Brussels at the global congress on combating counterfeiting.

Main Picture: A policeman adds fake and pirate software disks to the large pile to be destroyed at a factory in Xian in Shaanxi Province, China, in 2005. Police destroyed more than 100,000 confiscated disks during the operation.

The FBI estimates that this illegal trade costs Americans about $250 billion a year, and other research found some 750,000 US jobs have been lost to fake products.

Michel Danet, the secretary general of the World Customs Organization, warns that the production of fake products is a serious criminal offence and should be considered as an act of economic sabotage.

COUNTERFEIT

It can be extremely difficult to distinguish between genuine and counterfeit products. As well, almost any item has been illegally copied, from doorknobs and shoe polish to food, drugs, watches, cigarettes, clothing, electronic equipment, perfume and even airplane engines. Worldwide research in 80 countries in 2005 by the Business Action to Stop Counterfeiting and Piracy (BASCAP), part of the International Chamber of Commerce located in Paris, found that 40 per cent of counterfeited brands involve software giants, clothes designers, pharmaceutical companies, printer manufacturers and luxury goods retailers.

SUPPORTING CRIME

'In some counterfeit goods the quality is so good that it really takes a forensic expert to tell if it's fake or not', says Michelle Moore, a spokeswoman for the International Anti-Counterfeiting Coalition (IACC). She adds, 'And even though these places may look like innocent mom-and-pop shops, they're often connected to organized-crime rings.'

The IACC, located in Washington, DC, points out that counterfeiters do not pay taxes or fair wages and often use forced child labour. The profits have also been linked to organized crime, drug trafficking and terrorist activity. 'When you purchase a fake', it warned, 'you become part of the cycle of counterfeiting and your money directly supports these things you would never want to support.'

CUSTOMS

Every country is facing a nightmare battle. In 2007 India had 44 fake versions of Vicks VapoRub. In Malta during the first two months of 2007, customs officials intercepted over half a million counterfeit products. In Virginia police raided 11 Newport News stores, and found that 90 per cent of the goods were fakes.

RECOGNIZING FAKES

Each type of product (diamonds, pearls, designer bags, etc) has been counterfeited in a different way, so it is impossible to list specific advice on detecting a fake. Consumers can follow a few general rules to educate themselves, and Ed Kelly, an intellectual property rights attorney in Thailand, says shoppers should keep the 'Three Ps' in mind:

- **Package:** Look at the quality of the product and its packaging. Watch for things such as poor stitching or incorrectly spelled brand names or logos.
- **Price:** If the price is too good to be true, it probably is.
- **Place:** Brand name products are sold in shops or through the official company website, not on the streets or open-air markets.

The quality of some counterfeit goods is so high that it really takes a forensic expert to tell if it's fake or not.

Sources of Fake Goods

The US government estimates that US companies lose from £200 billion to £250 billion a year to counterfeiting and piracy, which floods markets with low-cost fake products, mostly made in China.

Even in China, losses from counterfeiting are estimated at about one-fifth of the total sales for top brands.

As with drug crime, customer demand fuels the counterfeit industry. A fake $13,000 Swiss watch is being sold on New York streets for $10, while Louis Vuitton bags, normally about $2,000, are offered for $50 on the street and $800 on the Internet.

SEIZURES

Fake goods have become so prevalent that in one recent 10-day period, EU officials seized two million counterfeit products which had been made in China. More than 70 per cent of all fake goods seized in the EU and 81 per cent seized in the US come from that country.

US customs figures showed that Chinese fakes had increased from 2005 to 2006 by 62 per cent with apparel jumping 709 per cent and footwear by 669 per cent. These seizures are more than from all other countries combined.

Other sources of fake luxury goods include India, Malaysia and Indonesia, with much of the merchandise reaching Europe through traders in intermediate countries including Afghanistan, Guinea and the UAE.

FORENSICS AND FAKE DRUGS

A new way of detecting fake drugs without opening the package was announced in 2007 by Dr Pavel Matousek and Dr Charlotte Eliasson of the Rutherford Appleton Laboratory in Oxfordshire.

Spectroscopy can provide an accurate fingerprint of a molecule. The scattered light from a molecule illuminated by a laser is collected by a lens and sent through a monochromator to a detector for analysis. But packaging material and the drug's coatings and inactive ingredients may add too much 'noise' to read a drug accurately.

Spatially offset Raman spectroscopy, however, avoids this problem. It can probe deep layers of material and separate out the interfering signals to authenticate the actual content of the drug. Successful tests have been done on blister packs and plastic bottles.

Left: The laser is an excellent Raman source, because it provides a narrow, highly monochromatic beam of radiation which can then be focused accurately into a small sample.

CHINA'S FREE INTERNET MUSIC

Research reveals that as much as 85 per cent of all music in China is pirated. In March 2007 11 companies sued Yahoo's China division for some 5.5 million yuan ($710,690), accusing it of violating copyright. China claimed it supports the campaign against piracy, but noted that Internet site owners are not liable for the actions of their users, which was decided in a previous suit against Baidu.com, China's biggest Internet search engine, based in Beijing. Baidu, in fact, had agreed in 2005 to remove links to websites offering pirated music. It had links to more than 50,000 files. They removed 3000 music files alone that involved a single Chinese song. Baidu said that 22 per cent of traffic on its website came from users of its search facility for music files.

Left: Chinese trade enforcement officers raid a display stand in 2004 at the annual China International Clothing and Accessories Fair in Beijing. Fake Pierre Cardin leather jackets were found.

The traces of a polygraph, or lie detector, may indicate false statements, but this is disputed.

Right: A woman undergoes a polygraph test as part of her application to work at the FBI headquarters in Quantico, Virginia, USA. All new recruits must take a lie-detector test.

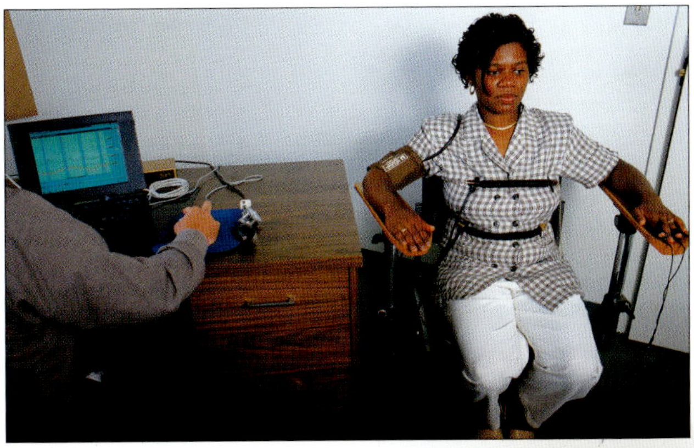

Below: Pulse meters are attached to a man's fingers for a polygraph test. The meters measure his heart rate, and under the subject's hands are the traces produced by the polygraph. These results are combined with measurements of blood pressure and respiration rate.

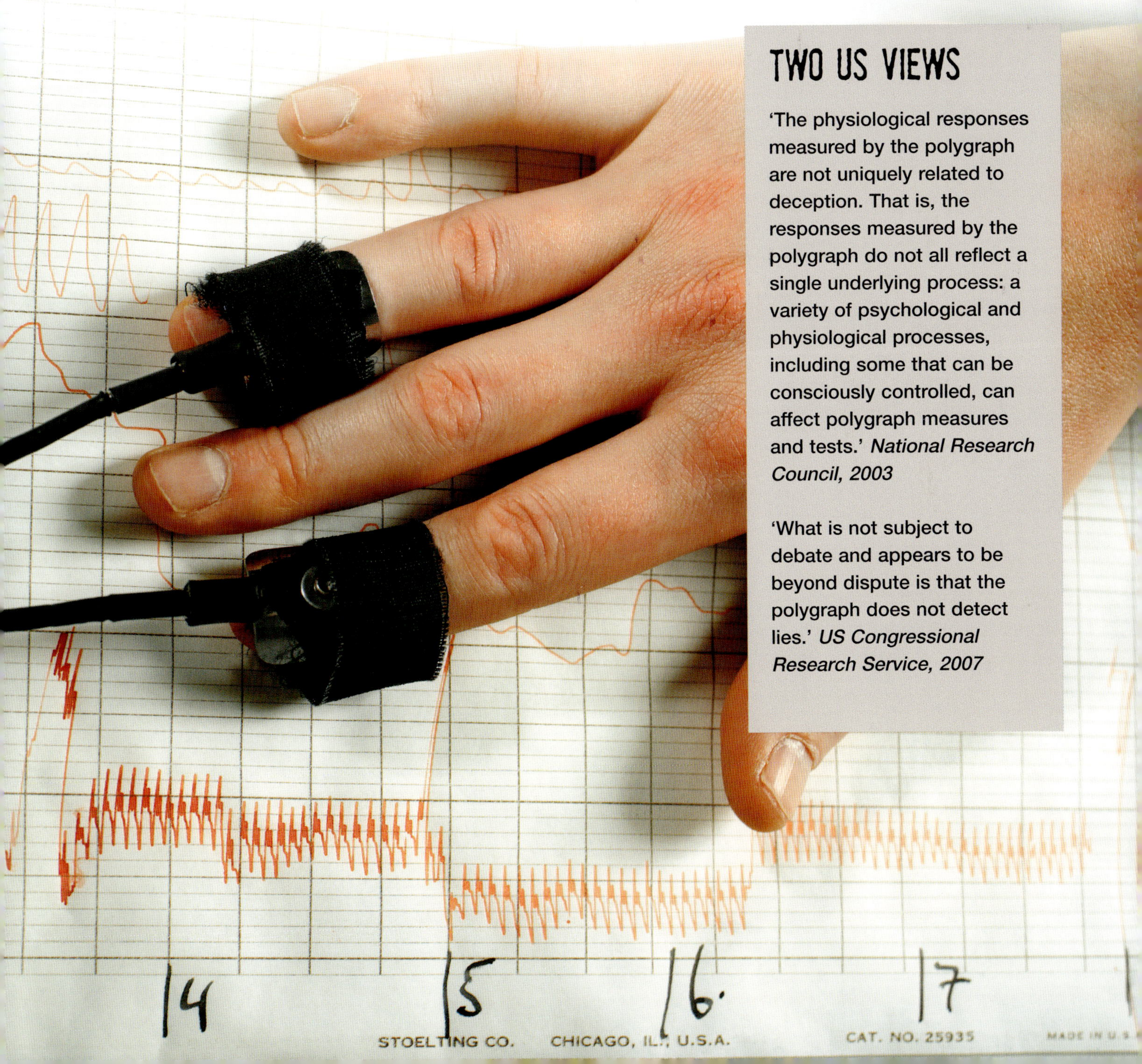

TWO US VIEWS

'The physiological responses measured by the polygraph are not uniquely related to deception. That is, the responses measured by the polygraph do not all reflect a single underlying process: a variety of psychological and physiological processes, including some that can be consciously controlled, can affect polygraph measures and tests.' *National Research Council, 2003*

'What is not subject to debate and appears to be beyond dispute is that the polygraph does not detect lies.' *US Congressional Research Service, 2007*

Polygraph Cases

The American middleweight boxer Rubin 'Hurricane' Carter, a suspect in a triple murder in 1966 in Paterson, New Jersey, took a polygraph test just hours after the murder and failed.

Police polygraph examiner John J. McGuire. had asked a series of questions twice, and Carter had failed both times.

Carter and John Artis were convicted in 1967 of firing shots at the Lafayette Bar and Grill, which killed the bartender, and a male and female customer. Both men received life sentences, but were granted a new trial in 1976 because deals between the prosecution and witnesses were never disclosed to the defense.

Then the prosecution made an offer, saying they could take another lie detector test. If they passed, the charges would be dropped and they could go free. If they failed, the test would not be used against them in court.

Rubin 'Hurricane' Carter (right) and his co-defendant John Artis face newsmen outside the Passaic County Courthouse in Paterson, New Jersey, in 1967 after their murder trial went to the jury. Both were convicted.

Both were re-tried because deals between the prosecution and witnesses had not been disclosed to the defence.

Before he took polygraph tests about Saddam Hussein having weapons of mass destruction, Ahmad Chalabi travelled the world seeking support for opposing the dictator.

Amazingly, both men chose to decline the offer made to them.

Carter and Artis were released from prison in 1985. Carter, who still claims he passed the initial polygraph test, now lives in Toronto, Canada.

MISTAKES

A polygraph test that had worldwide repercussions involved the Iraqi leader Ahmad Chalabi, who told US intelligence agents that Saddam Hussein possessed weapons of mass destruction.

Chalabi headed the Iraqi National Congress (INC), an exile group in London. He said Hussein had mobile biological weapons laboratories, and he passed a lie detector test that seemed to back up his information. In 2002, however, he failed another polygraph test, but intelligence analysts missed a warning that his information now was unreliable.

EDWARD GELB

Edward Gelb, a renowned American polygraph examiner, has administered more than 30,000 tests, and has been in the investigative field since 1956. His famous clients include O. J. Simpson, who was accused in 1994 of killing his wife and her friend. Simpson failed the test but was not convicted. Gelb also tested John and Patsy Ramsey, who were under suspicion in the 1996 murder of their daughter, JonBenet. They passed and were never indicted.

Here are crucial questions Gelb asked the Ramseys, who successfully answered 'No' to all of them:

'Did you inflict any of the injuries that caused the death of JonBenet?'

'Are you concealing the identity of the person who killed JonBenet?'

'Did you write the ransom note that was found in your house?'

John and Patsy Ramsey talk with reporters in 2001 after John was assaulted by a thief attempting to rob their home in Atlanta.

It has since been found that the INC had coached Chalabi to pass the first test. Though he lost friends in Washington, he is now a member of the Iraqi Governing Council, and in 2007 said his erroneous claims had achieved the aim of toppling Saddam Hussein. 'We are heroes in error', he said. 'What was said before is not important.'

Electroencephalograph

If the polygraph has its doubters, the electroencephalograph (EEG) has few. It has been used since the 1930s to track electrical waves coursing through our brains.

Computer-based 'Brain Fingerprinting', invented in the USA by Dr Lawrence A. Farwell, uses the Memory and Encoding Related Multifaceted Electroencephalographic Response (MERMER). This is a brain reaction that kicks in when the person being examined recognizes something of personal significance.

An electrical signal, known as P300, surges from the brain about 300 milliseconds after it confronts a significant image, such as a victim's face. This signal does not depend on the emotions of the suspect, only information stored in the brain. There is no testing to see if the suspect is telling the truth. The test can only indicate if he or she has certain information stored in their brain.

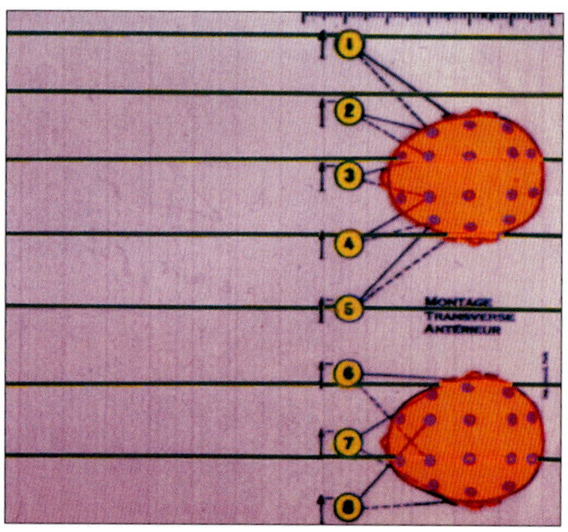

A coloured electroencephalograph (EEG) indicates a brain death. The eight brainwaves are flat because there are no electrical impulses being produced by the brain.

BRAIN FINGERPRINTING

In a Brain Fingerprinting test a suspect wears a headband with electronic sensors that measure the EEG from several locations on the scalp. He or she is shown images, words and phrases on a computer screen, some innocent and some connected to a crime. Brain Fingerprinting thus matches evidence at the crime scene with evidence in the brain.

The innocent images are used to establish the baseline response. The brain wave alters when an image is recognized, and guilty suspects cannot suppress their reaction as they can with a polygraph. A computer is then used to analyze the reaction.

Innocent suspects have no MERMER reaction when, for example, they are shown a crime scene they do not know.

In tests run on FBI and CIA agents, Brain Fingerprinting proved one hundred per cent accurate. In the FBI test 17 agents were separated from four non-agents by displaying images that only the FBI agents would recognize.

A MERMER CONVICTION

Brain Fingerprinting was instrumental in obtaining a confession and guilty plea from serial killer James Grinder in 1999 in Missouri. Dr Farwell gave the test to Grinder, showing him images connected to an unsolved murder, and the suspect's brain reaction confirmed a match. Grinder pled guilty to the rape and murder of Julie Helton and was given a life sentence without parole. He has since also confessed to killing three other women.

DR LAWRENCE A. FARWELL

The inventor of Brain Fingerprinting technology, Lawrence A. Farwell, is a former research associate at Harvard University. He is now the chairman and chief scientist of the Brain Fingerprinting Laboratories in Seattle, Washington. He also invented the Farwell Brain Communicator. This allows a paralyzed person to communicate directly to a computer and speech synthesizer using electrical brain activity.

Dr Farwell also has undertaken research that demonstrates the direct effect of human consciousness on matter at the quantum-mechanical level. As a result of his work he wrote the book *How Consciousness Commands Matter: The New Scientific Revolution and the Evidence that Anything Is Possible (2001).*

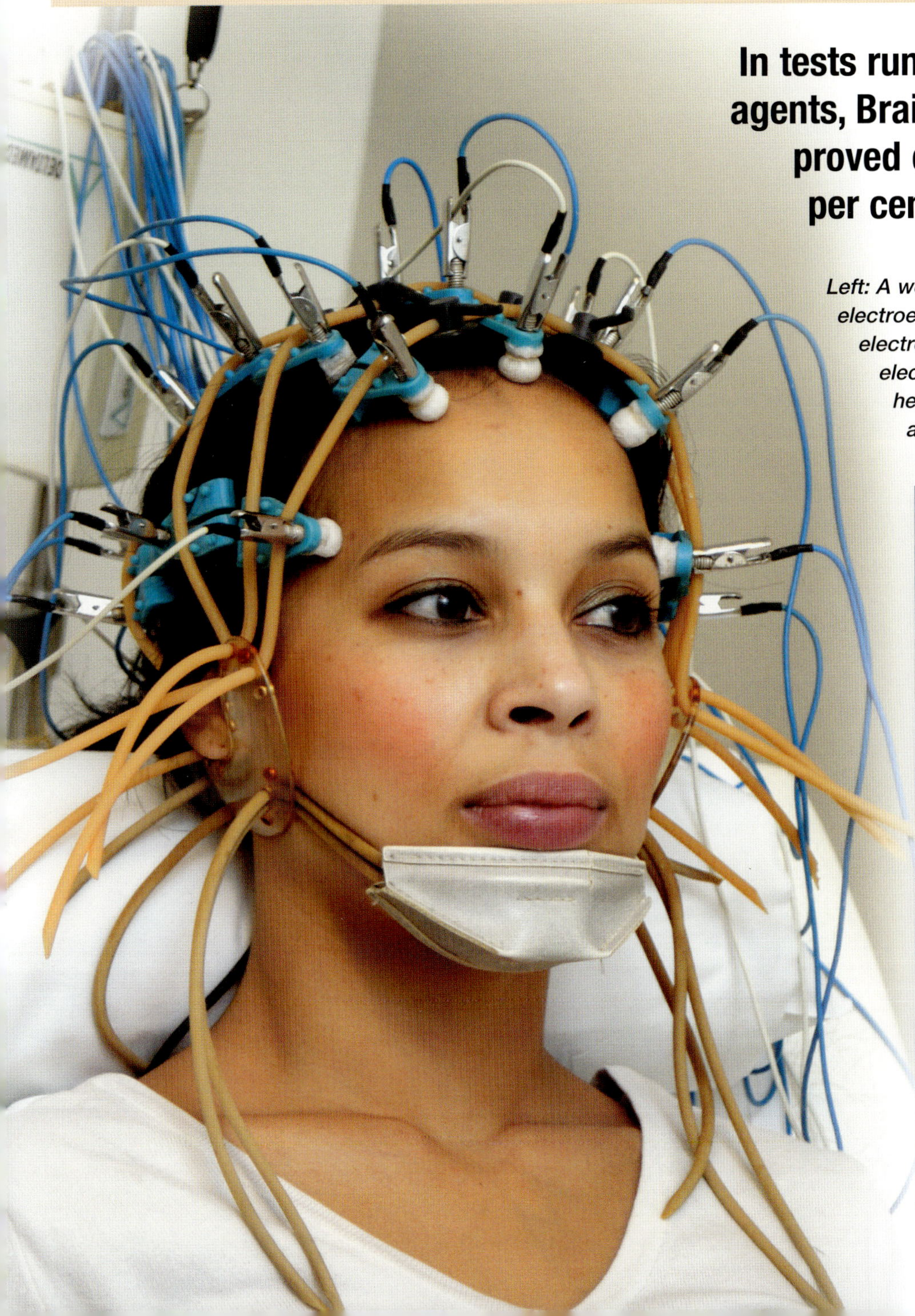

In tests run on FBI and CIA agents, Brain Fingerprinting proved one hundred per cent accurate.

Left: A woman undergoes an electroencephalograph. The numerous electrodes attached to her head record the electrical activity from different parts of her brain as it reacts to external visual or auditory stimuli.

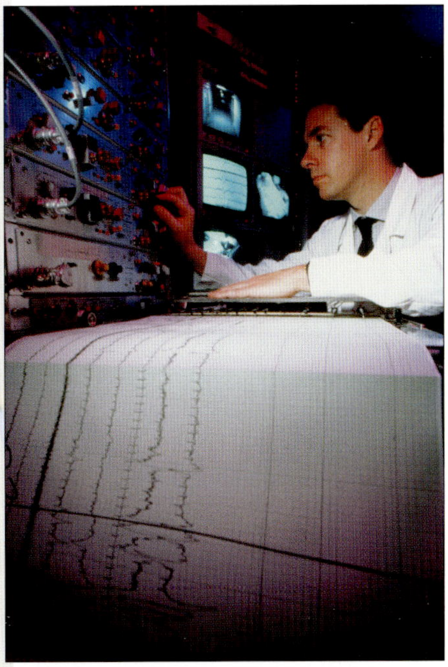

Above: A routine check is made of an EEG machine, which is recording a subject's brain activity by producing a printout with the characteristic wave patterns.

Psychological Stress Evaluator

It seems logical that the stress in one's voice can indicate a lie or at least anxiety when questioned about a crime. This idea of using a 'voiceprint' as a lie detector has intrigued investigators for years and led to the invention of a psychological stress evaluator (PSE).

This works on the assumption that a suspect's voice will reach a higher pitch when telling a lie. The voice emits inaudible vibrations called micro-tremors. Stress, which may exist when lies are told, causes the vocal muscles to tighten and the micro-tremors to decrease, producing flattened lines on a computer screen.

Voice stress analysis began in the 1970s when three retired US Army intelligence officers developed a system. All that is needed is a microphone and tape recorder, and a machine, which picks up differences

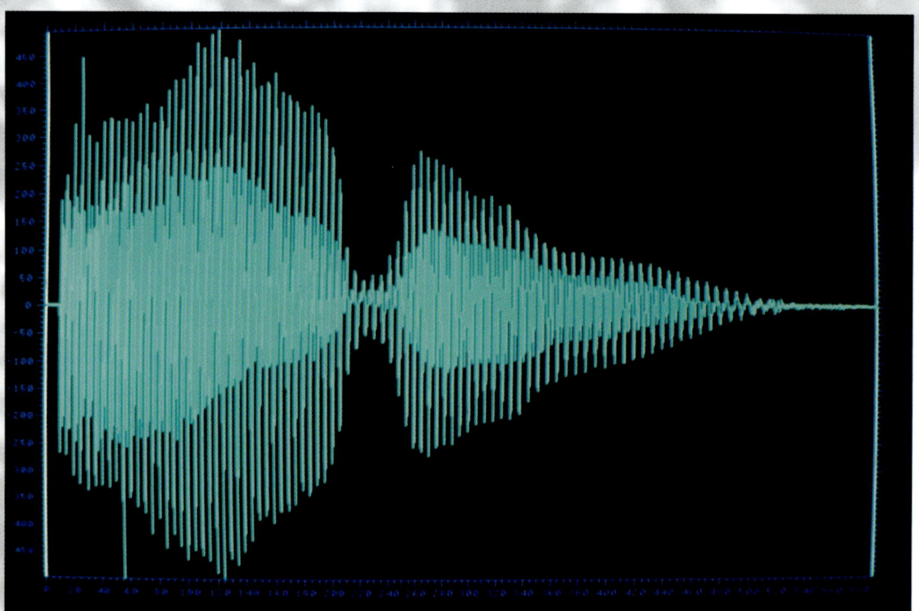

'A computer graphics image of the amplitude waveform of the word 'baby' is produced on a speech synthesizer. Amplitude means loudness, and a measurement of this could indicate stress.

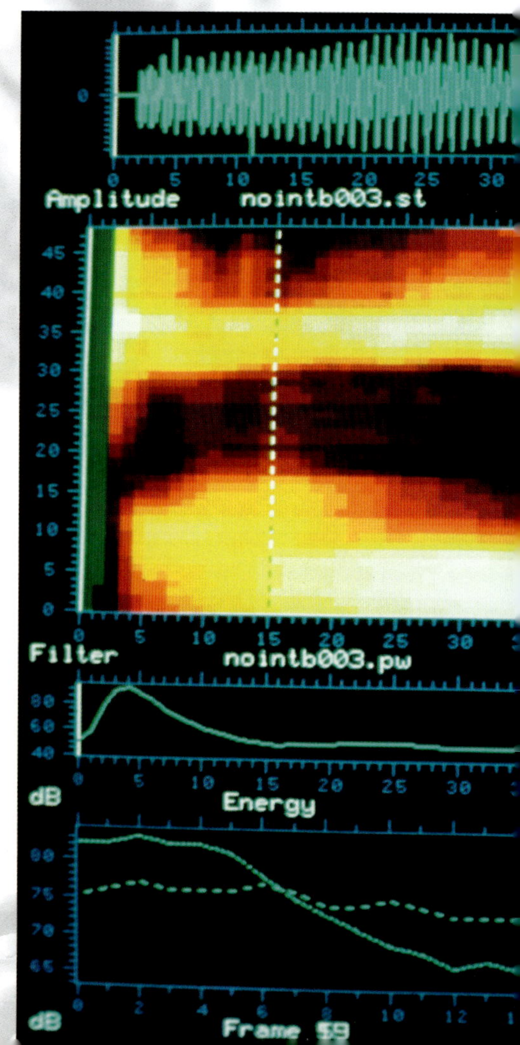

not heard by the human ear, analyzes the sound of a voice. The result is printed out onto a 'voiceprint' graph.

'MODERN-DAY OUIJA BOARD'?

Unfortunately most scientists do not believe the system can detect lies, with one calling it a 'modern-day Ouija board'. Frank Horvath, a professor of criminology at Michigan State University who has studied lie detectors for more than 30 years, says the PSE detection rate is at 'chance levels, the same as guessing. There's no merit to it, whatsoever.' Ian Christopherson, a lawyer in Las Vegas, adds, 'There may be something there that's measurable, but there's nothing there that correlates with the truth.'

Hundreds of US police departments, however, have recently bought one version, the Computer Voice Stress Analyzer (CVSA), in which a computer programme checks for minute vocal shifts.

The National Institute for Truth Verification of West Palm Beach, Florida manufactures the machine. The company, founded in 1986, has sold the product to more than 1200 police department and has trained nearly 5000 CVSA operators in the use of the machine.

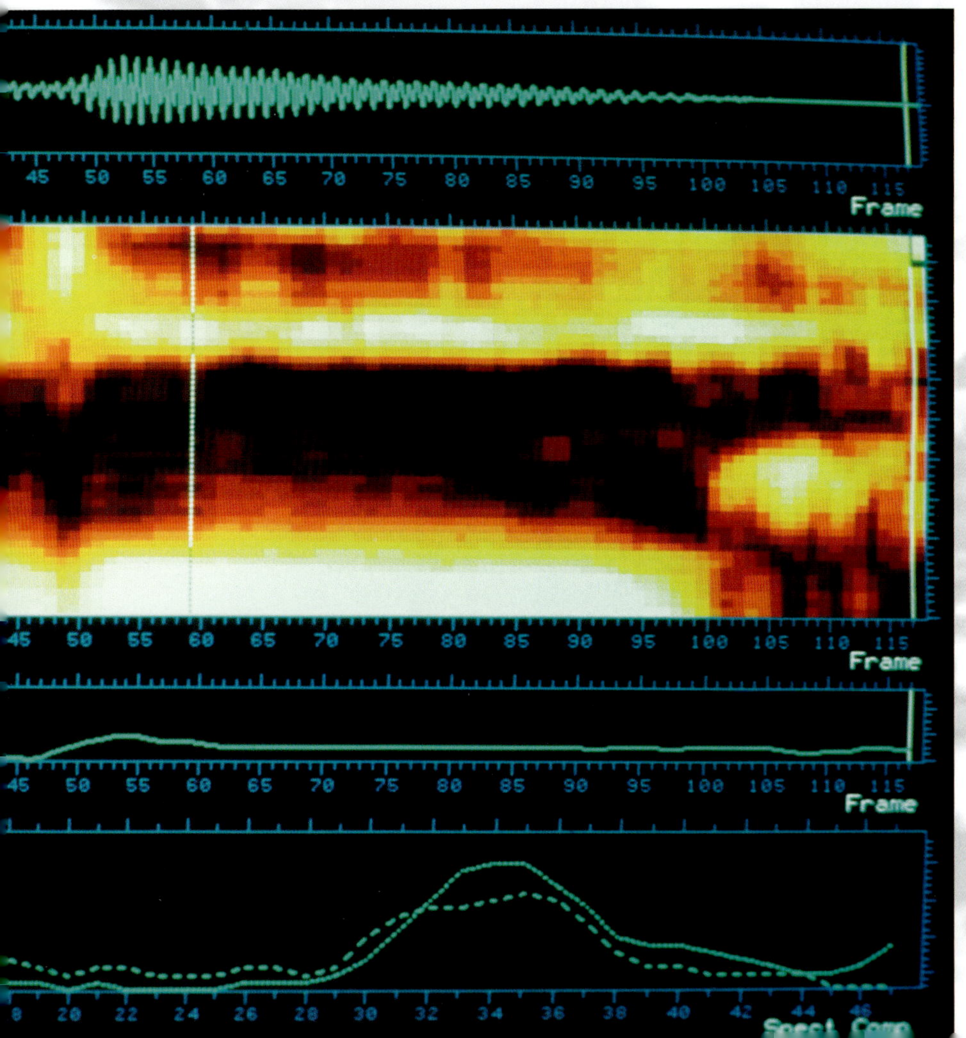

THE VOICE OF CRIME

Almost immediately after it was invented, the Psychological Stress Evaluator (PSE) was given credit for helping solve a crime. Gloria Carpenter's body was found in her bath in 1973 in Modesto, California, with a mark around her neck indicating she had been strangled by a nylon stocking. She had also been raped. Detectives visited her local bar and found John Wayne Glenn, her recent drinking partner. He admitted to taking her home but vowed he had never entered her apartment. No evidence linked him to the crime, but detectives persuaded him to submit to the new PSE test. The results indicated stress in his voice, so the investigators decided to target Glenn, returning to the bathroom and finally turning up a palm print that was matched to Glenn's. He now admitted he had visited the apartment, and the jury convicted him. The PSE evidence could not be used in court, but the detectives had doubled their efforts because of it.

A screen image captures waveform representations of the voiceprint for the word 'baby'. From top to bottom are indications of amplitude, filtered presentation, energy level and a spectral representation.

Criminal Insanity

'Not guilty by reason of insanity' is a shaky defence that covers various mental states. The law believes a criminal cannot be held responsible for his or her actions if that person has no perception of reality.

Other definitions include whether or not the person could tell right from wrong, whether they could control their behaviour and if they intended to act the way they did.

Forensic psychiatrists and psychologists know that it is not easy to explain the mind of the criminal within these terms. Many with mental health problems do know right from wrong, have a grasp on reality, are not subject to irresistible urges and can anticipate the results of their actions.

When ordinary neighbours commit insane crimes, they are often living in their own realities. A loving mother smothers her children to save them from the wicked world, or a reliable co-worker turns out to be a schizoid serial killer.

If a disturbed or mentally ill person commits a crime but lives in our reality, courts will often find them criminally responsible. In the USA, this may land them on death row. Several prisoners described as 'mentally retarded' have been executed, but the US Supreme Court ruled in 2002 that executing retarded prisoners violated the Constitution's protection against 'cruel and unusual punishments'.

Psychiatrists have pointed out other differences in the minds of violent offenders. Some have a distinctive lack of empathy for their victims, some are unable to control their behaviour and others have predisposing factors such as a history of a violent father.

SON OF SAM

David Berkowitz, nicknamed 'Son of Sam', was a serial killer who terrorized New York City in the 1970s. He wrote a strange letter to the police saying he was the 'Son of Sam' and 'Papa Sam keeps me locked in the attic too.' He was eventually caught in 1977 after receiving a parking ticket close to the scene of his latest murder. A search of his car revealed the gun. Berkowitz said that howling dogs in the neighbourhood were possessed by ancient demons that ordered him to go out and kill. This suggested a plea of insanity, but he confessed to killing six people and in 1978 received six life sentences.

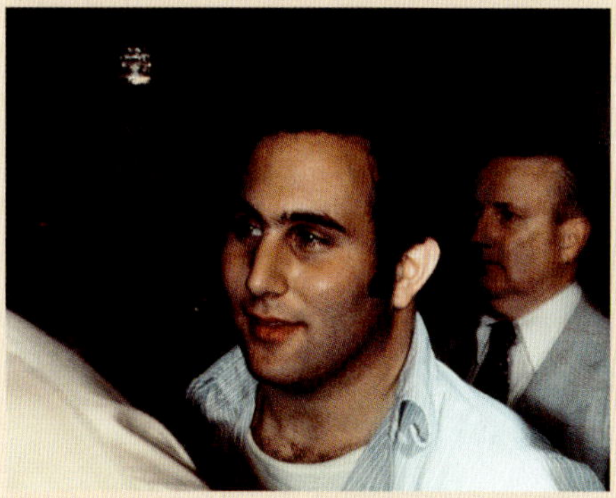

David Berkowitz arrives at the Brooklyn Criminal Courts Building after his arrest on 10 August 1977 outside his Yonkers home, New York.

Right: US Attorney Wendell Odom delivers his closing arguments in the second murder trial of his client Andrea Yates, in which she was found not guilty of murder by reason of insanity.

Above: Two men, later identified as terrorists Mohammed Atta (right) and Abdulaziz Alomari, are captured on CCTV going through security at Portland airport on the morning of 11 September 2001. The pair would later hijack American Airlines Flight 11, which Atta would pilot into one of the towers of the World Trade Center in New York City.

THE PSYCHOLOGY OF FEAR

Psychologists analyzing the tactics of terrorist agree that their battle is being waged with the psychological weapon of fear. This seemed to be the tactic when Khalid Sheikh Mohammed confessed in March 2007 from the US prison in Guantanamo, Cuba, that he had planned 31 terrorist attacks, including those of 9/11. He might have exaggerated the number to spread 'the message of fear', according to Jerrold M. Post, director of the Political Psychology Program at George Washington University.

The same tactic was seen in January 2007 after Britain foiled a terrorist plot in Birmingham to abduct, torture and murder a British Muslim soldier on film. Noted Professor David Wilson, a specialist in the mind of criminals and terrorists: 'They would have been saying, "nowhere is safe, not even your home".' He added, 'Terrorists are seeking to destroy the sense of safety and security normally associated with coming home.'

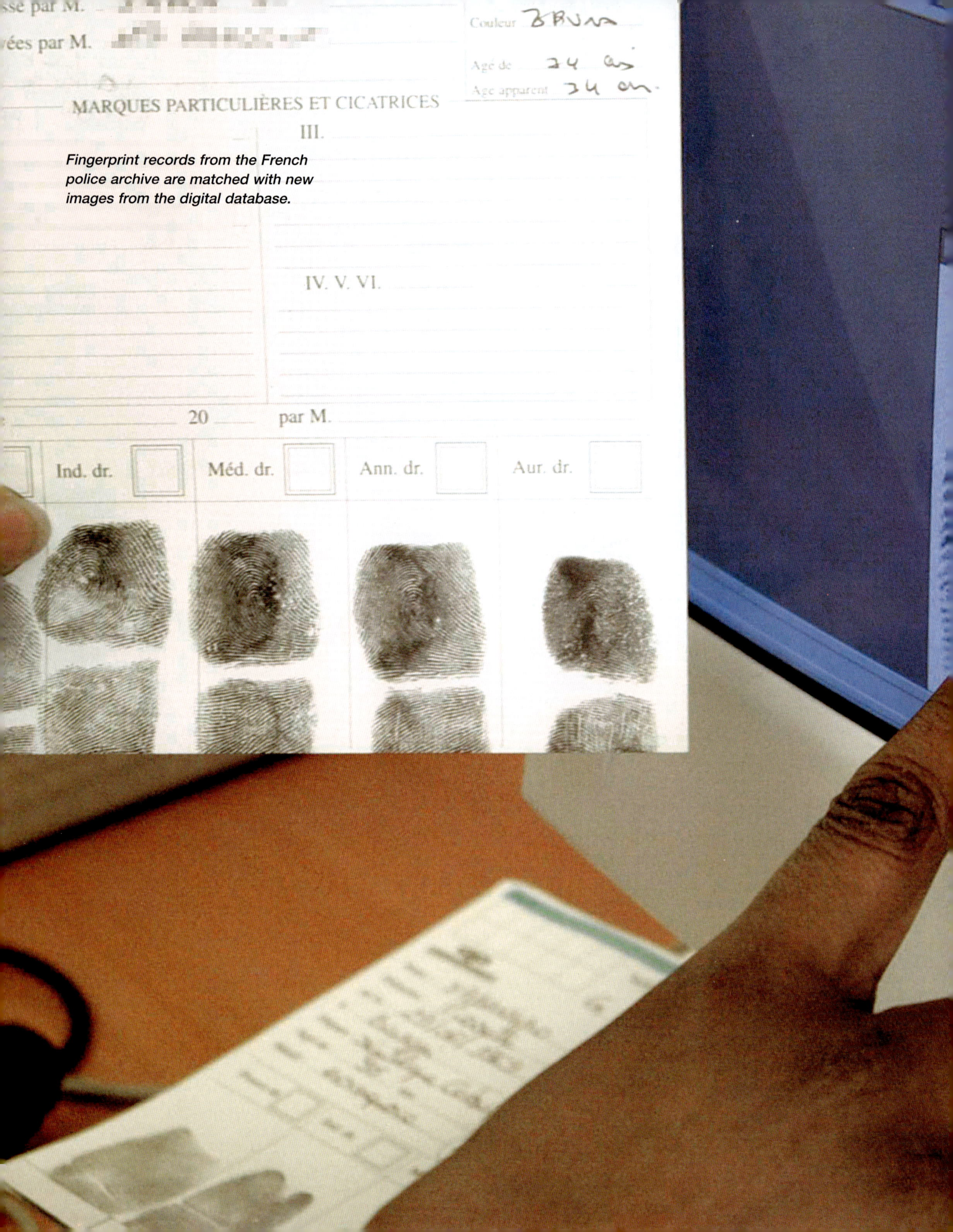

Fingerprint records from the French police archive are matched with new images from the digital database.

Chapter Twelve

History of Forensic Detection

FORENSIC EXAMINATIONS OF A SORT HAVE BEEN RECORDED SINCE ANCIENT times, when a Roman pathologist, Antistius, performed an autopsy on the corpse of the slain Julius Caesar. But the first true book of forensic science did not appear until 1247 in China.

Amateur work was seen in North America in the eighteenth century, with Paul Revere identifying the body of General Warren by his false tooth. Arthur Conan Doyle's fictional Sherlock Holmes popularized detection through observation in the latter nineteenth century. At that same time the Frenchman Alexandre Lacassagne was doing impressive forensic work in his laboratory at the University of Lyon.

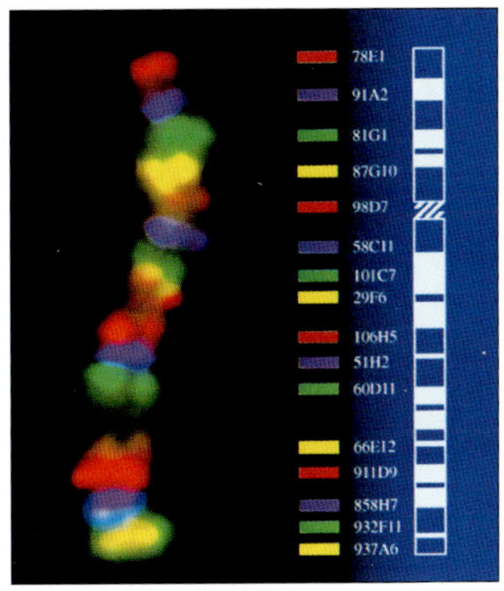

A chromosomal rainbow is created in this fluorescent light microgram and diagram of human chromosome 10.

In 1902 in England fingerprints were accepted as evidence for the first time. By 1932 the FBI had established its Technical Crime Laboratory, and in 1967 started its National Crime Information Center.

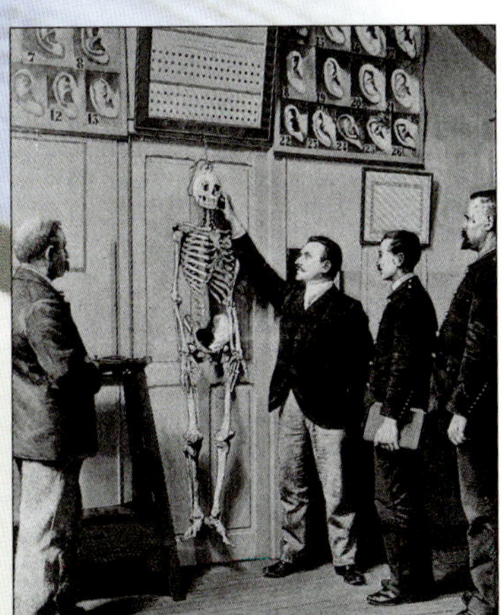

French criminologist Alphonse Bertillon at the Paris police headquarters shows his Bertillon System of identifying criminals by using anthropometric measurements.

Forensics in the Ancient World

Early civilizations had an awareness of the value of fingerprints for identification. The ancient Babylonians impressed their fingers into clay tablets when conducting business.

By 200 BCE Chinese rulers were using thumbprints for identification on important documents sent to government officials, who knew the distinctive imprint. In the seventh century the Arab merchant Soleiman described how a debtor's fingerprints were placed on a bill and given to the lender as legal proof of the debt.

The Greek mathematician Archimedes (*c.*287–212 BCE) perhaps recorded the first forensic evidence, when he exposed a fake product by testing its displacement in water. By measuring its buoyancy, he was able to prove that a crown, which people had claimed was made of gold, was in fact a fake.

EVIDENCE IN EGYPTIAN COURTS

The ancient Egyptians placed great importance on the use of evidence in their courts, using specialists to examine documents. One case was recorded in which examiners decided to falsify the documents of a property dispute. The petitioner, Moses, brought in witnesses to testify that his father had cultivated the land and paid taxes. Ultimately though Egyptian courts believed that witness testimony was more important than documents. Judges would also visit a crime scene to collect evidence, taking along the accused to the scene where he or she would be asked questions about the alleged crime.

It was also a Greek, the physician Erasistratus (*c.* 250 BCE), and founder of a school of anatomy at Alexandria, who developed the first known lie detection test. During his medical examinations he discovered that his patients' pulse rates increased when they told him falsehoods.

JULIUS CAESAR'S MURDER

The ancient Romans further developed the Greek knowledge of anatomy and applied it to crime. Antistius, the Roman pathologist, made a careful examination of Julius Caesar's body after his assassination in 44 BCE. He reported that Caesar had been stabbed 23 times but only 1 wound, found on his chest, had been fatal.

By 100 CE Romans were introducing crime-scene evidence in court. One famed orator, Quintilian, was able to demonstrate that bloody palm prints had been left to incriminate a blind man for his mother's murder.

Two types of written documents are exhibited at the Khotan Museum in China. One is a confidential document with a sealed cover that is made of clay. The other document is on a piece of wood.

In the seventh century the Arab merchant Soleiman described how a debtor's fingerprints were placed on a bill and given to the lender as legal proof of the debt.

EARLY POSTMORTEMS

The Greek anatomist Erasistratus of Chios, who taught in Alexandria conducted some of the first recorded postmortem examinations, although these were done to explain the human body, not to solve crimes. He dissected and examined the human brain, and was near to discovering blood circulation. However he had it circulating in the wrong direction. He believed the veins carried the blood, the arteries the 'vital' spirit and the nerves the 'animal' spirit.

Left: This artwork shows the Greek scientist Archimedes in his bath where he supposedly discovered that a body in a fluid displaces fluid equal to its own volume.

Forensics in the Middle Ages

The first recorded account of an investigator using insects to find a perpetrator occurred in thirteenth-century China. The victim had been slashed to death in a rural village, but no one confessed.

The investigator, Sun T'zu, asked all of the villagers to bring their harvesting sickles and lay them on the ground. He knew that flies have the ability to sense odours not detectable by humans. Soon the insects, attracted by tiny traces of blood and tissue remaining from the murder, began to settle on one sickle. Sun T'zu accused the man who owned the sickle, who confessed immediately.

This account was included in the first written report of medicinal knowledge being used to solve criminal cases, entitled *Xi Yuan Ji Lu* ('Collected Cases of Injustice Rectified'). Song Ci (1186–1249), a presiding judge in the Chinese high courts, wrote the book in 1247. It also describes how to clearly distinguish between drowning and strangulation. The work became a coroner's textbook.

OPIUM AND WINE

In Italy surgeons were beginning to use their skills to assist in legal cases in Bologna. Hugh of Lucca, surgeon to the Crusaders, founded the school of surgery at the University of Bologna. He introduced the idea of using wine to clean wounds, and became a medico-legal expert for the city in 1249. His son and pupil, Theodoric of Lucca, also taught at Bologna. Theodoric introduced the use of sponges soaked in opium as an anaesthetic.

By 1302 Bartolomeo de Varignon had performed a medico-legal autopsy to verify a suspected murder of a nobleman named Azzolino.

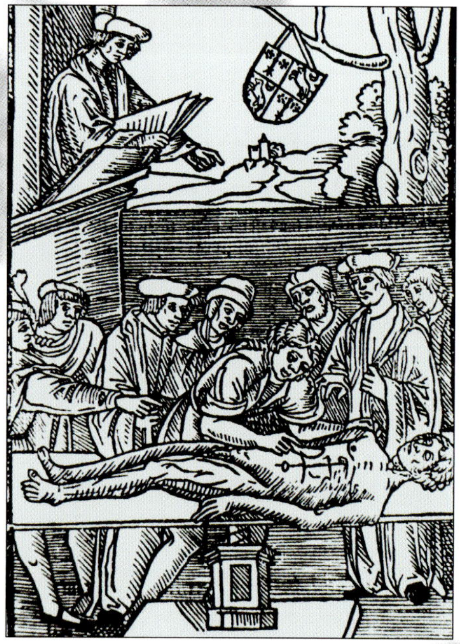

This historical print depicts a demonstrator performing a dissection of a corpse for students enrolled at a medical school during the fifteenth century.

THE FIRST MEDICAL EXPERTS

Although medical evidence had sometimes been introduced in the courts of antiquity, the thirteenth century saw its general acceptance in the legal matters of northern Italy. New laws allowed for the appointment of medical experts to advise the courts, and rules were even listed for someone to qualify as an expert medical witness. During these years, police surgeons were also becoming recognized as new professionals and were appointed to law-enforcement bodies.

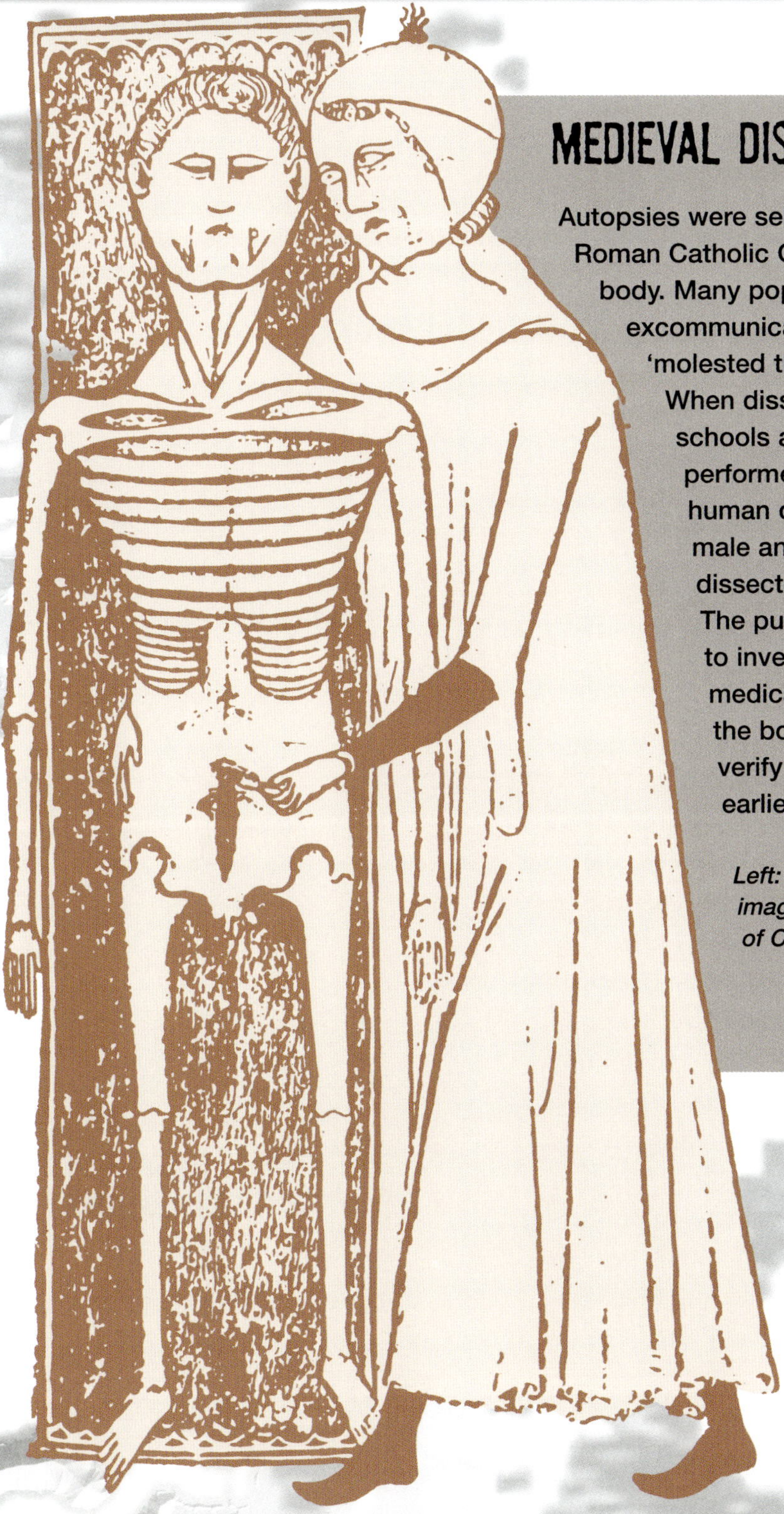

MEDIEVAL DISSECTIONS

Autopsies were seldom done in the Middle Ages because of the Roman Catholic Church's belief in the resurrection of the whole body. Many popes condemned dissection and threatened to excommunicate or even burn at the stake anybody who 'molested the dead'.

When dissections were done in the famous medical schools at Bologna, Padua and Montpellier, they were performed as rapidly as possible, and in the winter. Few human dissections occurred – Padua recorded one male and one female each year – so surgeons often dissected pigs.

The purpose of Medieval dissections was normally not to investigate why a person died or to advance medical treatment, but rather to do research on how the body functions, especially its organs. This was to verify or disprove information about anatomy from earlier philosophers and scientists such as Aristotle.

Left: A dissector works on a suspended cadaver. This image appears in a manuscript by Guy de Vigevano of Chantilly, dated 1345.

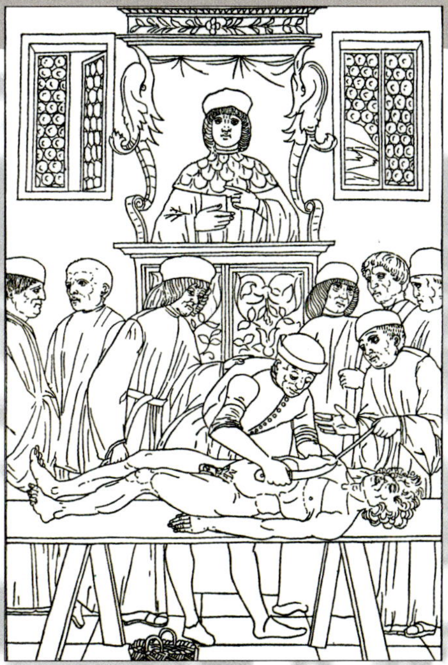

Right: A fifteenth-century woodcut shows an anatomical lecture at the famous University of Padua, Italy, showing the professor standing in his professorial chair (background) and presumably lecturing to the group of students below.

Early Forensic Breakthroughs

A renowned French surgeon, Ambroise Pare, published a court report on legal medicine in 1575, but Italy was again in the forefront of forensics in the sixteenth century.

PAOLO ZACCHIA

Italian physician Paolo Zacchia (1584–1659) first defined forensic medicine in his nine-volume work, *Quaestiones medico-legales* (Medico-legal questions). In it he covered such topics as malpractice and legal and medical ethics. Strongly advocating more authority for physicians, his method in legal cases was to follow a crime's sequence of events in order to establish its medical chronology.

Zacchia was the personal physician to the popes Innocent X and Alexander VII and legal advisor to the Rota Romana, the second-highest ecclesiastical court of the Roman Catholic Church, so his views were influential. His comprehensive medico-legal textbook remained in print into the late eighteenth century.

In 1598 the Italian physician Fortunatus Fidelis began to use 'the application of medical knowledge to legal questions', and another Italian doctor, Paolo Zacchia, gave legal medicine its name between 1621 and 1651 when he published *Quaestiones medico-legales* (Medico-legal questions).

In England in 1658 Sir Thomas Browne, a physician often considered an early forensic archaeologist, discovered the formation of adipocere, a waxy substance that forms in decaying corpses. Today, forensic scientists analyze adipocere to estimate time of death. That same year in Italy, at the University of Bologna, a professor of anatomy, Marcello Malpighi, carefully described the

Christiaan Huygens (1629–1696), Dutch physicist and astronomer, invented the two-lens eyepiece for microscopes in about 1684. Here he is shown colliding balls to derive the laws of elastic collisions.

ridges, spirals and loops in fingerprints, but did not consider their unique nature and possible application in identification.

MICROSCOPES

Microscopes, so vital to forensics, were now being developed. The first practical one was devised in 1590 by the Dutch spectacle-maker Zacharias Janssen and his father, Hans Janssen. In Germany in 1628 Christoph Scheiner, a professor of mathematics and Hebrew, refined the compound microscope, a prototype for modern microscopes. Innovation returned to Holland when the amateur scientist Anton van Leeuwenhoek invented the first precision microscope in 1670, using a single lens to achieve a magnification up to 270x. The physicist Christiaan Huygens devised a two-lens eyepiece about 1684.

Ambroise Pare (1504–1590), the French surgeon, wrote influential reports concerning legal medicine. He was a barber-surgeon in the army and is considered to be the father of modern surgery. He greatly improved the treatment of sword and gunshot wounds.

Adipocere, a waxy substance that forms on corpses, was discovered in 1658 and is still examined today to estimate time of death.

ANTON VAN LEEUWENHOEK

Though he started out counting threads in a dry goods shop, Anton van Leeuwenhoek (1632–1723) is today often called the 'father of microscopy'. Born in 1632 in Delft, Holland, as an apprentice he became frustrated with the weak magnifying glass he was forced to use to count threads in cloth.

Intent on developing a more powerful instrument for his work, Leeuwenhoek taught himself how to grind and polish lenses and even created a new way of increasing the curvature of the glass. This produced the strongest magnification of his day. The threads were forgotten as Leeuwenhoek concentrated on producing beautiful gold and silver instruments with a single lens of very short focus. These instruments bettered the performance of all the existing microscopes, assuring Leeuwenhoek of his place in history.

This drawing of human sperm by Anton van Leeuwenhoek was in a letter he sent to the Royal Society in London.

Global Forensics

The national forensic science laboratories and systems established in the twentieth century are now working together as efficient international networks of forensic scientists.

FBI agents instruct a group of Eastern European police officers in 2000 at the International Law Enforcement Academy in Hungary.

Authorities are able to access various types of criminal evidence in the powerful databases of the FBI in the USA, the FSS in the UK and Interpol in Europe.

Individual countries are also joining forces more often to help identify victims of natural disasters and to apprehend criminals who move across borders. Since it was founded in 1995, the International Law Enforcement Academy (LEA) in Budapest, Hungary, has taught forensic techniques to more than 2000 professionals from 27 nations,

INTERNATIONAL COURTS

Forensic scientists work closely with the two major world courts, both based in the Hague in the Netherlands: the International Court of Justice, which is the principal judicial body of the United Nations, and the International Criminal Court, an independent agency. The latter compiles and maintains a list of expert witnesses that includes those in forensic medicine and ballistics.

The forensic identification of victims of war atrocities has provided evidence for cases by both courts such as the indictment and highly publicized trial of Serbian President Slobodan Milosevic for war crimes. Extensive evidence was presented, but the case ended when he died in his prison cell on 11 March 2006.

from Albania to Uzbekistan. Terrorism has been a catalyst in speeding up cooperation around the globe.

SHARING INFORMATION

Forensic scientists share the latest technical advances through many international organizations. The European Network of Forensic Science Institutes, begun in 1995, holds regular meetings for its membership of forensic laboratories. The American Society of Crime Laboratory Directors maintains an International Liaison so lab directors can collaborate across the global forensic community.

Many specialist associations also exist such as the International Association of Bloodstain Pattern Analysts, with headquarters in Tucson, Arizona, and the International Association for Identification, based in Mendota Heights, Minnesota, with some 6700 members and 60 divisions worldwide.

Educational institutions are doing their part. In 2006, for example the University of Florida Global Forensic Science programme in the USA signed an agreement to exchange academic and research information with the Centre for Forensic Science at the Canberra Institute of Technology in Australia.

Below: The impressive International Court of Justice building is in the Hague, in the Netherlands. The court, also known informally as the World Court, was established in 1945 and began work the next year. Its 15 judges serve for nine-year terms.

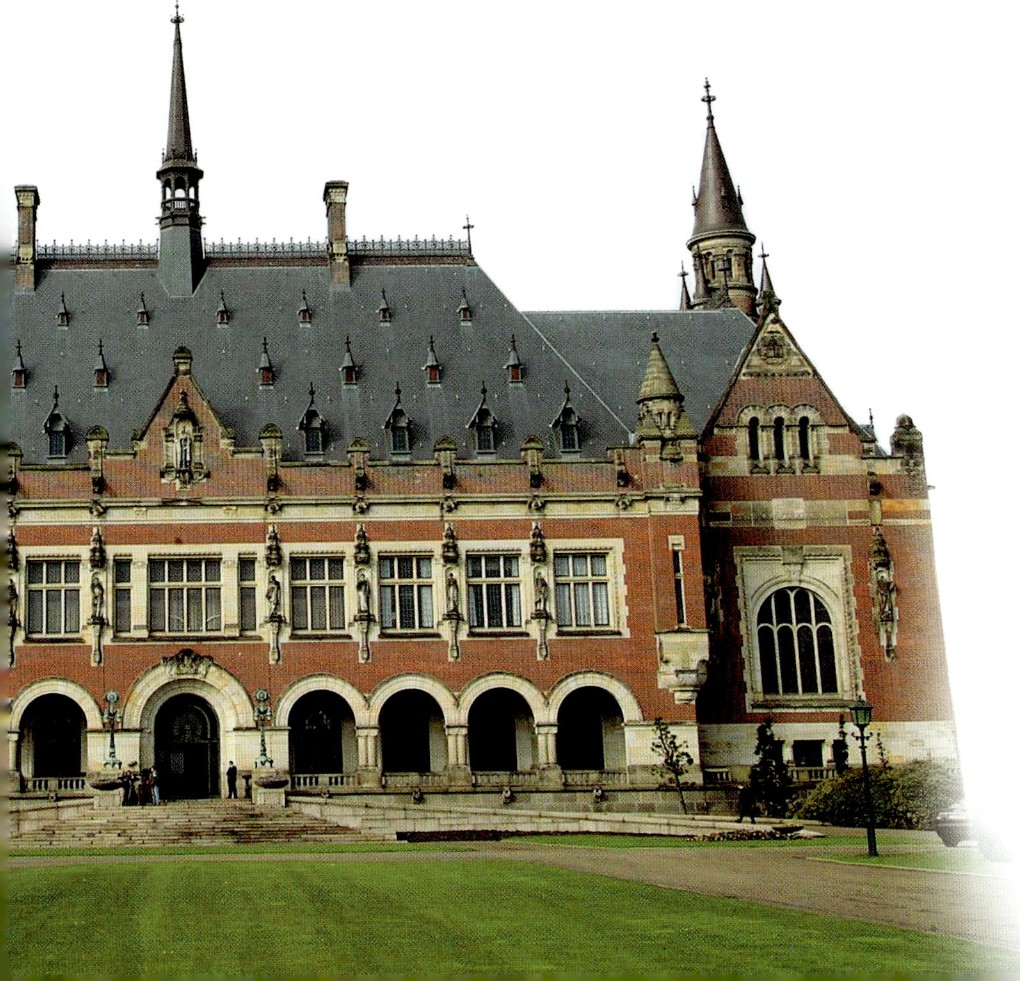

ORGANIZED CRIME AND POLLUTION

Interpol has undertaken an international project to see whether pollution crimes are linked to organized crime. In the first phase surveys were taken with five participating countries: the UK, USA, Canada, Sweden and the Netherlands. The results released in 2006 confirmed a connection, based on data from 1995 to 2005.
For example, 36 case studies involved organized crime in the illegal import and export of waste, illegal hazardous waste disposal and illegal movement of ozone-depleting substances. Some cases linked terrorism and pollution crimes such as the illegal waste disposal by terrorist groups in Northern Ireland.

Above: A child in a Third World country walks beside a wall of bags containing electronic waste illegally transported from developed nations.

Establishing Forensic Standards

Forensic medicine, also known as 'legal medicine' and 'medical jurisprudence', was a recognized field by the early nineteenth century, but had developed no specialties. The two about to emerge were forensic pathology and toxicology.

Physicians were routinely performing autopsies, but information and training was scarce, so most practitioners developed their own postmortem procedures.

The growth of forensic work in the late 1800s in Britain was due in part to the new organization and bureaucracy of criminal investigation, with the expansion of the court system and police. Photography was first used in the 1860s to document crime scenes.

Europeans also made advances in standardizing evidence collection.

This historical illustration is from the title page of the 1892 book Finger Prints *by the renowned British anthropologist Sir Francis Galton (1822–1911). The prints shown are his own. Galton was largely responsible for the introduction of fingerprinting as a means of identifying individuals in criminal investigations.*

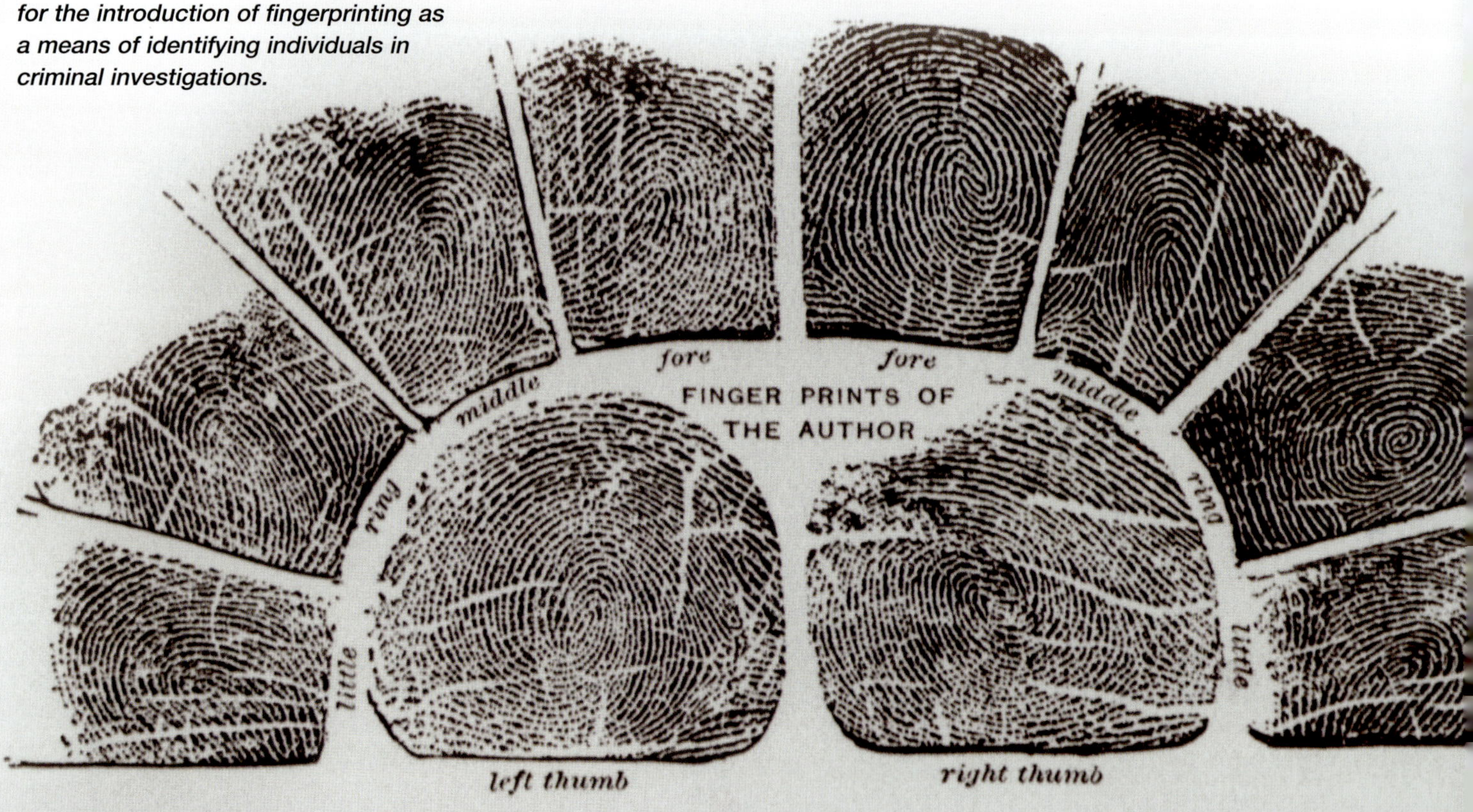

Dr Henry Faulds's Guide to Fingerprint Identification *(1905) included this artwork. Faulds (1843–1930), a Scottish missionary and scientist, was an early developer of fingerprint analysis. Convinced that the patterns of ridges on fingertips were unique, he set about trying to develop a system of analysis by describing several identifying features.*

In 1879 the German pathologist Rudolph Virchow became the first scientist to test hair as evidence, yet warned that it had limitations in court testimony. In 1891Hans Gross, an Austrian professor of criminal law at the University of Graz, wrote *Criminal Investigation*, the first definitive volume on physical evidence used to solve crimes.

FINGERPRINTING

Equally important, fingernail technology was being introduced into police and court procedures. Sir William James Herschel, a British chief administrative officer in Bengal, India, began to use fingerprinting to identify prisoners in 1877, and two years later Dr Henry Faulds, a Scottish missionary working in a Tokyo hospital, used fingerprints to identify a thief who stole the hospital's alcohol. He wrote about the forensic use of fingerprints in 1880 in the scientific journal *Nature* but failed to interest Scotland Yard in this type of identification because they could not establish the individual uniqueness of fingerprints. The British anthropologist Francis Galton proved this, however, when he announced his results in 1892 in his textbook, *Finger Prints.*

FINGERPRINTS IN FICTION

The acceptance of fingerprint evidence by the public (including juries) was accelerated by popular fiction in the late nineteenth century. In 1883 in his book *Life on the Mississippi*, Mark Twain had a murderer identified this way. He used this idea again in his serialized novel *Pudd'nhead Wilson* in 1893 and 1894.

The British author Arthur Conan Doyle used his stories of the brilliant fictional detective Sherlock Holmes to stress the importance of fingerprints and other trace evidence, with the first volume published in 1887.

JUAN VUCETICH

The Argentine policeman Juan Vucetich was the first person to develop a system of classifying fingerprints and the first to convict a murderer by fingerprints.

He developed the first criminal fingerprint identification system in 1891, and a year later, he investigated the case of Francisca Rojas, who had murdered her two sons and cut her own throat, saying they were attacked by an intruder. At the crime scene, however, Vucetich found a bloody fingerprint that matched hers and led to her conviction.

The Argentine police adopted his method of classification, and it was soon used in police departments worldwide.

Juan Vucetich (1858–1925) wanted to fingerprint the whole population of Argentina. He had emigrated from Croatia to Argentina as a young man.

The Twentieth Century

The turn of the century ushered in the total acceptance of fingerprint identification. Scotland Yard adopted the system in 1901, and the following year the New York Civil Service Commission initiated the first systematic use of fingerprints.

The New York State Prison System first used this for criminal identification in 1903.

In France the forensic scientist Edmond Locard presented his theory that 'every contact leaves a trace' in 1904. At the Sorbonne in Paris, Victor Balthazard, professor of forensic medicine, and Marcelle Lambert published the first comprehensive study on identifying hair, *Le poil de l'homme et des animaux* (Human and Animal Hair) in 1910, and three years later Victor Balthazard published the first article on identifying bullet markings.

The power and resolution of microscopes were now evolving rapidly. In 1925 the Americans Philip Gravelle and Calvin Goddard invented the comparison microscope used to compare trace evidence side by side, and in 1931 Ernst Ruska co-invented the powerful electron microscope, which can view objects as small as the diameter of an atom.

SIR EDWARD RICHARD HENRY

While serving in 1891 as the Inspector-General of Police of Bengal, India, Edward Richard Henry became convinced that fingerprints could be used for identification if they were divided into groups. He devised a classification system of 1024 primary groups and instituted it in Bengal in 1897. That same year, the Indian government adopted his system.

It proved so successful, a British committee in 1900 recommended that it replace the Bertillon anthropometric system then used. The next year Henry was transferred to England. There he set up Scotland Yard's Central Fingerprint Bureau, Britain's first, and published *Classification and Uses of Fingerprints*. In 1903 he was appointed the Commissioner of the Metropolitan Police.

Sir Edward Richard Henry (1850–1931) was born in London. His Henry Classification System is still used in many nations, including the UK and the USA.

THE COMPARISON MICROSCOPE

The comparison microscope is a staple of the crime laboratory. It consists of two compound light microscopes with a magnification of 40x to 400x. The optical bridge, a series of lenses and mirrors, projects images of two different specimens into a single eyepiece so a known sample such as a suspect's hair can be compared to a sample from the crime scene. It is often used to compare fibres, tool marks and ballistic evidence.

Two years after the instrument's invention in 1925 in the USA by Philip Gravelle and Calvin Goddard, a comparison miscroscope matched bullet casings to uphold the convictions of the anarchists Nicola Sacco and Bartolomeo Vanzetti.

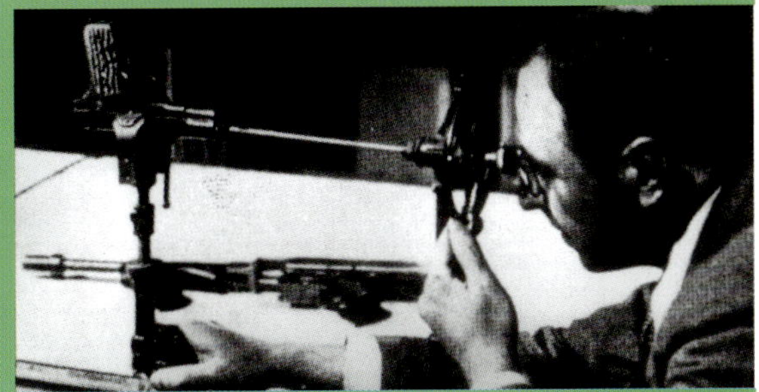

Calvin Goddard, inspecting a gun barrel, was also a pioneer in forensic ballistics and helped the FBI apply science to detective work.

CRIME LABS

Perhaps the most valuable contribution of the twentieth century was the evolution of crime laboratories. This began in France on a small scale in 1910 with Edmund Locard's laboratory in Paris. The first US crime lab was created in 1923 in the Los Angeles Police Department, and the high-tech FBI crime lab was created two years later. In 1935 London's Metropolitan Police forensic laboratory was opened.

Below: Discoverers of the DNA double helix James Watson (left) and Francis Crick (next to him) and Ernst Ruska (fourth from left), co-inventor of the electron microscope, join other scientists in San Francisco, California to receive the 1960 Albert Lasket Awards for medical research and public health advances.

The Advent Of Crime Labs

Edmund Locard's small technical laboratory, first established in 1910 in the attic of the Paris police station, used the best scientific techniques of its day, including microscopes and photography.

Before it created a fingerprint computer database, the FBI's forensic scientists had to compare samples in a time-consuming way.

Another police laboratory, the USA's first, was put together in 1923 in the Los Angeles Police Department by August Vollmer, who had also begun the School of Criminology at the University of California, Berkeley. The first private forensic laboratory was established in 1929 at Northwestern University in Evanston, Illinois, as the offspring of an investigation into the city's infamous St Valentine's Day Massacre.

In 1932 the United States Bureau of Investigation established its Technical Crime Laboratory in

THE BONE DETECTIVES

When the FBI began setting up its first crime lab in Washington, DC, in 1932, its agents were delighted to find a collection of 'bone detectives' just across the street in the red Gothic towers of the nation's Smithsonian Institution. These anthropologists were already working with the world's largest collection of human skeletons, and were more than happy to lend their expertise to the new laboratory, helping the FBI with such tasks as distinguishing between human and animal bones. The partnership also helped develop the field of forensic anthropology.

Washington, DC, conducting some 1000 forensic examinations the first year, and then moved a year later to larger premises under the new name of the Division of Investigation. The final name change occurred in 1935 as the Federal Bureau of Investigation (FBI), and its laboratory was given its own division within the bureau in 1942.

In 1935, London's Metropolitan Police Forensic Science Laboratory was opened. It retained its name in 1996 when it merged with the Forensic Science Service.

Right: The FBI began to emphasize science when it established a crime laboratory in 1932 in the Southern Railway Building in Washington, DC.

A LABORATORY CREATED BY GANGSTERS

They did not build it, but Chicago's gangsters were responsible for the creation of the first private US forensic laboratory. It began with Dr Calvin Goddard, the co-inventor of the comparison microscope, who investigated the bloody St Valentine's Day Massacre in a warehouse on 14 February 1929 when Al Capone's gang dressed as policemen to trap and murder seven members of the rival gang of George 'Bugs' Moran.

The crime scene yielded shell casings from some 200 bullets fired from submachine guns, and Goddard put them under his new microscope and found they did not match those from submarine guns issued to the police. After this was revealed, police raided the home of a Capone gang member and found two guns that Goddard used to successfully match the shells.

Goddard's impressive work with firearm identification attracted the interest of two businessmen on the coroner's inquest jury. They subsequently provided the funds for the private laboratory that opened in 1929 as the Laboratory Corporation. One year later it was renamed as the Scientific Crime Detection Laboratory.

Right: Moran's gang was lured to the garage by a promise of cheap whisky. After murdering them, the Capone men fled in a stolen police car, having missed killing Moran, who arrived late.

Left: The Smithsonian Institution has given the FBI generous assistance through the years. Known as 'the nation's attic', the Smithsonian was established by the US Congress in 1846 and undertakes considerable scientific research.

Recent Forensic Advances

DNA fingerprinting has been hailed by forensic scientists as the greatest forensic advance since fingerprinting. To some its impact ranks with the invention of the Gutenberg printing press.

As discussed in Chapter 5, constant refinements in DNA testing are assuring faster and more accurate testing. Among the important new innovations are mitochondrial DNA (mtDNA) tracing ancestry through mothers, familial DNA searches to find family members, polymerase chain reaction (PCR) to multiply DNA samples, DNAboost to improve poor samples, and ever more sophisticated instruments such as the miniaturized lab-on-a-chip device.

HUMAN GENOME PROJECT

The future of DNA forensic investigation seems limitless and will be accelerated by such giant strides as the 2003 completion of the Human Genome Project, which identified all of the genes in human DNA. 'Forensic DNA analysis is not a single technique', Dr. Lee said. 'It is a swarm of techniques based on the vast expanse of the human genome.'

Technical advances in other areas of the forensic sciences have been impressive, such as a three-dimensional computer reconstruction of a crime scene, including a house and garden. New innovations continue in the field of fingerprinting. Once it depended on a brush to dust for prints, but now it uses any of 250 different chemicals and instrument techniques. Two advances include:

A new generation of portable lasers that speed trace evidence recovery at crime scenes. This third-generation laser system is an optically pumped semiconductor (OPS) laser that can find trace evidence under the most adverse conditions, including old fingerprints and those on porous materials such as paper and stone. The traditional lower-power ion laser could miss such evidence.

Nanoparticles only one-billionth of a meter in length are being used by scientists at the University of Sunderland to produce a wipe-proof fingerprinting technique that provides a much clearer image than fluorescent powder now being used. Each nanoparticle has a sticky surface that attaches tightly to oily residue left by a fingertip. They are also dyed to assist scene-of-the-crime officers identify prints.

Below: A DNA autoradiogram is formed by fragmenting a DNA sample using enzymes, then separating the fragments under an electric current to form banding patterns.

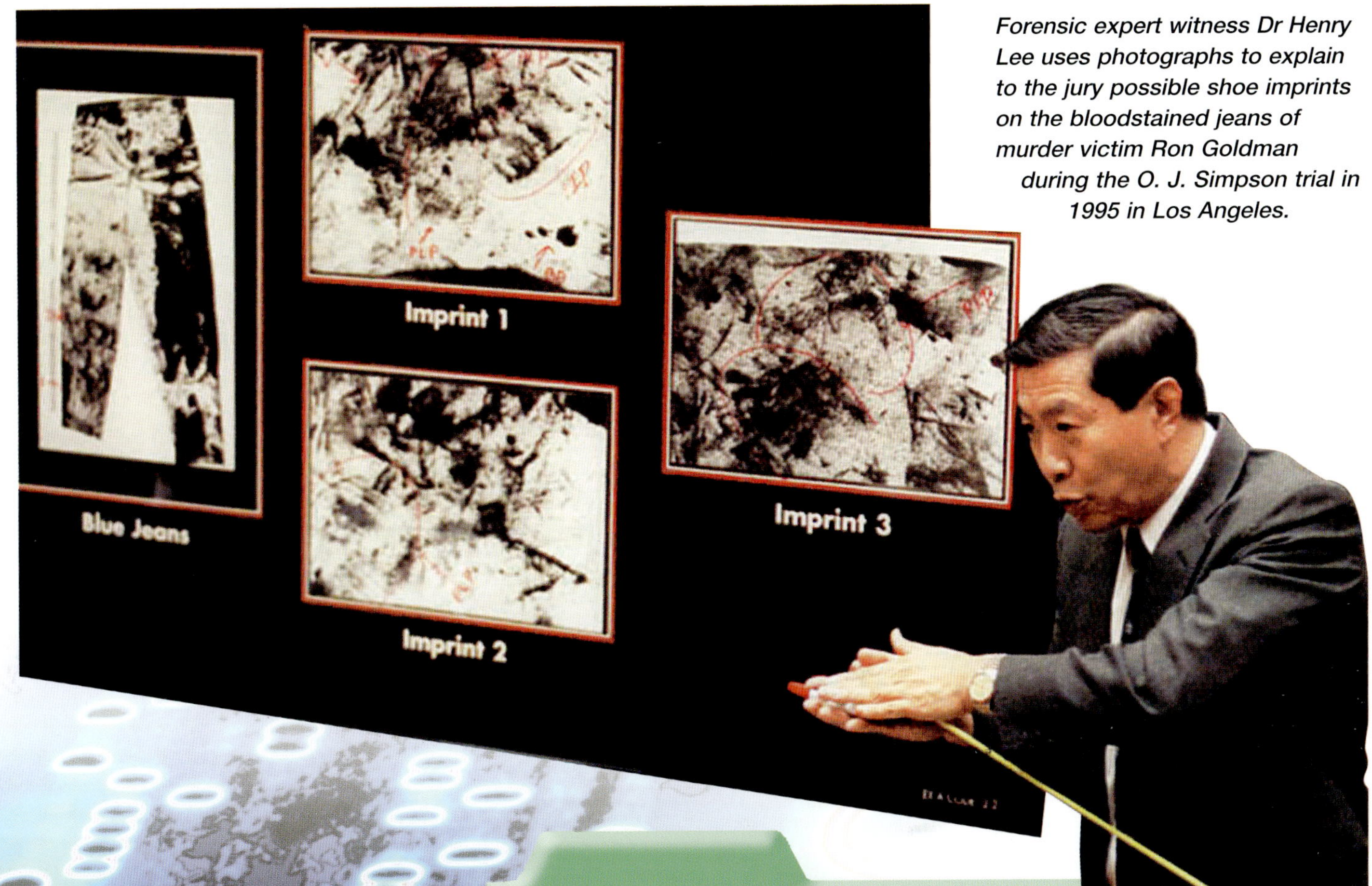

Forensic expert witness Dr Henry Lee uses photographs to explain to the jury possible shoe imprints on the bloodstained jeans of murder victim Ron Goldman during the O. J. Simpson trial in 1995 in Los Angeles.

A BETTER PICTURE

Image enhancement, as used by NASA to improve images sent from space, is now a common technique in forensic science. Videotape or photographs can be scanned into a computer and improved. Images of robbers' faces caught on security cameras are often of poor quality, making a positive identification impossible. In many recent cases colour enhancement and other technologies have clarified the images and led to identifications. Other non-destructive photographic techniques are used to enhance impressions on hard surfaces and imprints in soft materials such as mud, sand and snow. These techniques include filters and alternate lighting techniques such as ultraviolet light, polarized light and infrared light.

NASA's Retinex Image Processing technology makes images brighter, sharper and clearer, as seen in this view of Jupiter's moon Io.

Advanced DNA Databases

Forensic scientists throughout the world are able to use databases to help solve cases that would have remained mysteries a few years ago.

The two major criminal databases are the Combined DNA Index System (CODIS) of the FBI in the US and the National DNA Database (NDNAD) of the Forensic Science Service in the UK.

CODIS has an impressive sharing system of DNA profiles kept in the FBI's National DNA Index System (NDIS), which numbered 9,355,834 in October 2010. Through 2008, CODIS had produced some 54,000 hits and assisted in more than 260,000 investigations. The system has a Forensic Index with DNA profiles from crime-scene evidence, and an Offender Index with DNA profiles of those convicted of violent crimes and sex offences. All of the profiles originate at the local level and are then sent to state offices and on to the FBI.

MATCHING THE EVIDENCE

Matches among the profiles of the Forensic Index can link crime scenes together and possibly identify serial offenders. After a match, police in various jurisdictions can co-ordinate their investigations and share leads. Matches made between the Forensic and Offender indexes provide the identity of the perpetrator(s). After CODIS identifies a potential match, DNA analysts in the laboratories contact each other to validate or reject a match.

CODIS began in 1990 as a pilot project. Four years later, the US Congress DNA Identification Act gave the FBI authority to establish a national DNA index for law

CODIS is in the FBI building at 935 Pennsylvania Avenue NW in Washington, DC. Officially the J. Edgar Hoover Building, it was occupied in 1975 after the bureau had spent its first 67 years in the US Department of Justice Building.

enforcement purposes. NDIS became operational in 1998.

KEEPING A RECORD

The Forensic Science Service, part of the Home Office, runs the UK's National DNA Database. NDNAD was established in 1995 and now contains about 3.6 million profiles, more than five per cent of the country's population. This is expected to climb to 4.25 million profiles by 2008.

The Criminal Justice and Police Act 2001 allowed police to take DNA from anyone charged with a crime, but it had to be destroyed if the person was proved innocent. Under the Criminal Justice Act 2003, the police may now retain the DNA.

Most British criminals have their DNA on record. Police receive over 3,500 DNA matches a month, doubled from 1998–1999. NDNAD evidence led in 2008 to life sentences for Ipswich prostitute murderer Steve Wright and for Mark Dixie, who killed an 18-year-old London girl.

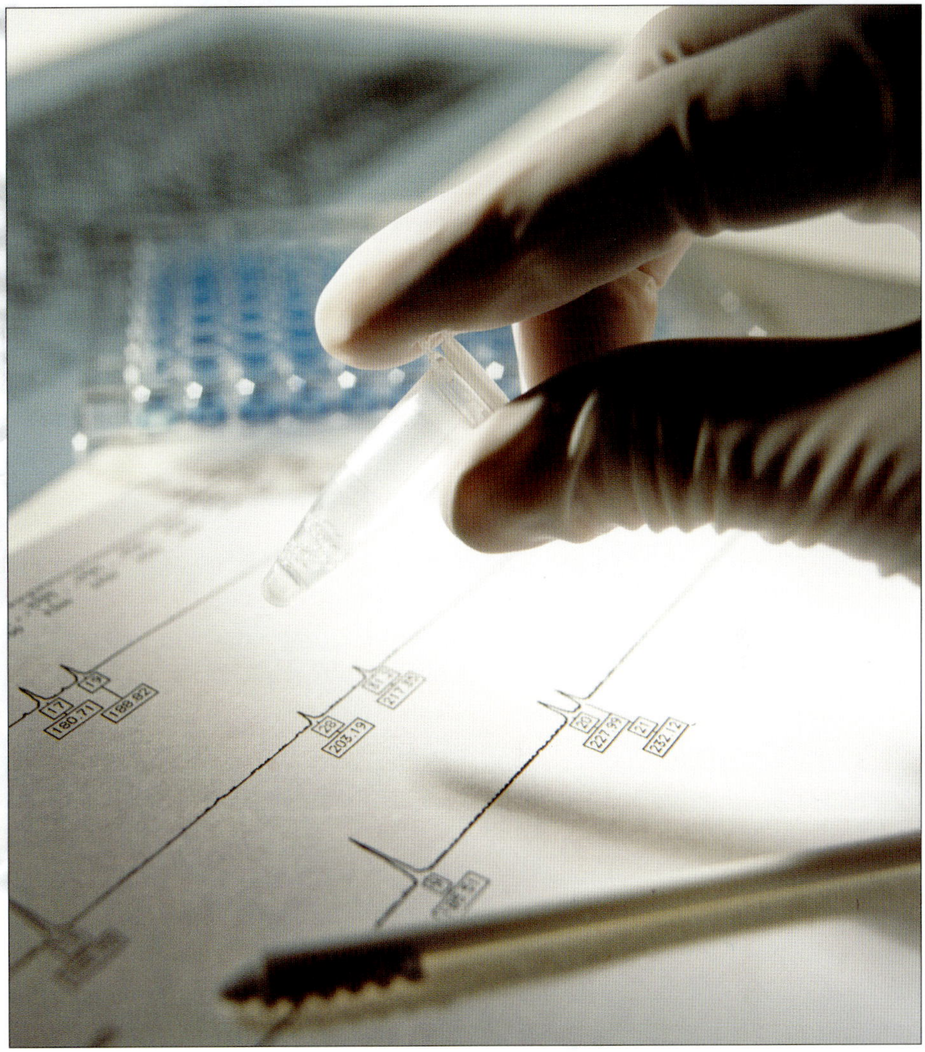

A gloved hand holds a sample tube containing DNA above the graph that shows the results of this particular DNA analysis.

AUTOMATED FINGERPRINT IDENTIFICATION

In 1999 the FBI placed into service its Integrated Automated Fingerprint Identification System (IAFIS). In 2007 it had grown to a data resource of more than 43 million 10-print records. Some 60,000 queries are now received electronically each day, and 80 per cent are answered in less than 40 minutes. New technology is coming that will shorten this response time further still. Interpol, the International police force, has an experts group studying the Automated Fingerprint Identification System (AFIS) in order to inform member states on how to acquire and develop their own system.

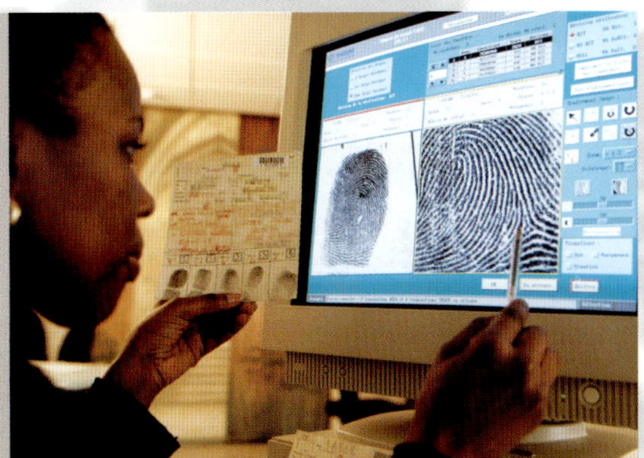

Computer technology has dramatically sped up the identification of criminals and victims through DNA profiles and fingerprint records.

DNA Database Failures

Despite their reputation for accuracy, DNA databases can in rare cases yield an incorrect result.

One wrongful arrest confirmed by the UK's Forensic Science Service involved Raymond Easton, who had given a blood sample 1995 after a minor domestic dispute. Four years later police investigating a burglary asked for another blood sample.

Easton was not worried, because he had been with his family on the night in question and he also had advanced Parkinson's disease. Yet the police returned to arrest him after the DNA database matched his sample to that left by the robber. The database's six genetic loci system supposedly had only 1 chance in 37 million of wrongly linking Easton to the DNA recovered.

Easton spent seven hours in a cell. Because of his situation, his lawyer successfully applied for a more sophisticated DNA test with ten genetic loci. It was able to discriminate between Easton's DNA and that found at the scene, so the charges were dropped. For its part the FSS upgraded its database to ten loci.

In a different type of database failure, research by the American newspaper *USA Today* revealed that investigators failed to pursue potential suspects whose DNA on the FBI's CODIS system had matched evidence from crime scenes in nearly three dozen cases from 2001 to 2006. This happened because of backlogs of unsolved 'cold cases' or was a result of basic police mistakes. 'Once a mistake has been made,' warns Australia's Federal Privacy Commission Malcolm Crompton, 'it is very difficult to fix or to undo the damage.'

Right: A scientist examines a sample of DNA on a computer database.

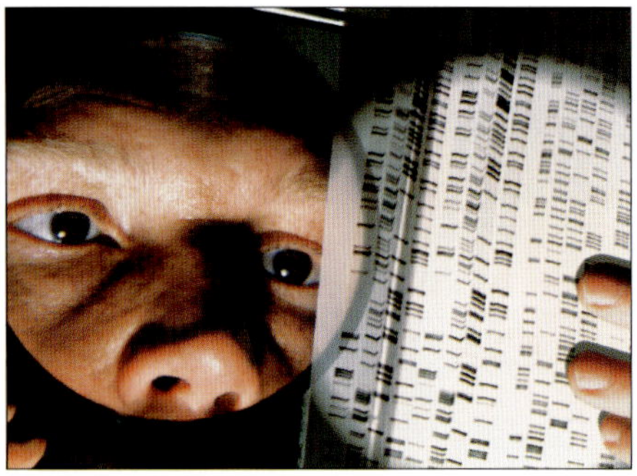

A scientist uses a magnifying glass to study a series of DNA sequencing autoradiograms, or genetic fingerprints. He is determining the sequence of base pairs (cytosine, guanine, adenine and thymine) that form the code for a section of DNA.

'A SILENT PROBLEM'

The FBI has begun creating a database of DNA from unidentified corpses, with one source estimating the USA has at least 40,000 cases. These include murder and accident victims, vagrants and runaways. Some are buried in paupers' graves or kept in local crime laboratories. Reporting unidentified remains is not required of coroners and medical examiners, but some states such as Nevada and Pennsylvania now require DNA to be taken before an unidentified body can be buried.

'It's a silent problem', said Michael Murphy, coroner in Clark County, Nevada. 'But these are also homicides that could be solved, accidents that could be cleared up, families whose questions could finally be put to rest.'

ESTABLISHING A EUROPEAN DNA DATABASE

No European DNA database exists, and the urgent need for one was realized in 1996 when an English schoolgirl was murdered in France. The perpetrator was caught in the USA, helped by American DNA testing, and this brought changes to the French DNA database. The UK put forward a proposal for a European database in 2004, and the following year, seven European countries announced they would sign an agreement to allow access to each other's DNA and fingerprint databases. In 2007 EU ministers from all 27 of the member states informally said they would explore the possibility of exchanging DNA and fingerprint data.

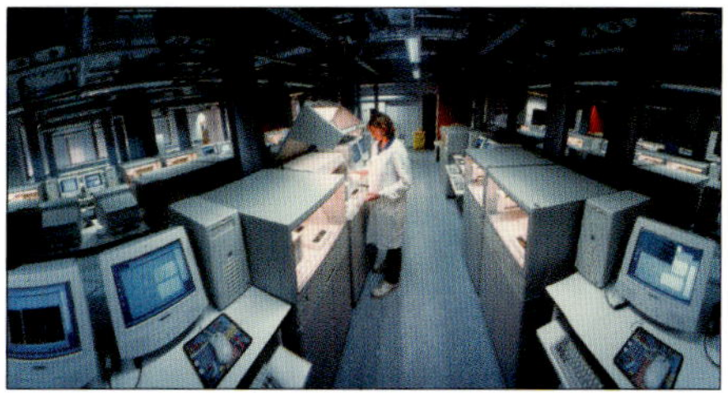

A technician at the Sanger Centre in Cambrige loads samples into automated DNA sequencers used for the Human Genome Project.

In 2005 seven European countries announced that they would allow access to each other's DNA and fingerprint databases.

Forensic scientists analyse unknown car paint on a slide by comparing it to the known samples on the desk.

Chapter Thirteen

The Forensic Career

AS THE VARIOUS FORENSIC SPECIALITIES HAVE expanded, so have the opportunities for employment in this rewarding career, which serves the interests of society, justice and public safety. The large umbrella of forensic science covers a fascinating assortment of jobs, from surgeon to fire investigator to administrator. All are involved in applying science to the law, so a good scientific background and an understanding of police work are both necessary.

Forensic scientists from the Institute Recherche Criminelle in France join a policeman to investigate the scene of a crime in a forest.

An inquisitive nature and stamina are required, too. 'You also have to learn to use deductive and inductive logic', says Dr Henry C. Lee, the American recognized as one of the world's leading forensic scientists. 'You need to have curiosity. You can't have an eight-to-four attitude. You have to have that persistence.'

Forensic scientists are totally responsible for their examinations and results, but they work closely with police, lawyers and other investigators. The result of their expert opinions will often influence the judge and jury to the point of determining the outcome of a court case. On the other hand forensic scientists may reduce the number of cases in the overloaded court system by proving that an issue does not merit a court hearing.

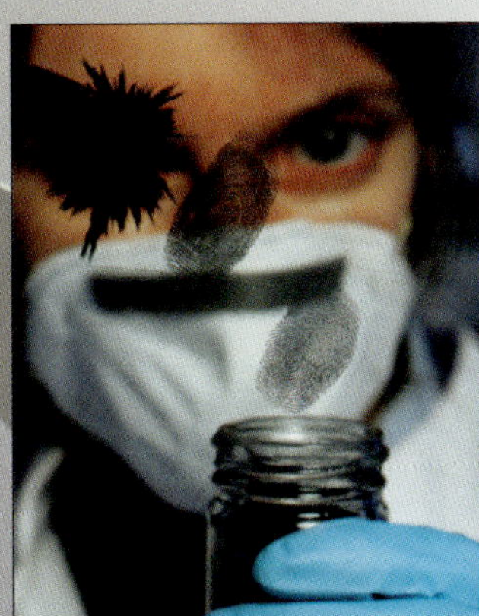

A forensic scientist uses powder to reveal fingerprints on a pane of glass at a crime scene. This will determine if a suspect was there.

Fact And Fiction

While slick television shows such as 'CSI' and 'Bones' glamorize the work of forensic teams, the hour-long format also gives the impression that investigators provide strong results after brief examinations.

In fact a former supervisory scientist with the FBI Laboratory, Max Houck, has identified what he calls the 'CSI Effect', which gives juries unrealistic expectations about what forensic laboratories can do. 'Defence attorneys now worry about the CSI Effect, as well', he noted, 'because they think that the jurors come in and have this view of science as this juggernaut, this infallible objective method that is always right and spells doom for their client.'

However, reality is not so neatly programmed in laboratories, which

Above: On this 'CSI: Miami' episode, Adam Rodriguez portrays a forensic scientist investigating a suspicious accident of a man decapitated doing a daring car stunt.

Left: Fictional forensic science must create ever original storylines. Here on 'CSI: NY,' the actors (left to right) Hill Harper, Carmine Giovinazzo and Melina Kanakaredes, track a serial killer who uses codes on T-shirts as inspiration for murder.

are often understaffed and overworked. Many traditional labs are suffering because the demand for DNA services has concentrated money and talent in that field.

A GRUESOME JOB

Also, television does not depict the often bloody, gruesome and smelly conditions prevailing in the lab or at a crime scene, where investigators must sift through dirt and mud to find blood droplets, bullet fragments and other trace evidence.

'There are certainly unpleasant scenes at crime scenes,' said the US forensic scientist Dr John DeHaan, a fire and explosives expert in Vallejo, California. He himself once had to crawl through a tight space in a home past the rotting body of the victim. 'You're cold and wet, or you're hot, and you're out there examining blood spatter or shovelling ashes and thinking, "Maybe Mom was right – maybe I should have been an accountant."'

Perhaps because of his humorous outlook, Dr DeHaan has persevered with his job for more than 30 years. The great majority of forensic experts are dedicated scientists, intrigued by their work of using intuition and high-tech science to find and convict criminals.

'CSI: Crime Scene' has popularized forensic science careers. Here it premiered its seventh season with a story about an aspiring dancer being killed backstage.

TELEVISION ERRORS

The basic science is normally correct in fictionalized forensic plots on television, but many liberties are taken. Some that have been pointed out by real laboratory workers are:

- Technicians in real labs do specific work and hand in the results. Unlike the television version, they do not work outside the lab or talk with police investigators about the case, and most certainly never draw conclusions on the guilt of the suspect.
- In a real lab, only about half the crimes are solved by forensic evidence, while television always solves every crime.
- Television experiments always work on the first try, whereas in reality reruns are often required.
- In a real lab, investigators often find DNA and fingerprints without knowing to whom they belong, so no match is made. A television series always has a suspect.
- Television lab workers never spend any time analyzing the data as is needed, but just wait for a printout from a test that gives them an immediate, clear result.

Duties of a Forensic Scientist

The main function of a forensic scientist is to provide scientific and impartial evidence for use in courts of law, and this means they will work closely with the police and may be required to go to a crime scene, such as a murder or fire.

Forensic scientists and reporting officers may attend crime scenes and have some supervisory responsibility within the lab. Most work concerns using all forms of analysis to examine trace evidence and relate it to a suspect.

Left: A forensic artist uses a wire frame and wax to reassemble a human skull. The face may also be reconstructed.

Forensic scientists who are reporting officers provide impartial scientific evidence for use in the courts.

OTHER FORENSICS STAFF

Assistant forensic scientists aid forensic scientists in biology- and chemistry-based analytical work, predominately based in the lab.

Forensic pathologists carry out routine coroners' autopsies and suspicious deaths autopsies. They also supervise the pathology lab or even the entire crime lab, such as the new Department of Forensic Medical Sciences in the UK's Forensic Science Service.

Forensic document experts looks at questioned documents to identify an individual by the handwriting or signature, or by the paper, ink, and indented impressions.

Forensic administrators review the development and implementation of leading technology, seek the legal and political context of forensic science, and study how to reduce error rates by reorganizing the existing processes.

INTERNATIONAL FORENSIC ORGANIZATIONS

The American Academy of Forensic Sciences (AAFS), founded in 1948, is headquartered in Colorado Springs, Colorado. It has members from all 50 US states and 62 other countries. It publishes the Journal of Forensic Sciences and is committed to 'the promotion of education and the elevation of accuracy, precision and specificity in the forensic sciences'.

The Forensic Science Society, based in Harrogate, North Yorkshire, is an international professional body founded in 1959 with more than 2500 members from over 60 countries. It publishes the journal Science & Justice and arranges scientific conferences.

Most work concerns using all forms of analysis to examine trace evidence and relate it to a suspect.

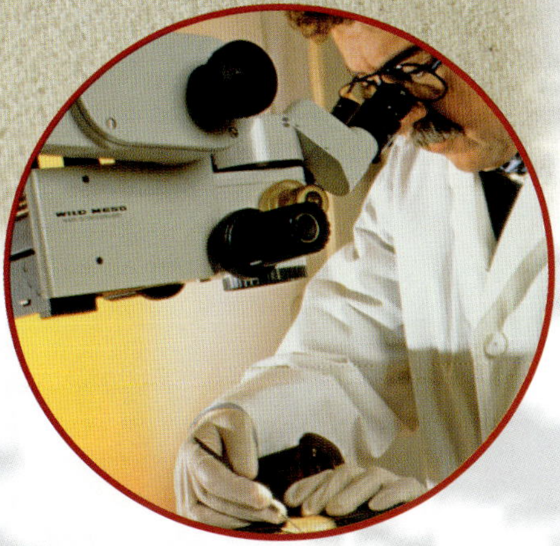

Investigators deal with a large variety of objects. The scientist above is taking a blood sample from a hammer found at a murder scene in order to make a DNA analysis, while the forensic expert at the right is using a microscope to study the sole of a suspect's boot.

COMMON LABORATORY WORK

The UK's Forensic Science Service lists the following eight common tasks found in a forensic lab:

- Identification of blood, semen and other body fluids; the blood grouping of dried stains; and the use of DNA profiling to compare samples.
- Identification and comparison of textile fibres.
- Identification and comparison of plant and animal materials, including hairs.
- Analysis of blood and urine samples for their drug or alcohol content in driving offences.
- Analysis of body fluids and organs in cases of suspected poisoning.
- Identification of illegal drugs such as amphetamine, heroin and cannabis. The purity of these drugs is determined and samples can be compared.
- Comparison of materials used to package drugs.
- Examination of paint and glass fragments using microscopy, and physical and chemical methods.

Forensic Scientists In Court

Unlike the ordinary fact witness, the forensic scientist is an expert witness, whose evaluation of the scientific tests performed must be presented in everyday language anyone could understand.

Often, this does not come easily, and forensic training normally teaches how to rephrase complex science into simple terms.

A jury is normally in some awe when confronted by a scientist, and it is important that his or her qualifications are brought out in questioning, including the number of years of experience in the field, the degrees received, participation in professional organizations and any

Opposing lawyers seek to find flaws in the forensic scientist's tests.

Dr Randall Alexander, an expert child-abuse witness for the prosecution, points to a doll representing six-year-old Tiffany Eunick and describes the deadly injuries she received in 2001 in Fort Lauderdale, Florida.

professional books or articles the scientist has published.

DISCREDITING SCIENTISTS

Facts in the testimony of a scientist are open to be challenged in court, with opposing attorneys seeking to find flaws in the scientific tests or the interpretation. It is not easy to discredit forensic facts or the science upon which they are based, but lawyers have had some successes. For this reason the forensic scientist must be aware of the court's rules of evidence on the admissibility of opinions and conclusions. And throughout the testimony, a forensic expert must maintain an impartial professionalism, no matter which side is helped or harmed by the presentation.

An expert in court is an impressive witness but, in reality, forensic scientists are required to appear in court in a very few number of cases. For most cases they write up comprehensive reports of the forensic examinations. The side that has retained the scientist will present these, so, as with an oral testimony, they should be written in such a way that anyone could easily understand the report.

Left: Defence attorney Roger Diamond shows a bottle of herbal Ecstacy to expert prosecution witness Dr. Jo Ellen Dyer, a toxicologist, at the date rape trial of Max Factor heir, Andrew Luster, in 2003 in Ventura, California.

WRONGFUL TESTIMONY

If a forensic scientist becomes too eager to back up the police view of a case, the result can be a terrible miscarriage of justice. This happened in Chicago, Illinois, in 1986 during the trial of two African-American defendants, Donald Reynolds and Billy Wardell, for the rape of a University of Chicago student and the attempted rape of another.

The testimony came in 1988 from the Chicago Police forensic serologist Pamela Fish. Fish testified that semen recovered from one victim could have come from only 38 per cent of the male population, including Reynolds, when actually 80 per cent of black males could have been the source. She also did not disclose to the jury that another Chicago Police crime lab analyst had examined hairs recovered from Reynolds and determined that they could not have come from either victim. The accused, who had been identified by the victims, were found guilty and given a total of 69 years in prison. The judge denied their request for DNA tests, but in 1996 new attorneys were able to ensure the tests were carried out, and these proved the men were innocent after spending 11 years behind bars.

Acquiring a Forensic Job

Media attention to forensic science in the court has created a rapidly expanding job market, resulting in numerous well paying jobs being available to university graduates with degrees in the field.

This is the opinion of Loyola University in Chicago, which offers a major in forensic science. The university prospectus adds: 'Recent published studies report an ever-increasing demand for forensic scientists and estimates suggest that 10,000 new forensic scientists will be required in the next five years to sufficiently staff the nation's forensic laboratories.' For its positions on offer, the UK's Forensic Science Service (FSS) recommends that a scientific qualification, often to degree level, is the best route, but even applicants with university degrees should gain paid work in a laboratory to gain experience.

Forensic scientists in New York collect evidence at the scene of a murder. Everything of the remotest importance must be photographed and recorded.

PROFESSIONAL QUALIFICATIONS

Applicants for some specialist positions such as a crime scene investigator, who must have an

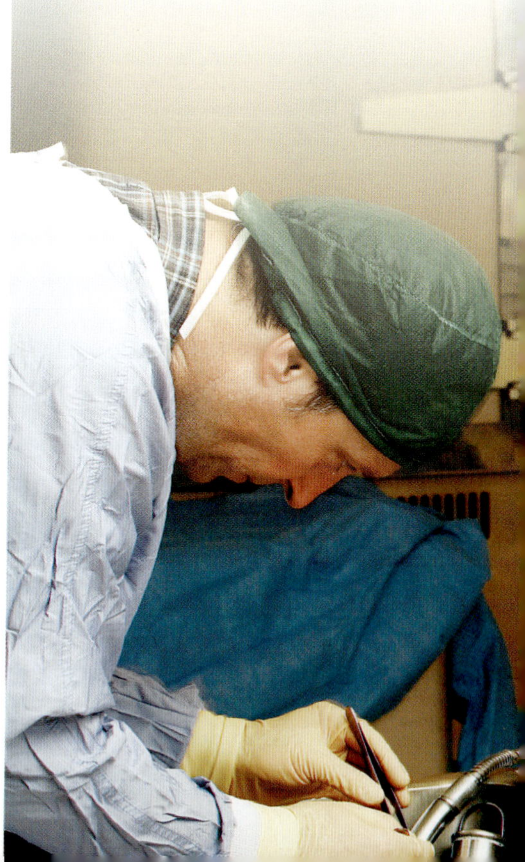

UNIVERSITY FORENSIC COURSES

The UK only offered three undergraduate courses at three universities in 1993, but by 2006 an explosion of courses saw more than 460 being offered by more than 60 universities and institutions of higher education. These included the Universities of the West of England at Bristol, Chester, Coventry, East London, Wales at Bangor, and at Lampeter, Greenwich, Manchester, Plymouth, Strathclyde and Worcester.

Among the many US universities with degree courses in forensic sciences are the University of Alabama at Birmingham; California State University, Sacramento; George Washington University in Washington, DC; the University of New Haven in Connecticut; and the University of Texas Southwestern Medical Center in Dallas. Courses at university level in Canada are offered at the University of Toronto and Laurentian University in Sudbury, (both of which are in Ontario), and at Mount Royal College in Calgary, Alberta.

Tomate

Fotografie von Luzia **Ellert**
Rezepte und Foodstyling von Gabriele **Halper**
Text von Elisabeth **Ruckser**

Collection Rolf Heyne

Inhalt

Einleitung

Die Pflanze der Pioniere

Es gibt sie in der farbenprächtigen Vielfalt tausender Sorten, und ihr Name steht seit Anbeginn (auch) für Liebe und Erotik. Und das, obwohl sich die kulinarische Begeisterung zunächst in Grenzen hielt: Als die spanischen Eroberer sie zusammen mit vielen anderen Pflanzen aus der Neuen Welt mit nach Hause brachten, hielt man die Tomate lange Zeit für giftig. Dennoch bahnte sich die schöne Beerenfrucht ihren Weg in die botanischen Gärten der Reichen und Mächtigen. Die Europäer nannten sie »Pomodoro« (Goldapfel), Paradies- oder Liebesapfel und sagten ihr aphrodisierende Kräfte nach, ja sogar, dass sie »Liebestollheit« bewirke.

Wir freuen uns heute vor allem über ihre lukullischen Verführungskünste. Und beobachten eine Entwicklung, die uns gerade in den letzten Jahren die wunderbar vielfältige Geschmackswelt der Tomate eröffnet beziehungsweise wieder zurückbringt. Das beliebte Fruchtgemüse feiert ein großes Comeback, und immer mehr Menschen sind auf der Suche nach dem »Geschmack von früher«. Nach Jahren, in denen Tomaten eher den Ruf einer Art »vierten Aggregatzustands von Wasser« innehatten, wie es eine österreichische Autorin launig formulierte, wird nun wieder Wert auf Duft, Geschmack, Vielfalt und Qualität gelegt. Die Verbraucher suchen Exemplare, die wie sonnenreif von der Staude gepflückt schmecken, und die Nachfrage vor allem nach alten Sorten steigt. Meist von kleinen, regionalen Betrieben und Produzenten oder auf dem eigenen Balkon hergestellt, sind sie aufgrund ihres unvergleichlichen Aromas gefragter denn je. Und das Spiel mit den bunten Erscheinungsformen von rot, gelb, violett bis grün gestreift erfreut Hobbygärtner wie Gourmets. Ebenso wie die Tatsache, dass sich aus ihnen so viel mehr Köstliches zubereiten lässt als Salat & Sauce …

Ein Siegeszug rund um die Welt

Die beispiellose Karriere der Tomate begann in Südamerika. Ganz genau lässt sie sich zwar nicht dingfest machen, aber man geht davon aus, dass Peru, Ecuador und Bolivien das Ursprungsgebiet der Tomate sind. Hier wächst sie bis heute auch in zahlreichen wilden Formen – auch wenn sie längst die ganze Welt erobert hat. Erstmals kultiviert wurde die Tomate vermutlich in Mexiko in der Gegend um Vera Cruz. Auch ihre heute in vielen Sprachen geläufige Bezeichnung geht auf die Sprache der Azteken zurück: Abgeleitet von »tomana«, was so viel wie »anschwellen« bedeutet, wurde die Frucht »Tomatl« genannt. (Mit diesem Begriff wurden dabei sowohl Tomaten als auch verschiedene Physalisarten bezeichnet.) Apropos Namen: In den östlichen Regionen Österreichs verwendet man heute vor allem die Bezeichnung »Paradeiser«. Sie geht wohl auf den paradiesischen Namensursprung zurück, ebenso wie das ungarische »Paradicsom«.

Nach Europa gelangte die Tomate jedenfalls 1523 und galt fürs Erste hauptsächlich als schön, aber ungenießbar. Das mag an ihrem Gehalt an Solanin – jener giftigen Verbindung, die auch in den Blättern der verwandten Kartoffel enthalten ist – liegen, und der sich beim Verzehr von unreifen Früchten schon mal gesundheitsschädlich auswirken kann. Was den Spaniern aber scheinbar relativ egal war, denn hier erobert sich die Tomate schnell einen Platz als häusliche Nutzpflanze. Kein Wunder, viele heimkehrende Seefahrer hatten sie schließlich in der Neuen Welt nicht nur gesehen, sondern auch gekostet und bemerkt, dass sie weder gefährlich noch giftig war. Auch die Italiener liebten das neue Gemüse vom Fleck weg und fanden alsbald heraus, dass seine bloße Verwendung als Zierfrucht eine ziemliche Verschwendung war. So wurden Tomaten bereits in der Mitte des 16. Jahrhunderts rund um Neapel angebaut. Der italienische Apotheker und Botaniker Petrus Matthiolus beschreibt sie 1544 in seinem umfassenden Botanikbuch – ein echtes Standardwerk seiner Zeit – als »... zunächst grüne und, sobald sie reif sind, goldene Früchte«. Er empfiehlt, sie in Öl wie Pilze zu braten, und gibt der gelb-orangen Frucht den Namen »Pomo d'Oro«, goldener Apfel. (Rote Sorten waren erst etwas später bekannt.) Die Tomate breitete sich in Windeseile bis nach Indien und in den Fernen Osten aus, im gesamten mediterranen Raum gilt sie ab dem Beginn des 17. Jahrhunderts als heimisch.

In Mittel- und Nordeuropa blieb man allerdings, was ihre Genießbarkeit betrifft, noch länger skeptisch. So findet sich hier die Erwähnung der Tomate in wissenschaftlichen Werken meist nur als Zierpflanze mit dekorativem und medizinischem Nutzen. Aber ihre oft zitierte aphrodisierende Wirkung ließ sie dennoch zu einem begehrten Objekt werden, etwa für Gartenlauben, einem beliebten Treffpunkt für Verliebte. Noch anno 1770 findet sich so zum »Liebesapfel« im »Universalwörterbuch der Pflanzen, Bäume und Sträucher Frankreichs« folgende Erläuterung: »Seine Früchte gelten als giftig und betäubend, sie finden kaum Verwendung.« Knapp zehn Jahre später taucht die Tomate dann allerdings auch hierzulande erstmals in einem Saatgutkatalog als »Gemüse« auf und hält schließlich Einzug in Gastronomie und Kochbücher.

Den Weg zurück nach Nordamerika nimmt sie übrigens von Europa aus: Auswanderer dürften die Tomate einfach mitgenommen haben. Und sie fanden auch gleich berühmte Bewunderer, wie den späteren amerikanischen Präsidenten Thomas Jefferson. Er kultivierte Tomaten bereits 1781 auf seinen Plantagen im Bundesstaat Virginia.

Warum Tomaten so gesund sind

100 g rohe Tomaten enthalten etwa 17 kcal, 0,2 g Fett, 2,9 g Kohlenhydrate, 1 g Eiweiß, 1,8 g Ballaststoffe und 0,2 g Fett. Frische, ausgereifte Früchte bestehen außerdem zu 94 Prozent aus Wasser und sind damit die ideale Basis für eine leichte Küche. Sie sind schmackhaft und ausgesprochen gesund. In den Tomaten stecken jede Menge Vitamine (B_1, B_2, B_6 und E, Folsäure sowie Vitamin C), Mineralstoffe, Fruchtsäuren und sekundäre Pflanzenstoffe.

Diese wertvollen Inhaltsstoffe der Tomate stärken auf natürlichem Wege das Immunsystem und helfen damit, Abwehrkräfte gegenüber Infektionen zu mobilisieren. Eine mittelgroße Tomate kann fast 40 mg Vitamin C liefern, was etwa der Hälfte des Tagesbedarfs eines Erwachsenen entspricht.

Die Tomate enthält auch sehr viel Kalium, ein Gegengewicht zu Natrium, das wie dieses eine wichtige Rolle im Wasserhaushalt des Körpers spielt. Kalium verhindert, dass sich zu viel Wasser in den Körperzellen ansammelt, es reguliert die Wassermengen außer- und innerhalb der Zellen und wirkt blutdrucksenkend. Typische Kaliummangelerscheinungen sind weiters Schlafstörungen, Nervosität oder Kopfschmerzen.

Der Eisengehalt der Tomate ist zwar nicht besonders hoch, aber durch ihr im Gegensatz dazu reichlich vorhandenes Vitamin C kann das für die Bildung der roten Blutkörperchen wichtige Spurenelement besonders gut verwertet werden.

Ein ganz besonderes gesundheitliches Plus der roten Früchtchen ist das zu den Carotinoiden zählende Lycopin. Dieser sekundäre Pflanzenstoff kommt vor allem in kräftigen roten Tomatensorten vor. Lycopine gelten mittlerweile als echte Geheimwaffe gegen die Entstehung von Krebs und als wirksamer Schutz vor Infarkten. Lycopin ist ein »Radikalfänger« und stabilisiert unsere Zellwände. Diese bioaktiven Substanzen wurden vor allem in den letzten Jahren eingehend erforscht, seit den 1990er-Jahren gibt es dazu etwa in den USA zahlreiche groß angelegte Studien. Besonders der Verzehr von Tomatenprodukten zeigt sich dabei als wirkungsvoll, da Lycopin gut aufgenommen werden kann, wenn die Früchte möglichst stark zerkleinert und am besten auch erwärmt werden. Vor allem das Erhitzen in Verbindung mit Öl macht das Lycopin für unseren Körper leicht aufnehmbar – so betrachtet ist auch Ketchup gar keine so ungesunde Sache.

Aber die Tomate kann noch mehr: Sie verschafft uns gute Laune, und das liegt in der Hauptsache an einer Substanz namens Tyramin, die in vollreifen Tomaten reichlich enthalten ist. Tyramin hebt den Blutzuckerspiegel und sorgt für positive Stimmung. In der einschlägigen Literatur wird daher durchaus empfohlen, täglich sehr reife bis fast überreife Tomaten roh zu verzehren, wenn man unter schlechter Laune und Stimmungsschwankungen leidet.

Ebenfalls gut für Gemüt: Folsäure. Dieses B-Vitamin ist wichtig für die Produktion von »Glückshormonen«, es regelt den Seratoninspiegel. Besonders während der Schwangerschaft sollten Frauen ausreichend davon zu sich nehmen.

Weniger gesundheitsförderlich ist dagegen die Tatsache, dass sich in unreifen Tomaten das giftige Solanin findet. Und zwar in einer Konzentration von 9 bis 32 mg pro 100 g Frucht. Nimmt man Solanin in geringen Mengen (ab 25 mg) zu sich, spürt man lediglich ein Kratzen oder Brennen im Hals. In größeren Mengen genossen, kann es zu Übelkeit, Durchfall und Krämpfen führen, in schweren Fällen auch zu Atemnot und Bewusstlosigkeit. Eine Dosis von 400 mg ist tödlich.

In reifen Tomaten (auch in ausgereift grünen Sorten) ist Solanin vollständig abgebaut, lediglich im Stielansatz finden sich Spuren davon. Deshalb ist auch in manchen Rezepten angegeben, den Strunk zu entfernen. Aber auch Gerichte mit unreifen Tomaten können in normalen Mengen ruhig verzehrt werden, da der Solaningehalt wie beschrieben gering ist. Solanin wird übrigens durch Kochen zu rund einem Drittel abgebaut bzw. gelöst, allerdings nicht durch Tiefkühlen.

Manche Menschen meiden Tomaten wegen ihres Gehaltes an Oxalsäure. Die Oxalsäure bildet mit Kalzium nicht lösliche Salze, die zur Entstehung von Nierensteinen führen können. Der Oxalgehalt der Tomate ist allerdings mit 5,3 mg pro 100 g geringer als von Kopfsalat (17 mg/100 g) und daher als niedrig anzusehen. Darüber hinaus wirkt die Tomate harntreibend und blutreinigend, was die Nierentätigkeit eher erleichtert.

So viele Sorten …

Oder: 10 000-mal genetische Identität

Die Tomate ist eine krautige, robuste, aber sehr frostempfindliche Pflanze. In kälteren Regionen wird sie meist als einjähriges Gewächs kultiviert, in warmen Regionen kann sie sehr langlebig sein und auch mehrere Jahre hintereinander Früchte tragen. Tomaten sind botanisch gesehen eigentlich Beeren, also Früchte. Sie enthalten reichlich Fruchtsäuren und Zucker, werden allerdings kulinarisch eher wie Gemüse verwendet. In den Einteilungen der Anbaufachbücher finden sie sich daher oft unter der Bezeichnung Fruchtgemüse.

Sie gehören zur Familie der Nachtschattengewächse – zu der auch die Kartoffel, die Paprika, der Tabak, die Aubergine, die Petunie oder die Chili gehören – und zur Gattung Lycopersicon. Diese Gattung wiederum wird in neun Gruppen je nach verschiedenen Kriterien wie Farbe, Kerngröße, Struktur der Blattränder und des Stiels oder Samenanzahl unterteilt. Die Art *Lycopersicon esculentum* gilt dabei als Ursprungspflanze der meisten heute angebauten Sorten.

Die Früchte sind meist rot, können aber auch in vielen anderen Varianten von orange bis gelb und von weiß oder violett bis grün gestreift auftreten. Die zarten, rund 1,5 Zentimeter großen Blüten dagegen sind immer gelb gefärbt, und die Bestäubung erfolgt durch die eigenen Pollen jeder Blüte. Zum Beispiel durch jene Erschütterungen, die der Flügelschlag der Hummeln auslöst, jenen häufigen Besuchern der Tomatenblüten. Es kommt auch zu Fremdbestäubung, besonders leicht etwa bei Sorten, die weit aus der Blüte herausragende Griffel haben – was bei der Zucht nicht immer erwünscht ist, nämlich wenn Sorten samenecht erhalten werden sollen.

Der typische und manchmal sehr intensive Tomatengeruch geht übrigens vom Stiel und nicht von der Blüte aus. (Das ist wohl mit ein Grund, warum im Handel die Nachfrage nach Rispentomaten in den letzten Jahren so sprunghaft gestiegen ist. Nicht nur in Deutschland greifen die Verbraucher aufgrund des intensiven Geruchs gern zu den mit Stiel angebotenen Früchten. Allerdings sind es gar nicht die Früchte, die so betörend duften, sondern die grünen Rispen – was über die Qualität der einzelnen Tomaten naturgemäß relativ wenig aussagt.)

Tomaten gehören zu den am weitesten verbreiteten Kulturpflanzen der Erde und sind von großer wirtschaftlicher Relevanz. Seit tausenden Jahren werden sie kultiviert und dabei jeweils besondere Vorzüge gefördert. Menschen suchten nach besserem Geschmack oder größerem Ertrag, man wollte Sorten, die robust gegen Wetterkapriolen, Krankheiten oder Schädlinge waren. Bestehende Sorten wurden gekreuzt, neue hervorgebracht, ausgesuchtes Samenmaterial vermehrt und wieder angebaut. Eine aufwendige Angelegenheit, die Erfahrung und Wissen voraussetzte.

Spätestens seit dem Beginn der Massenproduktion zu Beginn des 20. Jahrhunderts rückten dann andere Kriterien ins Zentrum der Aufmerksamkeit, da Märkte in kälteren Regionen das ganze Jahr über mit den beliebten frischen Früchten versorgt werden wollten. Die Tomaten sollten lange haltbar sein, dabei wie frisch gepflückt aussehen und sich über weite Strecken transportieren lassen. Geschmackliche Qualität oder Erhaltung der Artenvielfalt trat – wie bei vielen Nutzpflanzen – in den Hintergrund. Vor allem der Einsatz der Gentechnik schien in der Folge ungeahnte Möglichkeiten zu eröffnen und Produkte wie die »Anti-Matsch-Tomate« wurden entwickelt. Sie war das erste genmanipulierte Gemüse, das 1994 in den USA angeboten wurde – und bei den Konsumenten gewaltig floppte. (Hauptsächlich, weil es sich als geschmacklich äußerst dürftig herausstellte.) Weitere Entwicklungen waren zum Beispiel die »Antivirus-Tomate« des Saatgutherstellers Monsanto und Ähnliches.

Viele der heute im weltweiten Erwerbsanbau verwendeten Sorten sind sogenannte »Longlife-Tomaten«. Diese Sorten können sowohl lange Zeit reif am Stock hängen als auch bis zu 20 Tage, manche sprechen sogar von bis zu sieben Wochen, gelagert werden. Geschmacklich schneiden sie allerdings meist weniger gut ab.

Das vorläufige Ende vom Lied: Wir beklagen mittlerweile einen weltweiten Rückgang der Artenvielfalt. So spricht etwa die internationale Slow-Food-Vereinigung von einem unwiederbringlichen Verlust von 75 Prozent (!) an Nutzpflanzen in den letzten 100 Jahren, ähnlich dramatisch sind die Zahlen auch bei Nutztierrassen. Vereinigungen wie »Slow Food« setzen sich daher vehement für den Erhalt dieses »Weltkulturerbes des Essens« ein – und können dabei auf steigende Nachfrage bewusster Verbraucher bauen. »Alte Sorten kommen total gut an«, weiß auch Margit Lamm, Biobäuerin und Absolventin der Universität für Bodenkultur aus Oberösterreich. Sie hat sich im Rahmen der großen Genusslandessausstellung »Mahlzeit« speziell mit dem Thema Tomaten auseinandergesetzt. Ihr Resümee: Die Menschen wollen wieder Ursprüngliches, Echtes und zwar nicht nur als fertiges Produkt gekauft, sondern auch selbst gezüchtet. »Vor allem in Zeiten von Finanzkrisen und wirtschaftlichen Unsicherheiten bauen Menschen ihr Gemüse wieder gern selbst an«, so Lamm. Privat gepflanzt wird dabei längst nicht nur in ländlichen Regionen, sondern auch in großen städtischen Ballungszentren, wo »City Gardening« der große Trend ist, manchmal sogar von der öffentlichen Hand gefördert. Schätzungen sprechen davon, dass in Deutschland mittlerweile genauso viele Tomaten daheim auf Fensterbänken und in Gärten gezogen werden wie im erwerbsmäßigen Anbau.

Ein ganz besonders spannendes Thema in dem Zusammenhang ist die Herstellung von Saatgut. Margit Lamm: »Viele Menschen wissen heute gar nicht, wie sehr wir da von internationalen Multis abhängig sind.« Saatgut wird nicht mehr von Landwirten selbst hergestellt, sondern Jahr für Jahr von wenigen großen internationalen Herstellerfirmen bezogen. Der überwiegende Teil davon in Form von sogenannten »Hybridsorten«, die nicht oder nur sehr eingeschränkt selbst vermehrungsfähig sind. (Im Gegensatz zu sogenannten »samenechten Sorten«, die wie seit Jahrtausenden zur Herstellung von neuem Saatgut aus den Früchten der Pflanze herangezogen werden können.)

Die österreichische Organisation »Arche Noah« hat es sich in diesem Zusammenhang als eine der ersten in Europa zur Aufgabe gemacht, altes Saatgut und damit die Vielfalt der Kulturpflanzen zu erhalten. Im Laufe der letzten 20 Jahre wurde ein gewaltiges Archiv von Samen der verschiedensten Obst- und Gemüsesorten aufgebaut. Zahlreiche Erwerbsgärtnereien und landwirtschaftliche Betriebe arbeiten eng mit der »Arche Noah« zusammen und unterstützen durch den Anbau dieser Raritäten die Arbeit des gemeinnützigen Vereins. Alljährlich wird auch ein großer Pflanzenmarkt im niederösterreichischen Schiltern veranstaltet. Das Lieblingsgemüse Paradeiser steht dabei ganz oben auf der Wunschliste der vielen Tausend Besucher. Unglaublich viele verschiedene Sorten werden auf dem Markt angeboten, und sie werden verkauft wie die sprichwörtlichen warmen Semmeln.

Die Erhaltung der Vielfalt hat dabei weitreichende Bedeutungen, wie Obst- und Beerenexperte Bernd Kajtna der »Arche Noah« erläutert. Und das geht weit über geschmackliche Vorlieben hinaus. Nicht alles, was eine alte Sorte ist, schmeckt schließlich auch automatisch gut – und durchkosten kann sich durch die weltweit insgesamt geschätzten 10 000 Tomatensorten ja wohl auch niemand mehr. Warum also Tausende Sorten aufwendig erhalten?

Die Antwort ist einfach: »Jede Sorte«, so Experte Kajtna, »hat ihre eigene genetische Identität und gibt diese an ihre Nachkommen weiter.« Das sei vor allem für Neuzüchtungen und Kreuzungen wichtig. Etwa, wenn es darum geht, Tomaten an geänderte Klimabedingungen anzupassen oder widerstandsfähig gegen Krankheiten zu machen. Und nur durch möglichst große Vielfalt an genetischen Identitäten können auch vielfältige neue Sorten mit neuen Eigenschaften entstehen. Dabei kommen in manchen Fällen auch sogenannte »verborgene Eigenschaften« zum Tragen. Eigenschaften, die unter Umständen bei einer Pflanze gar nicht ausgeprägt sind, aber sehr wohl in der nächsten Generation auftreten können. Kajtna: »Es kann zum Beispiel sein, dass Sie zwei rote Tomatensorten kreuzen und heraus kommt eine grüne.« Allen Anforderungen kann aber natürlich nur mit den vorhandenen genetischen Informationen begegnet werden – je größer also der vorhandene Genpool, desto besser.

Die Bestrebungen, alte Sorten vor dem Aussterben zu retten, gibt es dabei vielerorts: Eine wiederentdeckte Rarität ist zum Beispiel die unter Gourmets so beliebte italienische San-Marzano-Tomate. Viel zu zart für die industrielle Massenproduktion war sie vor zwei Jahrzehnten fast ganz verschwunden. Mit Hilfe der örtlichen Regierung und Slow Food Italien gelang es quasi in letzter Minute, ihr Saatgut zu sichern, und inzwischen gibt es wieder einige Kulturen, die unter geschützter Herkunftsbezeichnung vor allem als Konserven vermarktet werden.

Ab in die Küche

Hier befinden wir uns auf ganz und gar erfreulichem Terrain: Die Tomate ist ein echtes Küchen-Multitalent, sie verträgt fast alles und sich mit fast allem – ob sauer oder süß, bitter, würzig oder scharf. Gabriele Halper, Food-Stylistin und Autorin zahlreicher wunderbarer Rezepte, so auch für das vorliegende Buch, formuliert es so: »Ein Allround-Genie, das alles kann.« Am besten frische, sonnenreife Früchte verwenden, dann kann – fast – nichts mehr schiefgehen.

Besonders gut steht den Tomaten immer ein wenig Zucker, Süße hebt das Tomaten-Aroma zusätzlich. Eine weitere sehr harmonische Kombination sind Tomaten mit Orangenschale und Minze. Gabriele Halper: »Das passt zum Beispiel sehr gut für Saucen, die Orangenschale betont die Fruchtigkeit der Tomate noch zusätzlich.«

Tomaten verfügen auch über ein natürliches Säure-Zucker-Verhältnis, das sich besonders positiv auf viele Gerichte auswirkt. Es schafft harmonisch-aromatischen Ausgleich, gibt Saucen eine wunderschöne Farbe und bringt immer eine leichte Säure mit ins Spiel. Sind die Tomaten wirklich ausgereift, entsteht auch allein schon durch den karamellisierenden Fruchtzucker eine optimale Saucenbindung. Und apropos gut ausgereift: »Ich kann nur sagen, wer's einmal probiert hat, wird wahrscheinlich nie wieder etwas anderes verwenden. Eine Sauce aus einer sonnenreifen, üppigen Sommertomate ist eine herrliche Sache – aus einer wenn auch frischen, aber wässrigen Winterfrucht dagegen eine traurige Angelegenheit.« Halpers Tipp daher: Wenn Tomaten gerade nicht Saison haben, lieber auf hochwertige Dosenware zurückgreifen. Oder aber im Sommer selbst einlegen – Rezepte dazu finden Sie in diesem Buch – und in der kalten Jahreszeit Selbstgemachtes aus dem Glas genießen.

Gelagert werden sollten Tomaten am besten bei Zimmertemperatur oder maximal im gemäßigten Zonenfach des Kühlschrankes. Bitte nicht direkt im Kühlschrank, da geht viel vom Aroma verloren. Interessant dabei: Gut reife Tomaten werden auch bei ungekühlter Aufbewahrung nicht faulig. Müssen sie ausnahmsweise einmal unbedingt doch in den Kühlschrank – dann vor dem Verarbeiten kurz ins Rohr oder noch besser in die pralle Sonne legen.

Aromaintensive Sorten eignen sich am besten für den frischen Genuss. Da können sich zarte Geschmäcker oder ein raffiniertes Säure-Zucker-Spiel voll entfalten. Beim Kochen würde das Aroma zum Beispiel einer zarten Ananastomate aber einfach untergehen. Zum Einkochen oder für die Saucenzubereitung passt daher eher eine kräftige, rotschalige Sorte, wie etwa die klassische Flaschen- oder Eiertomate. Da stimmt auch das Säure-Zucker-Verhältnis ganz von selbst perfekt. Gute, reife Sommertomaten sollte man, so Expertin Halper, auch lieber nicht entkernen oder schälen, denn auch dabei geht viel Geschmack verloren.

Was nicht so gut funktioniert: Tomaten tiefkühlen – da bleibt beim Auftauen nur noch Matsch übrig. Und auch der Prozess des Tomatentrocknens an der Luft ist leider nicht unbedingt für unsere Breiten geeignet, das klappt eigentlich nur wirklich gut in der sizilianischen Turbosonne. Selbst im Ofen und ohne professionelle Geräte ist es eine eher schwierige Angelegenheit für den Privatgebrauch. Die Früchte nehmen die vorhandene Luftfeuchtigkeit einfach immer wieder auf – und können daher später leicht faulig werden, wenn sie nicht wirklich durch und durch getrocknet sind.

Aber ob Salat, Sulz, Suppe, Sorbet oder Drink, ob mit Fleisch, Huhn, Fisch oder solo, ob einfach und schnell für den Familienalltag oder aufwendig und verführerisch für erlesene Gäste zubereitet: Die Tomaten-Küche erfüllt von Gesundheit bis Geschmack und von traditionell bis trendig einfach immer und in jeder Form eine Menge an hohen kulinarischen Ansprüchen.

In diesem Sinne: Willkommen im Paradeiser-Paradies!

Tomaten selbst züchten

Die eigene Tomatenstaude vor der Haustüre wird immer beliebter. Vor allem alte Sorten sind frisch gepflückt ein wahres Geschmackserlebnis – und die Samen fürs nächste Anbaujahr sind all inclusive. Wer es selbst versuchen will: Die Herstellung von Samenmaterial für den Hausgebrauch lässt sich relativ leicht machen, wie die Wiener Expertin für alte Obst- und Gemüsesorten Eveline Bach erklärt. Sie hat den Großteil der in diesem Buch gezeigten Prachtexemplare in ihrer Gärtnerei kultiviert und gibt dazu folgende Tipps zur Samengewinnung:

- Die kräftigste und schönste Pflanze voll ausreifen lassen
- Dann die Früchte aufschneiden und die Samen in einem Sieb kurz waschen
- Schließlich auf hartem Untergrund (zum Beispiel Glas oder Porzellan) trocknen lassen und in Papiertütchen bis zur Aussaat im März luftig und trocken aufbewahren.

In der Fachliteratur wird empfohlen, die Samen vor dem Trocknen in Wasser gären zu lassen, um dadurch die Samenhülle quasi zu »knacken«. Dabei muss man aufpassen, dass die Samen ja nicht zu lang im Wasser bleiben, »und es geht auch ohne, das kann ich aus Erfahrung sagen«, so Gärtnerin Bach.

Ins Glas

Eingelegte Kirschtomaten mit Rosmarin

Ergibt 4 Gläser à 250 ml

1 kg Kirschtomaten
2 EL Olivenöl
Salz
4 Knoblauchzehen
2 EL Pinienkerne
2 EL schwarze Oliven (mit Stein)
2 EL frische Rosmarinnadeln
250 ml Olivenöl extra vergine zum Auffüllen

Zubereitungszeit: ca. 30 Minuten plus 5 Stunden Zeit zum Trocknen

1 Die Kirschtomaten waschen und gut trocknen lassen.

2 Die Kirschtomaten halbieren, mit der Schnittfläche nach oben auf ein mit 2 EL Olivenöl bestrichenes Backblech legen und leicht mit Salz bestreuen.

3 Den Knoblauch schälen, in dünne Scheiben schneiden, über die Kirschtomaten geben und im auf 100 °C vorgeheizten Backofen etwa 5 Stunden trocknen. (Dabei die Ofentür einen Spalt offen lassen.)

4 Die getrockneten Kirschtomaten mit den Pinienkernen, den schwarzen Oliven und dem beim Trocknen ausgetretenen Saft in 4 Gläser geben, mit den Rosmarinnadeln bestreuen und mit dem restlichen Olivenöl auffüllen.

5 Die Gläser fest verschließen und die eingelegten Tomaten mindestens 3 bis 4 Tage ziehen lassen.

Tipp: Die eingelegten Kirschtomaten sind ein feines Antipasto, sie passen auch zu kaltem Braten, dünn aufgeschnittenem rohem Schinken oder Salami.

Eingelegtes Lauch-Tomaten-Gemüse mit Dörrzwetschgen

Ergibt ca. 800 ml

500 g vollreife Tomaten
2 große Lauchstangen (ca. 500 g)
200 g entsteinte getrocknete Zwetschgen
500 ml Gemüsefond
2 Zweige Rosmarin
5 EL Olivenöl extra vergine
Saft von 1 Zitrone
Salz
frisch gemahlener Pfeffer

Zubereitungszeit: ca. 70 Minuten

1 Die Tomaten am Stielansatz kreuzweise einschneiden.

2 Reichlich Wasser in einem großen Topf zum Kochen bringen. Die Tomaten darin portionsweise je 1 Minute blanchieren.

3 Die Tomaten kurz in Eiswasser abkühlen lassen, dann häuten, vierteln und entkernen.

4 Den Lauch putzen und in 3 cm große Stücke schneiden.

5 Die Tomaten, den Lauch und die Zwetschgen mit dem Gemüsefond in einen großen (am besten gusseisernen) Topf geben. Die Rosmarinzweige und das Olivenöl hinzufügen und das Gemüse bei geringer Temperatur etwa 40 bis 45 Minuten weich schmoren.

6 Das gare Gemüse mit dem Zitronensaft, Salz und Pfeffer abschmecken und heiß in saubere Einmachgläser füllen. Die Gläser fest verschließen und das Gemüse abkühlen lassen. (Im Kühlschrank hält sich das eingelegte Gemüse etwa 2 Monate.)

Tipp: Das eingelegte Lauch-Tomaten-Gemüse passt gut zu gegrilltem Fleisch oder leicht erwärmt zu Schafkäse. Auch ist es eine feine Omelettefüllung.

Eingelegte Steinpilz-Tomaten

Ergibt 2 Gläser à 400 ml

500 g kleine, ovale Tomaten (»Mini-Ovalis«)
500 g frische Steinpilze
2 kleine Knoblauchzehen, geschält
1 TL Meersalz
250 ml Olivenöl extra vergine
2 Zweige Rosmarin
4 EL weißer Aceto balsamico

Zubereitungszeit: ca. 1 Stunde 40 Minuten

1. Die Tomaten am Stielansatz kreuzweise einschneiden.
2. Reichlich Wasser in einem großen Topf zum Kochen bringen. Die Tomaten darin portionsweise je 1 Minute blanchieren.
3. Die Tomaten kurz in Eiswasser abkühlen lassen, dann häuten, vierteln und entkernen.
4. Die Steinpilze putzen und in etwa 1/2 cm breite Scheiben schneiden.
5. Die Tomatenviertel mit den Pilzen und dem Knoblauch in einen ofenfesten gusseisernen Topf geben, mit dem Meersalz bestreuen und mit dem Olivenöl übergießen.
6. Die Rosmarinnadeln von den Zweigen zupfen, zu den Tomaten geben und im auf 80 °C vorgeheizten Backofen etwa 1 Stunde ziehen lassen.
7. Die Steinpilz-Tomaten-Mischung mit dem Öl in 2 saubere Einmachgläser füllen und je 2 Esslöffel Aceto balsamico zugeben. Die Gläser in einen großen Topf oder eine Fettpfanne stellen, reichlich heißes Wasser angießen, sodass die Gläser zu 3/4 im Wasserbad stehen, und im auf 120 °C vorgeheizten Backofen 20 Minuten sterilisieren. Die eingelegten Steinpilz-Tomaten einige Tage ziehen lassen.

Tipp: Die eingelegten Steinpilz-Tomaten sind ein feines Antipasto. Auch leicht erwärmt mit Parmesan bestreut und frischem Weißbrot ergeben sie eine tolle Vorspeise.

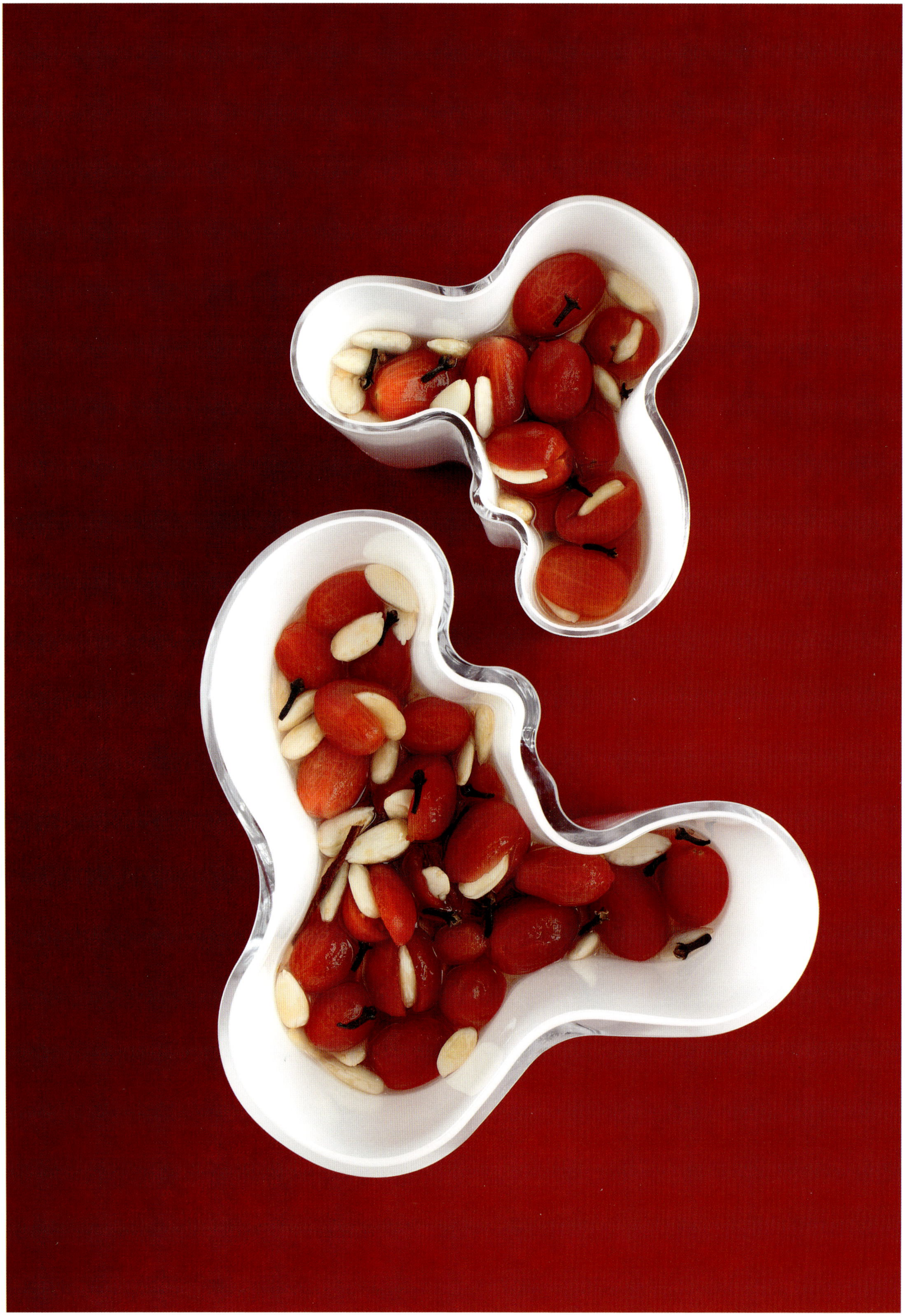

Kirschtomaten mit Mandelkernen in Nelkensirup

Ergibt 4 Gläser à 350 ml

1 kg feste, ovale Kirschtomaten

300 g geschälte Mandelkerne

Saft von 2 Zitronen

500 g Gelierzucker (3 : 1)

1 Zimtstange

5 Gewürznelken

2 Pimentkörner

fein geriebene Schale von 1 kleinen Zitrone (Bioware)

Zubereitungszeit: ca. 1 Stunde

1 Reichlich Wasser in einem Topf zum Kochen bringen. Die Tomaten darin portionsweise je 10 Sekunden blanchieren.

2 Die Tomaten aus dem Wasser nehmen, in Eiswasser abschrecken, häuten und auf Küchenkrepp abtropfen lassen.

3 Den Stielansatz der Tomaten herausschneiden. Vorsichtig die Kerne aus den Tomaten drücken.

4 Jede Tomate mit einem Mandelkern füllen. Die gefüllten Tomaten in eine Schüssel legen und mit dem Zitronensaft beträufeln.

5 Den Gelierzucker mit 750 ml Wasser, der Zimtstange, den Gewürznelken und den Pimentkörnern in einen Topf geben, aufkochen und 3 bis 4 Minuten sprudelnd kochen lassen.

6 Die Tomaten aus dem Zitronensaft nehmen, erneut auf Küchenkrepp abtropfen lassen, in den heißen Sirup legen und 6 bis 7 Minuten darin ziehen lassen.

7 Die Tomaten mit einem Schaumlöffel aus dem Sirup nehmen und in 4 Einmachgläser füllen, bis jedes Glas zu 2/3 gefüllt ist.

8 Die fein geriebene Zitronenschale und die restlichen Mandelkerne in den heißen Sirup geben. Den Sirup erneut aufkochen und 2 bis 3 Minuten kochen lassen.

9 Den Sirup kurz abkühlen lassen und die Zimtstange entfernen. Den Sirup über die Tomaten in den Gläsern gießen und die Gläser fest verschließen. Die eingelegten Tomaten mindestens 14 Tage ziehen lassen. Sie sind im verschlossenen Glas bis zu 1 Jahr haltbar.

Tipp: Diese Tomaten passen zu griechischem Joghurt, Vanilleeis, Grießpudding oder als süße Beilage zu herzhaftem Käse.

Mit Zitronenthymian gefüllte Tomaten in Olivenöl

Ergibt 3–4 Gläser à 350 ml

12 Flaschentomaten
1 kleine rote Paprikaschote (ca. 150 g)
4 Knoblauchzehen
2 EL frische Zitronenthymianblättchen
1 TL fein geriebene Zitronenschale (Bioware)
1 EL Meersalz
750 ml Olivenöl extra vergine

Zubereitungszeit: ca. 2 Stunden

1 Die Tomaten am Stielansatz kreuzweise einschneiden.

2 Reichlich Wasser in einem großen Topf zum Kochen bringen. Die Tomaten darin portionsweise je 1 Minute blanchieren.

3 Die Tomaten aus dem Wasser nehmen, in Eiswasser abschrecken, häuten und auf Küchenkrepp abtropfen lassen.

4 Die Tomaten der Länge nach halbieren, die Hälften dabei nicht ganz trennen und aufklappen. Die aufgeklappten Tomaten auf ein mit Backpapier belegtes Backblech legen und im auf 150 °C vorgeheizten Backofen 40 Minuten braten. (Die Ränder der Tomaten sollen leicht schrumpelig werden.) Das Blech aus dem Ofen nehmen und die Tomaten vollständig abkühlen lassen.

5 Für die Füllung die Paprika putzen, halbieren, von Stielansatz, Scheidewänden und Kernen befreien und in kleine Würfel schneiden.

6 Den Knoblauch schälen und fein hacken, dann mit den Paprikawürfeln, dem Thymian, dem Zitronenabrieb und dem Meersalz vermengen.

7 Je 1 Hälfte jeder aufgeklappten Tomate mit der Füllung bestreichen, dann vorsichtig zusammenklappen. Die Tomaten bei Bedarf mit Küchengarn zusammenbinden.

8 Die Tomaten in saubere Einmachgläser füllen und diese mit dem Olivenöl auffüllen. Die Einmachgläser fest verschließen und die Tomaten mindestens 2 Tage im Kühlschrank durchziehen lassen.

Tipp: Reichen Sie diese Tomaten als Vorspeise, auf einem Anti-Pasti-Teller oder als Snack mit frischem Weißbrot.

Grüne Tomaten im süßen Pfeffersud

Für 4 Gläser à 350 ml

1 kg kleine grüne Tomaten (unreife rote Tomaten)
350 g Zucker
1 EL Szechuanpfeffer oder 4 Stück langer Pfeffer
1 Zimtstange
1 EL Pimentkörner
5 Gewürznelken
1 Stück Ingwerwurzel (ca. 2 cm), in feine Streifen geschnitten
1 TL Salz

Zubereitungszeit: ca. 70 Minuten

1 Die Tomaten waschen, auf Küchenkrepp gut abtropfen lassen, dann jede Tomate mehrmals mit einer Nadel einstechen. Die Tomaten in 4 saubere Einmachgläser füllen, bis jedes Glas zu ca. 2/3 gefüllt ist.

2 Für den Gewürzsud 1 l Wasser mit dem Zucker, dem Szechuanpfeffer, dem Zimt, dem Piment, den Gewürznelken und dem Ingwer in einen Topf geben und aufkochen. Den Sud bei mittlerer Temperatur etwa 10 Minuten köcheln lassen, dann das Salz hinzufügen.

3 Den heißen Sud über die Tomaten gießen, die Gläser sofort verschließen und abkühlen lassen.

4 Die Gläser in einen ofenfesten Topf stellen und diesen mit heißem Wasser füllen, sodass die Gläser zu ca. 2/3 im Wasser stehen. Die Gläser im auf 120 °C vorgeheizten Backofen etwa 50 Minuten sterilisieren. (Bei kühler und trockener Lagerung halten sich die Tomaten etwa 3 Monate.)

Tipp: Die eingelegten Tomaten passen gut zu gebratenem Rind- oder Lammfleisch, aber auch zu würzigem Käse.

Schnelle Sommer-Pickles mit Tomaten

Ergibt 4 Gläser

350 g frische kleine Perlzwiebeln
300 g Kirschtomaten
1 große Salatgurke
1 l Reisweinessig
250 g Zucker
2 EL Salz
1 1/2 EL schwarze Pfefferkörner
1 Jalapeño-Chili
3 Zweige Thymian oder Rosmarin
1 frisches Lorbeerblatt
2–3 Fäden Safran

Zubereitungszeit: ca. 30 Minuten

1. Die Perlzwiebeln in kochendem Salzwasser etwa 8 Minuten weich kochen, dann herausnehmen und kurz in Eiswasser abschrecken. Die Perlzwiebeln schälen und beiseitestellen.
2. Die Kirschtomaten waschen und gründlich trocknen.
3. Die Gurke schälen, längs halbieren, vom Kerngehäuse befreien und in etwa 1 cm dicke Scheiben schneiden.
4. Für die Marinade den Reisweinessig mit dem Zucker, dem Salz, den Pfefferkörnern, der Chilischoteden Thymianzweigen, dem Lorbeerblatt und dem Safran in einen großen Topf geben, dann 100 ml Wasser zugeben und aufkochen. Den Topf vom Herd nehmen und die Chilischote herausnehmen.
5. Die Perlzwiebeln, die Kirschtomaten und die Gurkenscheiben in saubere Einmachgläser füllen, mit der heißen Marinade übergießen und die Gläser fest verschließen.
6. Die Pickles abkühlen lassen und bis zum Verzehr im Kühlschrank aufbewahren, wo sie sich 2 Wochen halten.

Tipp: Die Sommer-Pickles passen zu Gegrilltem und zu kaltem Braten.

Tomatensirup mit Chili

Ergibt ca. 1 l

2 kg vollreife Fleisch- oder Flaschentomaten
300 g Gelierzucker (3 : 1)
3 Zitronen
20 g Basilikumblätter
20 g gezupfte Minzeblättchen
2 Chilischoten

Zubereitungszeit: ca. 45 Minuten plus Abtropfzeit

1 Die Tomaten waschen, vierteln, von den Stielansätzen befreien und portionsweise im Mixer zu einem feinen Püree verarbeiten.

2 Ein großes Sieb mit einem sauberen Geschirrtuch auslegen und das Sieb auf eine dazu passende große Schüssel stellen. Das Püree hineingeben und 6 bis 7 Stunden (noch besser über Nacht) abtropfen lassen.

3 Den so entstandenen klaren Saft (Tomatenwasser, es sind ca. 1 1/2 l) in einen hohen Topf geben und um die Hälfte reduzieren.

4 Den Topf vom Herd nehmen. Den Gelierzucker mit einem Schneebesen zügig in die Reduktion rühren. Dann den Saft der Zitronen, das Basilikum und die Minze sowie die Chilis hinzufügen. Den Topf wieder auf den Herd stellen und den Sirup etwa 3 Minuten wallend kochen lassen.

5 Den heißen Sirup durch ein Sieb in Flaschen füllen und diese gut verschließen. Der Sirup ist bei kühler und trockener Lagerung ca. 3 Monate haltbar.

Tipp: Der Sirup eignet sich als Basis für Bowlen (z. B. Himbeer-Melonen-Bowle) oder als Prosecco-Spritz: 1–2 EL Tomatensirup mit 1–2 Blatt Basilikum oder Zitronenmelisse in ein Sektglas geben und mit gut gekühltem Prosecco oder Cava auffüllen.

Einfache Tomatensauce

Ergibt ca. 750 ml

1 1/2 kg vollreife Fleischtomaten
5 Knoblauchzehen
6 EL fruchtiges Olivenöl extra vergine
2 EL Kristallzucker
2 TL Salz

Zubereitungszeit: ca. 40 Minuten

1 Die Tomaten waschen, halbieren, vom Strunk befreien und in kleine Würfel schneiden.

2 Den Knoblauch schälen und fein hacken.

3 Das Olivenöl in einem großen Topf erhitzen und den Knoblauch darin kurz anschwitzen, dann den Zucker und die Tomatenwürfel zugeben und die Sauce kräftig aufkochen.

4 Die Herdtemperatur reduzieren und die Tomatensauce 20 bis 25 Minuten leicht köchelnd eindicken lassen, dann mit Salz abschmecken. (Wer eine besonders feine Sauce haben möchte, passiert die Sauce durch ein Sieb.)

5 Die fertige Tomatensauce abkühlen lassen. Sie hält sich in einem luftdicht verschlossenen Gefäß im Kühlschrank 3 Tage, im Gefrierfach 3 Monate.

Tipps: Diese einfache Sauce eignet sich bestens als Pizzabelag und als Basis für diverse Pastagerichte.
Kochen Sie die Sauce mit 2 Gewürznelken und 3 Pimentkörnern oder 1 Lorbeerblatt und einigen Pfefferkörnern.
Schmecken Sie die fertige Sauce mit gehackten Kapern oder Sardellen oder mit etwas frisch geriebener Orangenschale sowie frischen Kräutern (zum Beispiel Basilikum oder Minze) ab.

Mediterrane Tomatensauce mit kalt gepresstem Olivenöl

Ergibt etwa 850 ml

2 kg vollreife Fleischtomaten
2 große weiße Gemüsezwiebeln
2 Knoblauchzehen
4 EL Olivenöl extra vergine
3 EL Kristallzucker
250 ml trockener Weißwein
5 Zweige Oregano
1 daumengroßes Stück Zitronenschale

Zubereitungszeit: ca. 75 Minuten

1. Die Tomaten am Stielansatz kreuzweise einschneiden.
2. Reichlich Wasser in einem großen Topf zum Kochen bringen. Die Tomaten darin portionsweise je 1 Minute blanchieren.
3. Die Tomaten aus dem Wasser nehmen, in Eiswasser abschrecken, häuten, halbieren, entkernen und grob hacken.
4. Die Zwiebeln und den Knoblauch schälen und grob hacken.
5. Die 4 EL Olivenöl in einem kleinen Topf bei mittlerer Temperatur erhitzen und mit dem Zucker hellbraun karamellisieren. Die Zwiebeln und den Knoblauch darin anschwitzen, dann mit dem Weißwein ablöschen, die Tomaten, den Oregano und die Zitronenschale hinzufügen und alles bei mittlerer Temperatur 40 bis 50 Minuten zu einer dicken Sauce einkochen.

250 ml kalt gepresstes Olivenöl zusätzlich
Salz
frisch gemahlener Pfeffer

6 Den Topf vom Herd nehmen, die Kräuter und die Zitronenschale entfernen. Das Olivenöl langsam und gründlich in die Sauce rühren. Die Sauce mit Salz und Pfeffer abschmecken.
7 Die Sauce heiß in saubere Einmachgläser füllen und abkühlen lassen, dann kühl lagern.

Tipps: Wenn Sie die Sauce haltbar machen wollen, sterilisieren Sie die Gläser 30 Minuten im heißen Wasserbad im auf 120 °C vorgeheizten Backofen. Dann kann die Sauce auch bei Zimmertemperatur gelagert werden.
Diese Sauce eignet sich wegen ihrer dickeren Konsistenz als schnell zubereitete Pastasauce oder als Bruschettabelag, den Sie mit zerdrückten Sardellenfilets, Chili oder geriebenem Manchego verfeinern können.

Auberginen-Tomaten-Püree mit gebratenem Knoblauch

Ergibt ca. 450 ml

1 Melanzani (Aubergine, ca. 400 g)
2 Fleischtomaten (ca. 500 g)
5 Knoblauchzehen
5 EL Olivenöl extra vergine
4 EL fein gehackte Blattpetersilie
Saft von 1 Zitrone
Meersalz
frisch gemahlener Pfeffer

Zubereitungszeit: ca. 1 1/2 Stunden

1 Die Aubergine mehrmals mit einer Gabel einstechen, dann mit etwas Salz einreiben, in Alufolie wickeln und im auf 200 °C vorgeheizten Backofen (Ober-/Unterhitze) etwa 40 bis 50 Minuten weich garen. Die weiche Aubergine aus dem Ofen nehmen, die Alufolie entfernen und die Aubergine abkühlen lassen.

2 Die Tomaten waschen, halbieren, vom Stielansatz befreien und in kleine Würfel schneiden.

3 Den Knoblauch schälen und in feine Scheiben schneiden.

4 Das Olivenöl in einem Topf erhitzen und den Knoblauch darin hellbraun anbraten, dann die Tomatenwürfel hinzufügen und so lange köcheln lassen, bis alle Flüssigkeit verkocht ist. Den Topf vom Herd nehmen.

5 Die gare Aubergine aus der Folie nehmen und halbieren. Das Fruchtfleisch mit einem Löffel auslösen und grob hacken.

6 Das Auberginenfleisch mit den gekochten Tomaten vermengen, dann die Petersilie und den Zitronensaft hineinrühren. Das Püree mit Salz und Pfeffer abschmecken.

7 Das Püree in saubere Einmachgläser füllen und 3 bis 4 Tage ziehen lassen.

Tipps: Sterilisieren Sie die Gläser 30 Minuten im heißen Wasserbad im auf 120 °C vorgeheizten Backofen. Dann kann die Sauce auch bei Zimmertemperatur gelagert werden.
Dieses Püree ergibt eine tolle Pastasauce, einen Aufstrich für getoastetes Weißbrot oder einen Begleiter für weichen Käse.

Paprika-Tomaten-Sauce mit Vanillearoma

Ergibt ca. 1 l

1 kg vollreife Fleisch- oder Flaschentomaten
2 große rote Paprikaschoten (ca. 350 g)
4 Schalotten
4 Knoblauchzehen
125 ml Olivenöl extra vergine
2 Zweige Thymian
1 Zweig Rosmarin
1 Vanilleschote
1 Chilischote
500 ml Gemüse- oder Hühnerfond
Salz
frisch gemahlener Pfeffer

Zubereitungszeit: ca. 60–70 Minuten

1. Die Tomaten waschen, halbieren, vom Stielansatz befreien und grob hacken.
2. Die Paprika putzen, halbieren, von Stielansatz, Scheidewänden und Kernen befreien und in kleine Würfel schneiden.
3. Die Schalotten schälen und in kleine Würfel schneiden.
4. Den Knoblauch schälen und fein würfeln.
5. Das Olivenöl in einem Topf erhitzen. Die Schalotten und den Knoblauch darin kurz anschwitzen, dann die Paprika hinzufügen und 3 bis 4 Minuten mitschwitzen.
6. Die Tomaten, den Thymian, den Rosmarin, die ganze Vanilleschote und die ganze Chilischote hinzufügen und aufkochen, dann mit dem Gemüsefond aufgießen.
7. Die Sauce bei niedriger Temperatur etwa 40 Minuten köcheln lassen, dabei gelegentlich umrühren. Die Sauce dann durch ein Sieb streichen, nochmals erhitzen, mit Salz und Pfeffer abschmecken und heiß in saubere Einmachgläser füllen. Die Einmachgläser fest verschließen. Die Sauce ist im Kühlschrank ca. 3 Monate haltbar.

Tipps: Diese Sauce ist eine gute Basis für diverse Schmorgerichte oder kräftige Suppen, zum Beispiel eine Bouillabaisse. Bereiten Sie die Sauce mit 250 ml Fond und 250 ml kräftigem Rotwein zu – eine feine Variante!

Tomaten-Würzsauce mit Chili und Balsamico

Ergibt ca. 500 ml

1 kg vollreife Tomaten
6 EL Olivenöl
Salz
1 Zwiebel (ca. 100 g)
4 rote Chilischoten
3 EL brauner Rohrzucker
125 ml milder Aceto balsamico

Zubereitungszeit: ca. 70 Minuten

1. Die Tomaten vierteln, mit den Schnittflächen nach oben auf ein mit Backpapier bedecktes Backblech legen, mit 3 EL Olivenöl beträufeln und mit Salz bestreuen.
2. Die Tomaten im auf 200 °C vorgeheizten Backofen (Ober-/Unterhitze) etwa 30 Minuten braten, dann aus dem Ofen nehmen, abkühlen lassen, grob hacken und mit dem beim Braten entstandenen Saft in einen Topf geben.
3. Die Zwiebel schälen und in feine Würfel schneiden.
4. Die Chilischoten längs aufschlitzen, von den Samen befreien und fein hacken.
5. Das restliche Olivenöl in einer Pfanne erhitzen. Die Zwiebel und den Chili darin farblos anschwitzen, dann mit dem Zucker bestreuen.
6. Die Tomaten zu den Zwiebeln in die Pfanne geben und mit dem Aceto balsamico ablöschen. Die Sauce bei geringer Temperatur 20 Minuten leicht köchelnd reduzieren. Die Sauce mit Salz abschmecken.
7. Die heiße Sauce in saubere Einmachgläser oder Flaschen füllen und diese fest verschließen. Die Sauce vor dem Verzehr 2 bis 3 Tage durchziehen lassen. Die Sauce ist im Kühlschrank ca. 3 Monate haltbar.

Tipp: Diese Sauce passt zu kurz gebratenem Fleisch, Bratwürsten oder kaltem Braten (z. B. Roastbeef).

Tomatensauce »Santorini« mit Aranzini

Ergibt ca. 1 l

1 1/2 kg vollreife Fleisch- oder Flaschentomaten
250 ml frisch gepresster Orangensaft
2 Gemüsezwiebeln (ca. 180 g)
4 Knoblauchzehen
2 EL brauner Rohrzucker
2 Lorbeerblätter
1 kleine Zimtstange
50 g Aranzini (Orangeat)
65 ml Olivenöl extra vergine
Salz
frisch gemahlener Pfeffer
Olivenöl extra vergine zum Auffüllen

Zubereitungszeit: ca. 75 Minuten

1. Die Tomaten am Stielansatz kreuzweise einschneiden.
2. Reichlich Wasser in einem großen Topf zum Kochen bringen. Die Tomaten darin portionsweise je 1 Minute blanchieren.
3. Die Tomaten aus dem Wasser nehmen, in Eiswasser abschrecken, dann häuten, halbieren, entkernen und grob schneiden.
4. Die Tomaten mit dem Orangensaft in einen großen Topf geben und bei geringer Temperatur etwa 20 Minuten köcheln lassen. Dabei immer wieder den sich bildenden Schaum abschöpfen.
5. Die Zwiebeln und den Knoblauch schälen und grob hacken.
6. Die Zwiebeln und den Knoblauch mit dem Zucker, den Lorbeerblättern und der Zimtstange zu den Tomaten in den Topf geben und köcheln lassen, bis die Zwiebeln weich sind und zerfallen. Den Topf dann vom Herd nehmen und die Lorbeerblätter und die Zimtstange entfernen.
7. Die Aranzini fein hacken, mit dem Olivenöl verrühren und in die Tomatensauce rühren. Die Sauce mit Salz und Pfeffer abschmecken.
8. Die heiße Sauce in saubere Einmachgläser füllen, mit je 1 EL Olivenöl bedecken und die Gläser fest verschließen. Die Sauce ist bei kühler Lagerung ca. 3 Monate haltbar.

Tipp: Diese Sauce passt zu Pasta, Lamm und Geflügel, aber auch leicht erwärmt zu mildem griechischen Schafskäse.

Sauce Bolognese

Ergibt ca. 1–1 1/2 l

- 1 große Zwiebel (ca. 150 g)
- 2 Stangen Staudensellerie
- 1 Karotte (ca. 150 g)
- 125 ml Olivenöl extra vergine
- 800 g faschiertes (durchgedrehtes) Kalbfleisch (von der Schulter oder Wade)
- 3 EL dick eingekochtes Tomatenpüree oder Tomatenmark
- 5 Knoblauchzehen, fein gehackt
- 1 TL getrockneter Thymian
- 1 TL getrockneter Rosmarin
- 1 frisches Lorbeerblatt
- 750 ml Gemüse- oder Kalbsfond
- 1 kg vollreife Fleischtomaten
- Salz
- frisch gemahlener Pfeffer

Zubereitungszeit: ca. 2 Stunden

1. Die Zwiebel schälen und in kleine Würfel schneiden.
2. Den Staudensellerie waschen, von den Fäden befreien und in feine Scheiben schneiden.
3. Die Karotte putzen und in kleine Würfel schneiden.
4. Das Olivenöl in einem großen Topf erhitzen und die Zwiebeln darin glasig schwitzen. Dann den Staudensellerie und die Karotten hinzugeben und 5 bis 6 Minuten mitschwitzen.
5. Das Kalbsfaschierte zu dem Gemüse in den Topf geben, verteilen und 10 Minuten anbraten. Dabei hin und wieder umrühren.
6. Das Tomatenmark hineinrühren, dann den Knoblauch, den Thymian, den Rosmarin und das Lorbeerblatt hinzufügen, gut umrühren und mit dem Gemüsefond auffüllen. Die Sauce bei geringer Temperatur 30 Minuten köcheln lassen.
7. Die Tomaten waschen, halbieren, vom Stielansatz befreien und klein würfeln. Die Tomatenwürfel in die Sauce rühren. Die Sauce mit Salz und Pfeffer abschmecken und weitere 30 bis 40 Minuten köcheln lassen.
8. Die heiße Sauce in saubere Einmachgläser füllen und diese fest verschließen. Die Gläser in einen großen Topf oder eine Fettpfanne stellen, heißes Wasser angießen, sodass die Gläser zu 3/4 im Wasserbad stehen, und im auf 120 °C vorgeheizten Backofen 20 Minuten sterilisieren. Die Sauce Bolognese ist bei kühler Lagerung ca. 3 Monate haltbar.

Tipp: Die Sauce passt zu diversen Teigwaren und eignet sich zum Füllen von Gemüse oder Lasagne.

Tomaten »Passata«

Ergibt ca. 850 ml Sauce

2 kg vollreife Fleischtomaten oder vollreife fleischige gelbe Tomaten
2 EL Kristallzucker (bei gelben Tomaten 1 EL Kristallzucker)
Salz

Zubereitungszeit: ca. 1–1 1/2 Stunden

1 Die Tomaten am Stielansatz kreuzweise einschneiden.

2 Reichlich Wasser in einem großen Topf zum Kochen bringen. Die Tomaten darin portionsweise je 1 Minute blanchieren.

3 Die Tomaten aus dem Wasser nehmen, in Eiswasser abschrecken, dann häuten, halbieren, vom Stielansatz befreien, entkernen und klein würfeln.

4 Die Tomatenwürfel mit dem Zucker in einen Topf geben und bei geringer Temperatur leicht köchelnd um die Hälfte reduzieren.

5 Die Tomatensauce in der »Flotten Lotte« oder durch ein grobes Sieb passieren, dann erneut aufkochen und leicht salzen.

6 Die Tomatensauce in saubere Einmachgläser füllen und diese fest verschließen. Die Gläser in einen großen Topf oder eine Fettpfanne stellen, reichlich heißes Wasser angießen, sodass die Gläser zu 3/4 im Wasserbad stehen, und im auf 120 °C vorgeheizten Backofen 20 Minuten sterilisieren. (Alternativ die Tomatensauce in Plastikgefäße füllen und einfrieren.)

Tipps: Die Tomaten-Passata ist eine gute Basis für Suppen, Pastasaucen und Schmorgerichte.
Wenn Sie die Tomaten-Passata mit gelben Tomaten zubereiten, würzen Sie sie zusätzlich mit etwas frisch geriebener Zitronenschale und frisch gepresstem Zitronensaft.

Ofengetrocknete Kräutertomaten

Zutaten für 4 Personen

12 ovale Tomaten
3 Knoblauchzehen
4 EL Meersalz
1 Bund Thymian
20 Zweige Rosmarin
5 EL Olivenöl extra vergine, plus 200 ml Olivenöl extra vergine zum Auffüllen der Gläser

Zubereitungszeit: ca. 15 Minuten plus 12 Stunden Zeit zum Trocknen

1 Die Tomaten waschen und längs halbieren.

2 Den Knoblauch schälen und in feine Scheiben schneiden.

3 Eine große Bratform oder ein großes, tiefes Backblech mit Backpapier auslegen. Die Tomaten mit der Schnittfläche nach oben darauf verteilen. Die Schnittflächen mit dem Salz bestreuen, dann die Knoblauchscheiben, den unzerkleinerten Thymian und die Rosmarinzweige darübergeben. Dann alles mit dem Olivenöl beträufeln.

4 Die Tomaten in den Backofen geben und bei 60 °C 12 Stunden (am besten über Nacht) trocknen lassen.

5 Die getrockneten Tomaten in ein sauberes Glas füllen und mit Olivenöl übergießen. Die Tomaten bis zum Verzehr im Kühlschrank aufbewahren oder gleich als Pizzabelag, für Pastasaucen oder Pesto verwenden. Auch klein geschnitten im frischen Tomatensalat schmecken sie toll.

Tipp: Das Trocknen intensiviert den Tomatengeschmack – die getrockneten Tomaten eignen sich daher bestens zum Würzen von Tomatengerichten.

Scharfe Tomatenpaste

Ergibt ca. 400 ml

5 vollreife Tomaten (ca. 500 g)
1 kleine Zwiebel
80 g getrocknete Marillen (Aprikosen)
5 getrocknete Chilischoten
1/2 TL Anissamen
125 ml Olivenöl extra vergine
Salz
frisch gemahlener Pfeffer

Zubereitungszeit: ca. 30 Minuten plus 5 Stunden Ruhezeit

1 Die Tomaten am Stielansatz kreuzweise einschneiden.
2 Reichlich Wasser in einem großen Topf zum Kochen bringen. Die Tomaten darin portionsweise je 1 Minute blanchieren.
3 Die Tomaten aus dem Wasser nehmen, in Eiswasser abschrecken, dann häuten, halbieren, entkernen und in kleine Würfel schneiden.
4 Die Zwiebel in kleine Würfel schneiden.
5 Die Marillen fein hacken.
6 Die Chilischoten grob hacken.
7 Die Chilis, die Tomaten, die Zwiebeln, die Marillen und die Anissamen in eine Schüssel geben und mit dem Olivenöl vermengen. Die Schüssel abdecken und die Mischung 4 bis 5 Stunden ziehen lassen.
8 Die marinierte Mischung in einen Topf geben und bei geringer Temperatur etwa 20 bis 30 Minuten köcheln lassen. Dabei öfter umrühren. Den Topf dann vom Herd nehmen und die Tomatenmischung abkühlen lassen.
9 Die Tomatenmischung mit dem Stabmixer fein pürieren und mit Salz und Pfeffer abschmecken. Die Paste in kleine Gläser füllen und bis zur Verwendung im Kühlschrank aufbewahren.

Tipp: Die scharfe Tomatenpaste eignet sich zum Würzen von Schmorgerichten. Mit Joghurt verrührt ergibt sie eine scharfe Fondue- oder Grillsauce.

Tomatenöl

Ergibt ca. 750 ml

4 große vollreife Fleischtomaten (ca. 500 g)
2 Schalotten
2 Knoblauchzehen
1/2 kleine Fenchelknolle (ca. 100 g)
270 ml Olivenöl extra vergine
2 frische Lorbeerblätter
1 TL Salz
2 EL gehackter Oregano
2 EL grob gezupftes Basilikum

Zubereitungszeit: ca. 40 Minuten

1 Die Tomaten waschen, halbieren, von den Stielansätzen befreien, entkernen und fein würfeln.

2 Die Schalotten und den Knoblauch schälen und fein hacken.

3 Den Fenchel putzen und in kleine Würfel schneiden.

4 2 EL des Olivenöls (etwa 20 ml) in einem Topf erhitzen. Die Schalotten, den Knoblauch und den Fenchel darin anschwitzen, dann die Tomaten und die Lorbeerblätter hinzufügen. Den Topf abdecken und die Mischung etwa 15 Minuten schmoren. Dabei immer wieder den entstehenden Schaum abnehmen.

5 Das restliche Olivenöl (250 ml) langsam hineinrühren und die Mischung bei geringer Temperatur weitere 15 Minuten köcheln lassen. Dann den Topf vom Herd nehmen, das Gemisch salzen und den Oregano und das Basilikum hineinrühren. Den Topf abdecken und das Tomatenöl abkühlen lassen. Das Tomatenöl dann durch ein Sieb in eine Flasche füllen und bis zum Gebrauch im Kühlschrank aufbewahren. Vor dem Gebrauch gut schütteln, denn das Öl setzt sich oben ab. (Wer ein klares Öl haben möchte, streicht es durch ein Küchentuch.)

Tipp: Das Tomatenöl passt zu Frischkäse und Pasta, ergibt eine gute Salatmarinade und eignet sich bestens zum Verfeinern von gegrilltem Fisch und Meeresfrüchten.

Rosinen-Tomaten-Chutney

Ergibt ca. 250 ml

8 vollreife Strauchtomaten (ca. 600 g)
2 EL Sonnenblumenöl
1/2 TL Senfsamen
2 grüne Chilischoten
1/2 TL Kreuzkümmelsamen
2 EL brauner Rohrzucker
80 g große Rosinen
Salz

Zubereitungszeit: ca. 30–40 Minuten

1 Die Tomaten am Stielansatz kreuzweise einschneiden.

2 Reichlich Wasser in einem großen Topf zum Kochen bringen. Die Tomaten darin portionsweise je 1 Minute blanchieren.

3 Die Tomaten aus dem Wasser nehmen, in Eiswasser abschrecken, dann häuten, halbieren, entkernen und fein würfeln.

4 Das Sonnenblumenöl in einem Topf erhitzen, die Senfsamen hineinstreuen und so lange rösten, bis die Samen platzen.

5 Die Chilischoten längs aufschlitzen, entkernen und fein hacken.

6 Den Chili, den Kreuzkümmel, den Zucker und die Rosinen zu den Senfkörnern in den Topf geben und kurz mitrösten.

7 Die Tomaten hinzufügen und so lange köcheln, bis eine dicke Sauce entstanden ist, dann mit Salz abschmecken.

8 Das Chutney in kleine, saubere Einmachgläser füllen und diese fest verschließen. Das Chutney ist bei kühler Lagerung ca. 3 Monate haltbar.

Tipp: Das Chutney passt zu gegrilltem Fleisch, kräftigem Blauschimmelkäse und zu indischen Gerichten.

Tomaten-Boskop-Chutney

Ergibt ca. 600 ml

600 g vollreife Strauchtomaten
2 große weiße Gemüsezwiebeln
150 g Staudensellerie
2 Äpfel (z. B. Boskop)
5 EL Kristallzucker
2 TL fein geriebener Ingwer
Salz
Cayennepfeffer

Zubereitungszeit: 30–40 Minuten plus 1 Stunde Abtropfzeit

1 Die Tomaten vierteln, entkernen, salzen, in ein Sieb geben und 1 Stunde abtropfen lassen.

2 Die Zwiebeln schälen und in feine Würfel schneiden.

3 Den Staudensellerie putzen, von den Fäden befreien und klein schneiden.

4 Die Äpfel schälen und grob raspeln.

5 Die Tomaten, die Zwiebeln, den Staudensellerie und die Äpfel in einen Topf geben, mit dem Zucker bestreuen und bei geringer Temperatur zu einem dicken Chutney köcheln. Dabei öfters umrühren.

6 Den Ingwer in das Tomatenchutney rühren, dann mit Salz und Cayennepfeffer abschmecken.

7 Das heiße Chutney in kleine, saubere Einmachgläser füllen und diese fest verschließen. Das Chutney vor dem Verzehr mindestens 3 bis 4 Tage durchziehen lassen. Das Chutney ist bei kühler Lagerung ca. 3 Monate haltbar.

Tipp: Das Chutney passt zu gebratenem oder gegrilltem Fleisch und zu würzigem Käse oder Pasteten.

Tomaten-Mango-Gewürz-Sauce

Ergibt ca. 800 ml

1 kg vollreife Tomaten (z. B. Fleisch- oder Flaschentomaten)
2 vollreife Mangos (ca. 700 g)
200 g Mascobado-Zucker oder anderer brauner Rohrzucker
2 Chilischoten, fein gehackt
2 EL Currypulver
Salz

Zubereitungszeit: ca. 1 1/2–2 Stunden

1 Die Tomaten vierteln, mit den Schnittflächen nach oben auf ein mit Backpapier bedecktes Backblech legen und leicht salzen.

2 Die Tomaten im auf 180 °C vorgeheizten Backofen etwa 1 Stunde antrocknen lassen.

3 Die Mangos schälen, das Fruchtfleisch vom Kern lösen und in kleine Würfel schneiden.

4 Den Zucker mit 125 ml Wasser in einen Topf geben, aufkochen und so leicht karamellisieren.

5 Die Tomaten und die Mango hinzufügen, die Temperatur reduzieren und die Mischung dick einkochen. Dann die Chilis und das Currypulver hinzufügen, die Mischung salzen und mit dem Stabmixer fein pürieren.

6 Die heiße Sauce mithilfe eines Trichters in saubere Fläschchen füllen, diese verschließen und die Sauce 1 bis 2 Tage durchziehen lassen. Die Sauce ist bei kühler Lagerung ca. 2 Monate haltbar.

Tipp: Diese Sauce passt gut zu gegrilltem Huhn oder Lamm, eignet sich aber auch als Würzsauce für schnelle Currygerichte.

Ananas-Tomaten-Grillsauce

Ergibt 2 Gläser à 400 ml

500 g Tomaten, geschält und halbiert
2 Scheiben Ananas (je ca. 15 cm Durchmesser und 12 mm dick)
3 frische Chilischoten
1 Knoblauchzehe
1/2 TL Salz
1 EL Honig
4 EL gehacktes Koriandergrün
frisch gemahlener Pfeffer

Zubereitungszeit: ca. 20 Minuten

1 Die Tomaten, die Ananas und die Chilischoten im auf 250 °C vorgeheizten Backofen (Umluft) etwa 4 Minuten grillen, bis sie dunkel werden, dabei einmal wenden. Dann aus dem Ofen nehmen und beiseitestellen.

2 Den Knoblauch und das Salz im Mörser zu einer groben Paste zerdrücken.

3 Die Knoblauchpaste mit den Tomaten, den Chilis und dem Honig in der Küchenmaschine zu einer groben Paste verarbeiten. Die Paste in eine Schüssel geben.

4 Die Ananasscheiben würfeln und mit dem Koriandergrün zu der Tomatenpaste geben und vermengen. Die Sauce bei Bedarf mit Salz und Pfeffer abschmecken.

5 Die Grillsauce in sterile Einmachgläser füllen, diese sofort verschließen und die Sauce abkühlen lassen. Im Kühlschrank hält sich die Sauce bis zu 2 Wochen.

Tipp: Die Ananas-Tomaten-Sauce passt zu gegrilltem oder gebratenem Lamm und Geflügel. Auch zum Würzen von Geflügelcurrys ist sie bestens geeignet.

Salsa aus gerösteten Tomaten und Chipotle-Chili

Ergibt ca. 3 Tassen

3 getrocknete Chipotle-Chilis (geräucherte Chilis)
4 große Strauchtomaten
1 große weiße Gemüsezwiebel
1 Bund Koriandergrün
250 ml Sonnenblumenöl
1 TL Salz

Zubereitungszeit: ca. 20–30 Minuten

1 Die Chipotle-Chilis in einen kleinen Topf geben, mit kochendem Wasser übergießen, den Topf abdecken und die Chilis etwa 15 Minuten einweichen, dann die Stiele entfernen.

2 Die Tomaten waschen, halbieren, mit der Schnittfläche nach unten auf ein mit Backpapier belegtes Backblech setzen und im auf 250 °C vorgeheizten Backofen (Umluft) so lange grillen, bis sie beginnen, dunkel zu werden.

3 Die Zwiebel schälen und in kleine Würfel schneiden.

4 Die Chipotle-Chili, die heißen Tomaten, die Zwiebel und das Koriandergrün in der Küchenmaschine zu Püree verarbeiten, dann bei angeschalteter Maschine langsam das Sonnenblumenöl in das Püree fließen lassen. Das Püree mit Salz abschmecken.

5 Die heiße Salsa in kleine, saubere Einmachgläser füllen und diese fest verschließen. Die Salsa ist bei kühler Lagerung ca. 1 Monat haltbar.

Tipp: Die Salsa passt gut zu gegrilltem Rind- oder Lammfleisch.

Tomaten-Zitronen-Mus mit grünem Pfeffer

Ergibt ca. 800 ml

1 kg vollreife Strauchtomaten
2 Zitronen (Bioware)
650 g Gelierzucker (2 : 1)
1 Vanilleschote
1 Glas eingelegte grüne Pfefferkörner (ca. 50 g)

Zubereitungszeit: ca. 20 Minuten plus 3–4 Stunden Ruhezeit

1 Die Tomaten waschen, vierteln, von den Stielansätzen befreien und im Mixer oder der Küchenmaschine zu einem feinen Püree verarbeiten.

2 Das Tomatenpüree mit der fein abgeriebenen Schale sowie dem Saft der Zitronen und dem Gelierzucker in einen Topf geben und gut vermengen.

3 Die Vanilleschote längs aufschlitzen und das Mark auskratzen. Das ausgekratzte Vanillemark und die Vanilleschote zu den Tomaten geben. Den Topf abdecken und die Mischung 3 bis 4 Stunden durchziehen lassen.

4 Die eingelegten Pfefferkörner durch ein Sieb schütten, gut abtropfen lassen und grob hacken.

5 Die Tomatenmischung erwärmen und aufkochen. Dann die Temperatur leicht reduzieren und die Mischung 4 bis 6 Minuten kochen lassen. Den Topf vom Herd nehmen und die Vanilleschote entfernen.

6 Die gehackten Pfefferkörner in das Tomatenmus rühren.

7 Das heiße Mus in saubere Einmachgläser füllen und diese fest verschließen. Das Mus vor dem Verzehr 1 bis 2 Tage durchziehen lassen. Das Tomaten-Zitronen-Mus ist bei kühler Lagerung etwa 6 Monate haltbar.

Tipp: Dieses Mus passt zu Wildpasteten, gebratenem Fisch (Zander, Hecht) und ergibt einen würzigen Brotaufstrich.

Fünf-Gewürze-Tomatenketchup

Ergibt ca. 1 l

1 kg vollreife Fleischtomaten
1 große Gemüsezwiebel
1 große rote Paprikaschote (ca. 200 g)
5 EL brauner Rohrzucker
1/2 TL Korianderkörner
3 Gewürznelken
5 schwarze Pfefferkörner
1 Lorbeerblatt
1 kleine Zimtstange (ca. 2 cm)
Saft von 1 Zitrone
Salz

Zubereitungszeit: ca. 1 1/4–1 1/2 Stunden

1 Die Tomaten am Stielansatz kreuzweise einschneiden.

2 Reichlich Wasser in einem großen Topf zum Kochen bringen. Die Tomaten darin portionsweise je 1 Minute blanchieren.

3 Die Tomaten aus dem Wasser nehmen, in Eiswasser abschrecken, dann häuten, halbieren, entkernen und grob schneiden.

4 Die Zwiebel schälen und in kleine Würfel schneiden.

5 Die Paprika halbieren, von Stielansatz, Scheidewänden und Kernen befreien und ebenfalls in kleine Würfel schneiden.

6 Die Tomaten mit der Zwiebel, der Paprika, dem Zucker, dem Koriander, den Gewürznelken, den Pfefferkörnern, dem Lorbeerblatt und dem Zimt in einen großen Topf geben und bei mittlerer Temperatur etwa 45 Minuten köcheln lassen. Dabei öfter umrühren.

7 Das Lorbeerblatt entfernen und die Tomatensauce mit dem Stabmixer pürieren. Das Püree weitere 10 Minuten köcheln lassen, dann mit Zitronensaft und Salz abschmecken. Das Ketchup in heiß ausgespülte Flaschen füllen. (Bei kühler Lagerung hält sich das Ketchup etwa 2 Monate.)

Tipp: Bereiten Sie das Ketchup mit 2 EL Currypulver und 2 fein gehackten Chilischoten zu – dann erhalten Sie ein feuriges Ketchup.

Tomaten-confit

Ergibt ca. 250 ml

8 vollreife, aber feste Tomaten (ca. 600 g)
2 EL Gelierzucker (3 : 1)
3 Knoblauchzehen
4–5 Zweige Thymian
8 EL fruchtiges Olivenöl extra vergine
Salz
frisch gemahlener Pfeffer

Zubereitungszeit: ca. 1 Stunde

1 Die Tomaten waschen, vierteln, von den Stielansätzen befreien und entkernen.

2 Ein Backblech mit dem Gelierzucker bestreuen und die Tomatenviertel mit der Schnittseite nach unten darauflegen.

3 Den Knoblauch schälen, in feine Scheiben schneiden und über die Tomaten geben.

4 Den Thymian ebenfalls über die Tomaten geben.

5 Die Hälfte des Olivenöls über die Tomaten träufeln.

6 Die Tomaten im auf 100 °C vorgeheizten Backofen etwa 50 Minuten braten (bis sich die Haut leicht abziehen lässt), dann aus dem Ofen nehmen und den Thymian entfernen.

7 Die Tomaten mit dem beim Braten entstandenen Saft in eine Schüssel geben und mit einer Gabel durchmengen. Dabei die Tomaten zerdrücken. Das restliche Olivenöl hinzufügen und gründlich einarbeiten. Mit Salz und Pfeffer abschmecken.

8 Das Confit in ein sauberes Schraubglas füllen und bis zum Verzehr im Kühlschrank aufbewahren.

Tipp: Das Confit ist ein wunderbarer Belag für Crostini, aber auch eine tolle Beilage zu kaltem Braten, Frischkäse und ein fruchtiger Begleiter für viele Sommergerichte.

Tomatenmarmelade mit Anis und Fenchel

Ergibt ca. 800 ml

1 kg vollreife Tomaten (z. B. Fleisch- oder Flaschentomaten)
2 säuerliche Äpfel
2 Zitronen
250 g Gelierzucker (3 : 1)
1 TL Anissamen
1 TL Fenchelsamen
1 TL Meersalz

Zubereitungszeit: ca. 40 Minuten plus 2 Stunden Zeit zum Ziehen

1 Die Tomaten waschen, halbieren, von den Stielansätzen befreien und in kleine Würfel schneiden.

2 Die Äpfel schälen, entkernen und in feine Stifte schneiden.

3 Die Tomaten mit den Äpfeln in eine Schüssel geben und mit dem Saft der Zitronen und dem Gelierzucker vermengen. Die Schüssel abdecken und die Mischung etwa 2 Stunden durchziehen lassen.

4 Die Tomaten-Apfel-Mischung in einen großen Topf geben, die Anis- und Fenchelsamen hinzufügen und aufkochen. Die Temperatur reduzieren und die Mischung in etwa 30 Minuten zu einer dicken Marmelade einkochen, dann salzen.

5 Die heiße Tomatenmarmelade in saubere Einmachgläser füllen und diese fest verschließen. Die Marmelade vor dem Verzehr mindestens 2 bis 3 Tage durchziehen lassen.

Tipp: Diese Marmelade passt gut zu gegrilltem Fleisch oder Wild und zu Käse. Auch als Brotaufstrich schmeckt sie toll.

Tomatenmarmelade mit Papaya und Tonkabohne

Ergibt ca. 1 l

1,5 kg vollreife Eiertomaten oder Ochsenherztomaten
1 große Papaya (ca. 1 kg)
1 Stange Zitronengras, um die holzigen Enden gekürzt
2 Limetten (Bioware)
500 g Gelierzucker (2 : 1)
1/4 Tonkabohne, fein gerieben

Zubereitungszeit: ca. 20–30 Minuten plus 2–3 Stunden Zeit zum Ziehen

1 Die Tomaten am Stielansatz kreuzweise einschneiden.

2 Reichlich Wasser in einem großen Topf zum Kochen bringen. Die Tomaten darin portionsweise je 1 Minute blanchieren.

3 Die Tomaten aus dem Wasser nehmen, in Eiswasser abschrecken, dann häuten, halbieren, vom Stielansatz befreien, entkernen und in kleine Würfel schneiden.

4 Die Papaya schälen, halbieren, entkernen und klein würfeln.

5 Das Zitronengras längs halbieren.

6 Die Tomaten, die Papaya und das Zitronengras in einen hohen Topf geben.

7 Die fein geriebene Schale einer Limette darübergeben, dann den Saft beider Limetten und den Gelierzucker hinzufügen und gründlich vermengen. Den Topf abdecken und die Mischung 2 bis 3 Stunden ziehen lassen.

8 Die Mischung aufkochen, dann die Temperatur leicht reduzieren und die Marmelade 4 bis 5 Minuten sprudelnd kochen lassen.

9 Den Topf vom Herd nehmen, das Zitronengras entfernen und den Tonkabohnenabrieb in die Marmelade rühren.

10 Die heiße Marmelade in saubere Einmachgläser füllen und diese fest verschließen. Die Marmelade vor dem Verzehr 1 bis 2 Tage durchziehen lassen. Die Marmelade ist bei kühler Lagerung ca. 4 Monate haltbar.

Tipp: Diese Marmelade passt gut zu weichem Käse, aber auch zu frischer Brioche oder Weißbrot.

Zwiebel-Tomaten-Relish

Ergibt 1 Glas

400 g Flaschentomaten
3 große Haushaltszwiebeln (ca. 750 g), fein gehackt
2 EL Sesam- oder Erdnussöl
1 TL Zucker
4 EL Apfelessig
2 TL Salz
1 Prise Cayennepfeffer

Zubereitungszeit: ca. 45 Minuten

1. Die Tomaten am Stielansatz kreuzweise einschneiden.
2. Reichlich Wasser in einem großen Topf zum Kochen bringen. Die Tomaten darin portionsweise je 1 Minute blanchieren.
3. Die Tomaten aus dem Wasser nehmen, in Eiswasser abschrecken, dann häuten, halbieren, vom Stielansatz befreien, entkernen und grob schneiden.
4. Die Zwiebeln schälen und fein hacken.
5. Das Sesamöl in einem großen Topf stark erhitzen und die Zwiebeln darin etwa 7 Minuten anschwitzen. Achtung: Die Zwiebeln dürfen nicht bräunen, gegebenenfalls die Temperatur auf ein Minimum reduzieren.
6. Die Herdtemperatur reduzieren, die Tomaten in den Topf geben und unter gelegentlichem Rühren etwa 10 Minuten mitbraten.
7. Den Zucker, den Apfelessig, das Salz und den Cayennepfeffer hinzufügen und die Mischung etwa 10 Minuten köcheln, bis die Zwiebeln weich sind und die Sauce glänzt.
8. Das Relish warm oder zimmerwarm servieren. Das Relish ist luftdicht verschlossen im Kühlschrank ca. 3 Wochen haltbar.

Kalte Sommer-gerichte

Bohnen-Parmesan-Creme auf Tomatenbruschetta

Zutaten für 4 Personen

Für das Parmesanöl
125 ml Olivenöl extra vergine
etwas Rinde eines Parmesanstücks (Bioprodukt)

Für die Bohnen-Parmesan-Creme
80 g frisch geriebener Parmesan
200 g weiße Bohnenkerne (aus der Dose), gut abgetropft
1 EL weißer Aceto balsamico
Salz
frisch gemahlener Pfeffer

Für die Tomatenbruschetta
4 Scheiben Schwarzbrot
150 g Kirschtomaten, halbiert
50 g Rucola
Salz
frisch gemahlener Pfeffer
1 Knoblauchzehe, halbiert
Saft von 1/2 Zitrone
einige Zitronenspalten zum Servieren

Zubereitungszeit: 20 Minuten plus 3 Tage Zeit zum Ziehen für das Öl

1 Für das Parmesanöl das Olivenöl in einem kleinen Topf leicht erwärmen, dann die Parmesanrinde hinzufügen, den Topf abdecken und das Parmesanöl 3 Tage im Kühlschrank ziehen lassen.
2 Für die Bohnen-Parmesan-Creme den geriebenen Parmesan und die Bohnenkerne in der Küchenmaschine fein pürieren. Dann langsam und unter ständigem Rühren den Aceto balsamico und 8 EL Parmesanöl in das Püree fließen lassen. Das Püree mit Salz und Pfeffer abschmecken.
3 Das Schwarzbrot beidseitig goldbraun toasten.
4 Die Kirschtomaten waschen, trocknen und halbieren.
5 Den Rucola in feine Streifen schneiden, in eine Schüssel geben und mit den Tomaten vermengen. 2 EL Parmesanöl darübergeben und mit Salz und Pfeffer abschmecken.
6 Die getoasteten Brotscheiben beidseitig mit der Knoblauchzehe einreiben und mit der Bohnen-Parmesan-Creme bestreichen. Die Tomaten-Rucola-Mischung daraufgeben und alles mit dem restlichen Parmesanöl und etwas Zitronensaft beträufeln.
7 Die Bruschetta zusammen mit den Zitronenspalten garnieren und servieren.

Avocado-Joghurt-Creme auf marinierten Koriandertomaten

Zutaten für 4 Personen

Für die Koriandertomaten

500 g Kirschtomaten
4 EL Olivenöl extra vergine
3 EL Korianderkörner, grob gehackt
1 Prise Cayennepfeffer
Salz
frisch gemahlener Pfeffer

Für die Avocado-Joghurt-Creme

2 vollreife Avocados (à ca. 180 g)
1 EL frisch gepresster Zitronensaft
250 ml Naturjoghurt (3,5 % Fettgehalt)
250 g Crème fraîche
1 TL Kurkumapulver
1 kleine Knoblauchzehe, fein gehackt
Salz
frisch gemahlener Pfeffer
einige essbare Blüten

Zubereitungszeit: 10–15 Minuten plus 2–3 Stunden Kühlzeit

1 Die Tomaten waschen, trocknen und halbieren. Die Tomatenhälften auf 4 Gläser verteilen.

2 Das Olivenöl mit den Korianderkörnern verrühren und mit Cayennepfeffer, Salz und Pfeffer abschmecken. Diese Marinade über die Tomaten geben.

3 Für die Avocado-Joghurt-Creme die Avocados halbieren, entkernen und schälen. Das Avocadofleisch grob schneiden, in einen hohen Rührbecher geben und mit dem Zitronensaft beträufeln.

4 Den Joghurt mit der Crème fraîche, dem Kurkumapulver und dem Knoblauch glatt rühren und zu den Avocados in den Rührbecher geben. Mit dem Stabmixer zu einer glatten Creme verarbeiten. Die Creme mit Salz und Pfeffer abschmecken und über die marinierten Tomaten geben. Die Gläser mit Frischhaltefolie abdecken und 2 bis 3 Stunden im Kühlschrank erkalten lassen.

5 Die Avocado-Joghurt-Cremes jeweils mit einigen essbaren Blüten bestreuen und servieren.

Dipp mit Kirschtomaten und Mais

Zutaten für 4 Personen

3 frische Maiskolben
1 EL Milch
100 g Topfen (Quark, 40 % Fettgehalt) oder Frischkäse
1 EL frisch gepresster Limettensaft
250 g Kirschtomaten
2 EL fein geschnittene Blattpetersilienblättchen
Meersalz
frisch gemahlener Pfeffer

Zubereitungszeit: ca. 30–40 Minuten

1 Die Maiskörner mit einem kleinen, scharfen Messer von den Kolben lösen.

2 Die Maiskörner mit der Milch in einen kleinen Topf geben und aufkochen, dann bei geringer Temperatur 7 bis 9 Minuten köcheln lassen. Den Topf vom Herd nehmen und die Mischung vollständig abkühlen lassen, dann durch ein Sieb schütten.

3 1/3 der Maismischung mit dem Topfen und dem Limettensaft in einen hohen Rührbecher geben und mit dem Stabmixer (oder in der Küchenmaschine) fein pürieren.

4 Die Kirschtomaten waschen, vierteln und mit den restlichen Maiskörnern unter das Maispüree heben.

5 Die gehackte Petersilie unter den Dipp mengen und den Dipp kräftig mit Salz und Pfeffer abschmecken.

Tipp: Servieren Sie diesen Dipp mit Tortillachips und Gurkenstiften oder einfach als Brotaufstrich.

Tsatsikimousse mit lauwarmen Anis-Tomaten

Zutaten für 4 Personen

Für die Tsatsikimousse

4 Blatt weiße Gelatine
2 Salatgurken (à 350 g)
Salz
400 g griechischer Joghurt
4 EL Olivenöl extra vergine
1 Knoblauchzehe, fein gehackt
2 EL Ouzo (griechischer Anisschnaps)
frisch gemahlener Pfeffer

Für die Anistomaten

500 g kleine, ovale Kirschtomaten
2 EL Anissamen
8 EL Olivenöl extra vergine
Salz
frisch gemahlener Pfeffer
1 Spritzer Zitronensaft
einige frische Oreganoblüten zum Garnieren (nach Belieben)

Zubereitungszeit: ca. 30 Minuten plus Kühlzeit

1 Die Gelatine in kaltem Wasser einweichen.

2 Die Gurken schälen, längs halbieren, entkernen, grob raspeln, mit Salz bestreuen und 10 Minuten ziehen lassen, dann gut ausdrücken.

3 Den Joghurt mit dem Olivenöl und dem Knoblauch verrühren. Die Gurken unterheben.

4 Die eingeweichte Gelatine gut ausdrücken, mit dem Ouzo in einen kleinen Topf geben und bei geringer Temperatur auflösen, dann 3–4 EL der Gurken-Joghurt-Creme hineinrühren und alles unter die restliche Gurken-Joghurt-Creme rühren. Mit Pfeffer abschmecken. Die Mousse in 4 Gläser füllen, bis die Gläser halbvoll sind, und 4 bis 5 Stunden (am besten über Nacht) im Kühlschrank erkalten lassen.

5 Die Tomaten waschen und halbieren.

6 Die Anissamen ohne Fettzugabe kurz in einer beschichteten Pfanne anrösten. Die Pfanne vom Herd nehmen, das Olivenöl über die Anissamen geben und 10 Minuten ziehen lassen.

7 Die Tomatenhälften mit dem lauwarmen Anisöl vermengen und mit Salz und Pfeffer abschmecken.

8 Die Anistomaten auf die Tsatsikimousse geben und nach Belieben mit Oreganoblüten garnieren.

Karamellisierte Kirschtomaten auf Zucchinicarpaccio

Zutaten für 4 Personen

Für die karamellisierten Kirschtomaten

24 Kirschtomaten

125 g Kristallzucker

1 EL Pfeffer, grob geschrotet

Für das Zucchinicarpaccio

4 kleine, feste Zucchini (ca. 500 g)

8 EL Olivenöl extra vergine

4 EL weißer Aceto balsamico

1 EL fein gehackte Blattpetersilie

einige grob geriebene Chiliflocken

Salz

frisch gemahlener Pfeffer

frisch gehobelter Parmesan

frische Oreganoblättchen

Zubereitungszeit: ca. 30 Minuten

1 Die Kirschtomaten waschen und auf Küchenkrepp gut abtropfen lassen, dann jede Kirschtomate auf einen kleinen Holzspieß (Zahnstocher) stecken.

2 Den Zucker mit 200 ml Wasser in einem kleinen Topf aufkochen und bei geringer Hitze so lange köcheln, bis ein hellbrauner Karamell entstanden ist.

3 Den Topf vom Herd nehmen, die Kirschtomaten einzeln in den Karamell tauchen und mit dem groben Pfeffer bestreuen. Die Tomaten zum Trocknen auf ein mit Backpapier bedecktes Backblech oder Tablett legen.

4 Für das Zucchinicarpaccio die Zucchini waschen und mit dem Sparschäler (oder auf der Schneidemaschine) längs in dünne Streifen schneiden. Diese Zucchinispäne auf einem Teller anrichten.

5 Das Olivenöl mit dem Aceto balsamico und der Petersilie zu einem Dressing verrühren. Das Dressing mit den Chiliflocken, Salz und Pfeffer abschmecken.

6 Das Dressing über das Zucchinicarpaccio geben, die Tomaten darauf verteilen und nach Belieben mit frisch gehobeltem Parmesan bestreuen und mit Oreganoblättchen garnieren. Sofort servieren.

Bunter Tomatensalat mit roten Zwiebeln, Orangenzeste und Minze

Zutaten für 4 Personen

1 kg bunte Tomaten
2 rote Zwiebeln
etwas Meersalz
65 ml fruchtiges Olivenöl extra vergine
1 unbehandelte Orange
frisch gemahlener Pfeffer
2 Handvoll Minzeblätter

Zubereitungszeit: ca. 15 Minuten

1. Die Tomaten waschen, vierteln, von den Stielansätzen befreien und auf einer Servierplatte verteilen.
2. Die Zwiebeln schälen, halbieren, in Scheiben schneiden und über die Tomaten geben. Die Mischung mit Meersalz bestreuen und mit dem Olivenöl übergießen.
3. Die Schale der Orange zu feinen Zesten reiben und über den Tomaten-Zwiebel-Salat geben.
4. Die Orange halbieren und den Saft auspressen. Den Saft über den Salat träufeln. Den Salat kräftig pfeffern und mit den Minzeblättchen garnieren.

Tipp: Dieser Salat ergibt eine schnelle, leichte Sommervorspeise oder einen Beilagensalat. Bestreuen Sie ihn nach Belieben mit etwas grob gehobeltem, jungem Parmesan.

Salat vom Ochsenherz mit Pfirsichen und Honig

Zutaten für 4 Personen

6 Ochsenherztomaten (ca. 500 g)
4 weiße Pfirsiche (z. B. Saturn)
4 EL fruchtiges Olivenöl extra vergine
Saft von 1 Orange
2 EL sehr flüssiger Honig
1 TL frische Lavendelblüten
Meersalz

Zubereitungszeit: ca. 10 Minuten

1 Die Tomaten waschen, in 1/2 cm dicke Scheiben schneiden und leicht salzen.

2 Die Pfirsiche häuten, halbieren, entsteinen und in 1/2 cm dicke Würfel schneiden. (Vollreife Pfirsiche lassen sich leicht häuten. Klappt das nicht, die Pfirsiche kurz mit kochendem Wasser überbrühen, kalt abschrecken und dann häuten.)

3 Die Tomatenscheiben und die Pfirsichwürfel locker in einer Schüssel vermengen, dann das Olivenöl und den Orangensaft daruntermischen.

4 Den Tomaten-Pfirsich-Salat mit dem Honig überziehen und mit den Lavendelblüten bestreuen, dann erneut vorsichtig vermengen.

5 Den Salat auf 4 Tellern anrichten und mit etwas Meersalz bestreuen.

Tipp: Dieser Salat passt gut zu gegrilltem Huhn oder weißem Fisch und zu Frischkäse.

Lauwarmer Ananastomatensalat mit Rosmarin-Zabaione

Zutaten für 4 Personen

800 g gelbe Ananastomaten (aus dem Garten oder vom gut sortierten Gemüsehändler)

etwas Meersalz

4 Eigelb

125 ml fruchtiger Weißwein

1 EL Kristallzucker

2 Zweige frischer Rosmarin

1 TL fein geriebene Zitronenschale (Bioware)

2 EL Crème fraîche (ca. 80 g)

Salz

frisch gemahlener Pfeffer

Zubereitungszeit: ca. 30 Minuten

1 Die Tomaten halbieren, vom Strunk befreien, mit der Schnittfläche nach oben auf ein Backblech legen, mit Meersalz bestreuen und unter dem vorgeheizten Backofengrill 1 bis 2 Minuten grillen. Das Backblech aus dem Ofen nehmen und die Tomaten abkühlen lassen.

2 Die Eigelb mit dem Wein und dem Zucker in eine Rührschüssel geben und über dem warmen Wasserbad etwa 8 bis 10 Minuten zu einer dicken Creme (Zabaione) aufschlagen. Die Zabaione anschließend unter Rühren über einem kalten Wasserbad abkühlen lassen.

3 Für die Zabaione die Rosmarinnadeln von den Zweigen zupfen und fein hacken.

4 Den gehackten Rosmarin, die fein geriebene Zitronenschale und die Crème fraîche unter die Zabaione ziehen. Mit Salz und Pfeffer abschmecken.

5 Die lauwarmen Ananastomaten in tiefen Tellern anrichten und mit der kalten Zabaione überziehen.

Tipp: Legen Sie die halbierten Tomaten an heißen Sommertagen einfach 15 Minuten in die Sonne.

Rote-Rüben-Tomaten-Salat mit Mascarpone-Mohn-Creme

Zutaten für 4 Personen

Für den Rote-Rüben-Tomaten-Salat

6 junge rote Rüben, geputzt und längs halbiert

Olivenöl extra vergine zum Beträufeln

1/2 TL grobes Salz

4–6 dunkelrote Tomaten

Saft von 1/2 Zitrone

frisch gemahlener Pfeffer

Mohnöl zum Beträufeln

Für die Mascarpone-Mohn-Creme

120 g Mascarpone

125 ml Naturjoghurt

3 EL Mohnöl

2 EL Mohnsamen, fein gemahlen

Salz

frisch gemahlener Pfeffer

1/2 TL fein geriebene Zitronenschale (Bioware)

1 EL frisch gepresster Zitronensaft

Zubereitungszeit: ca. 50 Minuten plus Zeit zum Abkühlen

1 Die roten Rüben mit den Schnittflächen nach oben auf ein mit Alufolie bedecktes Backblech legen (die Alufolie dabei auf beiden Seiten weit überstehen lassen), mit dem Olivenöl beträufeln und mit dem groben Salz bestreuen. Die Alufolie über den roten Rüben zusammenschlagen und gut verschließen.

2 Die roten Rüben im auf 180 °C vorgeheizten Backofen etwa 35 Minuten weich garen, dann aus dem Ofen nehmen, abkühlen lassen und in Spalten schneiden.

3 Für die Mascarpone-Mohn-Creme den Mascarpone mit dem Joghurt, dem Mohnöl und den Mohnsamen vermengen. Die Creme mit Salz, Pfeffer, Zitronenabrieb und Zitronensaft abschmecken.

4 Die Tomaten waschen, vom Stielansatz befreien und in Spalten schneiden. Die Tomatenspalten mit den Rote-Rübe-Spalten auf einer Servierplatte anrichten, dann mit Olivenöl und dem Zitronensaft beträufeln und mit Salz und Pfeffer bestreuen.

5 Die Mascarpone-Mohn-Creme zu dem Tomaten-Rote-Rüben-Salat reichen. Den Salat nach Belieben mit etwas Mohnöl beträufeln.

Tomaten-Wassermelonen-Salat mit Zitronen-Vanille-Dressing

Zutaten für 4 Personen

- 2 unbehandelte Zitronen
- 3 EL brauner Rohrzucker
- 1 Vanilleschote
- 5 EL Olivenöl extra vergine
- Salz
- frisch gemahlener Pfeffer
- 1 rote Zwiebel (ca. 80 g)
- 400 g Wassermelone, geschält
- 5 vollreife Strauchtomaten (ca. 600 g)
- einige Korianderblättchen zum Garnieren

Zubereitungszeit: ca. 20–30 Minuten

1. Die Schale mit dem Zestenreißer von den Zitronen lösen.
2. Die Zitronen auspressen und den Saft mit den Zesten, dem Zucker und der ganzen Vanilleschote in einen kleinen Topf geben, bei mittlerer Temperatur aufkochen und etwa 6 bis 7 Minuten köcheln lassen. Den Topf vom Herd nehmen und das Dressing abkühlen lassen.
3. Die Vanilleschote aus dem Dressing nehmen. Das Olivenöl mit dem Schneebesen in das Dressing rühren. Mit Salz und Pfeffer abschmecken.
4. Die Zwiebel schälen und in feine Ringe schneiden.
5. Die Wassermelone entkernen und in mundgerechte Stücke schneiden.
6. Die Tomaten waschen, vom Stielansatz befreien, in Scheiben schneiden und mit den Melonenstücken auf einer Servierplatte anrichten.
7. Die Zwiebelringe und das grob gezupfte Koriandergrün darüberstreuen und das Dressing darübergießen.

Tipp: Servieren Sie den Salat gut gekühlt.

Kalte Tomatensuppe mit geräuchertem Paprikapulver

Zutaten für 4 Personen

1 kg vollreife Tomaten
2 große rote Paprikaschoten
5 große entsteinte grüne Oliven
1 Knoblauchzehe, fein gehackt
155 ml Olivenöl extra vergine
125 ml frisch gepresster Orangensaft
3 EL Semmelbrösel
1 TL Pimentón de la Vera (geräuchertes Paprikapulver)
Salz
frisch gemahlener Pfeffer
1 gelbe Paprikaschote

Zubereitungszeit: ca. 15 Minuten plus 3 Stunden Kühlzeit

1 Die Tomaten waschen, halbieren, vom Stielansatz befreien, entkernen und grob hacken.

2 Die roten Paprikaschoten waschen, halbieren, von den Kernen und Scheidewänden befreien und grob schneiden.

3 Die Paprikastücke mit den Tomaten, den Oliven, dem Knoblauch, 125 ml Olivenöl, dem Orangensaft, den Semmelbröseln und dem Pimentón de la Vera in der Küchenmaschine fein pürieren. Die pürierte Mischung mit Salz und Pfeffer abschmecken und 3 Stunden im Kühlschrank erkalten lassen.

4 Die gelbe Paprikaschote waschen, halbieren, von den Kernen und Scheidewänden befreien und in feine Streifen schneiden. Die Paprikastreifen leicht salzen und mit dem restlichen Olivenöl vermengen.

5 Die erkaltete Suppe in 4 großen Tassen anrichten, die marinierten Paprikastreifen daraufgeben und mit etwas Pimentón de la Vera bestreuen.

Tomaten-Gazpacho mit Ximénez

Zutaten für 6–8 Personen

1 kg leicht überreife Tomaten

500 g entrindetes Weißbrot oder Toastbrot

1 kleine Knoblauchzehe, fein gehackt

125 ml gut gereifter Sherry

65 ml Sherryessig (am besten Pedro Ximénez)

500 ml fruchtiges Olivenöl extra vergine

etwas Tabasco

Salz

frisch gemahlener Pfeffer

Olivenöl extra vergine zum Beträufeln

Zubereitungszeit: ca. 5 Minuten plus Kühlzeit

1 Die Tomaten waschen, halbieren, vom Stielansatz befreien und grob hacken.

2 Das Weißbrot grob schneiden.

3 Die Tomaten mit dem Weißbrot, dem Knoblauch, dem Sherry, dem Sherryessig und dem Olivenöl im Mixer fein pürieren. Das Püree mit Tabasco, Salz und Pfeffer abschmecken und mindestens 5 Stunden (am besten über Nacht) im Kühlschrank kalt stellen.

4 Die Gazpacho in Gläser füllen und mit einigen Spritzern Olivenöl beträufeln.

Tipp: Servieren Sie die Gazpacho mit kross gebratenem Rohschinken.

Geeiste Tomatensuppe mit Granatapfel und Ziegenkäse-Wan-Tan

Zutaten für 4 Personen

Für die Tomatensuppe

1 kg vollreife Tomaten
4 EL Olivenöl extra vergine
Saft von 1/2 Limette
1 TL Zucker
Salz
frisch gemahlener Pfeffer

Für die Ziegenkäse-Wan-Tans

100 g milder Ziegenfrischkäse
2 EL fein geschnittene Minze
Meersalz
8 kleine Wan-Tan-Blätter (erhältlich im Asialaden)
1 Eigelb
Pflanzenöl zum Ausbacken
4 EL frische Granatapfelkerne

Zubereitungszeit: ca. 30 Minuten plus 6–7 Stunden Kühlzeit

1 Die Tomaten waschen, vierteln, von den Stielansätzen befreien, grob hacken und im Mixer fein pürieren. Das Tomatenpüree kräftig und gründlich durch ein feines Sieb streichen.

2 Das Olivenöl, den Limettensaft und den Zucker in die passierten Tomaten rühren, alles mit Salz und Pfeffer abschmecken und 5 bis 6 Stunden im Kühlschrank erkalten lassen. Die Suppe etwa 45 Minuten vor dem Servieren aus dem Kühlschrank nehmen und ins Tiefkühlfach stellen.

3 Für die Ziegenkäse-Wan-Tans den Ziegenkäse mit der Minze verrühren und mit Meersalz abschmecken.

4 Die Wan-Tan-Blätter mit verquirltem Eigelb bestreichen. Auf jedes Blatt 1 TL Ziegenfrischkäse setzen. Die 4 Ecken jedes Teigblatts hochklappen und über der Füllung zusammendrücken.

5 Das Pflanzenöl in einem hohen Topf erhitzen und die Wan-Tans darin 2 bis 3 Minuten knusprig ausbacken.

6 Die eisgekühlte Tomatensuppe in 4 gut gekühlten Tassen anrichten, mit je 2 Wan-Tans und 1 EL Granatapfelkernen garnieren und servieren.

Geliertes Sommersüppchen mit Flusskrebsen

Zutaten für 4 Personen

Für die gelierte Suppe

4 Blatt weiße Gelatine
1 Karotte (ca. 120 g)
1 Zucchini (ca. 120 g)
2 Stangen Staudensellerie (ca. 100 g)
375 ml Gemüsebrühe
125 ml trockener Weißwein
2 Frühlingszwiebeln, in feine Ringe geschnitten
5–6 Blatt Basilikum, in feine Streifen geschnitten
Salz
frisch gemahlener Pfeffer
200 g sehr kleine Kirschtomaten

Für die Flusskrebse

250 g eingelegte Flusskrebse
2 EL Olivenöl
1–2 EL Weißweinessig
2 Frühlingszwiebeln, in feine Ringe geschnitten
2 EL Schnittlauchröllchen
Salz
frisch gemahlener Pfeffer

Zubereitungszeit: ca. 30 Minuten plus Kühlzeit

1 Die Gelatine in kaltem Wasser einweichen.

2 Die Karotte putzen und in feine Streifen schneiden.

3 Die Zucchini ebenfalls in feine Streifen schneiden.

4 Den Staudensellerie putzen, von den Fäden befreien und in feine Streifen schneiden.

5 Die Gemüsebrühe in einem kleinen Topf aufkochen, das Gemüse hinzufügen und 5 bis 7 Minuten bissfest kochen. Den Topf vom Herd nehmen.

6 Die eingeweichte Gelatine ausdrücken und in der heißen Gemüsesuppe auflösen. Die Suppe kalt stellen.

7 Den Weißwein, die Frühlingszwiebeln und das Basilikum in die Suppe rühren, bevor sie zu gelieren beginnt. Die Suppe mit Salz und Pfeffer abschmecken.

8 Die Kirschtomaten waschen und halbieren.

9 Die gelierende Suppe in tiefe Teller oder Schalen geben, die Tomaten darübergeben und die Suppe mindestens 4 bis 5 Stunden (am besten über Nacht) im Kühlschrank erstarren lassen.

10 Die Flusskrebse gut abtropfen lassen und in eine Schüssel geben. Die Flusskrebse mit dem Olivenöl, dem Weißweinessig, den Frühlimgszwiebelringen und den Schnittlauchröllchen vermengen und mit Salz und Pfeffer abschmecken.

11 Die Flusskrebse auf den gekühlten Sommersüppchen anrichten und servieren.

Tomaten-Aperol-Sulz mit Limettenjoghurt

Zutaten für 4 Personen

Für die Tomaten-Aperol-Sülze

8 vollreife Tomaten (ca. 1 kg)
50 g entsteinte schwarze Oliven
3 EL Olivenöl extra vergine
Salz
frisch gemahlener Pfeffer
10 Blatt weiße Gelatine
250 ml Gemüsebrühe
2 EL Tomatenmark
65 ml Aperol (italienischer Bitterlikör)
1 EL brauner Zucker
1 Spritzer frisch gepresster Zitronensaft
1 Spritzer Tabasco

Für den Limettenjoghurt

250 g Naturjoghurt
fein geriebene Schale von 1 Limette (Bioware)
1 Prise Zucker
Salz
frisch gemahlener Pfeffer

Zubereitungszeit: ca. 30 Minuten plus Kühlzeit

1 Die Tomaten am Stielansatz kreuzweise einschneiden. Reichlich Wasser in einem großen Topf zum Kochen bringen. Die Tomaten darin portionsweise je 1 Minute blanchieren. Die Tomaten aus dem Wasser nehmen, in Eiswasser abschrecken, dann häuten, vom Stielansatz befreien, vierteln und entkernen. Die Tomaten auf Küchenkrepp gut abtropfen lassen.

2 Die Oliven grob hacken, in einer Schüssel locker mit den Tomatenvierteln und dem Olivenöl vermengen und mit Salz und Pfeffer abschmecken.

3 Eine Kastenform (24 cm) mit Klarsichtsfolie auslegen. Die Tomaten-Oliven-Mischung hineinfüllen.

4 Die Gelatine in kaltem Wasser einweichen.

5 Die Gemüsebrühe mit dem Tomatenmark in einen Topf geben, aufkochen und 3 bis 4 Minuten kochen lassen. Den Topf vom Herd nehmen. Die eingeweichte Gelatine gut ausdrücken und in der heißen Flüssigkeit auflösen. Dann den Aperol hineinrühren und alles mit dem Zucker, Zitronensaft, Tabasco sowie Salz und Pfeffer abschmecken. Die Brühe in die Tomatenmischung geben. Die Kastenform mit Klarsichtfolie bedecken und die Sülze über Nacht im Kühlschrank gelieren lassen.

6 Für den Limettenjoghurt den Joghurt mit dem Limettenabrieb verrühren. Mit Zucker, Salz und Pfeffer abschmecken.

7 Die Sülze aus der Form stürzen, die Folie abziehen, die Sülze aufschneiden und mit dem Limettenjoghurt servieren.

Tomaten-Petit-Fours

Zutaten für 4 Personen

16 bunte, nicht zu kleine Kirschtomaten

Für die Parmesanfüllung

100 g frisch fein geriebener junger Parmesan

100 g Frischkäse (Doppelrahmstufe)

1 Spritzer frisch gepresster Zitronensaft

Salz

frisch gemahlener Pfeffer

Für die Ziegenfrischkäsefüllung

1 Rolle Ziegenfrischkäse (120 g)

fein geriebene Schale von 1/2 Orange (Bioware)

2 EL fein geschnittene Minzeblättchen

2 EL Olivenöl extra vergine

Chilipulver

Salz

frisch gemahlener Pfeffer

Zubereitungszeit: ca. 20–30 Minuten

1 Die Kirschtomaten waschen. Von jeder Tomate am Stielansatz einen Deckel abschneiden. Die Deckel beiseitestellen. Die Tomaten mit einem Parisienneausstecher oder einem Teelöffel aushöhlen.

2 Für die Parmesanfüllung den Parmesan mit dem Frischkäse glatt rühren. Die Creme mit Zitronensaft, Salz und Pfeffer abschmecken.

3 Die Parmesancreme in einen Spritzbeutel füllen und die Hälfte der Tomaten damit füllen. Auf die gefüllten Tomaten die Deckel setzen.

4 Für die Ziegenfrischkäsecreme den Ziegenkäse mit einer Gabel zerdrücken und mit der geriebenen Orangenschale, der Minze und dem Olivenöl glatt rühren. Die Creme mit etwas Chilipulver, Salz und Pfeffer abschmecken.

5 Die Ziegenfrischkäsecreme in einen Spritzbeutel füllen und die andere Hälfte der Tomaten damit füllen. Auf die gefüllten Tomaten die Deckel setzen.

Tipp: Wenn Sie keinen Spritzbeutel zur Hand haben, füllen Sie die Cremes jeweils in einen dickwandigen Gefrierbeutel, drücken Sie die Creme in eine Ecke und schneiden Sie die Ecke etwa 1/2–1 cm vor der Spitze ab.

Wachteleier in Tomatenvinaigrette

Zutaten für 4 Personen

24 Wachteleier
300 g sehr kleine, gelbe Kirschtomaten
3 Frühlingszwiebeln
4 Knoblauchzehen
250 ml Olivenöl extra vergine
2 EL Estragonessig
Salz
frisch gemahlener Pfeffer
4 Zweige Estragon

Zubereitungszeit: ca. 30 Minuten plus 1–2 Tage Kühlzeit

1 Die Wachteleier in einen Topf geben, mit kaltem Wasser bedecken und aufkochen. Den Topf vom Herd nehmen und die Wachteleier 5 Minuten ziehen lassen. Die Wachteleier aus dem Wasser nehmen, kalt abschrecken und schälen.

2 Die Kirschtomaten waschen. Die Hälfte der Kirschtomaten halbieren. Alle Kirschtomaten mit den Wachteleiern in eine Schüssel oder ein großes Schraubglas geben.

3 Die Frühlingszwiebeln putzen, in etwa 1 cm dicke Ringe schneiden und in die Schüssel bzw. das Glas geben.

4 Den Knoblauch schälen und in feine Scheiben schneiden. Den Knoblauch mit dem Olivenöl in einen Topf geben und leicht erwärmen. Den Topf vom Herd nehmen. Den Estragonessig hinzufügen und mit Salz und Pfeffer würzen. Die Marinade über die Wachteleier und die Tomatenmischung in der Schüssel bzw. dem Glas geben.

5 Die Schüssel mit Alufolie abdecken, bzw. das Schraubglas fest verschließen und die Wachteleier in der Vinaigrette 1 bis 2 Tage im Kühlschrank durchziehen lassen. Die Wachteleier mit den gezupften Estragonblättchen bestreuen und servieren.

Tipp: Die Wachteleier eignen sich gut für ein Picknick oder ein Sommerbuffet.

Tomaten mit Bonitofüllung in Petersilienöl und Chilifäden

Zutaten für 4 Personen

Für das Petersilienöl

30 g Blattpetersilienblättchen

125 ml Olivenöl extra vergine

1–2 EL Milch

1 Spritzer frisch gepresster Zitronensaft

Salz

frisch gemahlener Pfeffer

Für die Tomaten mit Bonitofüllung

150 g Thunfisch im eigenen Saft (aus der Dose)

2 EL Tomatenmark oder dick eingekochtes Tomatenpüree

1 Knoblauchzehe, fein gehackt

4 EL Olivenöl extra vergine

1 Spritzer frisch gepresster Limettensaft

Salz

frisch gemahlener Pfeffer

4 große Strauchtomaten

einige Chilifäden zum Garnieren

Zubereitungszeit: ca. 30–40 Minuten

1 Für das Petersilienöl die Petersilienblättchen mit kochendem Wasser übergießen, 1 bis 2 Minuten ziehen lassen, dann abseihen und kalt abschrecken.

2 Die Petersilienblättchen ausdrücken, mit dem Olivenöl, der Milch und dem Zitronensaft in einen Rührbecher geben und mit dem Stabmixer fein pürieren. Mit Salz und Pfeffer abschmecken.

3 Für die Bonitofüllung den Thunfisch gut abtropfen lassen, dann mit 3 EL des Petersilienöls, dem Tomatenmark, dem Knoblauch und dem Olivenöl in einen hohen Rührbecher geben und mit dem Stabmixer fein pürieren. Mit Limettensaft, Salz und Pfeffer abschmecken.

4 Die Tomaten am Stielansatz kreuzweise einschneiden. Reichlich Wasser in einem großen Topf zum Kochen bringen. Die Tomaten darin portionsweise je 1 Minute blanchieren. Die Tomaten aus dem Wasser nehmen, in Eiswasser abschrecken, dann häuten.

5 Von jeder Tomate eine Kappe (mit dem Stielansatz) abschneiden und das Tomateninnere vorsichtig mit einem Teelöffel aushöhlen.

6 Die ausgehöhlten Tomaten innen leicht salzen und mit dem Bonitopüree füllen.

7 Die gefüllten Tomaten mit der Öffnung nach unten auf 4 Teller setzen, mit dem restlichen Petersilienöl beträufeln und mit den Chilifäden bestreuen.

Steirischer Rindfleischsalat mit Bohnen, Tomaten und Kernöl

Zutaten für 4 Personen

300 g gekochtes Rindfleisch, z. B. mageres Meisel (Schulterscherzel)
300 g große weiße Bohnenkerne (aus der Dose)
4 große Tomaten
2 rote Zwiebeln
1 Bund Frühlingszwiebeln
125 ml Rindssuppe
65 ml milder Rotweinessig
1 Knoblauchzehe, zerdrückt
65 ml Kürbiskernöl
3 EL frisch geriebener Kren (Meerrettich)
Salz
frisch gemahlener Pfeffer
gehackte Blattpetersilie zum Bestreuen
frisch geriebener Kren zum Bestreuen

Zubereitungszeit: ca. 40 Minuten plus 1 Stunde Kühlzeit

1 Das Rindfleisch am besten in der Aufschnittmaschine in 2 mm dünne Scheiben schneiden. Die Scheiben in feine Streifen schneiden.

2 Die Bohnenkerne gut abtropfen lassen und mit den Rindfleischscheiben in einer Schüssel vermengen.

3 Die Tomaten waschen, halbieren, vom Stielansatz befreien und in Spalten schneiden und zu dem Fleisch und den Bohnen geben.

4 Die roten Zwiebeln schälen und in feine Ringe schneiden. Die Frühlingszwiebeln putzen und ebenfalls in feine Ringe schneiden. Beides ebenfalls in die Schüssel geben.

5 Für die Marinade die Rindssuppe mit dem Essig, dem Knoblauch und dem Kürbiskernöl in einen hohen Rührbecher geben und mit dem Stabmixer kurz durchmixen.

6 Die Marinade über den Salat geben und gut vermengen. Den frisch geriebenen Kren unterheben, mit Salz und Pfeffer abschmecken, die Schüssel abdecken und den Salat im Kühlschrank etwa 1 Stunde durchziehen lassen.

7 Den Salat auf 4 Teller verteilen und mit etwas gehackter Petersilie sowie frisch geriebenem Kren bestreuen.

Tipp: Statt mit Rindfleisch können Sie den Salat auch mit kaltem Braten zubereiten.

Rösttomaten auf Risoni-Kräuter-Salat mit Cacciatore

Zutaten für 4 Personen

Für die Rösttomaten

500 g kleine, gelbe Birnentomaten

2 EL Olivenöl extra vergine

fein geriebene Schale von 1 Zitrone (Bioware)

Für den Risoni-Kräuter-Salat

500 g Risoni (reisförmige Nudeln)

1 kleiner Bund Frühlingszwiebeln

125 ml Olivenöl extra vergine

50 g Blattpetersilienblättchen

50 g Basilikumblättchen

Saft von 2 Zitronen

Meersalz

frisch gemahlener Pfeffer

150 g Cacciatore (oder andere würzige Salami), fein aufgeschnitten

1 kleine rote Chilischote, fein gehackt

Zubereitungszeit: ca. 40 Minuten

1 Die Tomaten auf ein mit Backpapier bedecktes Backblech legen, mit dem Olivenöl beträufeln und mit der fein geriebenen Zitronenschale bestreuen. Die Tomaten im auf 200 °C vorgeheizten Backofen 8 bis 10 Minuten braten. Dann das Backblech aus dem Ofen nehmen und die Tomaten abkühlen lassen.

2 Die Risoni in reichlich Salzwasser al dente kochen, dann abschütten, mit etwas warmem Wasser abspülen und gut abtropfen lassen.

3 Die Frühlingszwiebeln putzen, in hauchfeine Ringe schneiden, mit dem Olivenöl vermengen, leicht salzen und etwa 10 Minuten ziehen lassen.

4 Die Risoni mit der Petersilie und dem Basilikum in eine Schüssel geben. Das Olivenöl mit den Frühlingszwiebeln hinzufügen und gut durchmischen. Den Salat mit Zitronensaft, Meersalz und Pfeffer abschmecken und kurz durchziehen lassen.

5 Den Salat auf 4 Tellern mit den Rösttomaten anrichten. Die Cacciatore und die fein gehackte Chilischote darüber verteilen.

Tipp: Bereiten Sie den Salat ohne die Cacciatore zu und reichen Sie ihn mit gegrilltem Fleisch.

Himbeer-Tomaten-Sorbet mit Karamellstangen

Zutaten für 4 Personen

Für das Sorbet

200 g brauner Rohrzucker
30 g Glukosepulver (Traubenzucker, erhältlich in der Apotheke)
3 Gewürznelken
6 große, reife Tomaten (ca. 800 g)
400 g frische Himbeeren
1 Vanilleschote
125 ml Prosecco
1 EL frisch gepresster Orangensaft

Für die Karamellstangerl

1 Packung TK-Blätterteig (320 g)
2 Eigelb
5 EL grober Kristallzucker
etwas gemahlener Zimt

Zubereitungszeit: ca. 1 Stunde plus 2–3 Stunden Kühlzeit

1 Den Zucker mit der Glukose und 200 ml Wasser in einem Topf aufkochen, dann 8 bis 10 Minuten einreduzieren. Den Topf vom Herd nehmen, die Gewürznelken in den Sirup geben und den Sirup abkühlen lassen.

2 Die Tomaten am Stielansatz kreuzweise einschneiden.

3 Reichlich Wasser in einem großen Topf zum Kochen bringen. Die Tomaten darin portionsweise je 1 Minute blanchieren.

4 Die Tomaten aus dem Wasser nehmen, in Eiswasser abschrecken, dann häuten, vierteln, vom Stielansatz befreien, entkernen und grob schneiden.

5 Die Himbeeren durch ein feines Sieb streichen. Die Gewürznelken aus dem Sirup nehmen. Das Himbeerpüree mit den Tomaten, dem Sirup und dem ausgekratzten Vanillemark im Mixer 1 bis 2 Minuten zu einem feinen Püree verarbeiten. Das Püree 2 bis 3 Stunden im Kühlschrank erkalten lassen.

6 Den kalten Prosecco und den kalten Orangensaft in das erkaltete Püree rühren. Die Mischung in der Eismaschine ca. 35 Minuten zu einem cremigen Sorbet gefrieren lassen.

7 Für die Karamellstangerl die aufgetauten Blätterteigplatten ausbreiten und mit verquirltem Eigelb bestreichen. Jede Platte in ca. 2 cm breite Streifen schneiden. Die Streifen auf ein mit Backpapier bedecktes Backblech legen, mit Zucker und Zimt bestreuen und im auf 200 °C vorgeheizten Backofen 10 Minuten goldbraun backen.

8 Das Himbeer-Tomaten-Sorbet in 4 Gläsern anrichten und mit den Karamellstangerln garnieren.

Frischer Tomatensaft

Ergibt 1 Glas (ca. 250 ml)

6 vollreife Tomaten (ca. 500 g)
1 EL frisch gepresster Zitronensaft
1 TL Zucker
Salz
etwas Worcestersauce (nach Belieben)

Zubereitungszeit: ca. 5 Minuten (Variante 1), 15 Minuten (Variante 2)

Variante 1

Die Tomaten von den Stielansätzen befreien, würfeln und im Entsafter zu Saft verarbeiten. Den Saft mit Zitronensaft, Zucker, Salz und Worcestersauce abschmecken.

Variante 2

Die Tomaten vierteln, von den Stielansätzen befreien, in einen hohen Rührbecher geben und mit dem Stabmixer pürieren. Das Püree durch ein feines Sieb tropfen lassen, dann das Fruchtfleisch durch das Sieb streichen und gut verrühren. Den Saft mit Zitronensaft, Zucker, Salz und Worcestersauce abschmecken.

Bloody Mary

Ergibt 1 Glas (ca. 250 ml)

2 Eiswürfel
1 Spritzer frisch gepresster Zitronensaft
1 Spritzer Tabasco
1 Spritzer Worcestersauce
50 ml Wodka
125 ml frischer Tomatensaft, gut gekühlt

Zubereitungszeit: ca. 1 Minute

Die Eiswürfel in ein hohes Glas geben. Den Zitronensaft, den Tabasco und die Worcestersauce hinzufügen, dann den Wodka darübergeben. Den Drink mit dem Tomatensaft auffüllen und mit einem langstieligen Löffel gut durchrühren.

Variante

Für eine Bloody Juanita bereiten Sie den Drink statt mit Wodka und Zitronensaft mit der gleichen Menge Tequila und Limettensaft zu.

UNSER
PARADEISS

Bowle von gelben Kirschtomaten mit Orangen und Ingwer

Für ca. 6 Gläser

50 g frischer Ingwer
100 g Rohrzucker
250 g kleine gelbe oder orange Kirschtomaten
5 große Orangen (ca. 1 kg)
125 ml Grand Marnier
1 Flasche Prosecco

Zubereitungszeit: ca. 30 Minuten plus Kühlzeit

1 Den Ingwer schälen, in feine Scheiben schneiden, mit dem Zucker und 500 ml Wasser in einen Topf geben und aufkochen. Die Mischung so lange köcheln lassen, bis ca. 500 ml Flüssigkeit übrig sind.

2 Die Kirschtomaten waschen und mehrmals mit einer Nadel einstechen. Die Kirschtomaten in eine Schüssel geben, mit dem lauwarmen Ingwersud übergießen, die Schüssel abdecken und die Tomaten einige Stunden ziehen lassen.

3 Die Orangen schälen, von den weißen Häutchen befreien, filetieren und zu den Tomaten geben, dann mit dem Grand Marnier aufgießen. Die Mischung mindestens 5 bis 6 Stunden (am besten über Nacht) im Kühlschrank ziehen lassen.

4 Die Bowle kurz vor dem Servieren mit dem gut gekühlten Prosecco aufgießen.

Warme Sommergerichte

Knusprige Selleriestäbchen mit Tomaten-Limetten-Öl

Zutaten für 4 Personen

Für das Tomaten-Limetten-Öl

6 vollreife rote Tomaten (ca. 500 g), blanchiert und gehäutet
1 EL Zucker
1 EL Tomatenmark oder dick eingekochtes Tomatenpüree
20 ml trockener Wermut
100 ml Limettenöl
Salz
frisch gemahlener Pfeffer

Zubereitungszeit: ca. 1 Stunde plus Abkühlzeit

1 Die Tomaten vierteln und entkernen, dann mit dem Zucker, dem Tomatenmark und dem Wermut in einen hohen Rührbecher geben und mit dem Stabmixer fein pürieren.

2 Die Tomatensauce in einen kleinen Topf geben und bei niedriger Temperatur leicht köchelnd um die Hälfte reduzieren. Den Topf vom Herd nehmen und die Sauce abkühlen lassen.

3 Das Limettenöl in die abgekühlte Tomatensauce rühren, mit Salz und Pfeffer abschmecken, den Topf abdecken und beiseitestellen.

Für die Selleriestäbchen

1 Knolle Sellerie (ca. 800 g)

Salz

2 Zitronen

80 g Parmesan, gerieben

50 g Pinienkerne, grob gehackt

3 Eier

120 g Weizenmehl (Type 405)

Butterschmalz zum Ausbacken

4 Den Sellerie schälen und halbieren. Den Sellerie in mit Salz und dem Saft der Zitronen versehenen Wasser weich kochen. Den weichen Sellerie im Sud abkühlen lassen.

5 Den abgekühlten Sellerie aus dem Sud nehmen, gut trocken tupfen und in 2 cm dicke Scheiben schneiden. Die Selleriescheiben in 1 cm breite Stäbchen schneiden. Die Selleriestäbchen salzen.

6 Den geriebenen Parmesan und die gehackten Pinienkerne auf einem Teller vermengen.

7 Die Eier verquirlen und in einen Teller geben.

8 Das Mehl auf einen Teller geben.

9 Die Selleriestäbchen nacheinander erst in dem Mehl, dann in dem verquirlten Ei und dann in der Parmesanmischung wälzen.

10 Das Butterschmalz in einer Pfanne erhitzen und die panierten Selleriestäbchen darin bei mittlerer Temperatur ausbacken. (Vorsicht: Bei zu großer Hitze verbrennt der Parmesan sehr leicht.)

11 Die Selleriestäbchen mit dem Schaumlöffel aus dem Schmalz nehmen, auf Küchenkrepp gut abtropfen lassen und mit dem Tomaten-Limetten-Öl auf 4 Tellern anrichten.

Frühstückstomaten

Zutaten für 4 Personen

4 rote Fleischtomaten (à ca. 150 g)
20 g Butter
etwas Kräutersalz
2 EL Olivenöl extra vergine
Butter für die Form
4 Eier
8 Scheiben Hamburger Speck (Frühstücksspeck), dünn aufgeschnitten

Zubereitungszeit: ca. 40 Minuten

1. Die Tomaten waschen und gründlich abtrocknen. Von jeder Tomate am Stielansatz einen Deckel abschneiden und die Tomaten mit einem Teelöffel aushöhlen.
2. Jede Tomate mit einem Stückchen Butter (5 g) füllen und mit etwas Kräutersalz ausstreuen.
3. Eine Auflaufform mit 1 EL Olivenöl und etwas Butter auspinseln. Die Tomaten in die Form stellen. Jedes Ei einzeln in eine Tasse aufschlagen und vorsichtig in eine Tomate gleiten lassen.
4. Die Tomaten etwa 30 Minuten im auf 180 °C vorgeheizten Backofen braten, bis die Eier stocken.
5. 1 EL Olivenöl in einer Pfanne erhitzen und den Speck darin knusprig braten.
6. Je 2 Scheiben Speck mit 1 Tomate auf 4 Tellern anrichten, nach Belieben salzen und servieren.

Tipp: Füllen Sie vor dem Ei etwas geriebenen Parmesan oder 1 Stück Blauschimmelkäse in die Tomaten.

Arme Ritter mit Parmesan-Oliven-Füllung und bunten Tomaten

Zutaten für 4 Personen

100 g Tapenade (Olivenpaste, erhältlich im gut sortierten Supermarkt)
2 EL frisch geriebener Parmesan
2 EL fein gehackte Blattpetersilie
8 Scheiben Toastbrot
3 Eier
250 ml Milch
Salz
Butterschmalz zum Ausbacken
1 kg bunte Tomaten
Meersalz zum Bestreuen
4 EL Olivenöl extra vergine
Saft von 1/2 Zitrone
einige Minzeblättchen

Zubereitungszeit: ca. 30–40 Minuten

1 Die Tapenade in eine kleine Schüssel geben und mit dem Parmesan und der Petersilie zu einer Creme rühren.

2 Die Oliven-Parmesan-Creme auf 4 Toastbrotscheiben streichen, dabei ringsum einen kleinen Rand frei lassen. Auf jede bestrichene Scheibe eine unbestrichene Scheibe legen. Diese »Armen Ritter« mit den Handflächen leicht zusammendrücken.

3 Die Eier mit der Milch verquirlen und leicht salzen. Die Mischung in einen tiefen Teller geben.

4 Die gefüllten »Armen Ritter« nacheinander in der Ei-Milch-Mischung wenden und kurz darin liegen lassen, bis sich das Brot vollgesaugt hat.

5 Das Butterschmalz in einer großen Pfanne erhitzen und die »Armen Ritter« darin von jeder Seite 3 bis 4 Minuten knusprig ausbacken, dann herausnehmen und auf Küchenkrepp abtropfen lassen.

6 Die Tomaten waschen, vom Stielansatz befreien, in Scheiben schneiden oder vierteln und auf eine Servierplatte legen. Die Tomaten mit Meersalz bestreuen, mit dem Olivenöl und dem Zitronensaft beträufeln und mit den gezupften Minzeblättchen garnieren.

7 Die »Armen Ritter« vierteln oder diagonal halbieren und mit den Tomaten servieren.

Sauerrahm-Tomaten-Schmarrn mit Schnittlauchgremolata

Für 4 bzw. 2 Personen (Vor- bzw. Hauptspeise)

Für den Sauerrahm-Tomaten-Schmarrn

350 g rote Kirschtomaten
4 EL Olivenöl extra vergine
4 Knoblauchzehen, fein gehackt
1 Prise brauner Rohrzucker
60 g Butter
Salz
frisch gemahlener Pfeffer
200 g Sauerrahm
5 Eigelb
3 EL glattes Weizenmehl (Type 405)
1 Msp. fein geriebene Zitronenschale (Bioware)
5 Eiweiß

Für die Gremolata

6 EL Schnittlauchröllchen
4 EL Olivenöl extra vergine
1 Msp. fein geriebene Zitronenschale (Bioware)
2 EL frisch gepresster Zitronensaft
Salz
frisch gemahlener Pfeffer
1/2 TL Chili- oder Tabascosauce

Zubereitungszeit: ca. 40 Minuten

1 Die Kirschtomaten waschen und halbieren.

2 Das Olivenöl in einer großen, beschichteten, ofenfesten Pfanne erhitzen und den Knoblauch darin anschwitzen. Die Tomaten hinzufügen und den Zucker darüberstreuen, alles 1 bis 2 Minuten weiterbraten. Die Pfanne vom Herd nehmen und 50 g Butterwürfel in die Tomatenmischung rühren. Mit Salz und Pfeffer abschmecken.

3 Den Sauerrahm mit den Eigelb und dem Mehl in eine Schüssel geben und glatt rühren.

4 Die restliche Butter (10 g) in einem kleinen Topf zerlassen und in den Teig rühren. Mit Salz, Pfeffer und Zitronenschale würzen.

5 Die Eiweiß zu steifem Schnee schlagen und locker unter den Teig ziehen.

6 Den Schmarrnteig über die Tomatenmischung in der Pfanne geben. Die Pfanne zurück auf den Herd stellen und den Schmarrn 2 bis 3 Minuten anbacken.

7 Den Schmarrn im auf 170 °C vorgeheizten Backofen etwa 20 Minuten fertig backen.

8 Für die Schnittlauchgremolata die Schnittlauchröllchen mit dem Olivenöl, dem Zitronenabrieb und dem Zitronensaft verrühren. Die Gremolata mit Salz, Pfeffer und Chilisauce abschmecken.

9 Den Schmarrn aus dem Ofen nehmen und mithilfe eines Esslöffels Nocken davon abstechen. Die Nocken in tiefe Teller geben und mit der Gremolata anrichten.

Tomatentarte Tatin mit Basilikumeis

Zutaten für 4 Personen

700 g gut reife rote Eiertomaten
4 EL Olivenöl extra vergine
3 EL Mandelblättchen
3 EL brauner Rohrzucker
3 Knoblauchzehen, fein gehackt
Salz
1 große rechteckige Platte Blätterteig (270 g)
20 g Basilikumblätter
400 ml Vanilleeis

Zubereitungszeit: ca. 1 1/2 Stunden

1 Die Tomaten waschen, halbieren und vom Stielansatz befreien. Die Kerne mit der Hand leicht herausdrücken.

2 Eine Tarteform (25 cm Durchmesser) mit 3 EL Olivenöl auspinseln. Die Mandelblättchen und 2 EL braunen Zucker hineinstreuen.

3 Die Tomaten mit der Schnittfläche nach oben dicht in die Tarteform schichten und mit dem Knoblauch und etwas Salz bestreuen.

4 Den gut gekühlten Blätterteig längs zusammenklappen, auf Backpapier legen und auf Größe der Tarteform ausrollen.

5 Den Blätterteig auf die Tomaten legen, mit den Handflächen gut andrücken und mit einer Gabel mehrmals einstechen.

6 Die Tarte im auf 200 °C vorgeheizten Backofen auf mittlerer Schiene etwa 50 Minuten backen.

7 Das Basilikum grob hacken, mit 2 EL heißem Wasser, 1 EL Olivenöl und 1 EL Zucker in einen hohen Rührbecher geben und mit dem Stabmixer fein pürieren.

8 Das leicht angetaute Vanilleeis in eine Schüssel geben, mit einer Gabel auflockern, dann grob mit dem Basilikumpüree vermengen und erneut tiefkühlen.

9 Die fertig gebackene Tarte aus dem Ofen nehmen, 6 bis 7 Minuten abkühlen lassen und aus der Form auf eine Servierplatte stürzen.

10 Die lauwarme Tarte in Stücke schneiden und mit dem Basilikumeis servieren.

Schmortomatensuppe mit Minzepesto

Zutaten für 4 Personen

Für das Minzepesto

2 EL Pinienkerne
1 Knoblauchzehe
2 Handvoll Minzeblättchen
80 ml Olivenöl extra vergine
1 TL Honig
1 EL frisch gepresster Zitronensaft
Salz
frisch gemahlener Pfeffer

Für die Schmortomatensuppe

1,5 kg vollreife rote Tomaten
1 rote Paprikaschote
2 EL Olivenöl extra vergine
750 ml Gemüse- oder Hühnerbrühe
1 TL brauner Rohrzucker
Salz
frisch gemahlener Pfeffer

Zubereitungszeit: ca. 50–60 Minuten

1 Für das Minzepesto eine Pfanne ohne Fettzugabe erhitzen und die Pinienkerne darin anrösten, dann herausnehmen und abkühlen lassen.

2 Den Knoblauch schälen und grob hacken.

3 Die Minzeblättchen grob hacken und mit den Pinienkernen, dem Knoblauch, dem Olivenöl und 1 EL heißem Wasser in einen hohen Rührbecher geben und mit dem Stabmixer fein pürieren. Das Pesto mit dem Honig, dem Zitronensaft, Salz und Pfeffer abschmecken und kalt stellen.

4 Die Tomaten halbieren und mit den Schnittflächen nach unten auf ein Backblech legen.

5 Die Paprika putzen, halbieren, von den Kernen und Scheidewänden befreien und grob schneiden. Die Paprikastücke zu den Tomaten auf das Backblech legen. Die Paprika und Tomaten mit dem Olivenöl beträufeln und mit Salz bestreuen, dann im auf 200 °C vorgeheizten Backofen etwa 30 Minuten braten.

6 Das gebratene Gemüse mit dem ausgetretenen Saft im Mixer fein pürieren.

7 Die Gemüse- bzw. Hühnerbrühe mit dem Püree in einen Topf geben und aufkochen. Die Suppe mit dem Zucker, Salz und Pfeffer abschmecken und 3 bis 4 Minuten köcheln lassen.

8 Die Suppe in 4 tiefe Teller schöpfen und mit dem Minzepesto servieren.

Tomatensuppe mit Kokos

Zutaten für 4 Personen

500 ml Gemüsebrühe
6 Pfefferkörner
1/2 TL Kreuzkümmelsamen
1–2 Chilischoten
500 g vollreife rote Tomaten, blanchiert und gehäutet
1 Dose Kokosmilch
Salz
frisch gemahlener Pfeffer
Koriandergrün zum Bestreuen

Zubereitungszeit: ca. 30 Minuten

1 Die Gemüsebrühe mit den Pfefferkörnern und den Kreuzkümmelsamen in einen Topf geben, aufkochen und 2 bis 3 Minuten kochen lassen. Dann den Topf vom Herd nehmen.

2 Die Chilischoten längs halbieren, entkernen, grob hacken und in die Brühe geben.

3 Die Tomaten halbieren, vom Stielansatz befreien und in Würfel schneiden. Die Tomatenwürfel in die Suppe geben und die Suppe bei geringer Temperatur 10 Minuten köcheln lassen.

4 Den Topf vom Herd nehmen, die Kokosmilch in die Suppe rühren und die Suppe in einen hohen Rührbecher geben. Die Suppe mit dem Stabmixer fein pürieren und zurück in den Topf geben.

5 Die Suppe nochmals langsam erhitzen, aber nicht aufkochen, dann mit Salz und Pfeffer abschmecken.

6 Die Suppe in 4 Suppenschalen schöpfen und mit gehacktem Koriandergrün bestreuen.

Weiße Tomaten-suppe mit Estragonöl

Zutaten für 4 Personen

Für das Estragonöl

20 g Estragonblättchen
100 ml Olivenöl extra vergine

Für die Suppe

1 kg vollreife Tomaten
5 Schalotten (ca. 80 g)
1 Knoblauchzehe
20 g Butter
700 ml Gemüsebrühe
125 ml Sahne
3 EL Crème fraîche
1 Msp. fein geriebene Orangenschale (Bioware)
Salz
frisch gemahlener Pfeffer
einige Estragonblättchen zum Garnieren

Zubereitungszeit: ca. 50 Minuten

1 Für das Estragonöl die Estragonblättchen mit kochendem Wasser übergießen, einige Sekunden ziehen lassen, dann kalt abschrecken, abtropfen lassen, trocken tupfen und mit dem Olivenöl in einen Rührbecher geben. Mit dem Stabmixer fein pürieren.

2 Die Tomaten waschen, vom Stielansatz befreien und in kleine Würfel schneiden.

3 Die Schalotten und den Knoblauch schälen und fein hacken.

4 Die Butter in einem Topf aufschäumen. Die Schalotten und den Knoblauch darin kurz anschwitzen, dann die Tomatenwürfel hinzufügen und mit der Gemüsebrühe auffüllen. Die Suppe bei geringer Temperatur 15 bis 20 Minuten köcheln lassen.

5 Die Suppe in ein mit Küchenkrepp oder einem Kaffeefilter ausgelegtes Sieb geben und langsam in eine Schüssel tropfen lassen – dadurch wird die Suppe klar.

6 Die klare Tomatensuppe nochmals aufkochen und 4 bis 5 Minuten köcheln lassen, dann die Sahne und die Crème fraîche zufügen. Die Suppe mit dem Orangenabrieb, Salz und Pfeffer abschmecken, dann mit dem Stabmixer aufschäumen.

7 Die Suppe in 4 tiefen Tellern anrichten, mit dem Estragonöl beträufeln und mit den Estragonblättchen garnieren.

Zucchini-Tomaten-Mus mit frittierten Sprotten

Zutaten für 4 Personen

Für das Zucchini-Tomten-Mus

1 Zucchini (ca. 150 g)
1 kleine Zwiebel
2 EL Olivenöl extra vergine
1 große Fleischtomate, blanchiert und gehäutet
1/2 TL getrockneter Oregano
3 Blatt weiße Gelatine
200 g Ricotta
Salz
frisch gemahlener Pfeffer
125 ml Schlagsahne, geschlagen

Zubereitungszeit: ca. 50–60 Minuten plus 4–5 Stunden Kühlzeit

1 Die Zucchini waschen und grob raspeln. Die Zwiebel schälen und in kleine Würfel schneiden.

2 Das Olivenöl in einer Pfanne erhitzen und die Zwiebeln darin anschwitzen. Die Zucchini hinzufügen und dünsten, bis alle Flüssigkeit verkocht ist. Dann die Pfanne vom Herd nehmen.

3 Die Tomate halbieren, entkernen und klein würfeln. Die Tomatenwürfel zu den lauwarmen Zucchini geben und den Oregano hineinrühren. Die Mischung rasch abkühlen lassen.

4 Die Gelatine in kaltem Wasser einweichen.

5 Den Ricotta unter die Zucchini-Tomaten-Mischung heben und alles mit Salz und Pfeffer abschmecken.

6 Die eingeweichte Gelatine gut ausdrücken, in einen kleinen Topf geben und bei geringer Temperatur erwärmen. Sobald sich die Gelatine aufgelöst hat, 2–3 EL des Tomaten-Zucchini-Muses hinzufügen und gut verrühren. Dann die Gelatinemischung in das restliche Tomaten-Zucchini-Mus rühren.

7 Die geschlagene Sahne unter das Mus ziehen. Das Mus in kleine, mit kaltem Wasser ausgespülte Förmchen füllen und 4 bis 5 Stunden im Kühlschrank erkalten lassen.

Für die frittierten Sprotten

300 g frische Sprotten oder Sardinen

Meersalz

Weizenmehl zum Wenden

neutrales Pflanzenöl zum Ausbacken

Zum Anrichten

Olivenöl extra vergine

gemischte Kräuter

8 Die Sprotten waschen, gründlich trocken tupfen und mit Salz bestreuen, dann in dem Mehl wenden.

9 Das Pflanzenöl in einem Topf erhitzen. Die Sprotten darin ausbacken. Die frittierten Sprotten mit dem Schaumlöffel aus dem Topf heben und auf Küchenkrepp abtropfen lassen.

10 Das Zucchini-Tomaten-Mus aus den Förmchen stürzen und mit den frittierten Sprotten anrichten. Mit Olivenöl beträufeln und nach Belieben mit frischen Kräutern garnieren.

Marinierte Scheiben vom Kalbsfilet mit Tomaten und Pesto

Zutaten für 4 Personen

Für das Pesto

10 g Blattpetersilienblättchen
10 g Basilikumblättchen
2 EL Pinienkerne
65 ml Olivenöl extra vergine
Salz
frisch gemahlener Pfeffer

Zum Nachwürzen des Pestos

etwas gehackter Knoblauch
etwas frisch geriebene Zitronenschale
Salz
frisch gemahlener Pfeffer

Zubereitungszeit: ca. 30 Minuten

1 Für das Pesto die Petersilie, das Basilikum und die Pinienkerne mit der Hälfte des Olivenöls in einen hohen Rührbecher geben und mit dem Stabmixer fein pürieren. Das Pesto mit Salz und Pfeffer abschmecken.

2 Das Kalbsfilet mit der Hälfte des Pestos bestreichen, in Frischhaltefolie wickeln und 2 bis 3 Stunden im Tiefkühlfach anfrieren.

3 Das restliche Pesto mit dem restlichen Olivenöl glatt rühren und nach Belieben mit etwas Knoblauch, geriebener Zitronenschale, Salz und Pfeffer nachwürzen.

4 Die Tomaten waschen und mit einem scharfen Messer in sehr dünne Scheiben schneiden.

5 Auf 4 Tellern einen Spiegel aus Pesto streichen, dabei etwas Pesto zurückbehalten. Die Tomatenscheiben auf das Pesto legen und leicht salzen.

Für das Kalbsfilet mit Tomaten

600 g küchenfertiges Kalbsfilet

6 vollreife ovale Tomaten (ca. 400 g)

Salz

3–4 EL Olivenöl

12 schwarze Oliven, entsteint

80 g frischer Parmesan (im Ganzen)

Salz

frisch gemahlener Pfeffer

6 Das angefrorene Kalbsfilet aus der Folie wickeln und mit einem scharfen Messer oder auf der Schneidemaschine in 1–2 mm dünne Scheiben schneiden. Die Fleischscheiben auf den Tomatenscheiben verteilen und mit etwas Olivenöl beträufeln.

7 Die Oliven längs in Spalten schneiden und über das Kalbfleisch streuen. Das restliche Pesto darüber verteilen.

8 Vom Parmesan mit dem Sparschäler dünne Späne abhobeln. Die Parmesanspäne über die Pestoschicht streuen. Alles nochmals mit etwas Salz und Pfeffer bestreuen.

Für den Fladenbelag

500 g geriebener Almkäse (z. B. milder Bergkäse)

450 ml Sauerrahm

125 ml Milch

4 Eier

2 EL griffiges Weizenmehl (Type 405)

Salz

frisch gemahlener Pfeffer

300 g bunte Tomaten

2 Zweige Rosmarin

7 Für den Belag den Käse, den Sauerrahm, die Milch, die Eier und das Mehl in eine Schüssel geben und gründlich vermengen. Die Füllung mit Salz und Pfeffer abschmecken und über die Zwiebeln geben.

8 Die Tomaten waschen, vom Stielansatz befreien und in ca. 1 cm dicke Scheiben schneiden. Die Tomatenscheiben auf der Almkäsefüllung verteilen. Die gezupften Rosmarinnadeln darübergeben.

9 Den Fladen im auf 200 °C vorgeheizten Backofen auf der mittleren Schiene etwa 30 Minuten backen, dann aus dem Ofen nehmen und leicht abkühlen lassen. Den Fladen in Stücke schneiden und lauwarm mit einem Glas Rotwein servieren.

Dolce-Latte-Omelette mit Salbeitomaten

Zutaten für 4 Personen

Für die Salbeitomaten

250 g Kirschtomaten
2 EL Olivenöl extra vergine
4 Blätter Salbei
1 TL Kristallzucker
Salz
frisch gemahlener Pfeffer

Für das Omelette

3 Eier
2 EL Mineralwasser
1 EL Stärkemehl
Salz
frisch gemahlener Pfeffer
1 Prise Cayennepfeffer
1 EL Butter
80 g Dolce Latte (sehr milder Gorgonzola)

Zubereitungszeit: ca. 20 Minuten

1. Die Kirschtomaten waschen und halbieren.
2. Das Olivenöl in einer großen Pfanne erhitzen und die Salbeiblätter darin 1 bis 2 Minuten anbraten. Die Tomaten in die Pfanne geben, mit dem Zucker bestreuen, mit Salz und Pfeffer würzen und bei niedriger Temperatur 4 bis 5 Minuten schmurgeln lassen. Dann die Pfanne vom Herd nehmen und beiseitestellen.
3. Für das Omelette die Eier in einer Schüssel mit dem Mineralwasser und dem Stärkemehl verquirlen. Den Omeletteteig mit Salz, Pfeffer und Cayennepfeffer abschmecken.
4. Die Butter in einer beschichteten Pfanne zerlassen und den Omeletteteig hineingeben.
5. Den Dolce Latte grob zerbröseln und über das flüssige Omelette geben. Das Omelette bei niedriger Temperatur etwa 5 bis 6 Minuten stocken lassen.
6. Das Omelette mit einem Pfannenwender zusammenklappen, auf einen großen Teller gleiten lassen, die Salbeitomaten darauf verteilen und servieren.

Tipp: Wenn Sie ein kräftigeres Omelette haben wollen, verwenden Sie statt Dolce Latte Roquefort oder kräftigen Gorgonzola.

Pasta mit Tomaten und Rosinen

Zutaten für 4 Personen

1 kleine Fenchelknolle (ca. 200 g)
2 Knoblauchzehen
4 EL Olivenöl extra vergine
1 TL Fenchelsamen
Salz
500 g Kirschtomaten
1 Döschen Safran
125 ml trockener Weißwein
1 Chilischote
2 EL Rosinen
3 EL gehackte Blattpetersilie
2 EL schwarze Oliven, entsteint
500 g Pasta (z. B. Spaghetti)
Olivenöl extra vergine zum Beträufeln

Zubereitungszeit: ca. 35 Minuten

1 Die Fenchelknolle putzen, halbieren und in feine Streifen schneiden.

2 Den Knoblauch schälen und in feine Scheiben schneiden.

3 Das Olivenöl bei mittlerer Temperatur in einer großen Pfanne erhitzen. Den Knoblauch und die Fenchelsamen darin kurz mitbraten, dann den Fenchel hinzufügen, leicht mit Salz bestreuen und alles ca. 10 Minuten schmurgeln lassen.

4 Die Tomaten waschen, halbieren, in die Pfanne geben und kurz anbraten. Dann den Safran hinzufügen und alles mit dem Weißwein aufgießen.

5 Die Chilischote fein hacken und mit den Rosinen in die Sauce rühren. Die Sauce weitere 5 bis 6 Minuten köcheln lassen. Bei Bedarf etwas Wasser hinzufügen.

6 Die Sauce mit Salz und Pfeffer abschmecken, dann die Petersilie und die Oliven hineinrühren.

7 Die Pasta nach Packungsanleitung in reichlich Salzwasser al dente kochen, dann abschütten und gründlich mit der Tomatensauce vermengen. Bei Bedarf erneut mit Salz und Pfeffer abschmecken.

8 Die Pasta in 4 tiefen Tellern anrichten, mit dem Olivenöl beträufeln und servieren.

Tipp: Belegen Sie die heiße Pasta mit 1 bis 2 Scheiben Ziegenfrischkäse oder italienischem Caprino di latte vaccino.

Brandteig-Petersilien-Gnocchi mit roher Tomatensauce

Zutaten für 4 Personen

Für die Tomatensauce

500 g Kirschtomaten
2 EL Zucker
125 ml Olivenöl extra vergine
Salz
frisch gemahlener Pfeffer

Für die Brandteig-Petersilien-Gnocchi

1 Bund krause Petersilie
2 EL Olivenöl extra vergine
1 EL Tiefkühlspinat, aufgetaut, passiert und gut abgetropft
1 TL Salz
150 g gesalzene Butter
300 g Weizenmehl (Type 405)
3 EL frisch geriebener Parmesan
6 Eier
etwas Weizengrieß für das Backblech
Olivenöl extra vergine zum Beträufeln
etwas frisch geriebener Parmesan zum Bestreuen

Zubereitungszeit: ca. 70 Minuten

1 Für die rohe Tomatensauce die Kirschtomaten vierteln, in eine Schüssel geben und mit dem Zucker und dem Olivenöl vermengen. Mit Salz und Pfeffer bestreuen, die Schüssel abdecken und die Tomaten bei Zimmertemperatur 1 Stunde ziehen lassen.

2 Für die Gnocchi die Blättchen von der Petersilie zupfen. Die Blättchen mit kochendem Wasser übergießen, kurz im Wasser ziehen lassen, dann abschütten, kalt abschrecken und trocken tupfen. Die Petersilie mit dem Olivenöl und dem Spinat in einen hohen Rührbecher geben und mit dem Stabmixer fein pürieren.

3 500 ml Wasser mit 1 TL Salz in einen großen Topf geben und aufkochen.

4 Die Butter in Stücke schneiden, in das heiße Wasser geben, schmelzen lassen und erneut aufkochen. Dann das Petersilien-Spinat-Püree hinzufügen.

5 Das Mehl auf einmal hinzufügen und die Mischung mit einem Holzkochlöffel so lange kräftig rühren, bis sich der Teig als Kloß vom Topfboden löst und sich am Topfboden eine weiße Schicht bildet.

6 Den Topf vom Herd nehmen, kurz abkühlen lassen, dann mit dem Handrührgerät (Knethaken) nach und nach den Parmesan und die Eier hineinkneten.

7 Den Brandteig in einen Spritzbeutel mit großer glatter Tülle füllen (Nr. 11).

8 Ein Backblech mit Backpapier bedecken und mit Grieß bestreuen. Den Gnocchiteig längs in langen Strängen aufspritzen.

9 Die Gnocchistränge mit einem befeuchteten Messer in etwa 3 cm lange Stücke schneiden.

10 In einem großen Topf reichlich Salzwasser aufkochen. Die Gnocchi in das kochende Wasser gleiten lassen (dabei eventuell mit einem Teigschaber nachhelfen) und aufkochen. Die Temperatur reduzieren und die Gnocchi 2 bis 3 Minuten ziehen lassen.

11 Die garen Gnocchi mit einem Schaumlöffel aus dem Wasser nehmen und in 4 tiefen Pastatellern anrichten. Die Gnocchi mit etwas Olivenöl beträufeln, mit etwas geriebenem Parmesan bestreuen und die rohe Tomatensauce darübergeben. Nach Belieben mit Pfeffer aus der Mühle würzen.

Safrangalette mit Zitronen-Crème-fraîche und Tomaten

Zutaten für 4 Personen

Für den Galetteteig
1 Döschen Safran
2 Eier
250 ml Milch
1/2 TL Salz
60 g glattes Weizenmehl (Type 405)
2 EL Buchweizenmehl
1 TL Koriandersamen, grob zerstoßen

Für den Galettebelag
400 g Kirschtomaten
2 EL Olivenöl extra vergine
1 TL brauner Rohrzucker
Salz
frisch gemahlener Pfeffer

Für die Zitronen-Crème-fraîche
300 g Crème fraîche
fein geriebene Schale von 1/2 Zitrone (Bioware)
3 EL Olivenöl extra vergine
Salz
frisch gemahlener Pfeffer

Zum Ausbacken und Garnieren
Sonnenblumenöl
gemischte Kräuter und Kräuterblüten

Zubereitungszeit: ca. 40 Minuten

1 Den Safran mit 3 EL heißem Wasser übergießen und 5 Minuten ziehen lassen.

2 Die Eier in einer Schüssel mit der Milch, dem Safranwasser und dem Salz verquirlen. Dann das Weizenmehl, das Buchweizenmehl und den Koriander hinzufügen. Alles zu einem glatten Teig verrühren. Den Teig 10 Minuten ruhen lassen.

3 Die Kirschtomaten waschen und halbieren.

4 Das Olivenöl in einer Pfanne erhitzen, den Zucker hinzufügen und leicht karamellisieren. Dann die Kirschtomaten in die Pfanne geben, salzen, pfeffern und 1 bis 2 Minuten anbraten. Die Pfanne abdecken und vom Herd nehmen.

5 Die Crème fraîche mit dem Zitronenabrieb und dem Olivenöl glatt rühren. Die Zitronen-Crème-fraîche mit Salz und Pfeffer abschmecken.

6 Etwas Sonneblumenöl in einer Pfanne erhitzen und nacheinander 8 dünne Galettes darin ausbacken.

7 Die Galettes mit je 1 EL Zitronen-Crème-fraîche bestreichen, 1 EL geschmorte Kirschtomaten darübergeben. Jede Galette zu einem rechteckigen Päckchen klappen.

8 Je 2 Galettes auf 1 Teller geben. Mit der restlichen Crème fraîche und den restlichen Kirschtomaten bedecken und mit frischen Kräutern und Kräuterblüten garnieren.

Info: Galettes sind Buchweizenpfannkuchen aus der Bretagne. Traditionell werden sie nur mit Buchweizenmehl zubereitet.

Mit Sommergemüse gefüllte Schmortomaten

Zutaten für 4 Personen

Für die Tomatensauce

6 reife Tomaten (ca. 500 g)
3 EL Olivenöl extra vergine
1 mittelgroße Zwiebel, fein gehackt
2 Knoblauchzehen, fein gehackt
3 EL dick eingekochtes Tomatenpüree oder Tomatenmark (oder 4 EL Tomatenconfit, siehe Rezept Seite 65)
2 Zweige Thymian
Salz
frisch gemahlener Pfeffer
1/2 TL Zucker

Zubereitungszeit: ca. 80 Minuten

1 Die Tomaten waschen, halbieren, entkernen und hacken.

2 Das Olivenöl in einer Pfanne erhitzen. Die Zwiebel und den Knoblauch darin glasig schwitzen. Dann die Tomaten, das Tomatenpüree und den Thymian hinzufügen und 8 Minuten köcheln lassen. Die Sauce mit 300 ml Wasser aufgießen, mit Salz und Pfeffer abschmecken und weitere 5 Minuten köcheln lassen. Die Thymianzweige entfernen, die Sauce nochmals abschmecken, dann den Zucker hineinrühren. Die Sauce vom Herd nehmen.

3 Für die Schmortomaten die Karotte schälen und fein würfeln. Den Staudensellerie putzen, von den Fäden befreien und fein würfeln. Die Zucchini putzen und fein würfeln.

4 Von den Tomaten jeweils das obere Drittel als Deckel abschneiden. Die Deckel beiseitestellen. Die Tomaten mithilfe eines Teelöffels aushöhlen.

5 Die Butter in einem Topf zerlassen. Die Zwiebel, den Thymian und das Lorbeerblatt darin etwa 3 Minuten anschwitzen. Den ungewaschenen Risottoreis hinzufügen und etwa 1 Minute anschwitzen.

Für die Schmortomaten

1 Karotte (ca. 120 g)

1 Stange Staudensellerie (ca. 100 g)

1 Zucchini (ca. 150 g)

4 große reife Tomaten

20 g Butter

1 Zwiebel, fein gehackt

1 TL frisch gehackter Thymian

1 frisches Lorbeerblatt

100 g Risottoreis

400 ml Hühnerbrühe

2 EL Sahne

85 g Gruyère (Schweizer Hartkäse), grob gerieben

1 EL natives Olivenöl

6 Den Reis mit der Hälfte der Hühnerbrühe aufgießen, salzen und pfeffern. Den Risotto gut aufkochen, dann die Temperatur reduzieren und den Risotto unter gelegentlichem Rühren 5 Minuten köcheln lassen.

7 Die Karotte, den Staudensellerie und die Zucchini in den Risotto geben, dann mit der restlichen heißen Brühe aufgießen und den Risotto unter gelegentlichem Rühren weitere 15 Minuten köcheln lassen.

8 Die Sahne und den Gruyère in den Risotto rühren. Den Risotto mit Salz und Pfeffer abschmecken, dann das Lorbeerblatt entfernen.

9 Den Risotto in die ausgehöhlten Tomaten füllen. Jede gefüllte Tomate mit dem Deckel verschließen.

10 Die Tomatensauce in eine Auflaufform geben. Die gefüllten Tomaten in die Sauce setzen und mit dem Olivenöl beträufeln. Die Tomaten im auf 180 °C vorgeheizten Backofen 25 bis 30 Minuten schmoren.

11 Die Schmortomaten mit der Sauce auf vorgewärmten Tellern anrichten und servieren.

Gefüllte Paprika mit Couscous

Zutaten für 4 Personen

8 gelbe Spitzpaprika oder 8 kleine grüne Paprika

500 ml Hühnerbrühe

1 Döschen Safran

150 g Instant-Couscous

50 g geröstete Mandelblättchen

50 g geröstete Pinienkerne

100 g Rosinen

1 EL Currypulver

1 TL Chilisauce

etwas gemahlener Koriander

Salz

frisch gemahlener Pfeffer

2 große Fleischtomaten (ca. 450 g)

3 Knoblauchzehen, geschält und gehackt

1 Sternanis

Olivenöl extra vergine zum Beträufeln

Zubereitungszeit: ca. 1 Stunde

1. Die Paprikas längs halbieren, entkernen und waschen.
2. 275 ml Hühnerbrühe mit dem Safran aufkochen, dann den Couscous hineinrühren, vom Herd nehmen und zugedeckt 10 Minuten quellen lassen.
3. Die Mandelblättchen, die Pinienkerne und die Rosinen zu dem garen Couscous geben und vermengen. Dann das Currypulver und die Chilisauce hinzufügen und erneut gut vermengen. Den Couscous mit Koriander, Salz und Pfeffer pikant abschmecken.
4. Die Tomaten waschen und in kleine Würfel schneiden. Die restliche heiße Hühnerbrühe (125 ml) über die Tomaten geben, dann den Knoblauch und den Sternanis hinzufügen. Die Mischung mit Salz und Pfeffer abschmecken und in eine Auflaufform geben.
5. Die Couscousmischung in die Paprikahälften füllen. Die gefüllten Paprikahälften auf das Tomatenbett in der Auflaufform setzen. Die Form mit Alufolie bedecken und die Paprika im auf 180 °C vorgeheizten Backofen etwa 20 Minuten garen. Dann die Alufolie entfernen und die Paprika weitere 20 Minuten garen.
6. Je 2 gefüllte Paprikahälften mit der Tomatensauce anrichten und alles mit etwas Olivenöl beträufeln.

Tipp: Servieren Sie die gefüllte Paprika mit Chilijoghurt – dazu 250 ml Schafmilchjoghurt mit 2 EL Zitronensaft, 1/2 TL Paprikapulver und 2 EL gehackter Petersilie vermengen. Mit Cayennepfeffer, Salz und frisch gemahlenem Pfeffer abschmecken.

Zitronenhuhn aus dem Wok mit grünen Schmortomaten

Zutaten für 4 Personen

Für die Zitronenmarinade und das Huhn

1 daumengroßes Stück Ingwer

4 EL frisch gepresster Zitronensaft

1 TL grüne Currypaste (erhältlich im Asialaden oder in gut sortierten Supermärkten)

3 EL Sonnenblumenöl

Salz

600 g Hühnerbrust (ohne Haut)

Für die grünen Schmortomaten

1 große Gemüsezwiebel (ca. 150 g)

200 g grüne Tomaten

1 kleine grüne Chilischote

6 EL Sonnenblumenöl

1/2 TL Kreuzkümmelsamen

Salz

3 EL gehacktes Koriandergrün

2 EL Honig oder geriebener Palmzucker

Zubereitungszeit: ca. 45 Minuten

1 Für die Zitronenmarinade den Ingwer schälen, fein reiben und in einer Schüssel mit dem Zitronensaft, der Currypaste und dem Sonnenblumenöl verrühren. Mit Salz abschmecken.

2 Die Hühnerbrust in etwa 2 cm dicke Streifen schneiden, in eine Schüssel geben und mit der Marinade vermengen. Die Hühnerbrust 20 Minuten ziehen lassen.

3 Für die grünen Schmortomaten die Zwiebel schälen und fein hacken.

4 Die grünen Tomaten waschen und vierteln.

5 Die Chilischote längs halbieren, entkernen und fein hacken.

6 3 EL Sonnenblumenöl in einem Wok stark erhitzen. Die Kreuzkümmelsamen darin anrösten, dann die Zwiebeln hinzufügen und glasig schwitzen.

7 Die Tomatenwürfel und die gehackte Chilischote in den Wok geben und die Mischung so lange dünsten, bis die Tomaten püreeartig sind. Mit Salz abschmecken, dann das Koriandergrün untermengen. Den Wok vom Herd nehmen.

8 3 EL Sonnenblumenöl in einer Pfanne erhitzen und das marinierte Fleisch darin portionsweise scharf anbraten.

9 Alles gebratene Fleisch zurück in die Pfanne geben. Etwa 125 ml Wasser und den Honig oder den geriebenen Palmzucker hinzufügen. Das Hühnerfleisch garen, bis alle Flüssigkeit verkocht ist und das Fleisch leicht karamellisiert.

10 Das gebratene Huhn mit den Schmortomaten anrichten.

Huhn mit Lavendelhonigglasur auf Schmortomaten

Zutaten für 4 Personen

Für die Gewürzmischung

1 EL Fenchelsamen

1 TL Koriandersamen

3 Gewürznelken

4 Pimentkörner

5 Pfefferkörner

1 getrocknetes Lorbeerblatt

1 TL Paprikapulver

1 EL getrockneter Thymian

Für das glasierte Huhn mit Schmortomaten

1 großes Freilandhuhn (ca. 1,3 kg)

Salz

4 EL Armagnac (französischer Weinbrand)

800 g Pflaumen-Rispentomaten (ovale Tomaten)

50 g gesalzene Butter

250 g Lavendelhonig

2 EL Sherryessig

frischer Lavendel zum Bestreuen

Zubereitungszeit: ca. 80 Minuten plus Zeit zum Marinieren

1. Für die Gewürzmischung alle Gewürze im Mörser grob zerstoßen oder in der Küchenmaschine grob vermahlen.
2. Das Huhn in 8 Stücke zerteilen. Diese in eine Auflaufform legen, leicht salzen, mit 2/3 der Gewürzmischung einreiben und mit dem Armagnac übergießen. Die Form abdecken und das Huhn mindestens 5 bis 6 Stunden (am besten über Nacht) im Kühlschrank ziehen lassen. Das Huhn 30 Minuten vor der Zubereitung aus dem Kühlschrank nehmen.
3. Die marinierten Hühnerteile in eine Fettpfanne legen.
4. Die Tomaten waschen und ganz in die Fettpfanne legen. Das Huhn mit den Butterflocken belegen und im auf 160 °C vorgeheizten Backofen etwa 40 Minuten braten.
5. Den Honig und den Essig in einen kleinen Topf geben und erwärmen, bis der Honig dünnflüssig wird. Dann die restliche Gewürzmischung hineinrühren.
6. Die Ofentemperatur auf 180 °C erhöhen. Die Hühnerteile mit der Honigglasur bestreichen und weitere 6 bis 7 Minuten braten. Die Hühnerteile erneut mit der Glasur bestreichen und weitere 6 bis 7 Minuten braten. (Wichtig: Der Honig soll nur leicht karamellisieren, keine Kruste bilden.)
7. Den Backofen ausschalten, die Ofentüre leicht öffnen und das glasierte Huhn etwa 5 bis 7 Minuten ruhen lassen.
8. Je 2 Hühnerteile mit den Schmortomaten und dem entstandenen (mit Salz und Pfeffer abgeschmeckten) Bratensaft anrichten und mit dem frischen Lavendel bestreuen.

Mariniertes Huhn in Curry-Tempura mit Grapefruit-Tomaten-Chutney

Zutaten für 4 Personen

Für das Chutney

5 große Strauchtomaten (ca. 500 g)
1 Zwiebel (ca. 80 g)
3 EL Olivenöl extra vergine
Salz
3 rosa Grapefruits
1/2 Chilischote
1 EL Honig
frisch gemahlener Pfeffer
2 EL fein gehackte Estragonblättchen

Für das marinierte Huhn

4 kleine Hühnerbrustfilets (à 140 g, ohne Haut)
4 EL Sojasauce
1 EL Honig
Saft von 1/2 Limette
fein geriebene Schale von 1 Limette (Bioware)
1 TL grob geschrotete Pfefferkörner
Salz
Pfeffer aus der Mühle

Zubereitungszeit: ca. 60 Minuten plus Marinierzeit

1 Für das Chutney die Tomaten waschen, halbieren, vom Stielansatz befreien und in kleine Würfel schneiden.

2 Die Zwiebel schälen und in kleine Würfel schneiden.

3 Das Olivenöl in einem Topf erhitzen und die Zwiebel darin glasig schwitzen. Dann die Tomaten hinzufügen und salzen. Die Tomaten köcheln lassen, bis die Flüssigkeit verkocht ist.

4 Die Grapefruits mit einem scharfen Messer schälen, von der weißen Haut befreien und filetieren. Die Grapefruitfilets zu den Tomaten in den Topf geben und einmal aufkochen. Dann den Topf sofort vom Herd nehmen.

5 Die Chilischote fein hacken, mit dem Honig vermengen und in das Chutney rühren. Das Chutney mit Salz und Pfeffer abschmecken, dann den Estragon hineinrühren. Das Chutney 1 bis 2 Stunden im Kühlschrank durchziehen lassen.

6 Die Hühnerbrustfilets längs in etwa 1 cm dicke Streifen schneiden, in eine Schale legen und leicht salzen.

7 Aus der Sojasauce, dem Honig, dem Limettensaft, der Limettenschale und den Pfefferkörnern eine Marinade rühren. Die Marinade über das Hühnerfleisch geben und dieses 30 Minuten ziehen lassen.

(Fortsetzung auf Seite 154)

Für den Tempurateig

5 EL glattes Weizenmehl (Type 405)

2 EL Stärkemehl

1/2 TL Backpulver

2 EL Currypulver

1 TL gemahlene Korianderkörner

Salz

Zum Ausbacken und Garnieren

reichlich neutrales Pflanzenöl

etwas gehackte Chilischote

(Fortsetzung von Seite 152)

8 Für den Tempurateig das Mehl, das Stärkemehl, das Backpulver, das Currypulver, den Koriander und etwas Salz in einer Schüssel vermengen. 200 ml eiskaltes Wasser hinzufügen und die Mischung zu einem glatten Teig verrühren. Den Teig 15 Minuten ruhen lassen.

9 Die Hühnerfleischstreifen im Zickzack auf lange Holzspieße stecken.

10 Reichlich Pflanzenöl in einem Topf erhitzen. Die Hühnerspieße durch den Tempurateig ziehen und sofort in dem heißen Öl knusprig ausbacken. Die frittierten Spieße mit einem Schaumlöffel aus dem Topf heben und auf Küchenkrepp abtropfen lassen.

11 Die Hühnerspieße mit dem Grapefruit-Tomaten-Chutney anrichten und mit etwas gehacktem Chili bestreuen.

Geschmorte Topfentomaten mit Sardellen und Melisse

Zutaten für 4 Personen

4 mittelgroße Fleischtomaten
250 g Topfen (Quark, 40 % Fettgehalt)
2 EL Sauerrahm
4 EL frisch geriebener Parmesan
2 EL Erdäpfelflocken (Instant-Kartoffelpüree)
4 Sardellenfilets
4 EL gehackte Blattpetersilie
4 EL gehackte Zitronenmelisse
Salz
frisch gemahlener Pfeffer
2 EL Butter für die Form und zum Bestreuen

Zubereitungszeit: ca. 40 Minuten

1 Die Tomaten waschen und am Stielansatz einen Deckel abschneiden. Die Deckel beiseitestellen. Die Tomaten mithilfe eines Teelöffels aushöhlen.

2 Den Topfen mit dem Sauerrahm, dem Parmesan und den Erdäpfelflocken in eine Schüssel geben und verrühren. Die Creme 5 Minuten ziehen lassen.

3 Die Sardellenfilets fein hacken und mit der gehackten Petersilie und der gehackten Zitronenmelisse in die Topfencreme rühren. Die Creme mit Salz und Pfeffer abschmecken.

4 Die Topfencreme in die Tomaten füllen und die Deckel auf die Tomaten setzen.

5 Die gefüllten Tomaten in eine mit Butter gefettete Auflaufform stellen. Auf jede Tomate 1 Butterflocke setzen. Die Tomaten im auf 180 °C vorgeheizten Backofen 20 Minuten schmoren.

6 Die Tomaten aus dem Ofen nehmen, abkühlen lassen und lauwarm servieren.

Tipp: Servieren Sie die Tomaten mit kross gebratenem Rohschinken oder mit der Paprika-Tomaten-Sauce (siehe Rezept Seite 46)

Gebratene Kalmare mit Tomaten-Reis-Füllung und karamellisierten Zitronen

Zutaten für 4 Personen

8 Kalmare
Meersalz
2 ganze Chilischoten
5 EL Olivenöl extra vergine

Für die Tomaten-Reis-Füllung

120 g Melanzani (Auberginen)
1 Knoblauchzehe
9 EL Olivenöl extra vergine
2 vollreife Rispentomaten (ca. 120 g)
2 EL Langkornreis
250 ml Hühner- oder Gemüsebrühe
5 Kapern, gehackt
8 schwarze Oliven, entkernt und gehackt
1 Sardellenfilet, gehackt
1 Chilischote, fein geschnitten
1/2 TL getrockneter Oregano

Zubereitungszeit: ca. 50 Minuten

1 Die Kalmare putzen, quer durchschneiden (sodass Tuben und Tentakel getrennt sind), von den Knorpeln im Inneren befreien, waschen und gut abtropfen lassen.

2 Für die Füllung die Melanzani waschen, putzen und in kleine Würfel schneiden. Den Knoblauch schälen und grob hacken. 2 EL Olivenöl in einer Pfanne erhitzen und den Knoblauch und die Melanzani darin kurz anbraten.

3 Die Tomaten waschen, vom Stielansatz befreien und in große Würfel schneiden. Die Tomatenwürfel und den Reis zu den Melanzani in die Pfanne geben. Alles mit der Hühnerbrühe aufgießen und 15 Minuten köcheln lassen.

4 Den Topf vom Herd nehmen und die Kapern, die Oliven, das Sardellenfilet und die fein geschnittene Chilischote hinzufügen. Die Füllung mit Oregano, Salz und Pfeffer abschmecken. Dann den Feta in große Würfel schneiden und untermengen.

5 Die Füllung in die Kalmartuben geben. Jeden gefüllten Kalmar mit einem Zahnstocher verschließen.

(Fortsetzung auf Seite 158)

Salz
frisch gemahlener Pfeffer
100 g milder Feta
etwas gehackte Petersilie

Für die karamellisierten Zitronen
2 Zitronen (Bioware)
2 EL Olivenöl extra vergine
2 EL brauner Rohrzucker

(Fortsetzung von Seite 156)

6 3 EL Olivenöl in einer Pfanne erhitzen und die beiden ganzen Chilischoten und die Kalmartentakel darin kurz anbraten, dann aus der Pfanne nehmen und warm stellen.

7 In der Pfanne erneut 2 EL Olivenöl erhitzen und die gefüllten Kalmare darin von allen Seiten 2 bis 3 Minuten anbraten, dann kurz ruhen lassen, mit der gehackten Petersilie bestreuen und leicht mit Salz abschmecken.

8 Für die karamellisierten Zitronen die Zitronen in 1/2 cm Scheiben schneiden. Das Olivenöl in einer Pfanne erhitzen und die Zitronenscheiben darin anbraten, dann mit dem Zucker bestreuen, wenden und 1 bis 2 Minuten braten. Die Zitronenscheiben dann aus der Pfanne nehmen und abkühlen lassen.

9 Die gefüllten Kalmare mit den gebratenen Tentakeln und den karamellisierten Zitronen auf 4 Tellern anrichten und mit 2 EL Olivenöl beträufeln. Nach Belieben mit rohen Tomatenscheiben und gehackten Oliven garnieren.

Meeresfrüchterisotto mit gegrillten Kirschtomaten

Zutaten für 4 Personen

300 g Meeresfrüchte (frisch oder TK-Produkt), geschnitten

8 EL Olivenöl extra vergine

2 kleine Knoblauchzehen, fein gehackt

1 TL frisch gepresster Zitronensaft

etwas Safransalz

frisch gemahlener Pfeffer

250 g Kirschtomaten

Salz

1 Zwiebel, fein gehackt

200 g Risottoreis (am besten Carnaroli)

125 ml trockener Weißwein

750 ml Rinderbrühe

40 g Butter

40 g frisch geriebener Parmesan

2 EL grob gehacktes Basilikum oder Estragon

Zubereitungszeit: ca. 50 Minuten

1 Die aufgetauten und abgetropften Meeresfrüchte mit 3 EL Olivenöl, der Hälfte des Knoblauchs und dem Zitronensaft in eine Schüssel geben und vermengen. Mit Safransalz und Pfeffer würzen, dann 10 bis 15 Minuten durchziehen lassen.

2 Die Kirschtomaten in eine Auflaufform legen, mit 1 EL Olivenöl übergießen, mit Salz bestreuen und unter dem vorgeheizten Backofengrill 10 bis 15 Minuten grillen.

3 Den Ofen ausschalten. Die marinierten Meeresfrüchte zu den Tomaten in die Form geben und vermengen. Das Ragout bis zum Weiterverarbeiten im Ofen gar ziehen lassen.

4 Für den Risotto 4 EL Olivenöl in einem großen Topf erhitzen. Die Zwiebel und den restlichen Knoblauch darin glasig schwitzen. Den Reis hinzufügen und unter Rühren anschwitzen, dann mit dem Weißwein ablöschen. Den Wein komplett verkochen lassen, dann den Risotto mit 1 Schöpflöffel heißer Brühe aufgießen. Die Brühe unter häufigem Rühren einkochen lassen, dann 1 weiteren Schöpflöffel heißer Brühe aufgießen. Diesen Vorgang so lange wiederholen, bis der Reis gar ist und der Risotto eine cremige Konsistenz hat.

5 Die kalte Butter und den Parmesan in den Risotto rühren, mit Salz und Pfeffer abschmecken und den Risotto kurz ruhen lassen.

6 Das Basilikum oder den Estragon unter das Meeresfrüchteragout mengen.

7 Den Risotto auf 4 vorgewärmten Tellern anrichten und das Tomaten-Meeresfrüchte-Ragout darübergeben.

Räucherlachsküchlein mit Brunnenkresse-Tomaten-Salat

Zutaten für 4 Personen

Für die Küchlein

350 g mehlig kochende Erdäpfel (Kartoffeln), geschält

Salz

2 EL Weißweinessig

2 Lachsfilets (à ca. 250 g)

140 g Räucherlachs, fein gehackt

frisch gemahlener Pfeffer

2 Eigelb

4 Frühlingszwiebeln, fein gehackt

2 EL Sonnenblumenöl

15 g Butter

Zubereitungszeit: ca. 1 1/4 Stunden

1 Die Kartoffeln in reichlich Salzwasser etwa 20 Minuten weich kochen.

2 Währenddessen eine tiefe Pfanne etwa 1 cm hoch mit Wasser füllen und den Weißweinessig hinzufügen. Das Wasser aufkochen, die Temperatur reduzieren, die Lachsfilets in das Wasser legen und mit einem Pfannendeckel abdecken. Die Lachsfilets 5 Minuten im leicht wallenden Wasser ziehen lassen.

3 Die Lachsfilets aus dem Sud nehmen, von der Haut befreien und in eine Schüssel geben. Die Lachsfilets mit einer Gabel zerpflücken, dann den Räucherlachs hinzufügen.

4 Die weichen Kartoffeln abschütten, mit etwas Lachskochwasser zerstampfen, salzen, pfeffern und zu dem Lachs in die Schüssel geben. Die Eigelb und die Frühlingszwiebeln hinzufügen und alles gut vermengen, dann mit Salz und Pfeffer abschmecken. Aus der Lachsmasse 12 Küchlein formen. Die Küchlein 30 Minuten im Kühlschrank erkalten lassen.

Für den Brunnenkresse-Tomaten-Salat

- 1/2 rote Zwiebel, geschält und fein gehackt
- 400 g Kirschtomaten, geviertelt
- 3 EL Schnittlauchröllchen
- Saft von 1/2 unbehandelten Zitrone
- 3 EL natives Olivenöl
- Salz
- frisch gemahlener Pfeffer
- 2 Bund Brunnenkresse (à ca. 90 g), geputzt

5 Für den Brunnenkresse-Tomaten-Salat die rote Zwiebel, die Kirschtomaten, die Schnittlauchröllchen, den Zitronensaft und das Olivenöl in einer Schüssel vermengen. Den Salat mit Salz und Pfeffer abschmecken, dann vorsichtig die Brunnenkresse unterheben.

6 1 EL Sonnenblumenöl in einer großen Pfanne erhitzen. Die Hälfte der Butter zugeben und aufschäumen. Die Lachsküchlein bei mittlerer Temperatur darin portionsweise von jeder Seite 2 bis 3 Minuten goldgelb anbraten

7 Auf 4 Teller je 3 Lachsküchlein geben, mit dem Brunnenkresse-Tomaten-Salat anrichten und servieren.

Wolfsbarsch im Tomaten-Muschel-Sud

Zutaten für 4 Personen

1 ganzer Wolfsbarsch, geschuppt und ausgenommen (ca. 1,3 kg)

Meersalz

6 Zweige Thymian

6 Zweige Blattpetersilie

3 Frühlingszwiebeln (ca. 100 g)

300 g kleine vollreife Tomaten

2 Handvoll Vongole (Venusmuscheln)

frisch gemahlener Pfeffer

5 EL Olivenöl extra vergine

1 Zitrone

Zubereitungszeit: ca. 1 Stunde

1. Den Wolfsbarsch trocken tupfen, innen und außen salzen.
2. Ein Backblech großzügig mit Alufolie belegen. Den Fisch daraufsetzen und mit je 3 Zweigen Thymian und Petersilie füllen.
3. Die Frühlingszwiebeln putzen und in feine Ringe schneiden.
4. Die Tomaten waschen, halbieren und mit den Frühlingszwiebeln auf dem Fisch verteilen.
5. Die Muscheln gründlich waschen, offene Muscheln wegwerfen. Die Muscheln auf die Folie um den Wolfsbarsch legen.
6. Den restlichen Thymian und die restliche Petersilie über den Wolfsbarsch geben. Alles mit dem Olivenöl beträufeln und mit Salz und Pfeffer bestreuen.
7. Die Alufolie über dem Wolfsbarsch zusammenschlagen und gut verschließen. Den Wolfsbarsch im auf 190 °C vorgeheizten Backofen etwa 40 bis 45 Minuten garen.
8. Den Wolfsbarsch aus dem Ofen nehmen, die Alufolie öffnen und alles mit Zitronensaft beträufeln. Den Wolfsbarsch filetieren, mit dem Muschelsud anrichten und nach Belieben nochmals mit etwas Olivenöl beträufeln und salzen.

Tipps: Dazu passt frisch geröstetes Weißbrot oder in Butter geschwenkte heurige (neue) Kartoffeln.
Garen Sie zusätzlich 3 bis 4 ganze Knoblauchzehen mit.

Gebratene Seeteufelmedaillons mit Orangeat und Tomaten-Fenchel-Gemüse

Zutaten für 4 Personen

Für das Tomaten-Fenchel-Gemüse

4 Tomaten (ca. 500 g)
1 kleine Fenchelknolle
3 EL Olivenöl extra vergine
2 Knoblauchzehen
2 EL weiches Orangeat, gehackt
2 Rosmarinzweige
Meersalz zum Bestreuen

Für den Seeteufel

8 dicke Medaillons vom frischen Seeteufel (ca. 600 g)
Salz
frisch gemahlener Pfeffer
3 EL Sonnenblumenöl
1 Stück Zitronenschale (Bioware)

Zubereitungszeit: ca. 30 Minuten

1 Reichlich Wasser in einem großen Topf zum Kochen bringen. Die Tomaten darin portionsweise je 1 Minute blanchieren. Die Tomaten aus dem Wasser nehmen, in Eiswasser abschrecken, dann häuten, vierteln, vom Stielansatz befreien und entkernen.

2 Den Fenchel putzen, halbieren und in 1/2 cm dicke Streifen schneiden, dann beiseitestellen.

3 Die Seeteufelmedaillons auf beiden Seiten mit Salz und Pfeffer bestreuen.

4 Eine ofenfeste beschichtete Pfanne erhitzen. Das Sonnenblumenöl und die Zitronenschale hineingeben. Die Seeteufelmedaillons darin von beiden Seiten 1 Minute anbraten.

5 Die Pfanne mit dem Fisch in den auf 70 °C vorgeheizten Backofen geben. Den Fisch darin 12 Minuten ziehen lassen.

6 Den Knoblauch schälen und in feine Scheiben schneiden.

7 Das Olivenöl in einer Pfanne erhitzen und den Knoblauch darin kurz anbraten, dann den Fenchel zugeben, salzen und bei niedriger Temperatur 5 bis 6 Minuten dünsten.

8 Die Tomaten, das Orangeat und die Rosmarinzweige in die Pfanne geben, alles gut durchschwenken, mit Salz und Pfeffer abschmecken und 4 bis 5 Minuten bei niedriger Temperatur ziehen lassen.

9 Das Tomaten-Fenchel-Gemüse in 4 tiefen Tellern anrichten, je 2 Seeteufelmedaillons daraufsetzen und nach Belieben mit Meersalz bestreuen.

Kabeljaufilet im Tomaten-Lavendel-Sud

Zutaten für 4 Personen

Für den Tomaten-Lavendel-Sud

6 vollreife Strauchtomaten, blanchiert und gehäutet
2 Schalotten
2 Knoblauchzehen
4 EL Olivenöl extra vergine
250 ml Fischfond (aus dem Glas)
1 Stück Orangenschale (Bioware)
3 Zweige Thymian
1/2 TL Lavendelblüten
1 kleine mehlig kochende Kartoffel
8 schwarze Oliven
Salz
frisch gemahlener Pfeffer

Für den Kabeljau

1 dickes Kabeljaufilet mit Haut (ca. 800 g)
Saft von 1 Zitrone
Salz
Pfeffer aus der Mühle
2 EL fein gehackte Blattpetersilie

Zubereitungszeit: ca. 50 Minuten

1. Die Tomaten vierteln, vom Stielansatz befreien und entkernen. Jedes Tomatenviertel erneut halbieren.
2. Die Schalotten und den Knoblauch schälen und fein hacken.
3. Das Olivenöl in einer ofenfesten Pfanne erhitzen. Die Schalotten und den Knoblauch darin glasig schwitzen.
4. Die Tomaten in die Pfanne geben und kurz mitschwitzen, dann mit dem Fischfond aufgießen.
5. Die Orangenschale, den Thymian und den Lavendel hinzufügen und alles bei niedriger Temperatur 10 bis 12 Minuten köcheln lassen.
6. Die Kartoffel schälen, fein reiben und in die Pfanne geben. Alles weitere 3 bis 4 Minuten köcheln lassen.
7. Das Kabeljaufilet in 4 gleich große Stücke schneiden, mit dem Zitronensaft beträufeln und mit Salz und Pfeffer bestreuen.
8. Den Kabeljau und die Oliven in den heißen Tomaten-Lavendel-Sud legen. Die Pfanne abdecken und den Kabeljau im auf 90 °C vorgeheizten Backofen 8 bis 10 Minuten ziehen lassen.
9. Den garen Kabeljau und den Sud auf 4 tiefe Teller verteilen und mit etwas gehackter Petersilie bestreuen.

Tipp: Dazu passt frisches Baguette.

Thai-Rindfleischsalat mit Tomaten und Kaffirmarinade

Zutaten für 4 Personen

Für das Rindfleisch

2 dicke Scheiben Roastbeef (à 250 g)
Salz
frisch gemahlener Pfeffer
2 EL Olivenöl extra vergine

Für die Kaffirmarinade

2 Kaffirlimettenblätter (erhältlich im Asialaden)
2 EL Thaibasilikum
8 EL frisch gepresster Limettensaft
8 EL Sesamöl
3 Chilischoten
Salz
frisch gemahlener Pfeffer
Sojasauce

Für den Salat

1 rote Zwiebel
150 g gemischte, junge Blattsalatblätter (Thai-Mischung)
2 EL gehacktes Koriandergrün
2 EL Thaibasilikum
400 g reife grüne Tomaten
Salz
2 EL schwarze Sesamsaat

Zubereitungszeit: ca. 25 Minuten

1 Das Rindfleisch etwa 30 Minuten vor der Zubereitung aus dem Kühlschrank nehmen. Dann kräftig salzen, pfeffern und mit dem Olivenöl bestreichen.

2 Eine Grillpfanne erhitzen. Die Rindfleischscheiben darin von jeder Seite 4 Minuten grillen. Die gegrillten Scheiben auf einen vorgewärmten Teller legen, mit Alufolie abdecken und 8 bis 10 Minuten ruhen lassen.

3 Für die Marinade die Kaffirlimettenblätter und das Thaibasilikum in sehr feine Streifen schneiden und in eine Schüssel geben. Den Limettensaft und das Sesamöl hinzufügen und alles gut vermengen.

4 Die Chilischoten längs halbieren, entkernen und fein hacken, dann in die Marinade rühren. Die Marinade mit Salz, Pfeffer und Sojasauce abschmecken.

5 Für den Salat die Zwiebel schälen, in feine Streifen schneiden und mit den Salaten und Kräutern locker vermengen.

6 Die Tomaten waschen, in Scheiben schneiden und auf 4 Tellern ausbreiten. Die Tomaten leicht salzen und jede Portion mit 1 EL Marinade übergießen.

7 Das Fleisch in dünne Scheiben schneiden und über die Tomaten legen.

8 Den Salat darüber verteilen, mit der restlichen Marinade beträufeln und mit Sesam bestreuen.

Tipp: Reichen Sie etwas Sojasauce und Sesamöl dazu.

Gegrillte Filetsteaks mit gebackenen grünen Tomaten

Zutaten für 4 Personen

4 Filetsteaks vom Rind (à ca. 200 g)
Salz
grob geschroteter Pfeffer
4–5 EL Olivenöl extra vergine
4 große reife grüne Tomaten (eine grüne Sorte, keine unreifen roten Tomaten)
80 g Weizenmehl (Type 405)
80 g Stärkemehl
1 EL brauner Rohrzucker
1 TL Salz
Sonnenblumenöl zum Ausbacken

Zubereitungszeit: ca. 30 Minuten

1 Die Steaks ca. 30 Minuten vor der Zubereitung aus dem Kühlschrank nehmen. Die Steaks auf beiden Seiten salzen und pfeffern, dann in eine flache Auflaufform legen und mit dem Olivenöl übergießen. Die Steaks im auf 60 °C vorgeheizten Backofen etwa 20 Minuten vorgaren.

2 Die Tomaten waschen und in etwa 1 cm dicke Scheiben schneiden.

3 Das Mehl in einer Schüssel mit dem Stärkemehl und dem Zucker vermengen.

4 Die Tomatenscheiben leicht salzen und in der Mehlmischung wenden.

5 Reichlich Sonnenblumenöl in einer Pfanne erhitzen und die mehlierten Tomatenscheiben darin schwimmend goldbraun ausbacken. Die gebackenen Tomatenscheiben mit dem Schaumlöffel aus der Pfanne nehmen und auf Küchenkrepp gut abtropfen lassen.

6 Eine Grillpfanne auf dem Herd erhitzen und die Filetsteaks darin von jeder Seite 2 Minuten grillen, dann nochmals salzen und mit den gebackenen Tomaten anrichten.

Gebackene Pancetta-Ricotta-Körbchen

Zutaten für 4 Personen

6 dünne Scheiben Pancetta arrotolata (italienischer Bauchspeck vom Schwein)

120 g frischer Ricotta

8 EL fein geriebener Parmesan

30 g Ziegenfrischkäse

2 Eigelb

4 EL feine Schnittlauchröllchen

Salz

frisch gemahlener Pfeffer

12 Kirschtomaten

Zubereitungszeit: ca. 20 Minuten

1 Ein Minimuffin-Blech mit 12 Vertiefungen leicht fetten. In jede Vertiefung eine halbe Pancettascheibe drücken.

2 Den Ricotta mit dem Parmesan, dem Ziegenkäse, den Eigelb und den Schnittlauchröllchen in eine Schüssel geben und vermengen. Die Creme mit Salz und Pfeffer abschmecken.

3 Die Käsecreme mithilfe eines Teelöffels in die Pancettakörbchen füllen. Je 1 Kirschtomate auf die Creme setzen.

4 Die Pancettakörbchen im auf 220 °C vorgeheizten Backofen (Ober-/Unterhitze) etwa 10 Minuten backen, bis der Speck kross und der Käse geschmolzen ist.

Tipp: Dazu passen marinierte Blattsalate.

Makkaroni mit Tomaten-Speck-Sugo

Zutaten für 4 Personen

450 g Makkaroni (z. B. Neapolitan Makkaroni)
Salz
200 g Hamburger Speck (Frühstücksspeck), gewürfelt
1 Knoblauchzehe, fein gehackt
600 g Kirschtomaten
5 EL Olivenöl extra vergine
3 EL fein gehackte Blattpetersilie
Salz
frisch gemahlener Pfeffer
4 EL frisch geriebener Parmesan (oder 1 EL cremiger Ziegenfrischkäse)

Zubereitungszeit: ca. 25 Minuten

1 Die Makkaroni nach Packungsanleitung in reichlich Salzwasser al dente kochen, dann abschütten (aber nicht abschrecken). Dabei 2 Schöpflöffel des Kochwassers für die Sauce auffangen und beiseitestellen.

2 Während die Pasta kocht, eine große Pfanne ohne Fettzugabe bei mittlerer Temperatur erhitzen. Die Speckwürfel darin anbraten. Dann den Knoblauch hinzufügen und kurz mitbraten.

3 Die Kirschtomaten waschen und halbieren.

4 Die Kirschtomaten zu dem Speck in die Pfanne geben. Alles gut vermengen und bei geringer Temperatur 6 bis 7 Minuten köcheln lassen.

5 3–4 EL des Makkaronikochwassers und das Olivenöl in den Sugo rühren. Dann die Petersilie hinzufügen. Die Makkaroni in den Sugo geben und alles gut vermengen, dann mit Salz und Pfeffer abschmecken und bei niedriger Temperatur 1 bis 2 Minuten ziehen lassen.

6 Die Makkaroni auf 4 vorgewärmten Pastatellern anrichten, mit dem geriebenen Parmesan bestreuen und servieren.

Gesottene Kalbszunge mit Tomaten-Balsamico-Vinaigrette

Zutaten für 4 Personen

Für die Kalbszunge

2 Kalbszungen (à ca. 300 g)
1 frisches Lorbeerblatt
3–4 Pfefferkörner
1 Bund Suppengemüse (ca. 250 g)
Salz

Für die Tomaten-Balsamico-Vinaigrette

4 Tomaten (ca. 400 g), blanchiert und gehäutet
Salz
6 EL fruchtiges natives Olivenöl
65 ml Gemüsebrühe
4 EL Aceto balsamico
frisch gemahlener Pfeffer
5 EL grob geschnittenes Basilikum

Zum Anrichten

150 g Rucola

Zubereitungszeit: ca. 2 Stunden 10 Minuten

1 Die Kalbszungen unter fließendem kalten Wasser gründlich waschen, dann mit dem Lorbeerblatt und den Pfefferkörnern in einen Topf geben und mit kaltem Wasser auffüllen.

2 Das Suppengemüse (Karotte, Petersilienwurzel, Knollensellerie) putzen, in grobe Stücke schneiden und zu den Zungen in den Topf geben. Die Kalbszungen bei mittlerer Temperatur etwa 1 1/2 bis 2 Stunden weich kochen. Den Kochsud nach der Hälfte der Kochzeit salzen.

3 Die garen Kalbszungen aus dem Sud nehmen, kurz in kaltes Wasser legen, dann häuten und bis zum Anrichten in dem Sud warm halten.

4 Für die Tomaten-Balsamico-Vinaigrette die Tomaten halbieren, entkernen und in kleine Würfel schneiden. Die Tomatenwürfel in eine Schüssel geben, salzen und kurz ziehen lassen.

5 Das Olivenöl mit der Gemüsebrühe und dem Aceto balsamico zu einer Marinade verrühren. Diese über die Tomatenwürfel geben und gut verrühren. Mit Salz und Pfeffer abschmecken, dann das geschnittene Basilikum darüberstreuen.

6 Die Kalbszungen aus dem Sud nehmen, längs in dünne Tranchen schneiden, auf einer Servierplatte oder einem flachen Teller ausbreiten, dann leicht salzen und pfeffern. Die Tomaten-Balsamico-Vinaigrette darübergeben und alles mit dem Rucola garnieren.

Kalbsleber mit Oliven-Zitrone und Tomaten in der Papillotte

Zutaten für 4 Personen

600 g küchenfertige Kalbsleber
1 grüne Paprikaschote
4 reife Strauchtomaten (ca. 350 g), blanchiert und gehäutet
4 Schalotten
2 Knoblauchzehen, geschält und in Scheiben geschnitten
60 g entsteinte schwarze Oliven
2 unbehandelte Zitronen
Salz
frisch gemahlener Pfeffer
125 ml Olivenöl extra vergine
4 Zweige Thymian

Zubereitungszeit: ca. 50 Minuten plus 2 Stunden Marinierzeit

1 Die Kalbsleber in fingerdicke Streifen schneiden. Diese in eine große Schüssel geben.

2 Die Paprikaschote waschen, halbieren, von Kernen und Scheidewänden befreien und in feine Streifen schneiden.

3 Die Tomaten vierteln, vom Stielansatz befreien, entkernen und jedes Viertel erneut halbieren.

4 Die Schalotten schälen und grob hacken.

5 Die Paprika, die Tomaten, die Schalotten, den Knoblauch und die Oliven zu der Kalbsleber in die Schüssel geben und gut durchmischen.

6 Den Saft einer Zitrone und die in Achtel geschnittene zweite Zitrone hinzufügen. Die Schüssel abdecken und die Leber 2 Stunden im Kühlschrank durchziehen lassen.

7 4 Stücke Backpapier auf ca. 40 x 50 cm zurechtschneiden.

8 Die Leber-Gemüse-Mischung auf die 4 Backpapierstücke verteilen. Alles mit Salz und Pfeffer bestreuen und mit dem Olivenöl beträufeln. Auf jede Portion einen Thymianzweig legen. Das Backpapier zu Päckchen zusammenklappen und die hochgeklappten Ecken mit Küchengarn fixieren.

9 Die Päckchen (Papillotten) auf ein Backblech legen und im auf 180 °C vorgeheizten Backofen (mittlere Schiene) etwa 30 Minuten garen.

10 Die Papillotten auf 4 Tellern anrichten und servieren.

Tipp: Dazu passt kräftiges Bauernbrot.

Sardisches Kaninchen

Zutaten für 4 Personen

1 Kaninchen (ca. 1,5 kg mit der Leber)
Salz
frisch gemahlener Pfeffer
5 EL Olivenöl extra vergine
4 Knoblauchzehen, grob gehackt
250 ml trockener Rotwein
10 g eingelegte Kapern
6 vollreife Tomaten (ca. 800 g)
3 Zweige Rosmarin
3–4 Zweige Thymian
3 frische Lorbeerblätter
100 g grüne Oliven (mit Stein)
frische Kräuter zum Garnieren

Zubereitungszeit: ca. 1 Stunde

1 Das Kaninchen in 10 bis 12 Stücke zerteilen und mit Salz und Pfeffer bestreuen. Die Kaninchenleber fein würfeln.

2 Das Olivenöl in einem Bräter erhitzen und die Kaninchenstücke darin von allen Seiten anbraten. Die Leberwürfel und den Knoblauch hinzufügen. Den offenen Bräter in den auf 190 ° vorgeheizten Backofen schieben und das Kaninchen etwa 10 Minuten braten.

3 Den Bratensatz mit dem Rotwein ablöschen, dann die Kapern und 3 EL der Kapernmarinade hinzufügen. Das Kaninchen salzen und kräftig pfeffern.

4 Die Tomaten waschen, vierteln, vom Stielansatz befreien und mit dem Rosmarin, dem Thymian, den Lorbeerblättern und den Oliven in den Bräter geben.

5 Den Bräter abdecken und das Kaninchen bei 190 ° weitere 25 Minuten im Backofen schmoren.

6 Das Kaninchen mit dem Schmorgemüse auf Tellern anrichten. Den Bratensaft mit Salz und Pfeffer abschmecken und um das Kaninchen geben. Nach Belieben mit frischen Kräutern garnieren.

Tipp: Dazu passt Parmesanbrot – ein Fladenbrot in 2 cm breite Streifen schneiden, mit frisch geriebenem Parmesan bestreuen, mit Olivenöl beträufeln und im auf 200 °C vorgeheizten Backofen kurz überbacken.

Süße Tomaten mit »Zwölf-Aromen-Füllung«

Zutaten für 4 Personen

- 2 Birnen (ca. 250 g)
- 100 g frische Ananas, geschält und vom Strunk befreit
- 50 grüne Pistazienkerne
- 50 g Mandelblättchen
- 1 EL Butter
- 2 EL brauner Rohrzucker
- fein geriebene Schale von 1/2 Orange (Bioware)
- Saft von 1/2 Orange
- 1 TL Rosinen
- 1 TL fein geriebener Ingwer
- 1 Msp. Nelkenpulver
- 1 Msp. Zimtpulver
- 1/2 TL Anissamen
- 1 Vanillestange
- 1 Prise frisch gemahlener Pfeffer
- 12 kleine reife rote Tomaten
- 2 EL Butterflocken
- etwas Puderzucker
- frische Minze zum Bestreuen

Zubereitungszeit: ca. 35 Minuten

1 Die Birnen schälen, entkernen und klein würfeln.

2 Die Ananas klein würfeln und mit den Birnenwürfeln vermengen.

3 Die Pistazienkerne und die Mandelblättchen grob hacken.

4 1 EL Butter in einer Pfanne zerlassen. Den Zucker darin leicht karamellisieren, dann die Birnen- und Ananaswürfel sowie die Pistazien und Mandeln zugeben, schwenken und 2 bis 3 Minuten karamellisieren.

5 Die geriebene Orangenschale darüberstreuen und den Orangensaft zugeben.

6 Die Rosinen, den Ingwer, das Nelkenpulver, das Zimtpulver und die Anissamen zugeben, alles gut durchmengen und weitere 1 bis 2 Minuten köcheln lassen.

7 Die Vanilleschote längs halbieren, das Mark auskratzen und zu der Fruchtfüllung geben. Die Fruchtfüllung pfeffern und die Pfanne vom Herd nehmen.

9 Von den Tomaten oben einen Deckel abschneiden. Die Tomaten mithilfe eines Teelöffels aushöhlen und die Füllung hineingeben.

10 Die Tomaten in eine Auflaufform setzen, mit den Butterflocken und dem Zucker bestreuen. Die ausgekratzte Vanilleschote in die Form geben. Die Tomaten im auf 200 °C vorgeheizten Backofen (mittlere Schiene) 8 bis 10 Minuten überbacken.

11 Die Tomaten auf 4 Tellern anrichten und mit dem Bratensaft übergießen, dann mit frischer Minze dekorieren.

PRODUIT D'ITALIE

Aus dem Glas

Tomatenbaguette mit Rosmarin

Für 4 Baguettestangen

50 g sehr saftige getrocknete Tomaten
2 EL frische Rosmarinnadeln
550 g Weizenmehl (Type 405)
1 Päckchen Trockenhefe
5 EL Olivenöl extra vergine
1 EL Salz
375 ml lauwarmes Wasser
etwas Weizenmehl für die Arbeitsfläche
etwas Olivenöl zum Bestreichen

Zubereitungszeit: ca. 2 1/2 Stunden

1 Die getrockneten Tomaten und den Rosmarin fein hacken.

2 Die Tomaten und den Rosmarin mit dem Mehl, der Hefe, dem Olivenöl, dem Salz und dem Wasser in eine große Rührschüssel geben und mit dem Handrührgerät (Knethaken) etwa 10 bis 20 Minuten zu einem glatten Teig verarbeiten. Die Schüssel mit einem Tuch abdecken und den Teig bei Zimmertemperatur etwa 40 Minuten gehen lassen.

3 Den Teig auf einer bemehlten Arbeitsfläche mit den bemehlten Händen durchkneten, dann in 4 gleich große Stücke teilen.

4 Jedes Teigstück nochmals so lange durchkneten, bis es glatt ist, dann jedes Stück zu einer Kugel formen.

5 Die Teigkugeln mit einem Tuch abdecken und bei Zimmertemperatur weitere 20 bis 30 Minuten gehen lassen.

6 Jede Teigkugel zu einem etwa 20 cm langen Teigstrang auseinanderziehen. Jeden Strang mit bemehlten Händen zu korkenzieherförmigen Baguettelaiben drehen. Die Baguettes auf ein mit Backpapier bedecktes Backblech legen, mit einem Tuch abdecken und bei Zimmertemperatur weitere 10 bis 15 Minuten gehen lassen.

7 Die Baguettelaibe mit Olivenöl bepinseln und im auf 200 °C vorgeheizten Backofen (Ober-/ Unterhitze) 30 bis 35 Minuten knusprig backen.

Tipp: Dieses Brot lässt sich gut einfrieren. Backen Sie das tiefgekühlte Baguette im auf 180 °C vorgeheizten Backofen etwa 20 Minuten auf.

Gerolltes Tomatenbrot mit Basilikum

Für 4 kleine Laibe

200 g in Öl eingelegte, getrocknete Tomaten, gut abgetropft

700 g griffiges Weizenmehl (Type 405)

1 gestrichener EL Salz

1 EL Trockenhefepulver

1 TL Zucker

300 ml lauwarmes Wasser

3 EL Tomatenpüree oder Tomatenmark

4 EL Olivenöl extra vergine

2 Handvoll Basilikumblättchen

Zubereitungszeit: ca. 3 1/4 Stunden

1 Die gut abgetropften Tomaten bei Bedarf mit Küchenkrepp trocken tupfen.

2 Das Mehl mit dem Salz, der Trockenhefe und dem Zucker in eine Rührschüssel geben und gut vermengen.

3 Das Wasser mit dem Tomatenpüree und dem Olivenöl verrühren und über die Mehlmischung gießen. Dann die gehackten Tomaten hinzufügen und alles in der Küchenmaschine mit Knethaken zu einem weichen, glatten Teig verarbeiten.

4 Die Schüssel mit einem Tuch bedecken und den Teig 1 1/2 Stunden bei Zimmertemperatur gehen lassen.

5 Den Teig auf eine bemehlte Arbeitsfläche geben und mit den Händen geschmeidig kneten. Den Teig in 4 gleich große Stücke teilen, diese mit einem Tuch bedecken und weitere 30 Minuten gehen lassen.

6 Die 4 Teigstücke mit den Handflächen flach drücken und mit den Basilikumblättchen bestreuen, dann grob verkneten und zu 4 Laiben formen. Die Laibe auf ein leicht gefettetes Backblech legen und weitere 20 Minuten ruhen lassen.

7 Die Brotlaibe mit etwas kaltem Wasser beträufeln und im auf 180 °C vorgeheizten Backofen 40 bis 45 Minuten backen. (Das Brot ist fertig, wenn es sich beim Klopfen an der Unterseite hohl anhört.) Das fertige Brot aus dem Ofen nehmen und auf einem Kuchengitter vollständig auskühlen lassen.

Stangenbruschetta mit Tomatencreme und Knusperartischocken

Zutaten für 4 Personen

Für die Tomatencreme

150 g eingelegte Tomaten, gut abgetropft
80 g entsteinte schwarze Oliven
150 g Frischkäse
1 EL frische Rosmarinnadeln
1 kleine Chilischote
Salz
frisch gemahlener Pfeffer

Für das Baguette

1 Baguette
2 EL Olivenöl extra vergine

Für die Artischocken

200 g eingelegte Artischocken
2 EL Olivenöl
4 EL gehackte Blattpetersilie

Zubereitungszeit: ca. 30 Minuten

1 Für die Tomatencreme die eingelegten Tomaten grob hacken, dann in einen hohen Rührbecher geben und mit dem Stabmixer fein pürieren.

2 Die Oliven grob hacken.

3 Den Frischkäse gründlich mit dem Tomatenpüree verrühren, dann die Oliven unterziehen.

4 Die Rosmarinnadeln und die nicht entkernte Chilischote fein hacken und in die Tomatencreme rühren. Die Tomatencreme mit Salz und Pfeffer abschmecken.

5 Das Baguette in 4 gleich große Stücke schneiden. Diese jeweils längs halbieren, mit den Schnittflächen nach oben auf ein Backblech legen, mit dem Olivenöl beträufeln und im auf 200 °C vorgeheizten Backofen 5 bis 6 Minuten knusprig aufbacken.

6 Die Artischocken gut abtropfen lassen, halbieren und gründlich mit Küchenkrepp abtupfen.

7 Das Olivenöl in einer Pfanne erhitzen und die Artischocken darin knusprig braten.

8 Das Baguette aus dem Ofen nehmen, etwas abkühlen lassen, mit der Tomatencreme bestreichen, die Artischocken darauf verteilen und mit gehackter Petersilie bestreuen.

Tomatengugelhupf mit Mandeln und Basilikumblättchen

Zutaten für 4 Personen

Butter für die Formen

einige geriebene Mandelblättchen zum Ausstreuen der Formen

120 g in Öl eingelegte getrocknete Tomaten, gut abgetropft

4 Eier

2 EL Staubzucker (Puderzucker)

1/2 TL Salz

5 EL Olivenöl

125 ml trockener Weißwein

80 g Mandelkerne, grob gehackt

2 EL grob geschnittenes Basilikum

200 g Weizenmehl (Type 405)

10 g Backpulver

Zubereitungszeit: ca. 30 Minuten

1 4 kleine Gugelhupfformen (ca. 10 cm Durchmesser) mit Butter ausfetten und mit den Mandelblättchen ausstreuen.

2 Die eingelegten Tomaten fein hacken.

3 Die Eier mit dem Staubzucker und dem Salz schaumig schlagen, dann nach und nach das Olivenöl und den Weißwein hineinrühren.

4 Die gehackten Mandeln und das Basilikum in den Teig rühren.

5 Das Mehl mit dem Backpulver mischen, in den Teig sieben und zügig unterrühren.

6 Den Teig in die vorbereiteten Gugelhupfformen füllen, die Oberflächen glatt streichen und die Gugelhupfe im auf 140 °C vorgeheizten Backofen 18 bis 20 Minuten backen.

7 Die fertigen Gugelhupfe leicht abkühlen lassen, aus den Formen auf ein Kuchengitter stürzen und vollständig erkalten lassen, dann servieren.

Tipp: Ideal fürs Picknick oder Sommerfest – der Gugelhupf lässt sich auch gut einfrieren.

Schwarzbrotterrine mit Saint Agur und getrockneten Tomaten

Zutaten für 4 Personen

250 g gesalzene Butter
200 g Saint Agur (oder ein ähnlicher Blauschimmelkäse)
80 g in Öl eingelegte getrocknete Tomaten, gut abgetropft
100 g Frischkäse
5 g Pinienkerne, angeröstet
1 EL gehackter Thymian
Salz
frisch gemahlener Pfeffer
500 g Vollkornbrot, in Scheiben geschnitten
einige grüne Weintrauben

Zubereitungszeit: ca. 15 Minuten plus 5–6 Stunden Kühlzeit

1. Die weiche Butter in einer Rührschüssel mit dem Rührquirl des Handrührgeräts 1 bis 2 Minuten schaumig schlagen.
2. Die schaumige Butter in 2 Hälften teilen.
3. Den Saint Agur mit einer Gabel zerdrücken und mit einer Hälfte der Butter vermengen.
4. Die eingelegten Tomaten fein hacken.
5. Die restliche Butter gründlich mit dem Frischkäse vermengen, dann die Tomaten, die Pinienkerne und den Thymian hinzufügen und gut verrühren. Mit Salz und Pfeffer abschmecken.
6. Eine Terrinenform (ca. 1 l Fassungsvermögen) mit kaltem Wasser auspinseln und mit Klarsichtsfolie auskleiden. Den Terrinenboden mit Vollkornbrot (etwa 1/3 der Menge) bedecken, die Tomatencreme daraufgeben und glatt streichen. Die Tomatencreme wieder mit Vollkornbrot bedecken, die Saint-Agur-Creme daraufgeben und glatt streichen. Die Saint-Agur-Creme erneut mit Vollkornbrot bedecken und mit den Handflächen leicht andrücken.
7. Die Terrine mit Klarsichtfolie verschließen und mindestens 5 bis 6 Stunden (am besten über Nacht) im Kühlschrank erkalten lassen.
8. Die erkaltete Terrine aus dem Kühlschrank nehmen, von der Folie befreien und in 1 cm dicke Scheiben schneiden. Die Scheiben nochmals halbieren, auf Tellern anrichten und mit Weintrauben garnieren.

Maccu – Sizilianische Bohnen-Tomaten-Suppe

Zutaten für 6 Personen

300 g getrocknete weiße Bohnenkerne
1 weiße Gemüsezwiebel (ca. 80 g)
2 gehäufte TL Fenchelsamen
2 Lorbeerblätter
frisch gemahlener Pfeffer
Salz
1 rote Zwiebel (ca. 80 g)
2 Knoblauchzehen
4 EL Olivenöl extra vergine
5 in Öl eingelegte Tomaten (ca. 80 g), gut abgetropft
2 EL fein gehacktes Basilikum
1 getrocknete rote Chilischote, zerbröselt

Zubereitungszeit: ca. 2 Stunden plus Einweichzeit der Bohnen

1 Die Bohnenkerne über Nacht in reichlich kaltem Wasser einweichen.
2 Das Einweichwasser abschütten und die Bohnen in einen Topf geben.
3 Die weiße Zwiebel schälen und fein würfeln.
4 Die Fenchelsamen, die weiße Zwiebel und die Lorbeerblätter zu den Bohnen geben, mit 2 1/4 l kaltem Wasser aufgießen und mit Pfeffer würzen. (Wichtig: Die Bohnen jetzt noch nicht salzen, sonst wird ihre Haut hart.)
5 Das Bohnengemüse aufkochen und 10 Minuten kochen lassen, dann die Temperatur reduzieren und die Bohnen 40 bis 90 Minuten leicht köcheln lassen, bis sie sehr weich sind. Die weichen Bohnen kräftig salzen, im Kochwasser belassen und mit dem Stabmixer pürieren, dann abschmecken.
6 Die rote Zwiebel und den Knoblauch schälen und klein würfeln.
7 Das Olivenöl in einer Pfanne erhitzen und die rote Zwiebel darin leicht bräunen. Dann den Knoblauch hineinrühren und die Tomaten, das Basilikum und den Chili hinzufügen und 1 bis 2 Minuten mitschwitzen, um die Tomaten zu erwärmen.
8 Die Bohnensuppe nochmals kurz erwärmen.
9 Die Bohnensuppe in 4 vorgewärmte Teller oder Tassen schöpfen, das Tomaten-Zwiebel-Röstgemüse darübergeben, leicht unterrühren und sofort servieren.

Burrata mit Bloody-Mary-Gelee

Zutaten für 4 Personen

4 Blatt weiße Gelatine
250 ml passierte Tomaten (siehe Rezept Tomate »Passata« Seite 51)
1 TL Kristallzucker
80 ml Wodka
2–3 EL Sojasauce
1 TL fein geriebene Orangenschale (Bioware)
1 Prise Cayennepfeffer
Salz
frisch gemahlener Pfeffer
2 große Kugeln Burrata (à ca. 250 g)
2 Handvoll Basilikumblättchen
etwas Olivenöl extra vergine

Zubereitungszeit: ca. 20 Minuten plus Kühlzeit des Gelees

1 Die Gelatine etwa 10 Minuten in kaltem Wasser einweichen.

2 Die passierten Tomaten mit dem Zucker in einen Topf geben und aufkochen. Den Topf vom Herd nehmen und den Wodka, die Sojasauce und die geriebene Orangenschale in das heiße Tomatenpüree rühren.

3 Die eingeweichte Gelatine ausdrücken und unter Rühren in dem heißen Tomatenpüree auflösen. Das Püree mit Cayennepfeffer, Salz und Pfeffer abschmecken, in eine flache Auflaufform füllen und mindestens 3 bis 4 Stunden (noch besser über Nacht) im Kühlschrank erstarren lassen.

4 Das erstarrte Bloody-Mary-Gelee mit einem in lauwarmes Wasser getauchten Messer in kleine Würfel schneiden.

5 Die Burratakugeln vierteln, auf 4 tiefe Teller verteilen und mit den Geleewürfeln garnieren. Alles mit den Basilikumblättchen bestreuen, mit etwas Olivenöl beträufeln und mit Salz und Pfeffer abrunden.

Info: Burrata ist ein Weichkäse aus Apulien. Wie der Mozzarella ist er ein Filata-Käse, doch im Gegensatz dazu wird der Burrata ausschließlich aus Kuhmilch gewonnen.

Tomatenpesto mit Mandeln und Chili

Ergibt etwa 400 ml

150 g in Öl eingelegte getrocknete Tomaten, gut abgetropft
60 g geschälte Mandelkerne
70 g junger Parmesan
2 Knoblauchzehen, geschält
1 getrocknete Chilischote
1 kleine Gewürznelke
200 ml fruchtiges Olivenöl extra vergine
Salz
frisch gemahlener Pfeffer

Zubereitungszeit: ca. 10 Minuten

1 Die Tomaten grob hacken und mit den Mandeln, dem zerbröckelten Parmesan, dem Knoblauch, der Chilischote, der Gewürznelke und dem Olivenöl im Mixer zu einer feinen Paste verarbeiten.

2 Das Pesto mit Salz und Pfeffer abschmecken und in saubere, fest verschließbare Gläser füllen und bis zur Verwendung im Kühlschrank aufbewahren.

Tipps: Wenn Sie das Pesto zusätzlich mit 1 EL getrockneten Tomatenflocken zubereiten, schmeckt es noch intensiver.
Das Pesto ergibt einen guten Aufstrich für Bruschetta, es passt auch zu Pasta oder zu einem Stück Ziegen- oder Schaffrischkäse. Auch als Saucengewürz eignet es sich bestens.

Kartoffel-Rapunzel-Salat mit Tomaten-Thymian-Marinade und geräuchertem Felchen

Zutaten für 4 Personen

Für die Marinade

1 große Zwiebel

1 große Knoblauchzehe

6 EL Olivenöl extra vergine

6 EL Weißweinessig

Für den Kartoffel-Rapunzel-Salat

1 kg festkochende Erdäpfel (Kartoffeln)

Salz

frisch gemahlener Pfeffer

50 g saftige getrocknete Tomaten

2 EL frisch gehackte Thymianblättchen

125–250 ml Rindssuppe

100 g Rapunzeln (Feldsalat), geputzt

Für den Felchen

300 g geräuchertes Reinankenfilet (Felchenfilet)

Zubereitungszeit: ca. 1 1/4 Stunden

1 Für die Marinade die Zwiebel und den Knoblauch schälen, fein hacken und gründlich mit dem Olivenöl und dem Weißweinessig verrühren.

2 Die Erdäpfel in reichlich Salzwasser weich kochen, dann schälen und in feine Scheiben schneiden.

3 Die Marinade über die Erdäpfelscheiben geben, vorsichtig vermengen und kräftig mit Salz und Pfeffer abschmecken.

4 Die getrockneten Tomaten gut abtropfen lassen, fein hacken und vorsichtig unter die Erdäpfel heben. Dann den gehackten Thymian hinzufügen. Den Erdäpfelsalat langsam mit der Rindssuppe auffüllen – dabei nach und nach gerade so viel Suppe hinzufügen, wie die Erdäpfel aufnehmen können. Den Salat etwa 30 Minuten ziehen lassen.

5 Das Reinankenfilet im auf 100 °C vorgeheizten Backofen etwa 10 Minuten erwärmen.

6 Den geputzten Feldsalat unter den Kartoffelsalat mengen und mit den Reinankenfilets anrichten.

Tipp: Statt Reinanke können Sie auch geräucherten Karpfen oder Saibling zu dem Salat servieren.

Bouillabaisse mit geräucherter Makrele und Zander

Zutaten für 4 Personen

2 geräucherte Makrelenfilets (à 150 g)
2 Fenchelknollen (ca. 250 g)
4 Knoblauchzehen, geschält
100 g Butter
7 EL Olivenöl extra vergine
Salz
125 ml trockener Wermut
250 ml Hühnersuppe
250 ml passierte Tomaten (oder Tomatenconfit, siehe Seite 65)
1 TL Anissamen
2 Briefchen Safran
frisch gemahlener Pfeffer
4 EL gehackter Estragon oder Dill

Zubereitungszeit: ca. 40 Minuten

1 Die Makrelenfilets häuten und die Haut beiseitelegen. Die Filets vorsichtig entgräten, in mundgerechte Stücke schneiden und zugedeckt beiseitestellen.

2 Den Fenchel putzen und in feine Streifen schneiden.

3 Die Knoblauchzehen in feine Scheiben schneiden.

4 Die Hälfte der Butter (50 g) in einem großen Topf zerlassen und 3 EL Öl hinzugeben. Den Knoblauch darin kurz anrösten, dann die Fenchelstreifen hinzufügen und ebenfalls kurz anschwitzen, dann salzen und mit dem Wermut ablöschen. Danach mit der Hühnersuppe auffüllen, die passierten Tomaten hineinrühren und die Makrelenhaut in den Sud geben. Den Sud etwa 15 Minuten kochen lassen.

5 Die Makrelenhaut aus dem Sud nehmen. Den Sud auf 2 Töpfe verteilen, eine Hälfte pürieren. Das Püree mit dem restlichen Sud zusammengeben und aufkochen. Den Safran und die Anissamen zufügen. Alles 2 bis 3 Minuten köcheln lassen, mit Salz und Pfeffer abschmecken und die gehackten Kräuter hineinrühren. Den Topf vom Herd nehmen.

(Fortsetzung auf Seite 204)

Tomatenschaum mit Forellenkaviargelee

Zutaten für 6 Personen

Für das Kaviargelee
3 Blatt weiße Gelatine
250 ml Fischfond (aus dem Glas)
1 Spritzer Zitronensaft
Salz
80 g Forellenkaviar

Für den Tomatenschaum
2 Schalotten
2 EL Traubenkernöl
300 g Dosentomaten
1 EL Tomatenmark
30 ml trockener Wermut
1 Zweig frischer Thymian
3 Blatt weiße Gelatine

Zubereitungszeit: ca. 45 Minuten plus Kühlzeit des Gelees

1 Für das Forellenkaviargelee die Gelatine etwa 10 Minuten in kaltem Wasser einweichen.

2 Den Fischfond in einem kleinen Topf leicht erwärmen.

3 Die eingeweichte Gelatine gut ausdrücken und in dem warmen Fischfond auflösen. Den Fond mit Zitronensaft und Salz abschmecken. Den Topf mit dem Fischfond auf ein Eiswasserbad stellen, bis der Fond zu gelieren beginnt. Dann vorsichtig den Kaviar unter den gelierenden Fond heben und den Fond auf 6 Gläser oder Tassen verteilen. Die Gelees 4 bis 6 Stunden im Kühlschrank erkalten lassen.

4 Für den Tomatenschaum die Schalotten schälen und fein würfeln. Das Traubenkernöl in einer Pfanne erhitzen und die Schalotten darin glasig schwitzen, dann die Dosentomaten (mit ihrem Saft), das Tomatenmark, den Wermut und den Thymian hinzufügen. Die Sauce 15 Minuten köcheln lassen.

5 Die Gelatine etwa 10 Minuten in kaltem Wasser einweichen.

6 Die heiße Tomatensauce durch ein Sieb passieren. Die eingeweichte Gelatine ausdrücken und in der heißen Tomatensauce auflösen. Die Sauce mit Salz und Pfeffer abschmecken und vollständig abkühlen lassen.

(Fortsetzung auf Seite 205)

4 Zanderfilets (à 125 g)
etwas gehackte Petersilie zum Garnieren
etwas Olivenöl extra vergine

(Fortsetzung von Seite 200)

6 Die Zanderfilets in etwa 3 cm breite Streifen schneiden und auf beiden Seiten mit Salz und Pfeffer bestreuen.

7 Die restliche Butter in einer beschichteten Pfanne zerlassen, das restliche Öl hinzufügen und den Zander darin auf der Hautseite 1 Minute anbraten. Die Pfanne vom Herd nehmen, zudecken, den Zander 2 bis 3 Minuten ziehen lassen.

8 Den Zander und die Makrele auf 4 tiefen, vorgewärmten Tellern anrichten, den Fenchelsud darumgießen, mit etwas Petersilie garnieren und mit Olivenöl beträufeln.

125 ml Sahne
Salz
frisch gemahlener Pfeffer
einige in Olivenöl extra vergine und Zitronensaft marinierte Kräuter zum Garnieren
etwas Kaviar zum Garnieren

(Fortsetzung von Seite 203)

7 Die Sahne steif schlagen und unter die Tomatensauce ziehen, bevor diese ganz geliert. Die Tomatensahne auf die Oberflächen der Kaviargelees streichen. Die Gelees erneut mindestens 2 Stunden im Kühlschrank erkalten lassen.

8 Die Gelees etwa 10 Minuten vor dem Servieren aus dem Kühlschrank nehmen. Die Tassen kurz in heißes Wasser tauchen und die Gelees auf Servierteller stürzen. Die Gelees mit den Kräutern und einigen Kaviarperlen garnieren.

Wandl-Brot mit getrockneten Tomaten und Schinkenspeck

Zutaten für 4 Personen

150 g in Öl eingelegte, getrocknete Tomaten, gut abgetropft

100 g entsteinte schwarze Oliven

50 g eingelegte grüne Pfefferkörner

500 g Weizenmehl (Type 405)

1 Päckchen Backpulver

1 TL Salz

250 g Topfen (Quark, 20 % Fettgehalt)

3 Eier (Größe L)

100 ml Olivenöl extra vergine

2 TL Anissamen

Butter und Mehl für die Form

100 g Schinkenspeck, dünn aufgeschnitten

Zubereitungszeit: ca. 70 Minuten

1. Die getrockneten Tomaten grob hacken. Die Oliven vierteln. Die Pfefferkörner grob zerstoßen.
2. Das Mehl mit dem Backpulver und dem Salz in eine Rührschüssel sieben. Den Topfen, die Eier, das Olivenöl und 1 TL Anissamen mit dem zerstoßenen Pfeffer zu dem Mehl in die Schüssel geben und alles in der Küchenmaschine (Knethaken) zu einem glatten Teig verarbeiten.
3. Eine Kastenform (26 cm Länge) mit Butter auspinseln und mit Mehl ausstäuben.
4. Den Teig auf einer bemehlten Arbeitsfläche zu einem Rechteck von ca. 26 x 25 cm ausrollen. Die Teigplatte mit dem Schinkenspeck belegen. Die gehackten Tomaten und die Oliven darüberstreuen und den Teig zusammenrollen.
5. Die Teigrolle mit der Nahtstelle nach unten in die Kastenform legen, die Oberfläche mehrmals mit einem Messer einritzen, mit dem restlichen Anis bestreuen und im auf 160 °C Umluft (180 °C Ober-/Unterhitze) vorgeheizten Backofen 50 bis 55 Minuten backen.
6. Das fertige Brot aus dem Ofen nehmen, etwas abkühlen lassen, auf ein Kuchengitter stürzen und erkalten lassen.

Tipp: Das Brot schmeckt am besten ganz frisch mit einem Glas Rotwein.

Tomaten-Kraut-Suppe mit Specksauerrahm

Zutaten für 4 Personen

500 g Weißkraut
1 große Zwiebel (ca. 120 g)
180 g Bauchspeck
3 EL Sonnenblumenöl
2 EL edelsüßes Paprikapulver
2 EL Tomatenmark
400 g passierte Tomaten (aus der Dose oder Tomaten »Passata« siehe Rezept Seite 51)
500 ml Rindssuppe
1/2 TL Kümmelsamen
3 Knoblauchzehen, fein gehackt
2 frische Lorbeerblätter
1 große mehlig kochende Kartoffel (ca. 180 g)
Salz
frisch gemahlener Pfeffer
375 ml Sauerrahm
2 EL fein gehackte Blattpetersilie

Zubereitungszeit: ca. 75 Minuten

1 Das Weißkraut putzen und in feine Streifen schneiden.

2 Die Zwiebel schälen und in dünne Scheiben schneiden.

3 Den Speck in kleine Würfel schneiden.

4 Das Sonnenblumenöl in einem Topf erhitzen und die Speckwürfel darin knusprig braten. Die Hälfte der Speckwürfel aus dem Topf nehmen und beiseitestellen.

5 Die Zwiebelscheiben in dem Topf mit dem Speck anbraten, dann mit dem Paprikapulver bestreuen und das Tomatenmark hineinrühren und kurz weiterbraten.

6 Das Weißkraut zu der Zwiebel-Speck-Mischung geben und gut vermengen, dann leicht salzen und alles 2 bis 3 Minuten weiterschwitzen. Danach mit den passierten Tomaten und der Rindssuppe auffüllen. Den Kümmel, den Knoblauch und die Lorbeerblätter zufügen und die Suppe bei mittlerer Temperatur etwa 30 Minuten köcheln lassen.

7 Die Kartoffel schälen, fein raspeln und in die Suppe geben. Die Suppe bei niedriger Temperatur weitere 20 Minuten köcheln lassen, dann mit Salz und Pfeffer abschmecken.

8 Die beiseitegestellten Speckwürfel fein hacken, mit dem Sauerrahm und der Petersilie vermengen und mit Salz und Pfeffer abschmecken.

9 Die Suppe in 4 tiefen Tellern anrichten und je 1 EL Specksauerrahm obenauf setzen. Den restlichen Specksauerrahm separat dazu reichen.

Geschmorter lila Blumenkohl mit Tomatenmasala

Zutaten für 4 Personen

2 Knoblauchzehen
20 g frischer Ingwer
3 EL Sonnenblumenöl
1 TL Kreuzkümmelsamen
3 EL dick eingekochtes Tomatenpüree oder Tomatenmark
200 g passierte Tomaten aus der Dose (oder Tomaten »Passata« siehe Seite 51)
1 Chilischote
1 TL Garam-Masala-Pulver (erhältlich im Asialaden)
1/2 TL Kurkumapulver
1 TL brauner Zucker
8 kleine lilafarbene Karfiolköpfe (lila Blumenkohl)
Salz
Sesamöl
4 EL gehacktes Koriandergrün

Zubereitungszeit: ca. 40 Minuten

1 Den Knoblauch und den Ingwer schälen und klein würfeln.

2 Das Sonnenblumenöl in einer Kasserolle erhitzen, den Kreuzkümmel darin kurz anrösten, dann den Knoblauch und den Ingwer zugeben und kurz mitrösten.

3 Das Tomatenmark zugeben und alles gut verrühren, dann die passierten Tomaten unterziehen.

4 Die Chilischote längs halbieren und fein hacken. Die gehackte Chili, das Garam-Masala-Pulver, das Kurkumapulver und den Zucker in die Tomatensauce rühren. Die Tomatensauce aufkochen.

5 Die ganzen Karfiolköpfe in die Tomatensauce geben, etwa 250 ml Wasser angießen und den Karfiol im geschlossenen Topf bei geringer Hitze etwa 30 Minuten weich garen. Den garen Karfiol salzen, mit dem Tomatenmasala auf 4 Tellern anrichten, mit etwas Sesamöl beträufeln und mit dem Koriandergrün bestreuen.

Tipp: Statt Tomatenmark und Chilischote können Sie 4 EL scharfe Tomatenpaste (siehe Rezept Seite 53) verwenden.

Kartoffelstrudel mit Steinpilzen und Tomaten-Zitronen-Pesto

Zutaten für 4 Personen

Für das Tomaten-Zitronen-Pesto

80 g in Öl eingelegte, getrocknete Tomaten, gut abgetropft

30 g geschälte Mandelkerne

30 g frisch geriebener Parmesan

1 Knoblauchzehe

120 ml Olivenöl

1 EL Aceto balsamico

1/2 TL frisch geriebene Zitronenschale (Bioware)

Salz

frisch gemahlener Pfeffer

Zubereitungszeit: ca. 1 1/4 Stunden

1 Für das Pesto die eingelegten Tomaten grob hacken und mit den Mandeln, dem Parmesan, dem Knoblauch, dem Olivenöl und 2–3 EL heißem Wasser in einen hohen Rührbecher geben. Die Zutaten mit dem Stabmixer zu einem groben Pesto verarbeiten. Das Pesto mit dem Aceto balsamico und dem Zitronenabrieb würzen und mit Salz und Pfeffer abschmecken. Das Pesto abdecken und beiseitestellen.

2 Die Kartoffeln schälen, in reichlich Salzwasser weich kochen, dann abschütten, kurz abkühlen lassen, dann mit einer Gabel zerdrücken.

3 Die Steinpilze putzen und grob hacken.

4 Den Knoblauch schälen und feinblättrig schneiden.

5 Die Butter in einer Pfanne zerlassen und den Knoblauch darin kurz anschwitzen. Die Pilze in die Pfanne geben und so lange braten, bis die entstandene Flüssigkeit verkocht ist.

Für die Füllung

500 g mehlig kochende Kartoffeln

400 g frische Steinpilze

2 Knoblauchzehen

50 g Butter

2 Eigelb

2 EL Crème fraîche

4 EL gehackte Blattpetersilie

Salz

frisch gemahlener Pfeffer

Für den Strudelteig

2 Blatt Strudelteig oder Filoteig (ca. 50 g)

80 g flüssige Butter

6 Die abgekühlten gebratenen Pilze mit den zerdrückten Kartoffeln, den Eigelb, der Crème fraîche und der gehackten Petersilie verrühren. Die Füllung mit Salz und Pfeffer abschmecken.

7 Das erste Strudelblatt auf ein leicht befeuchtetes Küchentuch legen und mit flüssiger Butter bepinseln. Das zweite Strudelblatt darüberlegen und ebenfalls mit Butter bepinseln. Die Steinpilz-Kartoffel-Füllung auf das untere Ende des Strudelteigs geben, dabei links und rechts einen Rand freilassen. Die Ränder auf die Füllung klappen. Den Strudelteig dann mit Hilfe des Küchentuchs einrollen.

8 Den Strudel auf ein gefettetes Backblech legen und im auf 190 °C vorgeheizten Backofen etwa 20 bis 25 Minuten knusprig braun backen.

9 Den fertigen Strudel aus dem Ofen nehmen, noch heiß in Stücke schneiden und mit dem Pesto servieren.

Tipp: Statt mit Pesto können Sie den Strudel auch mit dem Tomatenconfit (siehe Seite 65) servieren. Das Confit hier mit Salz, Pfeffer und Olivenöl abschmecken.

Pfifferlinge in Tomatencreme mit Serviettenschnitte

Zutaten für 4 Personen

Für die Serviettenschnite

400 g altbackenes Toastbrot oder Sandwichbrot
125 ml Milch
100 g Butter
3 Eigelb
3 EL fein gehackte Petersilie
Salz
etwas frisch geriebene Muskatnuss
3 Eiweiß
etwas flüssige Butter

Zubereitungszeit: ca. 1 Stunde

1 Das Brot klein würfeln, mit der zimmerwarmen Milch übergießen und 10 Minuten quellen lassen.

2 Die Butter zerlassen, etwas abkühlen lassen, dann in einer kleinen Schüssel mit den Eigelb verquirlen und über die Brotwürfel geben. Die gehackte Petersilie untermengen, mit Salz und Muskat abschmecken und locker vermengen.

3 Die Eiweiß steif schlagen und unter den Knödelteig heben.

4 Ein befeuchtetes Geschirrtuch mit etwas zerlassener Butter bestreichen. Den Knödelteig zu einem Striezel (Laib) formen, auf ein Ende des Tuchs legen, das Tuch locker eindrehen, und die Enden gut mit Küchengarn verknoten.

5 In einem großen, hohen Topf reichlich Salzwasser zum Kochen bringen. Den Serviettenknödel hineinlegen und im leicht wallenden Wasser etwa 30 Minuten gar ziehen lassen.

(Fortsetzung auf Seite 215)

Für die Sauce

1 kleine Zwiebel

1 Knoblauchzehe

50 g in Öl eingelegte, getrocknete Tomaten, gut abgetropft

40 g Butter

800 g Eierschwammerl (Pfifferlinge), geputzt

2 EL Weizenmehl (Type 405)

1 EL gehackte Thymianblättchen

125 ml Hühnersuppe

125 ml Sahne

Salz

frisch gemahlener Pfeffer

2 EL fein gehackte Blattpetersilie

(Fortsetzung von Seite 212)

6 Für die Sauce die Zwiebel und den Knoblauch schälen und fein hacken.

7 Die gut abgetropften Tomaten fein hacken.

8 Die Butter in einem Topf aufschäumen. Die Zwiebel und den Knoblauch darin kurz anschwitzen, dann die gehackten Tomaten hinzufügen und kurz mitschwitzen.

9 Große Eierschwammerl halbieren. Die Schwammerl in den Topf geben und mitschwitzen, bis alle Flüssigkeit verkocht ist. Mit dem Mehl bestäuben, dann den Thymian hinzufügen.

10 Die Pilze mit der Hühnersuppe und der Sahne auffüllen. Die Sauce 2 bis 3 Minuten köcheln lassen, dann mit Salz und Pfeffer abschmecken und die Petersilie untermengen.

11 Den Knödel aus der Serviette nehmen und in längliche Schnitten schneiden. Mit den Eierschwammerln anrichten.

Tiger Prawns in Ouzo-Tomaten-Sauce und gebackenem griechischem Käse

Zutaten für 4 Personen

800 ml Tomatensauce (siehe Rezept Tomatensauce »Santorini« Seite 48)

250 g milder Fetakäse

4 Frühlingszwiebeln

4 Knoblauchzehen

16 Tiger Prawns (Riesengarnelen), geschält

60 ml Olivenöl extra vergine

1/4 TL Anissamen

80 ml Ouzo (griechischer Anisschnaps)

frisch gemahlener Pfeffer

1 EL frisch gepresster Zitronensaft

Olivenöl extra vergine zum Beträufeln

etwas Meersalz

Zubereitungszeit: ca. 30 Minuten

1 Die Tomatensauce in eine flache Auflaufform füllen, den Fetakäse darüberbröckeln und 3 bis 7 Minuten in den auf 180 °C vorgeheizten Backofen geben. (Der Feta muss weich werden.)

2 Die Frühlingszwiebeln putzen und schräg in 1/2 cm dicke Scheiben schneiden.

3 Den Knoblauch schälen und in feine Scheiben schneiden.

4 Die Riesengarnelen der Länge nach halbieren und den Darm entfernen.

5 Das Olivenöl in einer Pfanne erhitzen und die Anissamen darin kurz anrösten, dann die Riesengarnelen hinzufügen und 1 bis 2 Minuten mitbraten. Danach den Knoblauch und die Frühlingszwiebeln dazugeben und bei sehr starker Hitze 1 bis 2 Minuten braten.

6 Mit dem Ouzo ablöschen, alles kurz durchschwenken und pfeffern. Die Mischung dann aus der Pfanne komplett in die Tomatensauce geben. Die Ofentemperatur auf 70 °C reduzieren und die Riesengarnelen in der Tomaten-Ouzo-Sauce 10 bis 12 Minuten im Ofen ziehen lassen.

7 Die Auflaufform aus dem Ofen nehmen, das Gericht mit etwas Zitronensaft und Olivenöl beträufeln, dann mit etwas Meersalz bestreuen und lauwarm servieren.

Tipp: Dazu passt Pitabrot oder frisches Weißbrot.

Lachswürfel in Knoblauch-Cashew-Bröseln auf Tomatenspinat

Zutaten für 4 Personen

Für die Knoblauch-Cashew-Brösel

50 g Cashewkerne (ungesalzen und ungeröstet)
2 Knoblauchzehen
60 g Butter
100 g Semmelbrösel
1/2 TL Kurkumapulver

Zubereitungszeit: ca. 30 Minuten

1 Für die Brösel die Cashewkerne grob hacken.

2 Den Knoblauch schälen und fein hacken.

3 Die Butter in einer Pfanne zerlassen und den Knoblauch darin kurz anschwitzen, dann die gehackten Cashewkerne hinzufügen und kurz mitschwitzen. Die Semmelbrösel und den Kurkuma in die Pfanne geben und die Mischung unter ständigem Rühren zu goldbraunen Bröseln braten. Die Pfanne vom Herd nehmen und beiseitestellen.

4 Für den Tomatenspinat den Knoblauch schälen und feinblättrig schneiden.

5 Die eingelegten Tomaten in feine Streifen schneiden.

6 Die Butter in einer Pfanne aufschäumen. Den Knoblauch und die Tomaten darin kurz anrösten, dann den Zucker darüberstreuen.

Für den Tomatenspinat

1 Knoblauchzehe

80 g in Öl eingelegte, getrocknete Tomaten, gut abgetropft

50 g Butter

1/2 TL brauner Rohrzucker

500 g Blattspinat, blanchiert (oder aufgetauter TK-Spinat)

1 Msp. gemahlener Zimt

Salz

frisch gemahlener Pfeffer

Für die Lachswürfel

4 Lachsfilets, ohne Haut (à 180 g)

etwas frisch gepresster Zitronensaft

Salz

4 EL Sonnenblumenöl

7 Den Spinat hinzufügen, alles gut durchmengen, dann mit Zimt, Salz und Pfeffer abschmecken und 4 bis 5 Minuten bei geringer Hitze durchziehen lassen.

8 Jedes Lachsfilet in 3 Stücke schneiden, mit dem Zitronensaft beträufeln und salzen.

9 Das Sonnenblumenöl in einer Pfanne erhitzen und die Lachswürfel darin von jeder Seite 1 Minute anbraten, dann in den Bröseln wälzen.

10 Die Lachswürfel mit dem Tomatenspinat auf 4 Tellern anrichten und servieren.

Tipp: Statt Spinat können Sie auch die gleiche Menge Mangold verwenden.

Zander im Tomatennetz mit Selleriesamt

Zutaten für 4 Personen

Für den Zander

1 kleines Schweinenetz (ca. 100 g)
2 EL Weißweinessig
4 dicke Zanderfilets (à 120 g)
fein geriebene Schale von 1/2 Zitrone (Bioware)
Salz
frisch gemahlener Pfeffer
150 g Bauchspeck
130 g Frühlingszwiebeln
200 g Mangoldblätter
80 g in Öl eingelegte Tomaten, gut abgetropft
1/2 TL Zucker

Zubereitungszeit: ca. 1 Stunde

1 Das Schweinenetz mit Wasser bedecken und den Essig hinzufügen.

2 Die Zanderfilets mit der fein geriebenen Zitronenschale, Salz und Pfeffer bestreuen, dann mit Frischhaltefolie bedecken und im Kühlschrank kalt stellen.

3 Den Bauchspeck klein würfeln.

4 Die Frühlingszwiebeln und den Mangold putzen und in feine Streifen schneiden.

5 Die eingelegten Tomaten in feine Streifen schneiden.

6 Eine Pfanne ohne Fettzugabe erhitzen, die Speckwürfel darin knusprig braten, dann mit dem Zucker bestreuen. Die Zwiebeln hinzufügen und kurz mitschwitzen, dann den Mangold zugeben. Das Gemüse garen, bis alle Flüssigkeit verkocht ist. Dann die Tomatenstreifen zugeben und eventuell etwas nachsalzen. Das Gemüse vom Herd nehmen und abkühlen lassen.

7 Das Schweinenetz aus dem Essigwasser nehmen, gut ausdrücken, auf einem feuchten Tuch ausbreiten und in 4 etwa 15 x 15 cm große Quadrate schneiden.

8 In die Mitte jedes Schweinenetzes ein Zanderfilet legen, die Gemüsemischung darauf verteilen, dann jedes Netz zu einem Päckchen einschlagen und die Päckchen kalt stellen.

Für die Fleischbällchen

4 Scheiben Weißbrot bzw. Toastbrot (ca. 100 g)
125 ml Milch
500 g gemischtes Faschiertes (Hackfleisch)
4 EL frisch geriebener Pecorino
4 EL frisch geriebener junger Parmesan
1 Ei
1 TL getrockneter Majoran
3 EL fein gehackte Blattpetersilie
4 EL Olivenöl extra vergine
Salz
frisch gemahlener Pfeffer

Für die Spaghetti

500 g Spaghetti
Salz
50 g weiche Butter
4 EL Olivenöl extra vergine
etwas frisch geriebener Pecorino oder Parmesan

(Fortsetzung von Seite 224)

7 Aus der Hackfleischmischung mit angefeuchteten Händen kleine Bällchen formen, diese in die köchelnde Sauce legen. Die Fleischbällchen etwa 20 Minuten bei geringer Temperatur ziehen lassen.

8 Die Spaghetti in reichlich Salzwasser al dente kochen, dann abschütten, mit der weichen Butter vermengen, in 4 tiefen Pastatellern anrichten und die Tomatensauce sowie die Fleischbällchen darauf verteilen. Jede Portion nach Belieben mit etwas Olivenöl beträufeln und mit geriebenem Pecorino oder Parmesan bestreuen.

Tipp: Wenn Sie eine schärfere Sauce servieren wollen, mengen Sie eine kleine gehackte Chilischote unter die Fleischbällchenmasse.
Servieren Sie das Gericht mit kurz angebratenen Cocktailtomaten – so ist es auf dem Rezeptfoto zu sehen.

Strozzapreti mit Entensugo und Herbsttrompeten

Zutaten für 4 Personen

2 Entenbrustfilets (à 200 g, mit Haut)
5 Wacholderbeeren
1 EL Pfefferkörner, grob geschrotet
1 Zwiebel
1 Karotte (ca. 80 g)
1 Petersilienwurzel (ca. 80 g)
60 g Selchspeck (Räucherspeck)
4 EL Olivenöl extra vergine
4 EL dick eingekochtes Tomatenpüree oder Tomatenmark (100 g)
1 TL brauner Rohrzucker
250 ml trockener Rotwein

Zubereitungszeit: ca. 1 1/2 Stunden

1 Die Entenbrustfilets in kleine Würfel schneiden.

2 Die Wacholderbeeren im Mörser zerdrücken und mit den geschroteten Pfefferkörnern mischen. Diese Gewürzmischung über die Fleischwürfel geben, gründlich vermengen und 30 Minuten ziehen lassen.

3 Die Zwiebel, die Karotte und die Petersilienwurzel schälen und in kleine Würfel schneiden.

4 Den Selchspeck ebenfalls in kleine Würfel schneiden.

5 Das Olivenöl in einem Topf erhitzen und das gewürzte Entenfleisch darin von allen Seiten 4 bis 6 Minuten anbraten, dann aus dem Topf nehmen und warm stellen.

6 Die Speckwürfel in dem Bratensatz anbraten, dann die Zwiebel-, Karotten- und Petersilienwurzelwürfel hinzufügen und kurz mitrösten. Das Tomatenmark und den Zucker hineinrühren, dann mit dem Rotwein ablöschen.

350 ml Hühnerfond
1 Zweig Rosmarin
Salz
frisch gemahlener Pfeffer
400 g Strozzapreti
120 g Herbsttrompeten
etwas Walnuss- oder Erdnussöl
100 g frisch geriebener Bergkäse

7 Das Röstgemüse mit dem Hühnerfond auffüllen, den Rosmarin hinzufügen, die Suppe leicht salzen und bei mittlerer Temperatur 40 bis 45 Minuten zu einem sämigen Sugo einköcheln. (Das Fleisch muss weich sein.)

8 Die Strozzapreti in reichlich Salzwasser al dente kochen, dann abschütten, mit dem Enten-Sugo vermengen und einige Minuten ziehen lassen.

9 Die Herbsttrompeten putzen. Das Walnussöl in einer beschichteten Pfanne erhitzen und die Herbsttrompeten darin scharf anbraten, dann salzen und pfeffern.

10 Die Strozzapreti in 4 Pastatellern anrichten, die Pilze darübergeben und mit dem Bergkäse bestreuen.

Zimtwachteln mit Tomatenpilaw

Zutaten für 4 Personen

- 1 EL Korianderkörner
- 8 küchenfertige Wachteln (à ca. 150 g)
- Saft von 1 Zitrone
- Salz
- frisch gemahlener Pfeffer
- 2 Zwiebeln
- 4 EL Olivenöl extra vergine
- 500 g passierte Tomaten aus der Dose (oder Tomaten »Passata« siehe Rezept Seite 51)
- 1 Zimtstange
- 250 g Langkorn- oder Basmatireis
- 700 ml Hühnersuppe
- 60 g Butterflocken
- 4 EL gehacktes Koriandergrün
- einige Cocktailtomaten

Zubereitungszeit: ca. 1 1/2 Stunden

1. Die Korianderkörner im Mörser zerstoßen.
2. Die Wachteln mit dem Zitronensaft beträufeln, dann mit den zerstoßenen Korianderkörnern einreiben und mit Salz und Pfeffer bestreuen.
3. Die Zwiebeln schälen und in kleine Würfel schneiden.
4. Das Olivenöl in einer großen Kasserolle erhitzen und die Zwiebelwürfel darin 2 bis 3 Minuten glasig schwitzen, dann mit den passierten Tomaten auffüllen, die Zimtstange hinzufügen und aufkochen.
5. Die Wachteln in die Tomaten-Zimt-Sauce setzen und in der zugedeckten Kasserolle im auf 160 °C vorgeheizten Backofen etwa 25 Minuten schmoren. Die Wachteln dann aus der Sauce nehmen, einzeln in Alufolie wickeln, beiseitestellen.
6. Den ungekochten Reis in die Tomaten-Zimt-Sauce geben und mit dem heißen Hühnerfond auffüllen, leicht salzen und auf dem Herd bei geringer Temperatur etwa 25 Minuten köcheln lassen.
7. Die Wachteln aus der Folie nehmen, auf das Reisbett in der Kasserolle setzen und die Butterflocken darüberstreuen. Die Kasserolle wieder schließen und alles bei 120 °C im Backofen 15 bis 20 Minuten fertig garen.
8. Den garen Pilaw mit einer Gabel auflockern, das Koriandergrün unterheben, nochmals mit Salz abschmecken und den Pilaw in 4 tiefen Tellern anrichten. Je 2 Wachteln daraufsetzen, mit einigen kurz angebratenen Cocktailtomaten garnieren und servieren.

Calzone mit getrockneten Tomaten und Fenchelsalami

Zutaten für 4 Personen

Für den Teig

350 g griffiges Weizenmehl (Type 405)
1 Päckchen Trockenhefe
$^1/_2$ EL Salz

Für die Füllung

1 Fenchelknolle (ca. 150 g)
80 g in Öl eingelegte, getrocknete Tomaten, gut abgetropft
200 g eingelegte gegrillte Paprikaschoten, gut abgetropft
2 EL Olivenöl
2 Knoblauchzehen, fein gehackt
30 g Kapern
Salz
frisch gemahlener Pfeffer

Zubereitungszeit: ca. 40 Minuten plus 3 Stunden Gehzeit

1 Für den Teig das Mehl mit der Hefe und dem Salz in eine Rührschüssel geben und gut vermengen, dann etwa 250 ml Wasser zugeben und mit den Händen zu einem glatten Teig verkneten. Den Teig zudecken und bei Zimmertemperatur etwa 2 Stunden gehen lassen. Den Teig nach der Ruhezeit nochmals gut durchkneten und mindestens 1 weitere Stunde gehen lassen.

2 Die Fenchelknollen putzen, halbieren und in feine Streifen schneiden.

3 Die eingelegten Tomaten und die Paprika in etwa 1 cm breite Streifen schneiden.

4 Das Olivenöl in einem Topf erhitzen und den Knoblauch darin anrösten. Die Fenchelstreifen hinzufügen, leicht salzen und weich dünsten. Dann die Tomaten, die Paprika und die Kapern hinzufügen und kurz mitdünsten, salzen und pfeffern. Den Topf vom Herd nehmen, bedecken und beiseitestellen.

5 Den Teig in 4 gleich große Stücke teilen und auf einer bemehlten Arbeitsfläche zu etwa 0,5 cm dicken Kreisen ausrollen.

Châteaubriand mit Gewürztraminer-Tomaten-Hollandaise

Zutaten für 4 Personen

Für das Châteaubriand
500 g Rinderfilet (gleichmäßig dickes Mittelstück)
Salz
frisch gemahlener Pfeffer
3 EL Olivenöl extra vergine
2 EL Sonnenblumenöl
50 g Butter
2 Zweige Rosmarin
3 Knoblauchzehen, geschält

Zubereitungszeit: ca. 1 1/2 Stunden

1 Das Rinderfilet mit Salz und Pfeffer bestreuen, mit dem Olivenöl einreiben, in eine Fettpfanne legen und im auf 80 °C vorgeheizten Backofen etwa 1 Stunde auf eine Kerntemperatur von 58 °C braten (Bratenthermometer).

2 Das Öl mit 50 g Butter in eine Pfanne geben, erwärmen und die Butter aufschäumen, dann den Rosmarin und die ganzen Knoblauchzehen hinzufügen. Das Fleisch aus dem Ofen nehmen und darin von allen Seiten scharf anbraten.

3 Die Ofentemperatur auf 60 °C reduzieren und das Fleisch im Backofen mindestens 30 Minuten ruhen lassen.

(Fortsetzung auf Seite 242)

In Barolo und Balsamico geschmortes Rindsragout

Zutaten für 4 Personen

Für das Rindsragout

800 g Schulterscherzel (Rinderschulter)
500 ml Barolo
65 ml Aceto balsamico
1 Gewürznelke
5 Pimentkörner
1 Zwiebel
80 g Karotte
100 g Knollensellerie
80 g Lauch
100 g Champignons
10 g Selchspeck (Räucherspeck)

Zubereitungszeit: ca. 1 1/2–2 Stunden plus Marinierzeit

1 Das Schulterscherzel in Würfel von ca. 2 cm Kantenlänge schneiden. Die Fleischwürfel in eine große Schüssel geben und mit dem Barolo und dem Aceto balsamico übergießen. Die Gewürznelke und die Pimentkörner hinzufügen. Die Schüssel abdecken und das Fleisch über Nacht im Kühlschrank ziehen lassen.

2 Das Fleisch ca. 30 Minuten vor der Zubereitung aus dem Kühlschrank nehmen und durch ein Sieb schütten. Die Marinade auffangen und beiseitestellen.

3 Die Zwiebel, die Karotte und den Sellerie schälen und in kleine Würfel schneiden.

4 Den Lauch putzen und in feine Ringe schneiden.

5 Die Champignons putzen und grob hacken.

6 Den Speck in kleine Würfel schneiden.

(Fortsetzung auf Seite 243)

Für die Hollandaise

150 g Butter
40 g in Öl eingelegte, getrocknete Tomaten, gut abgetropft
20 g entsteinte schwarze Oliven
3 Eigelb
1 TL scharfer Senf
1 TL Honig
150 ml Gewürztraminer
1 EL frisch gepresster Zitronensaft
Salz
frisch gemahlener Pfeffer
2 EL gehackter Zitronenthymian

(Fortsetzung von Seite 239)

4 Für die Hollandaise 150 g Butter klein würfeln, in einen kleinen Topf geben und bei niedriger Temperatur vorsichtig erwärmen, bis sich das Milcheiweiß am Topfboden abgesetzt hat. Die flüssige Butter kurz abkühlen lassen, dann durch ein Tuch passieren.

5 Die Tomaten und die Oliven fein hacken und beiseitestellen.

6 Die Eigelb mit dem Senf und dem Honig in eine kleine Schüssel geben und über dem warmen Wasserbad mit Hilfe eines großen Schneebesens 2 bis 3 Minuten gründlich aufschlagen. Den Gewürztraminer langsam in die Hollandaise rühren und schlagen, bis diese cremig wird.

7 Die geklärte Butter erneut erwärmen und langsam in die Hollandaise rühren. Dann die gehackten Tomaten und Oliven unterheben. Die Hollandaise mit dem Zitronensaft, Salz und Pfeffer abschmecken. Zum Schluss den Zitronenthymian in die Hollandaise rühren.

8 Das Fleisch in fingerdicke Tranchen schneiden und mit der Hollandaise servieren. Als Beilage passt Bohnengemüse.

4 EL Olivenöl
1 EL dick eingekochtes Tomatenpüree oder Tomatenmark
400 g Pelatitomaten (aus der Dose)
2 Zweige Rosmarin
50 g Butter
2 EL Weizenmehl (Type 405)
Salz
frisch gemahlener Pfeffer

Für die Tagliatelle
400 g Tagliatelle
Salz
50 g weiche Butter
etwas gehackte Petersilie

(Fortsetzung von Seite 240)

7 Das Olivenöl in einem Bräter erhitzen und die Zwiebeln und den Speck darin kurz anrösten. Dann das restliche Gemüse und die Pilze hinzufügen und 3 bis 4 Minuten mitrösten.

8 Das Tomatenmark hineinrühren, kurz mitrösten, dann alles mit der Marinade ablöschen.

9 Die Tomaten, die Fleischwürfel und den Rosmarin hinzufügen und aufkochen. Den Topf abdecken. Das Ragout im auf 150 °C vorgeheizten Backofen 80 Minuten weich schmoren.

10 Die weiche Butter mit dem Mehl verkneten. Das Ragout aus dem Ofen nehmen und die Mehlbutter in das Ragout rühren. Das Ragout auf dem Herd 2 bis 3 Minuten köcheln lassen, bis es sämig ist. Dann mit Salz und Pfeffer abschmecken.

11 Die Tagliatelle in reichlich Salzwasser al dente kochen, abschütten, mit der weichen Butter vermengen und mit dem Ragout in 4 tiefen Tellern anrichten. Mit etwas gehackter Petersilie bestreuen und servieren.

Marinierter Krustenschweinebraten mit Kartoffel-Tomaten-Gratin

Zutaten für 4 Personen

Für den Schweinebraten

1 kg Schweineschulter (mit Schwarte, ohne Knochen)
3 Knoblauchzehen
4 Zweige Rosmarin
4 Blätter Salbei
1 TL fein geriebene Zitronenschale (Bioware)
125 ml trockener Weißwein
1 TL edelsüßes Paprikapulver
1 TL Kümmelpulver
4 EL Olivenöl extra vergine
Salz
frisch gemahlener Pfeffer

Für das Röstgemüse

1 Zwiebel (ca. 100 g)
1 Karotte
1 Knollensellerie
2 EL Olivenöl
125 ml trockener Weißwein

Zubereitungszeit: ca. 1 1/2 Stunden plus Marinierzeit

1 Die Schwarte der Schweineschulter mit einem scharfen Messer im Abstand von jeweils 1 cm rautenförmig einschneiden.

2 Den Knoblauch schälen und fein hacken.

3 Die Rosmarinnadeln und den Salbei fein hacken und in der Küchenmaschine mit dem Knoblauch, der fein geriebenen Zitronenschale, dem Weißwein, dem Paprikapulver, dem Kümmelpulver und dem Olivenöl zu einer Kräuterpaste verarbeiten. Die Paste mit Salz und Pfeffer abschmecken.

4 Die Schweineschulter von allen Seiten mit dem Pesto bestreichen, zudecken und bei Zimmertemperatur zugedeckt etwa 1 Stunde ziehen lassen.

5 Für das Röstgemüse die Zwiebel, die Karotte und den Sellerie schälen und klein würfeln.

6 Das Olivenöl in einem Bräter erhitzen und die Gemüsewürfel darin 2 bis 3 Minuten anrösten, dann mit dem Weißwein ablöschen. Die marinierte Schweineschulter auf das Gemüsebett setzen und im auf 160 °C vorgeheizten Backofen etwa 50 Minuten braten. Die Ofentemperatur dann auf 200 °C erhöhen und die Schweineschulter etwa 20 Minuten weiterbraten, bis sie eine schöne Kruste hat.

Für das Gratin

250 g in Öl eingelegte, getrocknete Tomaten, gut abgetropft
600 g mehlige Kartoffeln
100 g frischer Parmesan
200 ml Milch
1 Knoblauchzehe, geschält
200 ml Sahne
Salz
Pfeffer aus der Mühle
Butter für die Form

7 Für das Kartoffel-Tomaten-Gratin die eingelegten Tomaten in feine Streifen schneiden.

8 Die Kartoffeln schälen, in dünne Scheiben schneiden und dachziegelartig in eine gebutterte Auflaufform schichten.

9 Die Tomatenstreifen und den geriebenen Parmesan über die Kartoffelscheiben geben.

10 Die Milch mit der ganzen Knoblauchzehe und der Sahne in einen kleinen Topf geben und aufkochen, dann kräftig mit Salz und Pfeffer würzen und die Mischung über die Kartoffelscheiben geben.

11 Das Gratin bei 160 °C 10 Minuten vor Ende der ersten 50 Minuten Bratzeit der Schweineschulter mit in den Backofen geben. Das Gratin mit der Schweineschulter 10 Minuten bei 160°C und dann weitere 20 Minuten bei 200 °C garen.

12 Den Backofen nach Ende der Garzeit ausschalten und den Krustenschweinebraten und das Kartoffel-Tomaten-Gratin weitere 10 Minuten darin ruhen lassen.

13 Den Krustenschweinebraten in Tranchen schneiden, mit dem Kartoffel-Tomaten-Gratin auf 4 Tellern anrichten und mit dem Bratensaft servieren.

Lammfilets in Kartoffel-Tomaten-Rolle

Zutaten für 4 Personen

Für das Lammfilet

4 Lammfilets (à 120 g)
Salz
frisch gemahlener Pfeffer
2 EL Olivenöl extra vergine
3 EL fein gehackte Blattpetersilie
2 EL fein gehackter Thymian
1 EL fein gehackter Rosmarin
1 Knoblauchzehe, geschält und gehackt

Für die Erdäpfel-Tomaten-Rösti

500 g mehlig kochende Erdäpfel (Kartoffeln)
50 g in Öl eingelegte, getrocknete Tomaten, gut abgetropft
80 g Bergkäse, geraspelt

Zubereitungszeit: ca. 50 Minuten

1 Die Lammfilets salzen, pfeffern und mit dem Olivenöl bestreichen.

2 Die gehackten Kräuter mit dem Knoblauch vermengen, die Lammfilets darin wälzen und bis zum Weiterverarbeiten zugedeckt bei Zimmertemperatur ruhen lassen.

3 Für die Erdäpfel-Tomaten-Rösti die Erdäpfel schälen und grob raffeln.

4 Die eingelegten Tomaten fein hacken und mit den geraffelten Erdäpfeln und dem Bergkäse vermengen. Die Mischung salzen, pfeffern und in 4 gleich große Portionen teilen.

5 Eine beschichtete Pfanne erhitzen, dann 1 EL Sonnenblumenöl darin verteilen und die Temperatur reduzieren. Die erste Portion der Erdäpfel-Tomaten-Mischung in die Pfanne geben, mit einem Pfannenwender flach drücken und von einer Seite 5 bis 6 Minuten knusprig braten. Den Röstitaler auf ein Stück Backpapier gleiten lassen. Auf diese Weise drei weitere Röstitaler backen.

Salz
frisch gemahlener Pfeffer
4 EL Sonnenblumenöl

Für die Sauce
250 ml Kalbsfond
125 ml trockener Rotwein
1 Prise Zucker
1 Zweig Rosmarin
50 g kalte Butterwürfel
Salz
frisch gemahlener Pfeffer

6 Auf die ungebratene Seite jedes Röstitalers 1 Lammfilet legen und den Taler vorsichtig einrollen. Die Rollen auf ein mit Backpapier bedecktes Backblech legen und im auf 200 °C vorgeheizten Backofen etwa 10 Minuten fertig braten. Das Backblech nach der Bratzeit aus dem Ofen nehmen und die Lammfilets noch 5 Minuten ruhen lassen.

7 Für die Sauce den Kalbsfond mit dem Rotwein, dem Zucker und dem Rosmarin in einen kleinen Topf geben und um die Hälfte reduzieren. Dann den Topf vom Herd nehmen und den Rosmarinzweig entfernen. Die kalten Butterstücke unter ständigem Rühren mit einem kleinen Schneebesen nach und nach in die Sauce rühren. (Achtung: Die Sauce nun nicht mehr aufkochen.) Die fertig montierte Sauce mit Salz und Pfeffer abschmecken.

8 Die fertigen Lammfilets in etwa 2 cm dicke Tranchen schneiden und auf 4 vorgewärmten Tellern mit der Sauce anrichten.

Zwiebelbuchteln mit Blutwurst-Tomaten-Füllung

Zutaten für 4 Personen

Für den Buchtelteig

400 g glattes Weizenmehl (Type 550)
40 g Kristallzucker
1 TL Salz
2 EL getrocknete Röstzwiebeln
40 g frische Hefe
1 TL flüssiger Honig
80 g flüssige Butter
150 ml Milch
2 Eigelb

Für die Füllung

150 g in Öl eingelegte, getrocknete Tomaten, gut abgetropft
3 Knoblauchzehen
1/2 EL getrockneter Thymian
2 EL fein gehackte Blattpetersilie

Zubereitungszeit: ca. 1 1/2 Stunden

1 Für den Teig das Mehl mit dem Zucker und dem Salz in eine Schüssel sieben und mit den Röstzwiebeln vermengen.

2 Die Hefe mit dem flüssigen Honig glatt rühren.

3 Die Butter zerlassen, mit der lauwarmen Milch vermischen, dann die Hefe-Honig-Mischung und die Eigelb hinzufügen und die Mischung mit dem Mehlgemisch vermengen. Alles in der Küchenmaschine (Knethaken) 7 bis 8 Minuten zu einem glatten Teig verarbeiten. Den Teig mit einem Küchentuch abdecken und 30 Minuten gehen lassen.

4 Für die Füllung die eingelegten Tomaten grob hacken.

5 Den Knoblauch schälen und fein hacken, dann mit dem Thymian und der Petersilie zu den Tomaten geben und gut vermengen. Die Crema di Balsamico, den Orangenabrieb und das Olivenöl hinzufügen, dann mit Salz und Pfeffer abschmecken und 15 Minuten ziehen lassen.

6 Die Blutwurst in kleine Würfel schneiden und unter die Tomatenfüllung heben.

2 EL dunkle Crema di Balsamico
1/2 TL fein geriebene Orangenschale (Bioware)
1 EL Olivenöl extra vergine
Salz
frisch gemahlener Pfeffer
400 g Blutwurst
200 g Butter

7 Den Teig auf einer bemehlten Arbeitsfläche durchkneten und mit etwas Mehl zu einer etwa 1 cm dicken Platte rollen. Die Teigplatte in Quadrate von 6–7 cm schneiden.

8 Die Butter in einem kleinen Topf zerlassen.

9 In die Mitte jedes Teigquadrats 1 EL der Tomaten-Blutwurst-Füllung geben. Die 4 Ecken jedes Teigquadrats hochklappen und fest verschließen, sodass kleine Kugeln entstehen.

10 Die Teigkugeln (Buchteln) vollständig in die flüssige Butter tauchen, dann nebeneinander mit der Nahtstelle nach unten in eine Auflaufform oder Fettpfanne (18 x 25 cm) legen.

11 Die Oberflächen der Buchteln nochmals mit flüssiger Butter bestreichen, die Buchteln weitere 10 Minuten gehen lassen, dann 45 Minuten im auf 170 °C vorgeheizten Backofen backen.

12 Die fertigen Buchteln aus dem Ofen nehmen, etwa 5 Minuten ruhen lassen, dann servieren.

Tipps: Dazu passt ein Rucola- oder Nussblattsalat (Salatrauke). Sie können die Buchtelmasse auch mit eingelegten Kirschtomaten (siehe Rezept Seite 26) zubereiten.

Kater-Killer

Zutaten für 4 Drinks

1 Bund Dill
1 Sardellenfilet
1 TL Fenchelsamen
1 l Tomatensaft
1 Msp. fein geriebene Zitronenschale (Bioware)
1 TL Honig
4–5 Eiswürfel
Salz
frisch gemahlener Pfeffer
1 Stange Staudensellerie

Zubereitungszeit: ca. 5 Minuten

1 Den Dill von den Stielen befreien und fein hacken.

2 Das Sardellenfilet mit einer Gabel zerdrücken.

3 Die Fenchelsamen im Blitzhacker fein hacken oder im Mörser fein zerstoßen.

4 Den Tomatensaft mit dem gehackten Dill, dem zerdrückten Sardellenfilet, den zerstoßenen Fenchelsamen, der geriebenen Zitronenschale, dem Honig und den Eiswürfeln im Küchenmixer (hoher Mixbecher) gut durchmixen.

5 Den fertigen Drink mit Salz und Pfeffer abschmecken, in 4 hohe Gläser füllen, mit einigen Staudenselleriestücken garnieren und sofort servieren.

Virgin Mary

Zutaten für 4 Drinks

1/2 Zitrone
2 EL Meersalz
1 l Tomatensaft, gut gekühlt
40 ml frisch gepresster Zitronensaft
1 EL Worcestershire-Sauce
etwas Tabascosauce
einige Gurkenscheiben

Zubereitungszeit: ca. 5 Minuten

1 Die Ränder von 4 Cocktailgläsern in der halben Zitrone befeuchten und anschließend in das auf einem Unterteller verteilte Meersalz tauchen.

2 Den Tomatensaft gut mit dem Zitronensaft und der Worcestershire-Sauce verrühren.

3 Die Virgin Mary mit Tabasco und Meersalz abschmecken, vorsichtig in die vorbereiteten Gläser füllen und mit Gurkenscheiben garnieren.

Tomaten-Joghurt-Lassi mit Korianderpaste

Zutaten für 4 Drinks

Für die Korianderpaste
1 Handvoll Koriandergrün
1 kleine Chilischote
1 TL Kreuzkümmelsamen

Für das Lassi
300 ml Naturjoghurt, gut gekühlt
5 EL fein passierte Tomaten
200 ml Mineralwasser, gut gekühlt
1 EL Honig

Zubereitungszeit: ca. 5 Minuten

1 Für die Korianderpaste das Koriandergrün und die Chilischote (mit Kernen und Scheidewänden) grob hacken, dann mit dem Kreuzkümmel und 1–2 EL heißem Wasser im Mörser zu einer groben Paste verarbeiten.

2 Für das Lassi den Joghurt, die passierten Tomaten, das Mineralwasser und den Honig mit der Korianderpaste in einen hohen Rührbecher geben und in der Küchenmaschine gut durchmixen.

3 Das Lassi in 4 Gläser geben und sofort servieren.

Tipp: Geben Sie zusätzlich 1 EL geröstete Sesamsaat zu der Korianderpaste – dann schmeckt sie noch exotischer. Sie können das Lassi nach Belieben mit Salz abschmecken.

Register

Vorspeisen mit Gemüse

Vorspeisen mit Fisch und Meeresfrüchten

Vorspeisen mit Geflügel und Fleisch

Hauptspeisen mit Gemüse

Hauptspeisen mit Fisch und Meeresfrüchten